ROSES,
in the
MOUTH OF A LION

Also by Bushra Rehman

Corona

Marianna's Beauty Salon

*Colonize This! Young Women of
Color on Today's Feminism*
(coeditor)

ROSES,
in the
MOUTH OF A LION

Bushra Rehman

FLATIRON
BOOKS
NEW YORK

This is a work of fiction. All of the characters, organizations, and events portrayed in this novel are either products of the author's imagination or are used fictitiously.

www.flatironbooks.com

Stories from *Roses, in the Mouth of a Lion* have appeared in the following:

Corona (Sibling Rivalry Press), *Everything All at Once* (Queens Museum of Art), *And the World Changed: Contemporary Stories by Pakistani Women* (Feminist Press), *NYC: Das vermessene Paradies Positionen zu New York* (House of World Cultures), *Aster(ix) Journal*, *The Blueshift Journal*, *ColorLines*, *The Feminist Wire*, and *Poets & Writers Magazine*.

Designed by Donna Sinisgalli Noetzel

Library of Congress Cataloging-in-Publication Data

Names: Rehman, Bushra, author.
Title: Roses, in the mouth of a lion / Bushra Rehman.
Description: First Edition. | New York : Flatiron Books, 2022.
Identifiers: LCCN 2022003578 | ISBN 9781250834782 (hardcover) |
    ISBN 9781250834799 (ebook)
Subjects: LCGFT: Novels.
Classification: LCC PS3568.E47623 R67 2022 | DDC 813/.54—dc23
LC record available at https://lccn.loc.gov/2022003578

Our books may be purchased in bulk for promotional, educational, or business use. Please contact your local bookseller or the Macmillan Corporate and Premium Sales Department at 1-800-221-7945, extension 5442, or by email at MacmillanSpecialMarkets@macmillan.com.

First Edition: 2022

10 9 8 7 6 5 4 3 2 1

For Rosina

BOOK ONE

Summer 1985

CORONA

Corona, I'm talking about a little village perched under the number 7 train in Queens between Junction Boulevard and 111th Street. I'm talking about the Lemon Ice King, Spaghetti Park, and P.S. 19. The Corona F. Scott Fitzgerald called the valley of ashes as the Great Gatsby drove past it on his night of carousal, but what me and my own know as home. And we didn't know about any valley of ashes because by then it had been topped off by our houses. You know, the kind made from brick this tan color no self-respecting brick would be at all. That's Corona.

And you know the song by Paul Simon? The one where he says, "*Goodbye to Rosie, the queen of Corona. Seein' me and Julio down by the schoolyard . . .*"

Well, at first, I couldn't believe it was Corona he was singing about, because why would Paul Simon be singing about Corona? I didn't see many white people there unless they were policemen or firemen, and I didn't think Paul Simon had ever been one of those. Then I saw these pictures of him standing in front of one of those tan brick homes. What I thought was a lie was true.

I once knew a Julio too. We didn't hang out down by the schoolyard like Paul Simon must have with his Julio. We didn't hang out anywhere at all, but I loved him the way you only could when you were a child. Julio had beauty marks all over, as if it wasn't obvious to everyone how he looked. He carried his body like fire, matchstick, rope.

All the girls in school showed off for Julio, cursing and fighting. In

Corona, girls learned early to flash skin, flirt, chew gum, and play games to bring the boys down to their knees, even though it usually ended up the other way around.

But I was not one of them. My mother didn't let me wear skirts, especially the short kind the other girls wore with their hairless legs and fearless way of flicking their hips. I watched them flirt with Julio, my back against the brick wall.

Julio was my next-door neighbor, and we were in the same fifth-grade class in school. We walked the same way home. Not together, of course. He walked ahead of me with his friends, who'd be whooping and laughing, pulling roses out whenever they went past this house that had so many roses they grew up and over, through the fence like they were some kind of convicts trying to scale the walls.

The Korean grandmother who lived there always stood in the yard as soon as the school bell rang and waved her stick and screamed at us, so we wouldn't pull out every last one. But Julio always managed to steal a rose. He was quick and thin. All the other boys rallied around him. He'd leap to the top of the fence, grab a rose, then fall back on the pack of boys, pushing them nearly into the street, partly from the impact and partly for the joy of it. Then he'd shake the hair out of his eyes and laugh.

One day, the Korean grandmother wasn't waiting inside the fence, yelling like she usually was. She was hiding behind a car across the street, and when Julio and his friends came around, she was right behind them. She grabbed Julio by one of his skinny arms and pulled him into the garden. "Bad boy!" She shook him. "Tell me where you live!"

Julio's friends stopped. Their hands were still pushed through the gaps in the fence. This was new. They didn't know whether to run away or run in. They stood like statues, waiting for someone to do or say something to make things normal.

Julio was the one who did. He pulled back with all his thin weight and said to her face, "I don't need to tell you where I live, you—"

The grandmother stopped. Her mouth opened, but what she wanted to say, she couldn't. Julio's and my eyes met, and I felt the thread of our shame pulse through me, a burning flame.

Just then, one of Julio's friends picked up a beer can from the street and threw it at her. He missed, but the next thing I knew, there was a howl and a rush. All the boys started picking up litter and glass bottles and throwing them.

The grandmother's fingers lost their grip, and when she ran into the house, the boys ran into the garden and started pulling roses off the branches. All of them: the tea lemon, the hot pink, the deep red, the little ones with flecks of gold in their skin. The thorns tore through their fingers, but they didn't let it stop them. It was their first time in the garden, and now it was theirs.

By this time, all the kids who walked home that way, and even some who didn't, had stopped to see what was happening. Unable to pull away, I stood with my face pressed against the chain links.

Then I saw Julio. His arms were full of tattered roses. He looked like a crown prince as he walked out of the garden, and started throwing flowers at the children who were too scared to run in. When he saw me, he stopped. For a second, I could see he didn't trust me not to tell.

Then he smiled, the first time he had ever really smiled at me. He picked out a rose. It was hot pink, stiff, just beginning to open.

"Here," he said, and threw the rose at my feet.

SKIN

It had poured rain and thundered all day like a hot summer storm should, and when I opened the door to my friends Saima and Lucy's house, the metal corners tugged on the grapevines, and cooled-down rain, which had pooled on the leaves, showered down on me, and wet my salwar kameez.

Lucy lived below Saima, and Saima lived above Lucy, and they both lived next to Shahnaaz, the neighborhood bully. I lived down the street, but in the summers, I spent all my time at Saima's and Lucy's. The grapevines lived everywhere, acting like they were trees. They grew when our mothers called us in to eat. They grew when we played in the back lot acting like junglees. They grew at night when we were asleep, and in the mornings, Lucy and Saima had to push against the doorjambs, pull and twist the doorknobs to get anywhere they needed to be.

The biggest argument Saima and Shahnaaz always had was whose grapevines they really were. They were rooted in Shahnaaz's yard, but the vines with their baby hair twists swung over the fence and knelt down and touched the ground on Saima's side of the fence.

I always sat with Saima on the red vinyl sofa her mother had put under the grapevines. All over Corona there were sofas like this, growing like mushrooms: yellow, red, orange, brown. Who could get rid of a sofa after paying so much?

I'd known Saima since she and I were born, and even before, because our fathers had been best friends in Pakistan. They'd met at Peshawar

University and had come to America together with their tight-fitting British suits, curly dark hair, and sunglasses. In Pakistan, they'd been scientists and worn white lab coats, but in Corona, they worked in stores. Now Saima's father wore tight pants and shiny shirts while he sold radios, VCRs, and illegal copies of Bollywood movies. My father wore his lab coat as a butcher at his Gosht Dukan: Corona Halal Meats. Whenever I visited him, his coat would be covered with blood.

Lucy's father was from the Dominican Republic. He worked so many jobs, Lucy couldn't keep track. He had a belly that hung out of his shirt and black curly hair all over his chest. When he was home, he sat under the grapevines, drinking. He'd learned how to make wine from the Italian neighbors, and on his days off, he drank homemade wine and yelled at us when we popped the sour green grapes into our mouths.

"Hey! You! Get away from my grapes!"

After it rained was the best because Lucy's father stayed inside watching TV. Then we pulled on the vines like hair and felt the rain run down our cheeks, soak our clothes, our salwar kameez. It always felt cold, sweet, and green, the air around us thick liquid, about to burst like a sneeze.

One afternoon, Shahnaaz was poking around in the old abandoned garage that had come with her house. Her family didn't have a car, so the garage was left to pile up with junk. It was the kind of place stray cats had babies. The kind of place rats lived. The kind of place you wouldn't go into by yourself, unless you thought you were a badass the way Shahnaaz did.

Our main way of getting money for candy was to look under the sofa cushions. There the loose change that leaked out of our fathers' and uncles' pockets slipped down and collected into secret pools of pennies, nickels, and dimes. Shahnaaz's brother, Amir, had just moved an old sofa into the garage, and she thought she'd find undiscovered treasure, but when she lifted the cushion, it wasn't George Washington's head or even Abraham Lincoln's she saw. It was a woman in a glossy magazine, her nipples pink and round as quarters, her mouth wide open, her head thrown back, nothing on her body but a thin sheet draped over her legs.

Shahnaaz didn't say this, but I'm sure her eyes popped. None of us had breasts, but Shahnaaz always acted like she did, pushing her chest out whenever we walked around the block. She thought she was the prettiest, and the only reason we agreed was because her brother was older and said he'd beat us up if we said she wasn't.

When Shahnaaz came up to the fence, Saima and I were sitting under the grapevines, pooling our cushion change. Lucy had gone to Top Tomato with her mother, and it would be a while till she got back. Every so often, Saima and I reached up and pulled down a handful of grapes. When we saw Shahnaaz, we weren't happy.

"Whatcha doing?"

"None of your business." Saima had less patience for Shahnaaz than I did.

"Oh yeah? Well, maybe it is my business because you're eating my grapes."

We rolled our eyes and ignored her, but she kept talking. "Well, what I found in the garage is none of your business either."

I tried to be tough. "So what then?"

It was useless. A few minutes later, I was sneezing from the dust in the garage, and Saima was trying to find a place to sit that wasn't covered with rat pee. Shahnaaz pulled out the magazines, and Saima's and my mouths dropped open. There were naked men and women in all sorts of positions. Some of them were doing everyday things like eating breakfast, just naked. One woman was spread out on a car.

"This is gross," Saima said with disgust, but she kept looking. I did too. I couldn't stop myself from flipping through the pages. I kept the tips of my fingers on the edges though, so I didn't have to touch the skin. Whenever I accidentally did, I could feel my fingers burning.

There was one lady I couldn't stop looking at. She was the only one who wasn't blonde. She was small with dark brown hair and brownish skin. Her body was thin, and she was sprawled out asleep on a bed, completely naked. Her eyebrows were wrinkled, and her hair was messy. There was brown hair, curly and thick, between her legs, brown hair thick underneath her arms, places where my skin was still as smooth as a baby's. The picture must have been taken by someone standing over her. She looked like she was sleeping and having a very bad dream.

"Are they your brother's?" Saima was the first to ask.

"No! My brother would never look at something like this. It's—"

"Guna," I said. It's what we learned from our mothers, who taught us the long lists of what was Guna and what wasn't. It was Guna to listen to music. Guna to talk to boys. Guna to cut our hair. Guna to miss any of our prayers: Fajr, Zohar, Asr, Maghrib, Isha. It was most definitely Guna to take off our clothes, lie on top of a car, and let people take pictures.

When my mother saw people in our neighborhood walking around wearing almost nothing, she always said, "They don't know any better. But you do. You think it's hot now? When you go to Hell, demons will take torches and set fire to all the places you left your skin naked. And as much as you scream and cry, or say please, please, Allah forgive me, Allah will say, 'You didn't listen to me when you were alive, why should I listen to you when you're dead?' But Allah is merciful, and when the demons have burned you enough, He'll forgive you, give you new skin, and bring you up to Heaven."

"But how long until I could go to Heaven?" I'd say, trying to push the images of demons out of my mind.

"In Hell, every day is an eternity," my mother would say, then leave me to go clean.

"We have to burn them." Shahnaaz's voice echoed the voice in my head. "Saima, does your mother have matches?"

Saima looked up at the windows of her house. We could all hear her mother screaming at her younger brother, Ziyad. "I don't want to go home. My mother won't let me come back out."

Shahnaaz turned to me. "Razia, go ask the man at the store."

"Why me?"

"Because you're the favorite."

It was true. The bodega owner always gave me free candy when my mother sent me there to get milk. The bodega was strange. The front windows were full of dish detergent, Ajax, Raid, and Mr. Clean, but the back shelves were barely stocked with anything. At some point, the owner must have realized he could carry dairy and get milk cheap for his family. He always said I was his best milk customer, even though I never saw anyone else buying milk there.

When I walked in, the bell rang loud and frantic, and the smell of wet cardboard hit me in the face. Inside, it was ten different shades of dark. A gray cat sat in the corner licking herself. Gold teeth flashed in the dim light and I saw the owner at the front counter, cleaning his fingernails with a match. His friend, the man with the black mustache, was next to him. They were laughing low.

The door slammed behind me and everyone looked up. "Ah, look who it is," the owner said. "My girlfriend!"

The man with the black mustache grinned. He was missing a number of front teeth. He must not have had enough money to replace them with gold.

"Could I please have a pack of matches?"

The owner leaned over the counter and looked down at me. "Baby, what you want matches for?"

I bit my tongue and lied. "They're for my father."

He smiled and passed them over the counter. I grabbed the pack, barely looking at him, said thank you, and ran out the door.

When I got back, Saima and Shahnaaz were pulling a metal garbage can into the back alley next to the railroad tracks. We'd had fire safety training in school, so we knew we had to be careful not to get caught.

We threw all the magazines in, but Shahnaaz insisted that she had to light the first match, since she'd found the magazines.

"But I'm the one who went to get them!"

"Yeah, but you'd have nothing to burn if I hadn't found them."

She was right. I looked inside the garbage can and saw my woman with brown hair still laid out on the bed. I wondered how she had ended up that way. My mother always told me it only took one step off the right path to start your downfall. Maybe one step like lying about matches.

"There's only one straight path," my mother would say, "and you need to pray to Allah you stay on it. It's the right path that looks difficult. All the others tempt you, but at the end of each one, there is a trapdoor that drops you into a burning, red-hot pit of fire filled with demons."

"But how do you know if you're walking the right path or the wrong path?"

"Listen to what I tell you," my mother would say, then leave me to go clean.

"Fine. You can light the first match," I said. "Stupidhead," I mumbled under my breath.

Shahnaaz struck the match against the flint and dropped it quickly into the garbage can. We all stepped back, thinking it was going to explode. But the magazines were thick and glossy, and the garbage can was damp. We watched as the flame burned, lowered, and then flickered away. Shahnaaz lit match after match, but each one flickered and went out.

"You have to get more matches." Shahnaaz acted annoyed, as if it was my fault she didn't know how to start a fire.

I didn't argue this time. I wanted the magazines to burn. I ran all the way to the bodega thinking of the woman in the garbage can. Where had she gone wrong? I thought of how easy it was to want to sleep instead of pray at dawn, to want to eat during Ramzaan. I thought of the boys I wanted to kiss: Julio, Phillip, Osman. Is that how it had started for her?

When I got back to the bodega, the owner was alone and this time he looked angry. The gray cat was still in the corner licking herself.

"Could I please have another pack of matches?"

He gave me a look. "Hey, what are you doing with these matches?"

"They're for my father," I lied again.

Something crossed his face. "Tell your father he's got to come here himself if he wants matches." Then he looked guilty. He'd never said no to anything I asked for before. "Here." He passed the matches and a square caramel over the counter. "Your favorite."

It was my turn to feel guilty. I couldn't believe how easily lying came to me. I thanked him and ran back to the alley behind Saima's house.

"This time I want to light it," I said. When Shahnaaz opened her mouth to argue, I cut her off. "We can't get any more matches, and you don't know how to light them."

Saima laughed and Shahnaaz gave her a look, but she stepped back. I walked up to the garbage can and looked down at my woman. Her mouth looked soft and sad. I struck the match and held it to the whole pack, until it became one big flame, a fireball in my hands.

I dropped it right on her. The flame kept and started burning a hole through the center. It turned into a hundred flames shooting up from the silver metal. We could barely see the orange, yellow, and blue of them in the light.

The smoke rose, and the fire reached higher and higher. The woman's skin began to submit, relent. The bed she was on, her sad eyebrows drawn together, her mouth melted away. Her body was being covered with smoke, and I knew her spirit was being lifted so she could fly clothed in fire all the way to Heaven.

THE OLD ITALIAN

Saima's house was crammed up next to the train tracks, and every time a train passed, it blasted through, blowing garbage and letting its long, wild siren fill the air. The houses were all by the railroad tracks like this:

railroadtracksrailroadtracksrailroadtracksrailroadtracksrailroadtracks
       Saima's house   Shahnaaz's house
       Lucy's house   Old Italian's house

When Saima and I ran outside, a train was just passing. The sound of her brother, Ziyad, crying was behind us, and we saw that Lucy and Shahnaaz were already hanging out under the grapevines. Ziyad was crying because his mother was forcing tablespoons of hot chili powder into his mouth. Saima's mother was always punishing them. Her methods were extreme even for our families, who believed in discipline.

It was hot hot hot. Lucy was sitting on a milk crate snapping gum and flipping her long, dark hair. She was wearing short shorts. Her belly was chubby as cake and pushed through her T-shirt. Shahnaaz was lying out flat, hogging the entire sofa under the grapevines. When she saw us, she got up. I could hear her skin unsticking from the red vinyl.

"I'm bored," Shahnaaz said.

"I'm bored too," Lucy said, snapping her gum.

"I'm bored three," Saima said. "Move over." She pushed Shahnaaz to the side.

"Whadda you want to do?" Shahnaaz asked. She must have been too hot to start a fight.

"We could go get some ices," I suggested.

"Anybody got money?" Lucy looked around, but we all shook our heads no. We were too young to work and our families didn't give allowances.

We heard the sound of Ziyad, now screaming, from one floor up. Saima and I looked at each other quickly, then looked away.

"You know when Amir crashed his bike into the fence?" Shahnaaz asked, ignoring Ziyad's cries.

"Yeah, so?" None of us liked Shahnaaz's bully big brother.

"So, stupid, there's a hole and we can look into the Old Italian's yard."

The Old Italian's yard was a field of sunflowers. He had started planting them years ago, cramming seeds next to each other, until the sunflowers grew so close, so tall, we could see them crowning their heads over the fence.

On summer days, the Old Italian wandered through his garden, a floating head among the sunflowers. But mostly he leaned out from his second-floor window and smoked his pipe, letting his belly hang out, scowling at the changes in the neighborhood: the new halal meat stores and Dominican mothers pushing wheelie carts.

Our neighborhood was a hand-me-down from the Italians. In the early days, gangs of Italian boys had roamed the streets attacking Pakistani boys they found alone in the playground or coming home from masjid. The more our families moved in, the more their families moved out. Now only the older Italians were left behind. They sat on their stoops with milky-white skin and let the sun drip over them or hid behind doorways with stacks of old newspapers and cold salads. They watched us all the time, frowning.

They'd spent a generation planting and creating gardens out of the hard rock soil of Queens. When mostly Italians had lived in Corona, hydrangeas and roses had grown. Cherry trees and magnolias had burst from the ground. But in our hands, these same gardens filled up with weeds, old sofas, and rusty cars.

Saima reached over her head and snapped some grapes off the vine. There were a few that had turned purple and sweet. She jumped up. "Let's go."

We were all experts at climbing fences. Once there had been a gate that separated the yards, but it had rusted shut, so we always had to climb. In a few minutes, we'd gotten into Shahnaaz's yard and were pushing against each other to press our eyes to the crack, a broken knot in the fence the size of a fist.

Up close, the Old Italian was a giant. There were puffs of white hair around his smooth, bald head. His face was sunburnt, cracked. The knees of his pants were worn from bending down in the dirt. He poured water and it caught the light. The sunflowers stiffened and straightened. The light moved through the flowers like lions set loose in Queens.

Lucy was the first to see the small shoebox at his feet. "Whadda you think's in that box?" she whispered, pressing her body against the fence.

"Maybe a dead baby," Saima said.

"Don't be stupid. It's a shoebox. He's probably got some old shoes in it. And stop hogging already." Shahnaaz pulled us out of the way.

"It could be a really small baby," Lucy insisted, shooting Shahnaaz a dirty look. She dusted off her legs. I could see that the hair on her legs had gotten longer and darker. Mine had too, but I always kept my legs covered.

All of a sudden, Saima screamed and pushed back so fast we fell over. The Old Italian's eye was pressed into the crack, looking at us. Just as quick as it had come, it disappeared.

Saima's salwar had gotten dirt on it, and she tried to rub it off. I knew her mother wouldn't be happy cleaning another dirty salwar. "Great idea, Shahnaaz."

Shahnaaz straightened her skinny body up. "Whatever. I'm not scared of him. Let him come."

"Oh yeah? What would you do?" Lucy asked.

Before she could answer, the Old Italian appeared before us. He moved slow with a limp. His pants were blue, splattered with paint, his belly big, as if he was pregnant. He held a shoebox out to us and said with a thick accent, "Hallo." It was the first time he'd ever spoken to us.

"Hello," we mumbled, shy all of a sudden.

We gathered around the box, and this time we didn't push. It was lined with newspaper, and in the center, there was a gray kitten. She was so tiny, she could've fit in my palm. Her fur puffed up all around her like a dusty halo.

We looked up at the Old Italian, becoming mute with the kitten so close. I'd never seen a kitten in real life, only on Scholastic posters we couldn't afford to buy. I reached out to feel her softness. She was as gray as the clouds on a thundery day, as the balls of dust that settled under the furniture in Saima's house.

When I touched her, a spark of electricity flew through my fingers. The world around me came into focus. I saw the chain links of the fence, the weeds that grew up and everywhere. Everything compared to the kitten felt harsh, dirty, covered with bad graffiti.

"You wan' her?"

"Oh yes, yes, yes." Our words tumbled all over each other.

He grunted, relieved we'd finally spoken.

Then, just like that, he became uncomfortable. He placed the box down under the grapevines and walked out, around the fence, back to his garden.

Like a pressure cooker bursting, everyone started talking at once.

"Stop touching her!"

"You stop touching her!"

Soon we were all fighting.

"You're scaring her!" Lucy yelled.

The kitten jumped and began to shiver.

I turned to Lucy. "Can you bring milk?" Only Lucy could go into her fridge without her mother yelling.

Lucy hesitated, but then said, "Only if one of you comes with me."

Saima and Shahnaaz looked at me. Our mothers wouldn't let us into anyone's house who wasn't Pakistani, but I lived two blocks away, so my mother was the least likely to find out.

We climbed the fence back to Saima and Lucy's side. My salwar snagged on the chain link and almost ripped, but I quickly untangled myself.

Inside Lucy's house, everything was different than I imagined. The way Saima's mother described it, I would have thought there were fountains of beer and drugs everywhere. I didn't know what drugs looked like, though, so while Lucy went into the kitchen, I looked around, searching for something that might be drugs.

There was an old table fan going in the living room, orange sofas with plastic, a TV with aluminum foil on the antenna, books, newspapers, and shoes scattered around a brown carpet. It could have been anyone's house. I followed Lucy into the kitchen and saw they even had the same fridge as Saima. When Lucy opened it, there was beer inside, and for some reason, I felt better.

"We better hurry. My mother's still in the bedroom putting her face on."

Before I could ask what that meant, I heard her mother call out, "Lucy?"

Lucy didn't answer, but she should've because just then her mother came in. Her hair was in pink curlers and her makeup was half-on, half-off. Lucy was just about to pour some milk into a cracked cereal bowl. Her mother smiled at me, then looked at Lucy and said something in Spanish. Lucy started talking to her mother in a hurried way.

From Lucy's hands, the way she moved them, I could tell she was telling her mother about the kitten. Her mother's smile got tighter and tighter, then finally snapped and fell apart. Lucy looked at me and I knew it was time to leave.

When we walked out, she carried the bowl carefully. There was just a little milk her mother had let her bring out. I climbed over the fence first. Lucy passed the bowl to me, then climbed over, concentrating on how to get her bare legs over the fence.

I decided not to ask what her mother had said. Even with Saima and Ziyad's mother, I never asked. She was always screaming at them in Pashto.

When we got back to Shahnaaz's yard, Saima and Shahnaaz were still playing with the kitten. Saima was saying "Meow" over and over, trying to speak in the kitten's language.

There wasn't enough room in the shoebox for the bowl. Everyone else was too scared to do it, so I lifted the kitten out of the box. I could feel her small bones in my palms. I put her under the grapevines. We watched as she explored the dirt and sticks scattered about. The kitten was still shivering, but when we put the milk next to her, her pink tongue came out like a snail.

I don't know how the whole day passed, but we couldn't feel the heat anymore. Saima, Shahnaaz, and I wanted to give her a Muslim name, but Lucy wanted to give her a Catholic name like Maria. We finally settled on Maria Perez Parvez Mirza, but since that was too long we just called her Miss Kitten.

We decided Lucy had to beg her mother to keep Miss Kitten. It had to be Lucy because we were Muslim and Muslims didn't have pets. Lucy looked doubtful, but she said she'd ask.

The next morning, I was up early. After I ate nashta, my mother let me go to Saima's. When I got there, Lucy was under the grapevines. The front of her T-shirt was wet with tears. By her feet was Miss Kitten's box, but I didn't hear any kitten sounds. The box was empty.

"What happened to Miss Kitten?"

Lucy didn't answer. She ran inside and slammed her door. I rang Saima's doorbell, but no one answered. I heard the sound of the train coming from the back alley next to the railroad tracks. I knew I shouldn't follow it, but I did.

At the end of the alley, there was a group of kids. Saima's brother, Ziyad, and his friends were in the center. There was a circle of blood at their feet. Ziyad was holding what looked like a rat in his hands.

The children were yelling, "Throw it! Throw it!"

"Ziyad!" I was only a few years older than him, but in our families that still had some power. "Ziyad!"

He turned and looked at me. There was terror in his face. I must have sounded like his mother. But the crowd was pushing. He turned his back on me and arched his arm. I saw it was our kitten in his hands. Her body sailed through the air and landed on the railroad tracks.

"Ziyad!" I screamed, and ran to grab him, but all the boys scattered down the alley laughing. "Ziyad! Ziyad!" My voice sounded like nothing under the tracks of the screaming train.

The Old Italian must have heard the noise. He limped into the back alley and stared at the blood on the cement. The horrible feeling in my stomach felt like vomit. He looked at me and the concern left his face. It became filled with the look I saw from all the other Italians. A look of hate, saying: We were bad. We were dirty. We didn't know how to take care of life. We didn't know how to grow anything, and when we touched the world, it died.

CORONA HALAL MEATS

It was the summer of young uncles. In villages all over Pakistan, young boys who'd been teenagers, kicking crows on dirt roads, had turned into men. Mustaches burst onto their faces. Their heads pushed out of the ceilings of their houses. Airmail letters crisscrossed the Atlantic. Mothers and wives were consulted or told. Permission was given or not given and young Pakistani men flooded the streets of Corona.

It was the summer all of Saima's uncles started appearing. They were like Russian nesting dolls made out of the same mold: some with red mustaches, some with brown, some short, some skinny, some fat, but they all had the same look. They were Pathans: pale skin, handlebar mustaches, and, like all Pathans, they carried their power around with them like wild cats. A few paired up with Dominican women who'd been in the country longer. Saima's uncles needed green cards, and they needed them fast.

I'd see one of her handsome uncles in front of Key Food or the library, and he'd be with a woman, beautiful as an air balloon. She'd bend down and say, "Oh, she's so cute." I'd pull away. I wasn't used to this kind of loving adult attention. When I'd see Saima's uncles coming with their ladies, I'd run and hide.

I felt guilty every time I saw them. These women loved the Pakistani uncles. They bought them new clothes, sunglasses, and shoes. In exchange, Saima's uncles walked with them down the street, their eyes wandering to all the younger girls who were off-limits. Next to their beds were pictures of the women they would be marrying back in Pakistan.

––––––

Saima's most handsome uncle, Azim, got a job at my father's Gosht Dukan: Corona Halal Meats. It was on the corner of 99th and National Streets. Before it was a halal meat store, it had been an Italian butcher shop, and even though my father didn't hang sausages and pigs' heads out front, the meaning was the same. Dead animals arrived there to be cut, sold, and eaten.

It was fine real estate for religion on National Street: an Episcopalian church, a Kingdom Hall, and our new masjid, crammed next to each other, wall to wall, skin to skin. And if you crossed the street, there was a Catholic store selling crucifixes and paintings of women and men in Hell burning. It was only right, then, that there should be a place for animal sacrifice as well. There could have been people slaughtering goats on that very spot for centuries. Men might have gathered, talked, and joked, the smell of blood and flesh making their jokes funnier, just like it did in the Gosht Dukan.

My mother always gave me chai to take to the store around four o'clock. I loved visiting my father. In this country, with so few people to love, he always showered me with affection until my mother said I was spoiled.

On the front door of the store there was a sign that said: OPEN, and on the other side, it said: OUT FOR PRAYER. A bell rang when I entered. My father looked up and smiled, a smile as large as an onion rack. He was standing at the back by the register with Azim and Shafiq Uncle, who worked as a mechanic in the gas station across the street. Shafiq Uncle always came at this time because he knew he'd get chai. He was sitting in one of the collapsible chairs my father had especially for him.

Shafiq Uncle tossed a bag of pistachios on the counter. I knew he wasn't going to pay for it. Azim looked to see if it was okay, but my father didn't hesitate. He opened the bag and brought out a plate for the pistachio shells. My father took the thermos from me, and Azim brought out Styrofoam cups. My father poured full cups for Shafiq Uncle and then Azim. There was only half a cup left for my father. Only I noticed this.

Shafiq Uncle started on one of his favorite subjects: comparative religion. Bits of pistachio fell out of his mouth. "The Yehovah's Witnesses came to the Garage!" He threw a handful of shells toward the plate, but they missed and fell to the floor.

"Why are they called that? Did they witness something?" Azim asked. He brought out the sugar, a half-pound bag torn open at the top. It had a hot-pink label and a plastic spoon with tea-soaked sugar crusted along the edge.

My father reached under the counter and took out a pamphlet that said: AWAKE!

"The Yehovahs gave it to me when they came to the Gosht Dukan. I tried to give them my Quran, but they wouldn't take it."

Azim and Shafiq Uncle laughed, imagining my father turning the tables on the Jehovah's Witnesses. I giggled too. I was usually quiet around the uncles, happy just to be near my father, a little moon circling around him. But this time I said, "They don't celebrate Christmas. The Jehovah's Witnesses."

Shafiq Uncle grabbed the spoon and loaded his cup full of sugar, then took a loud slurp. "This Christmas, I finally understand, but Easter—"

"I know Easter," my father said. "Easter is when Jesus goes upstate."

"Upstate how? On the bus?" Shafiq Uncle smiled.

My father pointed his cup in the air. "Upstairs, upstairs."

"Upstairs, acha," and they both started laughing.

Azim, who had only been in the country for a few months, smiled but then asked in all seriousness, "But what do eggs have to do with it?"

My father and Shafiq Uncle were laughing so hard, they didn't hear the door chime and Hafiz Saab walk in. Everyone quieted down and said salaam.

Hafiz Saab was our imam. Before he came to Corona, us children ran wild on the streets, but after, we were rounded up and sent to the basement of the masjid to learn Quran. Hafiz Saab had just come from Pakistan, but he might as well have come from a different planet, he was so strange to us. For our parents, though, looking at him reminded them of home. The men slapped him on the back and followed him around like lost puppies. The women hid behind doors and giggled whenever he passed.

Shafiq Uncle got up and offered his chair. "Here's Hafiz Saab. Ask him."

Azim, who hadn't touched his chai yet, handed his cup to Hafiz Saab, then asked, "What is it that the Yehovahs witness?"

Hafiz Saab took a sip of chai. His lips puckered. He said in Punjabi, "Don't make yourself crazy thinking about these things. Learn a little bit about Islam, why don't you?"

My father and the uncles looked down guiltily. "Haan, haan, yeh to hai." That is what Hafiz Saab was for, to keep them in line.

Hafiz Saab took another sip of chai. "Ek chicken kaat key dey do."

My father went into the back and sifted through the parts of chicken to give Hafiz Saab his favorite pieces: four legs, three necks, no breasts. He threw these into a plastic bag. Blood clung to the inside edges.

Hafiz Saab took the bag of chicken, wet and floppy. He made a half gesture to look in his pocket. He'd started a new fashion among the uncles, a kameez on top and pants on the bottom. That way, they could still look Pakistani but have pockets for all the things necessary to carry in this new country: keys, identification cards, money. All the men had started to dress like Hafiz Saab, all except Azim. He wore jeans and shiny polyester shirts.

After coming up empty-handed, Hafiz Saab looked at my father. "Write it in the Book."

My father didn't hesitate. For Pakistanis in Corona, there were two books. One was the Quran and the other was where my father fed everyone in the community for free. What everyone owed was written down in there. If my mother ever found out about the Book, she would go crazy.

At first, people only owed small amounts, but when they realized my father never asked them for payment, the sums got larger and the items went from packs of roti to burlap sacks of flour. From half a chicken to a whole goat. It was all written at first in my father's flowing handwriting, but now it was written in Azim's. Even though it was hard to tell the difference. To me, all men from Pakistan had the same handwriting.

"Chalo, it's time for namaaz." Hafiz Saab took one last long sip and put his cup down on a shelf next to the counter. He didn't bother to throw it in the garbage even though it was right next to his feet.

I drifted to the back of the store, touching all the different bags of daal by color. My father called me back to the front. "Do you want to come with me?"

I nodded excitedly and everyone laughed. The masjid had just gotten speakers, and today Hafiz Saab was going to give the azan so the whole neighborhood could hear. Our fathers had been slowly building the masjid for years, brick by brick. It wasn't even close to finished, but they were starting from the top and working their way down.

The uncles and Hafiz Saab went ahead. I waited while my father threw away the cups and put the towel back on the teakettle, where he thought the mice couldn't reach. He locked the door and turned the sign to OUT FOR PRAYER. We walked to the masjid, quiet, the way we always were when we were alone together.

We heard Hafiz Saab even before we got there. I didn't know his voice could sound like that, like a man's voice turning back into a boy's. He recited, "Allahu Akbar . . . Allahu Akbar . . ."

The azan came through the loudspeakers. Men and women everywhere spilled out onto the street. Everyone in the neighborhood tilted their heads and listened. Out of basement apartments and sixth-floor walk-ups, Muslim men started walking toward the sound, pulling their topis out of the back seats of their pockets.

The sun went down, and the clouds bent low over the buildings. I stood in front of the masjid and held my father's hand. The sky was turning pink and darkening, and I saw my father was weeping as a sleepy blue light settled on everything.

AJAX, RAID, MR. CLEAN

In my house, there was my mother, my father, me, and about fifty million roaches. My mother was mostly interested in them. While I was asleep, dreaming my Atari dreams, my mother was planning her attack. Ajax, Raid, Mr. Clean. Like any general, she got up at dawn with war on her mind. But as many souls as she took on the battlefield, hundreds more were being born. It was the roaches' primary method of attack, laying eggs squirming with babies.

During the day, the apartment was ours, but at night, the roaches took over. In the bathroom or kitchen, there were roaches covering every inch from the ceiling to the floor. There were the young ones that looked like the tips of exclamation points, with their eyes like little dots on the sides of their heads, and the older ones that looked like cheap wood paneling.

Some nights, my mother planned a sneak attack. She'd come into the kitchen quickly, quietly, and snap on the light. The roaches would be like lovers on the last night of summer, partying up and down the refrigerator, soft and crunchy underfoot. They'd be dancing on the countertops drunk on crumbs. That's when my mother would strike. The cockroaches would run and hide. Most of them survived.

"Let me tell you," Saima's mother said as she searched through Saima's hair. "After I used the bomb, I didn't see roaches for months. They're back, but that was a good summer."

Saima was next to me, watching TV, her eyes fixed on Woody

Woodpecker. The sun streamed in through the living room windows. There were orange curtains, and the light that came in was melting orange like an icy pop.

Our mothers were checking our hair for lice. It was the softest my mother ever touched me. I was torn between wanting to fall asleep and wanting to keep feeling her hands moving through my hair.

"Bugs, bugs everywhere." My mother pulled an egg out of my hair and cracked it against her fingernail. It made a popping sound. "These I don't mind. At least they're contained in her little head, and the ants, they only come in when it's raining. But the cockroaches—they're in the food, in the pots, everywhere."

Saima's mother agreed. "We never had these roaches in Pakistan."

"Hmmph."

Saima's mother squished another egg, then said, "You should do the bomb."

"The bomb?" My mother looked up, as if she hadn't heard Saima's mother the first time.

"You put it in all the rooms. Then you close the windows and take yourself and the children out of there. If you do it overnight, it kills all the roaches."

"All the roaches?" My mother stopped scratching through my head. I shifted closer to her fingers, so she wouldn't stop.

"You could stay with us." Saima's mother made a quick pinch. Saima winced and we both turned to look. A mother louse scampered across Saima's mother's palm. She grabbed it and snapped its head off.

"No," my mother said. "We couldn't stay at your house."

"Why not? We stayed with you."

Saima's family had lived with us last winter, for reasons I still didn't understand. My mother nodded and started on my hair again, but I could tell she was barely looking. She was thinking of the roaches.

My mother sent me to the bodega first to see if they had the bomb. She gave me enough money for a gallon of milk. Then, not knowing how much a bomb cost, she counted out ten ones. I walked to the corner carefully, as if I was carrying a basketful of eggs, afraid of dropping the extra money.

The bell rang when I walked in. The owner was at the front counter with his friend, the man with the black mustache. They were speaking in low, angry whispers. They stopped when they saw me. The owner smiled, but his eyes stayed serious.

I was embarrassed to ask for the bomb. Even though having roaches was no sin. Everyone in Corona had them. It's why all the bodegas stocked Raid. But buying Raid meant we had a little problem and buying the bomb meant the roaches were winning.

I hurried past the owner and his friend to the milk fridge in the back. It was humming fluorescent like an alien ship. I slid open the glass door. It was sticky with crumbs and black tar in all the corners. When I pulled down the gallon, the milk pulsed against the plastic, heavy and smooth.

The gray cat was watching the corner, intently. She pounced and caught something, a water bug or mouse. I didn't wait to find out. I ran back to the front, lifting the gallon of milk onto the counter. The owner and his friend stopped talking as soon as they saw me.

I swallowed the stone in my throat. "Do you sell the roach bomb?"

The owner leaned toward me. "You got a problem with the roaches, baby?"

"This country is full of roaches," his friend said, then cursed in Spanish.

The owner started pulling items off the shelf behind him. There were boxes and tubes, sprays and hoses. All of them had pictures of dead roaches, their antennas twisted and red.

His friend picked up the spray. "You see this? You know what they use to perfume this poison? Roses. They make it all romantic for the roaches before they murder them. Just like women who put on their perfume before they eat your heart out with their—"

"Hey, watch your mouth, brother," the owner said, "that's my girlfriend you're talking to. Don't turn her against love. I'm going to marry her someday."

"Marry!" His friend leaned over the counter until I could see each individual black hair of his mustache. "Don't ever let anyone trap you." He picked up a box that said ROACH MOTEL in large yellow letters. He started cracking up. "'Cause once you check in, you can't check out!"

I smiled. I'd seen the commercial too, where cartoon roaches pulled up to a cartoon Bates Motel and got trapped forever.

"You bastard," the owner said, but he was laughing.

The front bell rang, and we all turned. It was Julio. There was a cut on his lips that made me wince. After his parents had found out about the roses and his disrespect of the Korean grandmother, Julio had gotten such a beating from his father, I'd heard it from next door. As much as I tried to squash my feelings for Julio, they'd only swollen and spread.

The owner looked from Julio to me. He started laughing. His gold tooth shone out into swollen points of light. "Ah, man, love ain't a roach motel, it's—"

I didn't stay to hear what love was. I left everything on the counter and ran home. I told my mother they didn't have the bomb at the bodega, even though it meant I would have to go to the place I hated most in the world: Key Food with my mother.

My mother was ferocious in the house, a small demon woman. But outside, I'd watch her shrink. Like a forever-expanding-and-shrinking Shrinky Dink. She didn't know how to read English, so she brought me with her to make sure she bought the right bomb.

There was no sign dangling above the aisles that said "roach bombs," so we walked through the whole store. There were aisles with meat wrapped up in cellophane, aisles with boxes and boxes of cereals, and aisles filled with sponge cleaners, toilet brushes, and detergents. It was here we found an entire section for poison: sprays, gels, and Roach Motels.

I picked up a box and showed it to my mother. It said THE FOG: ROACH FUMIGATOR. It didn't say "bomb." Saima's mother must have imagined that part.

My mother had watched *Sesame Street* with us for years, so she knew "bomb" started with a *b*, not an *f*. "That doesn't say 'bomb,'" she said.

"Ammi, they call it 'the Fog.' Only Saima's mother calls it 'the bomb.' Look." I showed her the pictures on the back of the box: a hand putting the spray in a room, gas coming out, roaches lying dead on the floor. The pictures convinced her more than I could.

When we got to the checkout, the cashier, an older Italian lady, saw the roach bomb and glared at my mother. I saw my mother shrink in her eyes. I wanted to tell the cashier there were no roaches in Pakistan, but something stopped me. I tried to smile, to see if my charm would work like it did at the bodega, but the cashier only frowned. I moved closer to my mother until I felt stuck to her side like a mouse caught in a glue trap. My mother didn't seem to notice. She was just focused on getting the bomb and getting home.

When we walked out of the store, I looked at my mother. For a moment, the self she was inside our house became the self she was outside, powerful. People on the street stopped and looked. She was a bulb, a wetness, a wonder. She swelled with purpose, and I saw her the way the roaches must have seen her, as a giant.

Saima's mother came over the next morning to help my mother. They put all the dishes away in plastic bags and taped them up. They shut the food tight and opened all the doors of the cupboards and drawers. Then they carefully set bombs in each room, two on the tiles of the kitchen floor, one on the small dining room table, one in each bedroom, sentinels.

While our mothers busied themselves, Saima and I hid in the tiny space between the sofa and the radiator. Saima had brought over her Barbies. I was thrilled because my mother didn't let me have my own Barbies. She thought they looked too much like naked women.

Saima's Barbies could do anything: fly, swim, jump across valleys and ravines, have all kinds of adventures. But Saima wanted to play a new game where the Barbies had to run from a teddy bear who grabbed them and rubbed against them until they screamed. Our mothers were busy in the kitchen, so they didn't notice what we were doing. The Barbies' plastic legs thrashed against the bear.

Saima looked at me. "If you sleep at our house, you'll have to sleep with the spider."

"What spider?"

"It crawls up your legs and onto your stomach."

"There's no spider that does that!"

I could see my mother in the doorway of the kitchen. She was packing up the pots as if she was going to a new, better place. I swallowed my fear. I would do anything to make my mother happy.

"How do you stop the spider?"

Saima looked at the teddy bear. "You make yourself go to sleep. You just tell yourself it's a dream."

We slept at Saima's house that night. Our mothers outdid themselves making a feast: biryani, keema, chicken, samosas, and Peshawari kebabs. Afterward, the grown-ups sat around the tea table, stuffed and laughing, drinking chai. Saima's father told stories from our fathers' university days in Peshawar, and our mothers smiled, remembering the young men they had been. Soon, the table was covered with empty cups of chai and an almost-empty tin of Danish butter cookies.

A new uncle had just come from Pakistan, Saima's father's brother. He reached for the blue tin and ate the last sugar-crusted cookie. He was young and had a thick, bristly mustache. The crumbs from the cookie got lost in the hairs above his mouth. He kept looking at me over the table in a way that made me need to run to the bathroom and pee.

While our mothers took the empty teacups to the kitchen, Saima's father turned on the VCR and put in a Bollywood movie. "*Qurbani*. This is the one everyone's been buying at the store."

It was scandalous, filled with fight scenes and cabaret dance numbers. The heroine, Zeenat Aman, sang in a nightclub, wearing a red sequined dress. She held a microphone easily in her hands while disco lights swung above her head. The movie was long and soon among the *tashoom tashoom* of the disco and pistols, I fell asleep. A fight scene woke me up, but then I fell back asleep curled up next to my father. At some point, I was lifted up and put into a bed.

When I woke up, the room was cold and my parents were gone. I felt the bristle of hair, something against my leg, the tiny feelers of spiders. I froze. The spider crept up my leg and over my stomach. I wanted to cry out, but I couldn't move. Saima was asleep next to me. I could hear her breathe, but I couldn't move my head to look at her.

In my bedroom, poison fog was in the air. The roaches were

dying. Everywhere there were roach bodies, their feet worrying the air. I willed myself to sleep as Saima had told me to. I imagined myself in the sun with my mother gently searching my hair. I saw a mother louse scampering across her palm, getting smaller and smaller. Then I got smaller and smaller too, until I was gone.

SUGAR FIENDS

We became sugar fiends, Saima and me. We had sweet teeth and mouths full of cavities. We broke into kitchen cupboards when our mothers were busy on their sewing machines or vacuuming in a frenzy. The machines drowned out the creaks as we climbed onto the counters and rummaged through to find where the cookies were hidden. Cookies were expensive luxuries, and we had no qualms about being thieves.

Money was tight and our parents were trying to stem their losses where they could. The pools of change we used to find underneath the sofa cushions had dried up. Even the bodega owner didn't want to give me candy anymore. He was afraid it would have a different meaning now that I wasn't a child.

My body was changing. So was Saima's. There were buds growing on our breasts, painful and sore. Hair sprang from every crevice, every surface. It curled over our arms and legs in a thick carpet. It crawled down our backs and between our eyebrows, wild black grass with thick roots. We were stepping out of our husks, our wings dragging behind us, our skin darkening in the sun.

We were leaving the empty shells of our childhoods behind and becoming prey. Whenever we stepped onto the street, unshaven men with droopy eyes and skulking bodies emerged from corners and benches, buzzing, their hands tapping their torsos, their eyes red and bulging. This only made us fiend for sugar harder, for that sweet line that connected us to when we were still children, to the time before.

———

It was the summer Mayor Koch announced recycling. The buzzing of cicadas lay over the city like an electric blanket. Saima and I were lying under the oak tree, studying the prehistoric husk of a cicada shell we'd found. There were rips in the armor, where it'd come out of its skin.

For days, I'd been trying to convince Saima that we should do what the signs all over Key Food said: RECYCLE! TRADE IN CANS FOR MONEY! DO YOUR PART TO SAVE THE EARTH! For every can we returned, we could get a nickel, and with each nickel we could buy two caramel toffees, five Tootsie Rolls, two Mary Janes, or two Bazooka Joes. I dreamed of the penny candy display falling into our laps like the girl who counted her chicks before they hatched. Except instead of chicks, it was cans, covered with fingerprints and filled with spit.

But our mothers wouldn't let us recycle. Even though our families drank Coke like others drank beer and wine, our mothers' pride kept them from turning the cans in. I had no such useless pride.

While looking into the shell of the cicada's eyes, the answer came to me. "Saima! We could get cans from my cousin."

My cousin Osman Bhai had just arrived from Pakistan with his long hippie hair and a giant smile that filled his face. He lived nearby, sharing a room with three other men, their mattresses spread out on the floor. Osman Bhai and his roommates were even younger than the young uncles. Their bodies were strong, tireless. They could make money day and night, and pour it from stores and side businesses back to their mothers and sisters in Pakistan.

The front door was open, and we let ourselves in. Osman Bhai was sitting in the front room, smoking. One of his roommates was on a mattress with his eyes closed. The other was watching TV with the volume turned down low. The apartment smelled of cigarettes, spilled chai, and men's aftershave.

Osman Bhai was surprised to see me and quickly put out his cigarette. "Razia, is everything okay?"

I watched the smoke rising from the ashtray. "Yes, everything's fine." I tried not to look at the men on the mattresses. "Do you have any empty cans we could take?"

"Cans? What? Are you two becoming garbage collectors?"

I smiled. "We want to recycle them."

"You want to make a bicycle out of them?"

"No," Saima said, not knowing he was teasing us. "We get money if we bring them to Key Food."

"How much?"

"Five cents a can," she said, becoming embarrassed.

The ratty-looking roommate on the mattress opened his eyes. "Five cents a can? I'll take them to the store myself."

"Shut up, idiot," Osman Bhai said in Punjabi.

None of the other grown-ups cursed like the young cousins.

The roommate watching TV said, without taking his eyes off the screen, "In America even the children know how to make money."

"What are you going to do with all this money?" Osman Bhai asked.

"Buy candy," Saima and I said at the same time.

Osman Bhai and his roommates all started laughing. Not quite understanding what was so funny, Saima and I shifted uneasily, wanting to get the cans and leave.

"Come with me," Osman Bhai said, and we followed him into the kitchen. There were cans all over the counters and tables. He shook his head, looking at the mess. He filled two plastic bags for us. "Enjoy your candy," he said. "Life is nothing, if not sweet."

When Saima and I stepped back outside, we were each holding a plastic bag, cans popping out like blossoms. A fortune, but instead of feeling satisfied, the sugar demon in me wanted more.

"Do you think we could get some cans from Lucy's?" I asked.

"Lucy's in the Dominican Republic."

It was true. Families in Corona were starting to have enough money to go back home during the summer. Even Shahnaaz had gone to Pakistan after much showing off of her ticket.

"I know. But her dad didn't go. If we get more cans, we could buy our own cookies. Denmark's."

Saima's eyes widened. "Denmark's?" They were our favorite fancy cookie. We loved the crunchy sugar crystals on top of the pretzel shapes, the glazed brown of the buttered chessmen, the swirls of sugar and flour. "Could we really have enough?"

"Yes!" I said. "We're going to be rich!"

We knocked on Lucy's door quietly, hoping Saima's mother wouldn't look out the window and see us. When Lucy's father opened the door, he was in a soccer shirt and shorts, holding a beer can in one hand and a newspaper in the other.

The thought occurred to Saima and me at the same time. How could we touch a can that had touched alcohol?

"Lucy's not here," he said, hiding his surprise underneath gruffness.

Saima was too embarrassed to say anything, so I asked, "Do you have any cans we could recycle?"

"Recycle?"

The word was still new for all of us.

"We just need empty cans to bring to Key Food."

He finally understood. Key Food had been plastering signs all over Corona. "Sure." He tilted his head back and drank the rest of his beer, then held it out to us.

How strange we must have looked to him, two girls trembling at the sight of a beer can. Finally, I reached out my hand, wincing as I touched the cold, wet aluminum.

He closed the door, shaking his head.

The smell from the can was sour, rancid. It wasn't until we dropped it into the bag and watched it disappear, roll down to the bottom of the pile, that we allowed ourselves to breathe.

We'd stepped across some invisible line of morality by accepting the beer can. There was no going back now. I turned toward the back alley near the train tracks. I hadn't been there since Miss Kitten had died. Every time I thought of her broken body, my own body ached. But my desire for sugar was stronger than any suffering.

Saima's eyes followed mine.

"Should we?" I asked. "We'll just get the cans and go."

I took it for granted that Saima would always be by my side. Even when we'd been babies, and our parents had taken photos, she could only sit upright when her body was propped up against mine. I'd smile in a toothless way, but she'd look at the camera terrified. She had the same look on her face now, but I pretended not to see.

The back alley was filled with bottles and cans glinting in the sun. There was the scent of something dirty and undefinable. Vile. Glass vials, dirty clothes, newsprint. Every time I picked up a beer bottle and put it in our bag, I felt terrible. I began to promise myself just this once, just this once and then I'll never do it again.

I looked over at Saima. She was rounded down, intent on gathering bottles and cans as fast as she could. The air was filled with the light of dust. A train went by, loud, screeching. Newspapers and plastic bags flew up, tornadoes in the air.

Then I saw him, a man emerging from behind a dumpster, not far from Saima. He must have been waiting until the screams of the train would hide his sound. He shuffled, hunched a bit to the side as if one half of his body had been accordioned.

His pants were down and he had a thing coming out of them. Wet like a worm.

"Saima," I tried to say, but my voice couldn't leave my throat. He was getting closer and closer. I tried to run toward her, but my feet wouldn't move. The fear came barreling through me. With all my force, I threw the can I had in my hands. The beer flew through the air, like spittle.

Horrified at the rain of beer, Saima screamed, "Razia! What are you doing?"

The man was still moving toward her. She turned and saw him. I was finally able to move. I grabbed her hand and pulled her out of the alley.

Somehow, we ended up back on the street. Saima was still clutching her bag. I'd left mine behind. A cavern of fear opened up inside me. The man could've taken Saima, dragged her away. Without Saima, who would I be brave for?

"I'm sorry, Saima, I'm sorry," was all I could say.

She wouldn't look me in the face. "Let's just go get the money."

We walked to Key Food in silence.

———

It was the same older Italian woman, the cashier who'd sold my mother and me the roach bomb. She saw Saima's plastic bag full of cans and said in a voice barely hiding her contempt, "Go to the back."

In the back of the store, there was a line of Corona folk. I'd thought we'd gathered a lot of cans, but there were old women with five or six full garbage bags. The line was endless. The AC chilled us to the bone. A radio station played over the speakers, loud and jarring commercials that put my teeth on edge. I kept seeing the man's worm slithering toward Saima. She still wouldn't look at me. I wanted to crawl out of my body, exit my skin, but I was trapped, earthbound, unwieldy.

The Can Counter was stationed in the back. He was a heavyset man with thick, unshaven jowls. I remembered him from the deli meats department. Now he worked in can returns. He didn't seem happy about being assigned to this new position.

"How many?" he barked at each person. No matter what people said, whether they knew the count or not, he still counted each bottle and can slowly. Wearing thick gloves, he tossed them into a larger garbage container. "Disgusting," he said, as if he was referring to the recycling, but really he meant us. When there was any liquid left, he screamed, "Empty this shit out."

Now I understood why our mothers hadn't wanted us to do this.

When it was finally our turn, he leaned down over the counter. His eyes focused on my chest, and then on my face.

"How old are you?" he asked, his eyes narrowing. He was going to hold on to his little bit of power. He wasn't going to give us money without tormenting us.

"Why? There's nothing on the signs about age." But even as I said it, I realized we were the only children on the line.

"Razia, let's just go." Saima tugged on my sleeve.

He laughed, seeing he was getting to Saima. "I can take the cans, but I can't give you any money." He chewed on a toothpick. "I don't know if I can pay kids under eighteen. It's in the fine print."

The rage I'd been keeping inside ripped through me, searing me free. I hated men, every man, especially this man in front of me. "There's no fine print!"

People began to grumble. "Hey, what's the holdup?"

The crowd parted and the Key Food owner stepped up to us. He was a young Korean man. I could see the Can Collector's lips curl up in hate.

"What's the problem here?" the owner asked.

"These girls are too young to be selling cans."

The owner looked at us. His eyes softened. "Just give them the money and keep the line moving."

His pity felt even worse than the hate.

The Can Collector snarled, "Yes, sir." He counted out our cans, then pulled out the dirtiest dollar bills, the most rusted pennies.

I wondered if they had set up the register that way. As if we deserved nothing better.

When we left Key Food, our hands were empty of garbage but full of money. I could feel the rusty pennies sweating between my fingers. Saima let her bag go and we watched it float away in the wind.

Having been quiet in Key Food, the sugar demon rushed back into my body. It was sulky now, but still persistent. *Now can we get some candy?*

I looked at Saima. Her whole body slumped down. Her eyes scanned the cracks in the sidewalks. I took her hand. "Come on."

The bell rang as we opened the door to the bodega. The owner looked up from the newspaper he was reading. I threw our coins across the counter. They fell and spun, shone like planets.

"We want everything," I said.

The bodega owner laughed and Saima finally began to smile as he pulled out candy after candy and filled her hands. I could see sugar crystals in her eyes. She leaned toward me, and I held her body up with mine.

BOOK TWO

Fall 1985 – Summer 1986

SABAK

My mother taught Quran to all the neighborhood kids. Well, the Pakistani Muslim ones, at least: Saima, Ziyad, Shahnaaz, and me. Yes, even Shahnaaz had gotten roped in. Her mother had heard there was a place she could send Shahnaaz for a few hours where she could learn Quran (nothing wrong with that!) and be out of her mother's hair and trouble.

The other mothers knew my mother was the only one strict enough to keep us kids Allah-fearing. She kept a yellow plastic baseball bat at her side. She never used it, but the threat was real. Just seeing it made everyone scared enough to keep reading.

My mother taught us Quran as my grandmother had back in the mountains of Pakistan. When my grandfather's heart had burst inside his chest, my grandmother was left with four young children. Within a year, there was only my mother remaining. One child died of fever, his body heating up the cold house; one child died of hunger, her body slowly drifting away. The last son was murdered, flying off the mountainside, an imprint of a foot left on his back. His body was found by the village children who surrounded it, thinking it was a game. It was only when my grandmother flew through the crowd screaming that they knew it wasn't.

My grandmother survived by teaching Quran to the girls of the village. The girls' families paid her in eggs and milk from the buffalo. They washed my grandmother's dishes and clothes. They played with my mother, the baby, as if she was a doll.

My mother taught Quran in the same style as my grandmother. Well, almost. I couldn't imagine Saima, Ziyad, and Shahnaaz washing our dishes. But they did arrive every Saturday morning with their Qaidas or Qurans, just like the girls in the village. They sat cross-legged on the sheet my mother put on the floor and began reading in a language both achingly beautiful and indecipherable. None of us understood Arbi.

Each of us had our own way of reciting. I fell into my own meditation, loving the sounds, meaning or no meaning. Saima struggled, trying to untangle the letters like patterns of insect wings. Shahnaaz stared dreamily out the window, quickly looking down at her Qaida if my mother glanced at her. Experienced as a young fox, Shahnaaz was always one second ahead of my mother.

Ziyad rocked back and forth like the boys in Pakistani madrasas. When Ziyad's mother had found out about the death of the kitten and the company he was keeping, he'd been nearly skinned alive. His father had intervened and sent Ziyad to Hafiz Saab. He'd become too busy to teach the rest of us, but for Ziyad, he made an exception. Ziyad had become born again, one whom the light of Allah had forgiven.

I wondered sometimes what it would have been like if girls could go to our masjid. Would we be able to transform the darkness of our anger into gold, our mistakes into light?

My mother lavished the rooms in our house with artistic attention. We read Sabak in the living room, her study in orange. There was an orange carpet, orange walls, and orange sofas covered in plastic. The shelves were filled with beautiful objects, elephant figurines decorated with tiny mirrors and brightly colored plastic flowers in carved vases. The walls were covered with tapestries of Mecca and Medina and framed works of calligraphy, proclaiming "Allah, Allah, Allah" from every corner.

There wasn't any air-conditioning, and the air was sticky with heat and the buzz of insects. The fan blew warm air side to side. After an hour of everyone reading out loud, stumbling over words, or doing a soft hum of smooth sounds, our eyes were starting to close.

My mother had a thin film of sweat on her forehead. She corrected everyone, getting more and more frustrated. We were making more mistakes than usual. "What's wrong with you today? Have you left your brains in your shoes? Put away your saparahs and let's finish with taleem."

We gathered into a circle so my mother could tell stories from the Quran. Today she began with the creation story: "Adam was made from clay from the earth, from mud molded into shape, then Eve was made from his ribs . . ."

While she told the old story, I looked out the window. A ray of sun slanted in. On the branches of the oak tree, I could see the leaves dappled with light, with dark shadows underneath. I followed the trunk of the old oak deep into the earth where we came from. Its roots spread so far, I imagined them stretching through Corona all the way to Pakistan.

Shahnaaz interrupted my mother. "But, Aunty, how can people be made from dirt?"

I was afraid of how my mother would respond, but she surprised me by laughing. Her laugh was so beautiful and contagious, everyone started giggling. Everyone but me. In my mind, being made from dirt was as believable as any other story of how people came to be.

My mother was still laughing when the phone rang. She didn't answer Shahnaaz's question. She just said, "Go ahead. Go outside." Shahnaaz and Saima didn't wait another moment, but my mother held me back. "Razia, get the phone."

Ziyad got up slowly. "Aunty, can I go to masjid?" he asked. My mother looked at him with approval and I felt a twinge of jealousy.

When I answered the phone, it was Saima's mother. She said salaam and then asked in strained Urdu, "Is your mother free?" Unlike the other aunties who spoke Urdu and Punjabi, Saima's mother mostly spoke Pashto. My parents spoke Pashto too, but they hadn't taught me. It was their secret language. I handed my mother the phone and slipped out the door.

Saima and Shahnaaz had already settled under the oak tree, the only place with shade. The rest of the yard was doused in a golden autumn light. Their bodies glowed like incandescent lamps.

It had not rained in days and dust rose in the air. When we had first moved in, the yard had been well kept with hydrangeas, roses, and morning glories, but every year since, it had gotten wilder. In the mountains of Pakistan, everything grew wild and it was fine and beautiful. My parents didn't realize or accept that here, nature had to be tamed.

I joined Saima and Shahnaaz and fanned myself with the bottom of my kameez. In the last few years, Shahnaaz's family had become rich, their gas stations blooming all over Queens. She was always showing up to Sabak with a new gift from her father. Today she wore a golden heart-shaped locket around her neck. She pulled the locket away from her skin, pretending it was burning her, but I knew she was just showing it off. "My father bought me this." She opened it up to show a baby picture of her, next to a picture of her brother, Amir.

Saima looked with hunger. I wanted to tell her not to give Shahnaaz the satisfaction, but even I imagined for a brief moment having a locket like hers.

"I'm going to ask my father to get me a locket," Saima said.

Shahnaaz laughed. "Your family doesn't have that much money."

Saima's face turned red. "Yes, they do!"

Shahnaaz shook her head as if we were naive. "My father says he's going to buy both your fathers' stores when they go out of business."

Saima and I went silent. Shahnaaz often knew the secret things grown-ups talked about, and I was afraid it was true.

"That's why your mother has to take money for teaching Quran."

I grew hot, thinking of how my mother quickly slid the envelopes Saima and Shahnaaz brought into her purse.

Before I could think of a comeback, we saw Saima's mother hurrying down the street with Saima's baby brother, Ijaz, in a stroller. He was kicking his legs and crying. Her dupatta was in a strangle around her neck.

Shahnaaz jumped up. "I'm out of here." She wanted nothing to do with Saima's mother. Shahnaaz disappeared, like the fox she was, into the tall grass and out the gate.

"Asalaamu alaikum," Saima's mother said, tight-mouthed.

We mumbled, "Wa alaikum asalaam."

"Where's Ziyad?" Saima's mother asked in Pashto.

Saima looked terrified. "Masjid."

Her mother turned her gaze on me. "Ammi upar hai?"

"Yes, Ammi's upstairs."

She pulled Ijaz out of the stroller. He whimpered as they disappeared through the front door.

I turned to Saima. "What's going on?"

"I don't know," Saima said, looking down at her feet. I knew her well enough to know she was lying.

"Let's see what they're talking about."

Saima hesitated, but then followed me up the stairs.

We peeked into the living room from behind the curtain. Ijaz was in a pile of toys in the corner, sitting up, silent, as though he'd gone to a deep place inside himself. Tears rolled down his face.

At first, I couldn't tell if it was the Pashto or if it was what my mother and Saima's mother were talking about that made it sound so rough. The only words I could understand were "Azim . . . Gosht Dukan . . ." and "Azim" again.

Suddenly, curses flew across the room. Saima gripped my arm. Her mother turned away from my mother and picked up Ijaz abruptly. He came to from the suddenness and began wailing. "Khuda hafiz!"

Saima and I bolted down the stairs. When Saima's mother saw us sitting under the oak tree, rage clouded her face. "Saima! Dalta rasha!"

Saima got up and followed her mother without looking back.

When I got upstairs, my mother was on the phone. I knew from her tone that she was speaking to Taibah Aunty, a new aunty in the neighborhood.

I hid behind the door and listened while my mother told Taibah Aunty how she was never letting Saima's mother into our house again. "We gave her brother a job and this is how he repays us . . . by stealing."

I watched my mother, with the phone in the crook of her neck, the cord spirally as a pig's tail. Now it all made sense, the growing tension, the strained whispers between my parents in their secret language.

After the fight, my mother stopped teaching Quran. The sounds of children reading Sabak no longer filled the house. I sat alone in the living room, reading by myself. Waves of loneliness washed over me as I tried to burrow inside and find peace in the surahs.

Days turned to weeks, and our families still didn't talk.

The sadness was unbearable. Saima had been my best friend, the only friend my mother had allowed me to have. Without her, there was no one.

My father began to look like a shadow of himself. His face took on lines of worry I hadn't seen before. It was only my mother who seemed to grow big, angrily vacuuming the living room each day. She'd never really liked Saima's mother or the amount of attention my father gave her father, his best friend.

But we did not speak of it. In my family, we didn't speak.

On the last day I ever went to Saima's house, I carried a tray of lunch to the store. My father had worked a night shift at a hospital lab and then gone straight to the Gosht Dukan in the morning. When the store had begun to hemorrhage money, he had to find lab work and only the night shift was available. Rather than the store becoming a new life for him, it had become another mouth to feed. Without Azim, my father had to be there from opening to close. He didn't even have time to eat. I brought all his meals to the store.

When I entered, he was sitting at the counter, reading Quran with a peaceful expression on his face. The door was propped open, and the flies were coming in. My father had a blue flyswatter next to him and when a fly buzzed too close, he reached for the swatter and saw me. He didn't kill the fly.

"Razia." He put his Quran down and smiled.

I placed the tray on the wooden plank that lowered to separate the back of the butcher shop from the part where the dried goods were kept. He pulled off the kitchen towel. His smile grew when he saw the food. There was keema in a bowl and roti.

"Hungry?" he asked. I shook my head.

He dug in and I looked away, not wanting to see his hunger. There was a dusty fan blowing air around. I followed its rotating eye and saw how sooty the walls were from the passing cars, how the fresh paint my father had put on years ago had yellowed, especially since Azim had let his friends smoke inside. The store felt shabby in a way it hadn't when it had been filled with the uncles' laughter.

When my father finished eating, he got the plastic jug from the back and poured water into a small, almost-transparent plastic cup.

"Pani?" he asked.

I shook my head, then blurted out, "Ammi says Azim's stealing from the store."

My father was quiet for a second, then said, "Oh, you know, your Ammi, she worries too much."

"Was he? Was he stealing?" I persisted. I needed to know if it was true. Azim hadn't just been stealing from the store, he'd been stealing my father's time away from me.

"Money." My father shook his head, his eyes sad even though he was smiling. He put up his hands. "Money is nothing. This life is nothing. It's all about after." He put his finger up in the air and made it leap. I followed the line, the trace of it.

I wanted to say, "Money does matter," but my voice choked and my stomach tightened like the clasp of my mother's purse when I followed her around Key Food, never asking for anything I wanted to eat.

Money was why my father had to work day and night and was never home. Money was why girls like Shahnaaz got heart-shaped lockets and thought they were better than me. Money was why Saima and I couldn't speak.

He continued, "This is just a storm that'll pass. Your mother's anger will disappear. Then everything will be fine."

We were both silent. The fan turned around and around, blowing dust into our faces. I scratched my finger into the wood of the counter.

"Have you seen Saima?" he asked.

I looked up, my heart in my throat.

"Just because we're having problems doesn't mean you can't see her." I hadn't imagined it any other way.

"Why don't you go over there now?"

"But what about Ammi?"

"Don't worry about Ammi. I'll talk to her."

I ran to Saima's, feeling the sun on my face. The closer I came to her house, the more I felt my father was right. It would all blow over one day.

Saima and Shahnaaz were in the front yard, under the grapevines. Shahnaaz had taken my place beside Saima. Together, they were pulling down lush purple grapes, as if it didn't matter at all that I wasn't there.

I entered the yard as I always had, the gate closing behind me. Saima's body imperceptibly jerked as if she wanted to jump up and hug me, but she held herself back. She looked up to the window, to see if her mother was watching. I looked up too, but I didn't care about her mother anymore.

"What are you doing here?" Shahnaaz asked, an edge to her voice. "Did your mother let you come?"

"Saima," I said, ignoring Shahnaaz.

"I can't hang out with you," Saima said in a low voice. "Your mother called my uncle a thief and my mother a liar."

"So?" I didn't understand why Saima was taking sides in adult fights.

"So," she said, getting bolder, "it isn't true."

"I don't care if it's true or not."

Shahnaaz stood up as if she was going to fight me. "If your mother believes things that aren't true, your mother's crazy!"

"My mother's not crazy!" I stepped toward her, ready to fight.

Hearing the commotion, Saima's mother came outside. She didn't even bother to look at me. Instead, she said harsh words to Saima. With a look of pain, Saima followed her inside. Shahnaaz climbed back over the fence, laughing a cruel laugh.

I ran home, Shahnaaz's laughter trailing behind me like smoke and ash. What if there was something wrong with my mother? What if there was something wrong with all of our mothers? Would anyone but us children ever know?

I ended up back in my front yard, but I couldn't bear to go inside, to the stifling quiet that filled the house. I sat down at the foot of the oak tree, bitterness filling my throat.

The roots of the oak tree were exposed, pushing out the earth. I laid my head down on them and felt a wave of exhaustion coming over me.

I looked up at the branches heavy with leaves. I closed my eyes and saw the bodies of children flying off mountainsides, out of their burning skin, scratching the corners of the sky. Children soaring into the light, Saima among them, while I lay chained to the earth, the way Allah had cursed me to be.

EXORCIST

Without Saima, I was always alone on the streets. There were men on every corner. They hung around the sides of buildings and stared with the focused glares of wolves. They whistled and whispered dirty words. They knew they could overpower me. They knew it and I knew it. Whether I ignored them and said nothing or whether I got mad enough to scream, there was no winning. I'd feel dirty and stained, soiled, anytime I left my house.

The library was the only place I felt safe. There, the librarians sat close to the front doors at the circulation desk. As it became colder, they let some of the wandering men in, but only the ones who slept, their faces falling into the words of newspapers, their feet rotting in their dirty sneakers.

I always smiled at the librarians, and they looked back at me, a little puzzled that a girl in salwar kameez could be so obsessed with reading. But like the sleeping men, I was one of the regulars. Every week, I chose a pile of books from the "Classics" shelf, usually based on the cover illustrations.

I'd read *The Secret Garden* because of a drawing of a young girl opening a round doorway carved into a brick wall, ivy and roses dripping over her as she looked back, afraid of anyone seeing her. I'd read *From the Mixed-Up Files of Mrs. Basil E. Frankweiler* because of a drawing of two children with suitcases in their hands, staring up the steep stairs of what looked like a temple, but which I learned was the Metropolitan Museum of Art.

Today, though, I was looking for a book about something real. Jinns. Ever since the fight between my mother and Saima's mother, I'd been having strange dreams. I'd wake up frozen, paralyzed, my hands curled up in front of my face. I'd have no power to move them or any part of my body.

Then a shadow of a man would rise from the foot of my bed. His weight would travel over me like a slow earthquake. I'd hear whispers around me: "Razia, Razia." My bed would begin to shake, only a vibration at first, but then it would leap out of the frame.

"Ammi!" I'd try to scream, crying out for my mother in a way I hadn't since I'd been a kid, but I'd be unable to move my lips. I'd struggle until I'd fall into darkness.

Now I wandered between the library shelves, lost. Nonfiction books were labeled by number, not by author, and I couldn't figure out the formula matching numbers to books. I approached the librarian at the circulation desk. She was wearing bright red lipstick and glasses, thick ovals around her eyes.

There was a clock over her head. It ticked quietly, doing its job. She was busy checking in books and didn't notice me at first, or at least pretended she didn't. I waited, looking at the novels the librarians had chosen to highlight that week. They always placed two or three books on the wood paneling of their circulation desk. A book caught my eye. There was a tree spread across the cover. Its smooth skin shone in the sun, its limbs stretched toward Heaven. A young girl sat in its lap, reading.

"Can I help you?" the librarian finally asked.

"I . . ." I'd never asked a librarian for a book before. I was too in awe of them. "I'm looking for a book on—" But there was no exact translation for "Jinn." "I'm looking for a book on demons."

"Demons?" She raised her penciled-in eyebrows, and I saw myself in the reflection of her glasses: an awkward Pakistani girl wearing the brightest salwar kameez you could imagine.

"Ghosts," I said, backtracking, knowing ghosts were a more acceptable English term.

"Ah," she said, smiling. "Come with me."

I followed her, breathing in her smell of sweet perfume and cigarettes. The library wasn't large, but we wound through a maze of books before we came to an aisle I'd never seen before. There was a strange smell, books with curling binders, an eerie yellow glow coming from crinkly pages. I felt as if I'd stumbled into a forest, a dark hallway of trees.

"Dewey put the supernatural first," she said, and smiled. The tips of her front teeth were covered with lipstick.

I didn't know what she meant until I saw we were in the 000s–100s. I turned to thank her, but she'd already disappeared.

I took a deep breath and reached for the thickest book: *The Encyclopedia of Witchcraft and Demonology*. The pages were heavy with illustrations, images of possessions, bodies contorted in fear. I flipped through, horrified and fascinated.

Then I saw it. A black-and-white drawing of a young girl sleeping, a demon-man creeping over her, rising from the bottoms of her feet like an ominous cloud. Sweat broke out under my armpits. I felt like the creature was suddenly here, hiding behind the bookshelves. I closed the book and tried to calm myself with a prayer like my mother had taught me to do.

I opened the book again and became lost in stories of this demon-man who'd appeared to young girls for centuries. How could a creature have existed in 1638 England and then come to Queens in 1985?

A coughing fit from one of the sleeping old men brought me to my senses. I looked around, waking from my own daydream. How long had I been reading?

I rushed to the circulation desk and was shocked to see from the library clock that over an hour had passed. My mother had told me to be back before noon. I dropped the encyclopedia on the discard cart. I could never bring it home. My mother always looked through my books, and since she couldn't read English, she also judged them by their covers.

If I came home without a book, my mother wouldn't believe I'd gone to the library. The book with the tree was still on the circulation desk, open and ready. I brought it to the librarian.

"*A Tree Grows in Brooklyn*." She smiled. "I love this book. It's not about ghosts, though."

"That's okay," I said, looking back with fear at the book I'd discarded.

Outside, a cold autumn wind blew through the streets. I huddled into my coat, holding the library book close to my body.

When I got home, my mother was folding laundry in the living room. I wanted to go to my bedroom but was afraid. My mother looked over at me. "What's wrong?"

My longing for her protection outweighed my fear of what she'd say. "Ammi, there's a Jinn in my room."

Annoyance, then belief washed over her face. It was something she'd always suspected, something she blamed for the darkness that loomed over our house.

Her eyes narrowed and she walked quickly to my room. I followed her. As soon as she stepped in, she started picking up clothes from the floor. "What's wrong with you? Clean this mess!" Then, remembering what she'd come in for, she asked, "Where did you see the Jinn?"

"It was at the foot of the bed, saying my name . . ."

"Astaghfirullah. It knows your name." She prayed the Ayatul Kursi and blew it around. "This is what happens when you miss Fajr."

I remembered half in a dream that my mother had tried to wake me up for Fajr namaaz, but I'd kept going back to sleep. That was when the creature had come in, during the last hour before dawn.

"Go read Fajr now."

My mother knew Allah accepted late namaazes the way teachers accepted late homework: begrudgingly, but glad we'd put in the effort.

I went to the bathroom to do wuzu. I splashed water on my face and looked in the mirror. My body seemed to be melting into a strange squish ball of wax. My lips were shrinking, my nose was growing. Worst of all, my breasts had burst like mushrooms overnight. They were what attracted the Eyes. Maybe they were what attracted the Jinns. I wrapped my dupatta around my chest and went to the bedroom to pray.

I started off my namaaz with my intention. "Allah, I'm reading two rakaat for my late Fajr." I said "late" with the proper amount of apology in my voice.

These intentions always were odd to me. Shouldn't Allah already know what I was going to pray? When I'd asked my mother, she'd said,

"Of course Allah knows. But Allah wants to know if you know what you're doing."

When I was done, I cupped my hands for dua, my private time with Allah. "Oh, Allah! Please don't let me be possessed like that girl from *The Exorcist*. I don't think I could handle it. Life's already so hard without a Jinn coming into me. Please, Allah, protect me."

I wrapped up my prayer with two puffs of air to either side of my shoulder, so the angels could bring it up to Heaven.

When I got to the living room, my mother was already reading Quran. As soon as I sat next to her, she started reciting prayers over me. My mother knew a million prayers of protection. I began to feel calm. I didn't know how much time had passed before my mother stood up and said, "Keep reading."

She went to the phone in the kitchen, where she thought I couldn't hear her, but I knew from her tone that she was speaking to Taibah Aunty. Taibah Aunty had anointed herself the spiritual advisor for the women in the community, especially for issues that couldn't be brought to Hafiz Saab. I shivered, wondering what they had in store for me.

On the 7 train, some of the people stared at our salwar kameez, but most just minded their own business. My mother and I had never been on a subway together before, but Taibah Aunty was an expert at public transportation. She'd been a schoolteacher in Karachi, and the trains in New York City were nothing compared to the crowded open-air bus terminals in Pakistan, where barely anyone knew where the buses were going.

I could tell from the way my mother was quiet that she was nervous and trying not to show it. Taibah Aunty filled the air with chatter. Listening to her stories, I began to wonder how often she came to the Peer Saab and if she got a cut.

Every time she leaned close, I got a whiff of rose oil. "He's very good. When Jabeen was unable to have children, I took her to see him. Then Ali was born. And when Ghazala didn't want to get married, her mother brought her. Whatever taweez he gave her straightened her right out."

I understood now why my mother was taking me on a Sunday. It was the day my father worked at a lab and the Gosht Dukan. He wouldn't have approved of us seeing anyone who dealt in magic.

I longed for the train to go faster, but it was the 7, after all, and stopped every few minutes. More and more people got on. I could hear them cursing their lives under their breath. They held on to wheelie carts full of orange and yellow plastic bags of groceries. The smiling faces on their bags were the only faces smiling among them.

In the corner, a group of teenage girls were decked out in makeup like tropical birds, laughing and being loud. One of them caught me looking and smirked.

Embarrassed, I pulled out my library book and began reading: *Serene was a word you could put to Brooklyn, New York. Especially in the summer of 1912. Somber, as a word, was better. But it did not apply to Williamsburg, Brooklyn.*

I was transported to a world where children roamed the streets. They were gathering garbage to sell, and it all came back to me: the day Saima and I had gone recycling, the man in the alley, the cold air in Key Food, the cruelty of the Can Counter, and, afterward, how Saima had smiled, her hands full of penny candy. I'd never thought my life wouldn't include Saima. I buried myself in the book so I wouldn't think of her anymore.

Too soon, the conductor said, "74th Street–Roosevelt Avenue," and my mother poked me to get up. Taibah Aunty knew exactly where she was going. She took us through the main thoroughfare of Jackson Heights. The streets were bustling with desis, the smell of kebabs, incense, samosas. There were white mannequins dressed in salwar kameez and gararas and mountains of rainbow burfi filling the window displays. Old desi men hung outside shops with soft, thick blankets hanging down from the awnings.

We turned down an empty avenue and stopped in front of a lone house covered in dirty yellow vinyl siding. A dog barked in the distance. The top windows were boarded with wooden planks instead of glass. I panicked and made a move as if to run, but my mother held on to my shoulder and walked me up the stairs.

Although it was a sunny day, it was dark in the house. The radiators were sizzling and popping steam. The air was heavy with the stink of sweat. The Peer Saab was behind a curtain. I caught a glimpse of his enormous knee poking from underneath. A light shone behind him, and I could see his silhouette next to the silhouette of a thin man.

"There's something inside me, twisting my insides," the thin man said in a desperate voice. "It hurts like I'm being cut open. Like bombs going off in my behind. I can't stop them."

My mother and Taibah Aunty put their dupattas over their faces and struggled not to laugh. I was too scared to even smile.

After a silence, the Peer Saab said, "You have a Jinn inside you. Drink this morning and evening." There was the sound of movement, then a fridge opening. "Only eat foods cooked at home and avoid all milk. I will make you a taweez. Allah willing, the Jinns will leave you alone."

It was quiet for a few minutes. Then the thin man gave profuse thanks, and the curtain parted. Seeing us, he got embarrassed and scurried away. The curtain fell closed behind him.

"Asalaamu alaikum, sisters," the Peer Saab called out.

"Wa alaikum asalaam," my mother and Taibah Aunty said shyly, as if they were in the presence of a rock star.

"How can I help you?"

Taibah Aunty nudged my mother and she began. "My daughter is being visited by Jinns. They're coming to her when she sleeps."

The Peer Saab didn't say anything. He was quiet for so long I wondered if he was getting paid by the minute. His shadow picked its teeth with a toothpick.

My mother filled the silence. "I feel like someone has put an evil eye on her. I knew it would happen. She reads Quran so beautifully."

My mother was praising me. I couldn't believe it.

"Mashallah," the Peer Saab said, but I could tell from his tone that he didn't want my mother to talk.

"She was only seven when she finished the Quran for the first time," my mother continued. "Her father wanted her to have a big Ameen. I told him we should do something simple, but he wanted to invite everyone. Our whole community was there. That must have been when she got the evil eye."

"Yes, pride invites the devil," the Peer Saab said. My skin bristled.

He was insulting my father, but my mother didn't seem to notice. She was going through the guest list in her mind, wondering who had put the evil eye on me. "Please open the curtain."

My mother hesitated, but Taibah Aunty pulled aside the curtain for her.

My skin withered when I saw him. There were pockmarks on his face, holes the size of craters. He was wearing one of those white Arbi robes and underneath, there was just a mass of flesh.

I looked down while he stared at me without saying a word. Unlike the stares from the men on the street, his eyes seemed to peer beneath my skin, to the inner workings of my soul. I shivered, even though the room was unbearably hot.

Finally he said, "Allah, subhanahu wa ta'ala said Jinn were created from 'marijin min nar,' a smokeless flame of fire. They are in a world of their own, separate but connected to humans and angels. There are times they attach themselves to special persons. Is your daughter different from other children?"

My mother looked surprised. "She just . . . All of the children here are different."

Taibah Aunty looked nervous, as if my mother had been impertinent, but the Peer Saab laughed, a long, low laugh. "I understand. Does she ever seem different from children born here?"

I looked up. He'd said something true. I *was* different. I had no words for this difference. No way of explaining.

Without waiting for an answer, he continued, "Your child is loved by the Jinns. Her difference attracts them. You will need to work extra hard to protect her."

My mother and Taibah Aunty nodded, taking it all in.

"You mustn't let her watch television."

"She doesn't," my mother said slowly, looking guilty, probably remembering all the times she'd put me in front of the TV since I'd been a baby.

"She mustn't listen to American music."

"Of course not." Music was strictly banned in our house.

"She mustn't read books." He said "books" as if it was a curse word.

My mother straightened up but didn't respond. Finally she said, "She needs to read books for school. She's in junior high school now."

The Peer Saab cleared his throat as if he was going to spit, but then said with anger simmering underneath, "You mustn't let her read more books than she has to."

My mother looked at Taibah Aunty and then looked down. "Hmmmm, yes."

Rage rose through me, burning my throat. I knew I couldn't say anything. I could only pray. *Allah, please make Ammi not listen to him. Allah, please make Ammi not listen to him.* I hoped Allah would hear me even in this dark place.

The Peer opened the minifridge that was behind him. It was full of small bottles of water.

"Zam Zam," he said.

My mother and Taibah Aunty hummed in appreciation. Of course he'd have Zam Zam, the prized possession and delight of any Muslim. It was salty spring water, so even though it came from the ground, it tasted of the ocean.

He took the cap off a bottle and began to recite duas under his breath and blow on the water. I winced, wondering if his saliva germs were going into the bottle.

"Which duas are you reading?" my mother asked, seeing if she could add more to her repertoire.

But he ignored her. Instead he said, "Give her the Zam Zam every morning at dawn and every evening before she goes to sleep, until it's finished."

He pulled a slip of white paper from a pile, then a fountain pen from his shirt pocket. He began to write in Arbi. Blue ink soaked into the thin onionskin paper. He folded the paper into smaller and smaller folds. I was surprised at how his enormous fingers could be so precise.

He pulled a small black square of cloth from another pile, tucked the prayer in the opening, and pulled a threaded needle out of his shirt pocket. He handled the needle effortlessly, his whole body transformed by the sewing. He sewed up the paper in the cloth with a red thread. Finally, he knotted the thread around the cloth and placed the taweez along with the bottle on the floor in front of my mother.

"She must wear this taweez at all times and drink the Zam Zam. She mustn't read books anymore. Allah willing, the Jinns will leave her alone."

Before my mother could say anything, we heard the door open. A male customer walked in and sat down next to the Peer Saab. He gave us a look, then pulled the curtain closed.

"Anything else, sisters?" Peer Saab asked.

"How much?" my mother whispered to Taibah Aunty.

"Fifty," Taibah Aunty whispered back.

I felt faint with guilt as I watched my mother count out the bills and slip them under the curtain. It was a fortune. The Peer Saab's nimble fingers appeared and quickly took the money.

When we walked out of the house, I was stunned by the brightness of the day.

"I'm going to do some shopping," Taibah Aunty said to my mother. "Do you need anything?" She glanced at my mother's stomach. I felt something I couldn't identify pass between them.

My mother shook her head. She seemed lost in her own thoughts. Seeing the look on my mother's face, Taibah Aunty said, "Don't worry, it will be fine. The Peer Saab is very good." She smiled at me, then gave my mother directions back to the train.

We were quiet for the whole walk. I didn't trust my voice. We found the station and walked up the stairs to the platform. The benches were empty. Not many people were heading deeper into Queens at this time of day. My mother pulled her mini-Quran from her purse and started reading. I was too afraid to take out my library book.

My mother looked up. "Why aren't you reading?"

"But the Peer Saab said . . ."

"Razia." She sighed. "When I was growing up . . ." Her voice began to shift to her story voice. "Families didn't want their daughters to learn how to read because of what people would say. Even the families who wanted their daughters to learn thought it wasn't safe to let them travel to schools so far from home. You see, sometimes men bothered girls on the way." She whispered this, even though no one else was listening.

"After a time, some families started letting their daughters go to school, but not my family. You see, my mother was a widow and I had no father or brothers to protect me from—" She stopped, probably realizing she didn't want to tell me what it was she needed protection from. But I already knew.

"I begged my mother to let me go, but she always said no. I was so jealous of the girls who went to school with their uniforms, carrying tablets under their arms and chalk in their pockets. I'd collect rocks and pretend I was writing in the dirt." She laughed a dry laugh. "Then one day my mother was away, visiting a sick person in a nearby village. She was an important spiritual woman and sick people would want her to pray with them." There was always a hint of pride when my mother spoke of my grandmother. "She left me behind, and I followed the other girls to school. The teacher was so happy when she saw me. She thought my mother had changed her mind.

"But I've always been unlucky. It was the same day the headmaster came to visit. The headmaster was your Big Uncle and when he saw me, he lost his temper and shouted, 'What are you doing here?' He grabbed me by the ear in front of the class and pulled me out of the seat. He dragged me the whole way home. That was my first and last day of school."

"Why? Why did he do that?"

My mother became irritated. She thought I wasn't listening. "I told you. My family didn't think girls should go to school."

"But your uncle was the headmaster." I just couldn't understand something so unfair.

My mother sighed. "That made it worse for him."

None of it made sense to me. The train pulled into the station. We found seats and my mother opened up her mini-Quran. She had saved her place with her finger the whole time she was telling her story. "You'll wear the taweez and drink Zam Zam, but you'll also read."

With our books in our laps, we read together all the way home. The train rocked us into something that was almost like sleep, and the Jinns never bothered me again.

ABANDONED BREAD TRUCK

Every few weeks, an abandoned car showed up outside our dining room window. The car was left there sometimes on a Saturday night, whole for just a moment before it started to decay. Every morning after that, pieces went missing. The tires were the first to go. Then the windows were shattered and the insides gutted. Finally, the engine lid popped open and pieces of the car disappeared. As suddenly as the car had come, it was gone, but its space wasn't empty for long before another car showed up to take its place.

On winter mornings, I sat on the radiator and looked out our window. It was the only way to stay warm. I saw the abandoned cars and imagined I was living in the desert, or a high, distant plain, walking past the same dead animal laid to rest on the sand and in the heat. I imagined it stripped by secret claws and beaks. Pieces always disappeared while I was asleep.

One especially bitter January morning, a bread truck delivering fresh Italian bread stalled right outside of our house. The truck driver was a big man. He got out and cursed and kicked the truck. His curses made smoke in the air. He walked off to find a pay phone, but there were few working pay phones in Corona. He turned the corner and disappeared.

It was a snow day, and already children were coming outside to make snow angels and pretend they were skating on patches of ice. They came out in their boots and their cheap coats from Alexander's. I saw Julio with his friends, a group of boys who orbited him like wobbly planets.

They noticed the abandoned bread truck and began to circle it, as if it was a boy they were ready to gang up on. Julio jumped up on the step and tried to pull open the door, but it was locked. His friends threw snowballs at the truck. The white on white hit the metal and bounced off. Soon they got bored and wandered off to make trouble somewhere else.

I began to see faces in the windows of the buildings across the street: the three old Italian ladies who always wore black, the young Dominican mothers of the kids in my school, holding baby brothers and sisters on their hips. The bread truck had made the mistake of stalling on the street where all the abandoned cars were left.

Everyone was waiting to see what would happen.

The old Italian ladies were the first to arrive. As if they'd been given a signal, they all vanished from their different apartments, then showed up on the snow, like black crows on ice. They crept up to the back of the truck. I ran to tell my mother. She was in the kitchen scrubbing the counters with Mr. Clean. Her pregnant belly pushed against the counter.

We were going to have a baby, and I prayed it would be a little sister. I tried not to bother my mother as she always seemed overwhelmed, but I couldn't help rushing over to her now. "Ammi, something's happening."

By the time my mother washed her hands and came with me, there was a mob on the street. Julio had returned with his father and a crowbar. His father looked around for the driver. When he saw no one, he popped open the back like he was opening a can of soda and went into the truck. He emerged after a few moments, his arms full of loaves of bread. He threw an armful to Julio, who ran home with it.

Slowly other people started coming to the back of the truck. The old Italian ladies were at the head, but behind them was the Korean grandmother, the young Dominican mothers, and more kids from my school. Some of them waited for Julio's father to throw them bread. Others jumped in themselves and grabbed armfuls of Italian bread with or without seeds, whole loaves and rolls. They ran home hugging the fresh bread to their chests.

I looked up at my mother, waiting for her to say something about the people in our neighborhood, but instead she said, "Put on your coat."

"Kya?" I asked, afraid I'd get in trouble if I'd misheard. This was the same mother who made me walk back to the bodega to give back even five cents if they gave me too much change.

She looked at me again. "Put on your coat and get some bread."

It was as if someone had thrown a block party in the middle of the winter. I'd never seen my neighbors smiling at each other this way. I walked to the truck, feeling cold in my thin coat. But the ice was nothing when Julio's father put a loaf of steamy, soft bread in my arms. It was like a baby, a new baby, for us to have. The snow crunched under my feet, and I looked up to see my mother smiling down at me, her face pressed against the glass.

ASSEMBLY

Nothing in I.S. 61 was ever warm. The windows and vinyl pull-down shades rattled as a frigid wind blew through the streets. The world outside was icy, covered with layers of hardened, dirty snow. There was slush in the sewers and glaciers on the edges of the roads.

Ms. Cooperman, our teacher, frowned as she saw us shivering. "Bring your coats," she said. "We're having an assembly."

The whole class groaned. It had snowed heavily the night before, and so many teachers were absent, there wasn't enough staff to hold classes. It would be another day in the auditorium watching *The Red Balloon*.

The Red Balloon was a silent film about a lonely boy left to wander Paris streets by himself. That is, until he meets a magic red balloon. Wherever the lonely boy goes—home, church, school—he's punished for keeping company with the red balloon. I don't know why they showed us this movie over and over. It might have been the only movie the school owned.

We knew the drill. Boys in one line, girls in another, size order. Normally, I stood next to Nelson, a short boy who wore a headset and braces, and Salman, a boy who the teachers thought was a genius, but they were both absent, so I ended up next to Julio.

Ever since first grade, Julio and I had been tracked into the same honors classes. It was the same at I.S. 61. The only difference was that now he followed me around. Maybe it was because I was familiar, maybe it was my new body, the one that brought all the boys to trail after me.

When I hung my coat in the coat closet, Julio was right behind.

When I secretly read books under my desk, hoping no one would notice, he saw me and smiled. If I went up to the board to sharpen my pencil, he tried to catch my eye. I'd turn and pretend to study the bulletin board where our spelling tests were on display. Julio's and my tests, the ones with the highest scores, were stapled next to each other. Even my spelling test couldn't get away from him.

Ms. Cooperman sensed something and always made Julio and me partners or rivals. If there was a poster contest about the Statue of Liberty, we were the ones chosen to come up with designs to represent the school. If there was a spelling bee, we were captains of opposing teams. Even if a note had to be delivered to the main office, either me or Julio was sent.

It became a class joke. Whenever Ms. Cooperman said, "I need someone to—" a boy would yell out, "Julio!" Then another would shout, "No, Razia! It's Razia this time."

But today Ms. Cooperman wasn't showing any favorites. "Line up! Line up!" she shouted, practically pushing us out of the freezing room.

The entire sixth grade funneled into the auditorium. The teachers tried to get us into our designated rows of wooden seats. Normally girls sat with girls and boys with boys, but things were so chaotic, the lines got mixed up and Julio ended up sitting next to me. I held the wooden armrests between us and tried not to inhale his scent of Tide and boy sweat. It felt as if the school had turned up the heat, though I knew they never would.

Our principal, Mr. Nichols, walked to the front of the stage. He was skinny and pale, and always dressed in a tie and a jacket. "Boys and girls!" His voice boomed through the microphone, but we didn't listen. The teachers tried to shush us until they were noisier than we were. Mr. Nichols tried again. "Boys and girls! Pay attention! Today we're going to watch a movie about a very important topic." He said the words carefully, as if they would break in his mouth. "Acquired immunodeficiency syndrome. AIDS."

We stopped fidgeting and hushed. We'd been hearing about AIDS in whispers. Every night on the news the numbers of those who'd died were announced. They were in the thousands and rising. Still, no one told us what AIDS was, only that we should be afraid.

The teachers turned off the lights. The movie screen was blank at first. Then the music began, a slow mourning song. There were three men in hospital beds, thin as skeletons. Their skin clung to their bodies, blistered and wrinkled. I pushed back into my seat. It creaked. All through the auditorium, I heard echoes of creaks as if the entire auditorium had turned into a haunted house.

The men told stories of their lives, their dreams, what they'd hoped for themselves. They told stories of being put out of their homes when their landlords found out they were sick. They spoke of newspapers filled with obituaries of their friends and funerals every weekend. They spoke of mobs burning the ambulances they were carried in. They spoke of people blaming them, saying it was God's punishment.

"We die," they said, "and they do nothing."

The movie followed the men as they became sicker, as they struggled to do everyday tasks: to speak, to drink a glass of water, their Adam's apples bumping against the skin of their throats. Their cheeks grew more sunken and their eyes shone with blank light, the light of death. Their arms were thin as bones, like Jesus. Their veins were blue in their skin, like rivers thawing in the cold winter night.

I felt a connection to these men I couldn't explain. In between hospital scenes, the movie shifted to home videos and photos. Young and healthy, the men were the most handsome men I'd ever seen. Their hair was perfectly groomed. Their skin was soft, their smiles open.

By the end of the movie, we were glued to our wooden seats. In what we thought was the last scene, they showed a still of the first man. Underneath his name, they wrote: "Died, December 13, 1984." He was frozen in his hospital bed, the same man who'd been laughing with his friends just a few minutes before. We were stunned.

We thought the movie was over. We started clapping. Another picture came of the second man from the movie. "Died, December 26, 1984." We started clapping again, frantically, wanting to end the movie so the last man wouldn't die. Wanting to do something with our hands. When the third man died, there was a deep chill in the auditorium. What little warmth there'd been had evaporated. I wiped tears from my cheeks, relieved Julio wasn't looking at me.

When the lights turned on, there was silence. Mr. Nichols's face was red, and the teachers were flustered. Mr. Nichols's voice, always full of authority through the loudspeaker every morning and through the megaphone at lunch, wavered and broke. "Everyone return to your classrooms."

The entire sixth grade was unnaturally quiet as we exited the auditorium.

As soon as we got back to our room, Ms. Cooperman burst out, "How could you clap because those men were dying?" She looked like she was going to scream or cry, two things we'd never imagined her doing.

We defended ourselves. "We were clapping because we thought the movie was over!"

"Again and again? You're smarter than that!"

Were we? We still didn't know what AIDS was. We still thought we could catch it from holding hands. We still thought if we clapped, we could magically stop the last man from dying.

"You will not leave today until you write a letter of apology to Mr. Nichols. And," she added after a moment, "I will read all of your letters before sending them."

Normally, there would've been complaints, but a pall had fallen over us. We bent over our papers and began to write while a thick snow fell outside, white like the blankets that had covered the men.

One by one, we walked up to Ms. Cooperman and gave her our letters. Like penance. She gathered the dark, sweaty papers with their uneven handwriting, reviewed them, and then put them in a mustard-yellow interoffice envelope.

"Razia," she said, then added, "and Julio, make sure these letters get to Mr. Nichols."

I sighed. I wanted to be alone with my thoughts, not have to deal with Julio. Julio, too, was looking down. He got up slowly and followed me out.

The halls were empty as we walked down the stairwell to the principal's office. The secretary, Mrs. Dean, who normally guarded Mr. Nichols's office, wasn't there.

"Let's just leave it on Mrs. Dean's desk," Julio said.

But I didn't want to. She was as old as the school. She treated everyone with disdain, even Mr. Nichols. Her attitude toward him was: *I've buried more principals than you'll ever know.* Her attitude toward us was worse.

There was a window in Mr. Nichols's office door. I stood on my tip-toes to look through. Surrounded by papers and books, Mr. Nichols had his face in his hands. His body was shaking with sobs. I stepped back so fast, I almost fell on Julio. I could tell from his face that he'd seen too. Without another word, we dropped the letters in front of Mr. Nichols's door and ran into the hall.

Suddenly, Julio stopped and turned to look at me. His voice trembled. "Do you know anyone who—?"

I became still, suddenly knowing what he was going to say.

"My uncle has it," he said, his voice breaking, "but I can't see him. Nobody can see him."

I couldn't breathe. None of it seemed real, the empty hallways, Mr. Nichols with his face in his hands, Julio crumpling at my feet.

It started snowing again, and we were dismissed early, the teachers just giving up on us. We trudged home like wet turtles, walking single file through a narrow, barely shoveled path. The snow from last night had turned gray from cars and buses, yellow from dog piss. Now fresh snow was covering it, giving the world a new skin.

I felt Julio, even before I turned around. He was standing alone. How frail he looked, a thin tree in the middle of a snowstorm, his body like the bodies of the men, fading into white.

CHERRY TREE

My sister, Safia, was born in the spring, at the end of a cold, hard winter. Her wriggly body was long and thin, and it was hard for me to match her being with the round, hard melon my mother's stomach had been for months and months.

Safia cried day and night as if she too had a hard time connecting this world with the one she'd left behind. The nights were long, and although the dark should have reminded her of the darkness of the womb, she cried the most then. My father started sleeping in my room so he could get some rest before work, and I slept in the bedroom with my mother and sister. The three of us woke up every morning with heavy bags under our eyes, as if we'd been dragging matching sets of luggage along with us.

All night long there were stirrings. My mother got up countless times to warm up bottles of formula because the doctors had told her it was better than her milk. She carried her own breasts, heavy and painful as stones. The roundness of her stomach did not disappear. She still looked pregnant, but now she was full of melancholy and temper. She flew into rages for any small thing. She blamed me for everything: dishes unwashed, books left open, dust gathering in the corners.

The mother I had known was gone. This mother whisper-screamed at Safia, "Chup! Chup! Chup!" Then I'd pick up Safia and take her to any room other than the one my mother was in.

At first my mother cried secretly, when she thought I couldn't hear, and then she stopped trying to hide it and cried in the open. She sat on her janamaaz and wept. She cried at dawn when she was reading

Fajr, at noon when she was reading Zohar, in the afternoon when she was reading Asr, at sunset when she was reading Maghrib, and at night when she was reading Isha. My father came home after Isha, so she was still hiding it from him.

Those first few months of my mother's sadness, I took refuge in our cherry tree. There were two trees in our front yard, a cherry and an oak. The oak was over a hundred years old and had been in Corona before the subway lines, before the whole neighborhood had grown. But the cherry tree was young. The now-malnourished soil of Queens had kept it from growing too high. There was a knob at the fork that made a foothold, its limbs stretching out into a wobbly Y. It was the perfect tree to climb.

I had a favorite branch I sat on, halfway up the tree. When I was hidden among the leaves, no one could see me. I felt forgotten. I was no one, nobody, not in a way that hurt, but in a way where I felt free.

Spring began to unfold, slowly at first and then quickly. The cherry tree's charcoal stick branches were suddenly covered with white flowers and baby green leaves twisting open. I sat on a branch and watched bees climb inside flower petals, filling the golden bronze pistils inside with their whole bodies.

I got lost for hours daydreaming, until I heard the familiar call of my mother. "Razia!"

I said goodbye to the cherry tree and climbed down. My mother was in the kitchen, on the phone. She'd become attached to the phone as if it was another limb, as if she was trying to re-create a village in our house with her calls back home.

My sister had woken up and was crying in her crib, but my mother didn't want to hang up. I could tell from her words, she was talking to cousins in Pakistan, and once disconnected, she couldn't easily reconnect.

I got Safia and brought her to the living room. She liked it when I laid her down on a blanket in the sun. I brought out toys and entertained her by making voices for each one. Safia smiled, waved her arms, and kicked her legs in a frenzy of joy. I loved having a little sister more than I'd ever imagined I would.

My mother came into the room. "Watch Safia. I'm going to take a shower."

I didn't say I was already watching her.

When my mother came back, her hair was wet and open, reaching the small of her back. I never saw my mother's hair open except for right after her shower. She sat on the sofa and combed out the knots.

"Were you in the cherry tree?" she asked.

I was surprised. I thought she didn't know I was in the tree all the time. I nodded and she smiled. She combed her hair and began to tell a story. "When I was a child, we used to sneak into a neighbor's garden and steal fruit, my friends and me. We'd fill our dupattas with aam, lychee . . . jamun." I'd never heard of any of those fruits, but I didn't interrupt my mother to ask. I stayed absolutely still, not wanting to break the spell of her story. "You don't know what hunger is, but we were often hungry. My father died when I was just a baby, so it was just your Maji and me. There was never enough to eat. The fruits were so delicious, we'd sneak in and eat so much we'd get stomachaches." My mother started laughing. "One day, our neighbor saw us. He started to scream, 'Get away from my fruit!' When we didn't, he brought out his shotgun and started shooting."

My mother's stories always had a horrible twist, but I was surprised every time. "Weren't you scared?"

Even though it was still slightly damp, my mother began to braid her hair into one long braid. "Of course not. He didn't really want to shoot us. He was our neighbor. He was just trying to scare us away from his fruit."

"Why did he have a gun?"

"Everyone had a gun."

I remembered the pictures she'd shown me of my boy cousins, with their mustaches and films of dirt on their faces. All of them had held shotguns like third limbs.

My mother tied up her braid. Her voice changed from her story voice back to her everyday voice. "Go broom the front yard."

Brooming was my main chore. I loved the way it slowly but surely brought me out of the house. I liked to pretend I was making a waterfall of dust, a backward wave of how dirt flowed inside. I started in the kitchen, swept out the door, then down the hall and out the front, down the porch stairs and all the way outside.

In the front yard, white cherry blossom petals were everywhere, blowing into the streets, covering the sidewalks, filling up the gutters, gathering in the corners of our steps. I brushed them into the dustpan, then poured the dirt and flowers into the garbage.

When I was done, I decided to spend more time in the cherry tree. From my perch, I could see all the happenings of the neighborhood: the fire station with its burly firemen, the Armenian man who filled a tub with caught fish every week, and the old Greek couple who acted like they were still young and in love. The husband was round and wrinkly, bald with tufts of white floating over his ears like clouds. The wife wore muumuus like Mrs. Roper from *Three's Company*.

As soon as the weather became warm, they pulled their linoleum chairs out into the sun to feel the weak light that slanted between the buildings, landing right on their doorstep in the afternoon. Sometimes they left their chairs out front with an old-fashioned trust in the neighborhood and strolled hand in hand.

I climbed to my spot and began to spy on them. She was laughing and touching his arm as if they were sixteen, not sixty. The husband pointed into the branches and whispered something to his wife. I was wrong that no one could see me. They got out of their chairs and crossed the street. I didn't know whether to climb up higher or run down.

They stopped in front of our fence. The old man looked up. "Hey, little girl! You like to climb that cherry tree?" His fingers flashed with silver rings. He was laughing at me. I felt myself growing hot.

His wife smacked him on the arm. "Stop it. You're embarrassing her." She asked in a sweet voice, "You have a new baby in your house?"

"Yes," I admitted in a hoarse whisper.

"Beautiful!" This couple seemed thrilled by everything, cherry trees, babies.

When they figured out I wasn't going to leave the tree or talk to them, they shrugged and began to walk away. Before they turned the corner, the man looked back and shouted, "Don't eat all of the cherries when they're pink, or even red. Wait for them to get so red they're almost black, sweet and juicy!"

"How long will that take?" I blurted out, my mouth watering a little bit.

The Greek couple looked at each other and laughed, surprised I'd spoken. The man patted the air. "There's still time. Just watch them and wait. And don't forget to save us some cherries!" They turned the corner, still holding hands.

When I was sure they were gone, I swung down from the branch, landed with both feet on the dirt, and ran upstairs. My mother was just getting off the phone. "Where's the broom?" she asked, becoming annoyed. "Where's the dustpan?".

The days got longer and the nights shorter. The centers of the cherry blossoms became the hearts of hard green cherries. I tried to eat one, but it was bitter. Then I remembered what the Greek man had said and left the cherries alone. I distracted myself by watching the ants marching through the limbs of the tree, full of purpose.

Soon, the cherries softened, turned color, from yellow to peach to pink, here and there, especially on the higher branches. Some turned dark red like blood, but they were too high for me to reach. My mother too began to soften. Safia had started to sleep. Her crying subsided. We found a new rhythm, not a happy one, but one we could live with.

One day, while I was in the cherry tree in my perch, my mother came outside. She was holding Safia in her arms. "Watch her while I make dinner."

I started to climb down. She looked up, her eyes narrowing in the sun. "Are the cherries ripe?"

"Some, but they're too high to reach."

My mother turned her face up toward the highest branches and got a shiny look in her eyes. "I can reach them."

I remembered what the Greek man had said. "The neighbors asked if they could have some."

She smiled and her face blossomed like a river. "Of course they can."

She handed Safia to me and easily pulled herself up the tree. The branches shook as she climbed. I could hear the leaves rustle like money. Soon my mother was beyond the spot where I always rested. She ascended effortlessly to where the branches thinned out and the blackest, reddest cherries were hiding. She filled her dupatta and kept climbing up to the topmost branches, laughing. The higher she got, the more she laughed. The farther she went, the more afraid I became.

Safia cried in my arms and I yelled, "Ammi, stop!" but she didn't. She kept going, as if she could climb so far, she could climb back home, disappear into the light of the sun.

DAYS OF OUR LIVES

My mother had been in a mood all morning, angrily vacuuming, dusting so hard she'd knocked a shelf of elephant miniatures to the floor. Now, while Safia was napping, my mother was taking an hour to herself, to fold laundry and watch *Days of Our Lives*. I was not allowed to interrupt.

Days was her break from us, especially during the long summer months. On the dot, at one o'clock, I heard the music, "Doo doo doo doo, doo doo doo doo. Like sands through the hourglass, so are the days of our lives," and then my mother's voice: "Razia! Go broom the yard."

I knew why my mother didn't let me stay for *Days* because sometimes I hid behind the living room curtain and watched. This week, Bo and Hope were on the run from Hope's rich, evil husband. Hope looked like a Dominican princess, with her thick hair and red lipstick. Bo looked like my father, with his dark beard and handsome face. But I knew there were no Muslims or Dominicans on *Days*. The actors just had spray tans.

Bo cupped Hope's face in his hands, brushing her wet black hair from her eyes. Hope threw herself at Bo, nuzzling his neck, finding his lips with hers. My skin tingled. I wanted so much to know what it felt like for someone to run their hands through my hair, to touch my face as if it was the most beautiful face in the world, even if there were a million more beautiful faces. I wanted to be chosen by someone.

I sighed from behind the curtain.

My mother turned. "Razia! Did you go outside?"

I ran before she could see me, grabbing the broom on the way out. My father had just brought my mother an old-fashioned straw broom, replacing the cheap kind with blue plastic bristles. He'd given it to her like a bouquet of flowers. These were the ways my parents showed love to each other: not in words, never in passionate kisses, but with presents to make a home.

When I opened the front door to begin to sweep outside, I stopped short. There was a baby bird lying on the top step, its short feathers stuck up all around its body, wet and slick, in points. Its eyes were swollen, its eyelids dark. Its neck was twisted, its face all sharp beak and empty mouth.

I gently touched the bird with the tip of my finger and felt just the edge of heat. There was an ant crawling over her skin. The ants in Corona were ruthless. They formed roads with their bodies, feeding themselves through feats of impossible strength. The thought of them dragging the baby bird away made me sick.

On the far side of the fence, there was a pair of hydrangea bushes covered with bouquets of bluish-purple flowers. There was a plot of dirt between them, a perfect burial spot.

I couldn't bring myself to touch her, so I emptied the dustpan and nudged her gently in with the broom, wincing as the pointy bristles pinched her skin, swallowing the bitter taste in my mouth.

The ground was dark and wet from recent rain. Branches had fallen from the oak tree. I picked one up and began to dig.

"What are you doing?" It was Julio.

He'd just come from a pool and was wearing swimming shorts and no shirt. The sun went behind a cloud and the wind picked up. Julio's arms erupted into goose bumps. I became aware of how close he was. I began to feel warm, the way I felt when watching *Days of Our Lives* from behind the curtain. Is this how Hope felt when Bo returned?

Julio had been gone for months. Soon after he told me about his uncle, he stopped coming to school. I'd heard his family had gone back to the DR. Now here he was, leaning into the fence, pushing his fingers through, getting under my skin as soon as he asked, "Did you kill that bird?"

"What? No!"

"Can I help you bury it?"

"No."

Julio crossed his arms over his chest. "You always think you're better than everyone else."

I was shocked. "It's not that—it's . . ." I looked up at the living room window. If my mother looked out, she'd see us. My mother thought sex and betrayal were always happening in America from watching *Days*. I tried to tell her it wasn't true, but here I was with Julio, a boy, a half-naked boy.

"I'm just not allowed to talk to boys outside of school."

"So what if you're not allowed?"

I stalled. "Where have you been anyway?"

He frowned and his voice became flat. "We buried my uncle back home."

"Oh." I felt the air leave my body. I looked down at the baby bird. "I'm sorry."

I didn't know what else to say. I'd been spared from death so far. My uncles and aunties in Corona were still healthy and my relatives who died in Pakistan were strangers to me. There had been one uncle killed by the police, but my parents had gone to the funeral without us.

Julio shifted and the wire diamonds made shadows on his body. "We just came back to get our stuff. We're going back at the end of summer."

I looked up at him, feeling a sudden unbearable sadness.

He leaned into the fence and looked down at the baby bird. "I bet that bird's mother didn't like something about her and killed her so there could be more food for the other baby birds. That's what happens. Or sometimes father birds have more than one family and the other bird wife gets jealous and kills his other children."

Julio was changing the subject and I went along. "It sounds like *Days of Our Lives*."

He started laughing, and the tension between us burst. "*Days of Our Lives*? My mom's watching that right now."

I smiled. "So is mine."

"Can I help you bury it, then? Your mom won't even know." He looked at his watch. The silver gleamed on his skin. "It's only one thirty."

Half the sand was still left in the hourglass. I glanced at Julio, trying not to stare at his chest. He smiled a slow smile, already knowing I was going to give in.

"Okay," I said, "but you have to leave as soon as I say."

In a moment he was beside me, over the fence in two bounds. He found another stick, and without speaking any more, we both dug furiously into the ground. Whenever our hands touched, I felt heat rush through my body. A worm squiggled up my fingers, and I jumped back. Julio laughed as the worm disappeared into the dirt.

When the hole was done, I picked up the dustpan where the bird still lay. I was about to tip her in when Julio grabbed my wrist.

"Not like that." He picked her up gently in his hands and put her inside the grave.

He pulled flowers from the hydrangea bush. They were blue with just the hint of purple underneath, like a bruise. He put them on top of her. Knowing what to do now, I brushed the dirt over the baby bird, placing the flowers like a blanket.

Julio fell quiet and I felt remnants of grief pulse out of him. He took my hand, and I felt the same tingling I'd felt when Bo and Hope had kissed. Was he going to kiss me?

"For the prayer," he said, and I blushed for what I'd been imagining.

"You go first," he said. "Just say anything from your religion."

I was surprised. We'd never talked about me being Muslim. The only thing that came to my mind was the kalma, so I recited it out loud. Julio looked deep into my eyes. I felt the world become blurry.

"Razia!" my mother yelled down from the window.

I pushed Julio away. "Go!" He fell backward, hitting his elbow against the fence.

His face clouded over. "What's wrong with you?"

As angry as he was, he kept his promise. He was over the fence in less than a second. My longing for him reached over as he crossed to the other side.

He turned and looked at me through the metal. "You don't care for anyone but yourself."

Before I could respond, my mother yelled out the window again: "Razia! Where are you?"

My mother was agitated when I got upstairs. I was terrified she'd seen me with Julio, but she just said, "Take Safia."

Safia's eyelashes and cheeks were covered with tears. She'd cried so much, she'd turned red. My mother hadn't seen me. She was upset because she'd missed the last fifteen minutes of *Days*. Now she'd never get to see what had happened to Bo and Hope when Hope's evil husband found them. They didn't do reruns for soaps.

Her hour to herself was up and she had a million household tasks to finish before the end of the day. I didn't blame my mother for needing an escape. I felt guilty for my existence and the burden we were on her. I picked Safia up and brought her to look out the window.

The earth looked disturbed where we'd buried the baby bird, where I'd pushed Julio away. Small brown sparrows were everywhere, flitting from tree to tree, from tree to telephone pole. The poles were heavy with wires and the wires were heavy with sparrows.

Safia nestled in my arms. I began to calm down, just by holding her. "Bird," I said to her. "Bird." She gurgled sounds. "Bird," I said again, but even I couldn't find the words for what I wanted to say.

PAJAMA PEOPLE

It was a scorching hot August day. The trees were filled with purple flowers with their mouths wide open, pistils hanging out like dog tongues. The morning glories were napping and summer's last roses were bursting onto the scene, saying, *Is it too late? Is it too late?* Their petals wilted in the hot sun.

Taslima and I blended into the summer wilderness. It was the kind of day our loose cotton salwar kameez made sense. Taslima's salwar kameez was covered with green and purple flowers. Mine was composed of miniature roses on black.

Taslima was my new best friend. She filled the emptiness Saima had left behind. Her family had just moved to Corona from Brooklyn. Our mothers had met at Key Food and had struck up a friendship. My mother had asked Taslima's mother if she was Pakistani. Then they'd both started laughing. Surrounded by Italians and Greeks, they stood out like Technicolor holograms in their flowery salwar kameez.

Now they talked on the phone almost every day. It was funny to see my mother with a real friend. Usually, she didn't get close to anyone. There were plenty of aunties, but she spoke to them only about Islam or cooking. It was only with Taslima's mother that my mother laughed.

Taslima fanned herself. "Let's walk around the block. Maybe there'll be a breeze on the other side."

"Fine," I said, and steered her to the right, out the front gate. "I want to show you this dog that looks like a lion."

She gave me a look. "There's no dog that's a lion."

"Looks, looks! Not is!"

We passed the row of houses where our Italian neighbors lived.

They'd gotten older and barely ever came outside anymore. Sometimes I felt their eyes, but when I turned, there was no one there, just a curtain trembling slightly, as if it had fallen or been stirred by a breeze.

The cicadas were singing all around us. Their buzz vibrated in my whole being and filled me with joy. When we turned the corner and came to the lion's house, there were two trees filled with purple flowers, a carpet of buds on the ground. The buds looked like tightly wrapped lavender cocoons, twisted parachutes with red tips, children curling into themselves.

Beside them, the lion was even more beautiful, with a golden halo of fur around his head. He paced back and forth in the alley between the houses, a silver six-foot fence on either side. There wasn't enough room for him to take a running leap and escape. His dark eyes stared into mine. I saw boredom, longing, hunger. When he realized we had nothing for him to eat, he turned and walked back to the end of the alley.

Taslima started laughing. "That's a lion? Razia, I hate to break it to you, but that dog is not a lion."

"Looks! Looks like a lion!"

"He *looks* like a dog."

I tapped my fingers against the fence. "He looks sad."

"How do you know it's a he?"

"I don't know. I just think of all dogs as boys and all cats as girls. Except, if he's a lion, he's a cat too."

Taslima shook her head. "Razia. Sometimes I don't understand how you can be so smart and so dumb at the same time."

She was right. There was a lot of junk in my head. Still, I was disappointed Taslima didn't think the "lion" was as amazing as I did.

To hide my feelings, I bent down to pick up a few of the flower buds off the ground. I put them in the lap of my kameez. "Hey. Let's make jelly out of these."

My parents had taken me to Brooklyn over the weekend to see some friends, and the daughter had shown me how to squish the purple flowers with rocks to make a sticky paste she called Flower Jelly. How soothing it felt to hit a rock against something soft, the squoosh sound the flowers made when the jelly came out. But now that I thought of it, the girl had been a little strange, rough and edgy.

"Why would you want to make jelly out of flowers?" Taslima threw the buds back on the ground. "Come on, let's go."

I emptied my kameez too. "To make jelly?"

"No, Razia. Let's go back home. Where there are fans. It's hot."

Taslima didn't love the heat like I did. I wanted the sun to burn my skin and make me dark, so dark Taslima couldn't say I didn't look Pakistani. Whenever she said I didn't, I responded, "How could people not know I'm Pakistani when I'm wearing salwar kameez?"

I turned in the direction we'd just come from.

"What are you doing?" she asked. "Let's go the other way. It's faster."

"Right." I'd steered Taslima the long way to avoid passing Julio's house. On a day this hot, I knew he'd be hanging out on his front steps.

We'd only walked a block when his voice came to us loud and clear. Taslima smiled. "Ohhhh . . . now I see why you didn't want to come this way!" Even she knew about my crush.

"He's moving back to the Dominican Republic."

"Oh no, why?"

I shrugged, trying to hide my feelings. "I don't care why." I didn't tell her about his uncle. It felt like a secret I had to keep for Julio.

There was a group of kids squeezed between Julio's front stairs and the fence Julio's father had put around the stairs. There were three boys from the neighborhood and two girls with bright red hair and orange freckles whom I didn't recognize.

Julio smiled at me. "Hey, Razia."

The tall girl turned to look at me. Her eyes were like the razors of supervillains. Their power burned through my salwar kameez. She started laughing. "Look, it's the Pajama People!"

My stomach clenched, became a tight rope of knots.

"Ha! Pajama People!" Julio laughed, and all the kids joined him.

They began to chant: "Pajama People! Pajama People!" Julio didn't stop them. Instead, he smiled and leaned into their orange-whiteness like a blade.

Taslima and I walked away quickly, pretending we didn't hear their taunts. Once we turned the corner and they couldn't see us, I began to run, not caring if Taslima was keeping up with me.

Tears stung my eyes.

"Razia! Hey!" Taslima tried to catch up with me.

I wanted to scream at her, "I told you I didn't want to go that way!" Instead, I ran inside my house.

Taslima followed me into the kitchen and watched while I struggled to open the Everything Drawer, the drawer where my mother kept rulers, screwdrivers, silver twine rope, silver duct tape, pens, erasers, pencils, paper clips, and small pieces of broken appliances. It was stuck. I pulled harder and it flew open, objects flying out.

Taslima looked worried. "What are you doing? What are you looking for?"

I held up a half-filled bag of party balloons.

Taslima looked at me like I'd really lost it. She said carefully, "What are we going to do with balloons?"

"We're going to make boiling-hot water balloons."

It took her a second. Then she smiled.

We took turns filling them up with the hottest water from the kitchen sink. We watched the shriveled colors expand into wriggly bulbs. So beautiful, they didn't know they were going to be used for revenge. By the time we filled the last one, our fingers were withered and burnt.

The day had gotten even hotter. The voices of the cicadas came in waves, calling, calling, one rising and then another. I could feel their electric buzz in my head.

We'd taken so long that when we got to Julio's steps, there was just one girl left, the younger one of the orange sisters. The others had all gone inside. I could hear Woody Woodpecker cackling from the television.

When she saw us armed with water balloons, her eyes widened. Her freckles blotched out. I knew she hadn't been the one who started it, but she had been chanting like the rest.

Taslima and I walked back and forth in front of her, pacing. The water balloons between our fingers swung like breasts.

At first, the girl was too proud to leave. She looked sullen and defiant, but by our fourth round past her, she turned green and ran inside. I began to feel ill too. It didn't feel good at all to try to squish her.

I was about to say to Taslima "Let's go home" when Julio came outside.

His face was flushed. His hair was in his eyes. He lifted his hand to push it, then saw the balloons. His voice was hard. "Get out of here, Razia."

I heard Taslima but couldn't understand what she was saying.

"Get out of here," he said again, with more force. He looked over his shoulder and then I heard them too.

Taslima pulled my arm so hard, I thought she'd pull it out of the socket. "Razia, let's go!"

We ran. We didn't know what Julio's friends would do to us when they came back outside. Julio was trying to protect us from them and from the self he'd become as soon as they arrived.

Our mothers were in the yard, waiting for us.

"Where were you?" they both asked at the same time.

"Walking around the block," we said, not meeting their eyes.

We'd never tell them what had happened. They'd just blame us and tell us we couldn't take walks around the block anymore.

"Taslima, go get your things."

Taslima didn't hesitate. She ran upstairs.

My mother saw the balloons. "What's that?"

"Nothing." I tried to hide them behind my back.

Her eyes became sharp. "Give them to me."

Annoyance filled my body, but I gave them to her. I felt all the air drain out of me.

"Balloons?" The mothers started laughing. I burned all over again.

"You missed Asr," my mother said. "Go read namaaz."

I was more than happy to get away, but my hands ached for the water balloons.

Our mothers began their long goodbyes. I kept thinking of Julio's friends chanting, "Pajama People! Pajama People!"

"Razia, I told you to go read namaaz." My mother's voice snapped me out of my trance.

I said "Khuda hafiz" to Taslima's mother and went inside. Taslima was coming down the stairs as I was going up.

As we hugged goodbye, she leaned in and whispered, "You know, the dog did look a little like a lion."

I tried to smile.

"Razia!" my mother yelled. "Namaaz!"

Taslima had left her water balloons on the kitchen counter. I didn't know if she'd done it on purpose or by mistake, but I was grateful. I heard my mother coming up and I grabbed the balloons and ran to the bathroom.

The bathroom had a window looking out onto the street. I turned on the water, so if my mother listened at the door, she'd think I was doing wuzu. I twisted open the window lock and stuck my head out the window. Everything on the street looked miniature. Taslima and her mother were already down the block, Taslima's salwar kameez a purple splash against the cement and red brick. They were wrong, Julio and those orange girls. Our clothes were beautiful.

One by one, I threw the hot-water balloons out the window, wincing every time they burst. Each one exploded when it hit the ground, but the ropes in my stomach didn't loosen. I thought of the trapped lion, of Julio, of the purple flower buds, so tightly wound. I wondered if it hurt them too, when they fell to the ground.

STRAYS

Since the masjid had been built, more and more Pakistanis moved to the neighborhood. My mother began to meet aunties who were as religious as her. Together, they began to plan Vazes, religious parties where we prayed together and read an entire Quran. It was easy enough. There were thirty chapters and they were all laid out in little booklets, saparahs. If there were enough aunties, and a handful of young girls, it wasn't long before we were done reading an entire Quran.

The Vazes took place almost every weekend at Bahar's, another new family who'd moved to Corona. We met at Bahar's because their house was in the center of all of our homes, in the middle of a long, slanting hill. In Bahar's house, every single thing I touched, my fingers got stuck. The stove was covered with burnt milk that had spilled for chai, salan that left flecks of garam masala like dirty stars. Every countertop in the kitchen was sticky, stuck. The handle of the fridge was brown. The sink was a black hole, the stove a pit of roaches who lived like crocodiles.

It was a mystery to me because Bahar was beautiful but lived in a house that was ugly and old. When I first met her, I thought she was one of those fairy-tale princesses who'd been locked up in a kitchen with a curse. She had two soft, long braids that swung from her back down. Her eyelashes were thick over her dark eyes, bright and clear as an animal's.

It was a mystery because Bahar's mother wasn't beautiful at all. She had brown-tinted front teeth that turned out, colored from the paan she chewed. She wore brown saris wrapped around her body. Her voice was as loud as a car alarm. But our mothers always told us Bahar's mother had once been beautiful as well.

I wondered if her lost beauty had something to do with her husband, who was never home, and how in her basement there lived a family with two little girls, their heads grazing the basement ceiling when they played freeze tag in the dark. I wondered if it had something to do with the pack of stray dogs she fed cornflakes to, the ones who circled their house in the afternoon, snapping their teeth and their bleeding gums. Her favorite was Benji, a pregnant German shepherd. She'd named her Benji because it was the only dog name she knew.

When we got to Bahar's I helped my mother carry Safia and her stroller up the cement stairs. The front door was open and the hallway was already full of shoes: all the aunties' Bata chappals, little brothers' sneakers, and girls' jelly sandals. I kicked off my sky-blue jellies and was excited to see Taslima's purple ones.

As we walked toward the sitting room, I could hear the low hum of the aunties reading Quran. The furniture had all been moved to the side so the aunties could sit in a circle on the floor. The air smelled of jasmine and feet.

My mother carried Safia into the room, smiling. She loved Vazes. Every time she said "Asalaamu alaikum," her entire being glowed. When my mother allowed it, she was incredibly beautiful. The aunties didn't interrupt their reading, as this was considered disrespectful to praying, but they smiled and said, "Wa alaikum asalaam," then made space in the warm circle of their bodies.

There were two piles of saparahs: the chapters that had already been read and the ones still left to read. Bahar's mother gestured with her chin at the pile closest to the door. My mother put Safia down and took two saparahs. She handed one to me. I didn't take it right away. Instead, I whispered, "Can I read with Taslima?"

Taslima was sitting cross-legged near the edge of the carpet, struggling over the Arbi. My mother nodded. She knew she needed the help. I gently put the saparah back on the pile and squeezed in beside Taslima. Our knees pushed up against each other.

Taslima flipped through the pages. The paper inside was white with a hint of gray, almost translucent. The calligraphy of the scriptures floated above a lined mint-green background.

"Thank God you're here. I'm never going to finish this."

I smiled. "Don't worry. I'll read it fast."

"I know you will," she said, both gratefully and begrudgingly.

Taslima and I had our own way of reading Quran. Whoever was sitting on the left side of the saparah would read the left page and whoever was sitting on the right side would read the right. I'm pretty sure this wasn't allowed by Allah, but we did it anyway. Our hurry was that as soon as we were done, we could leave the circle of aunties and hang out.

While reading, I fell into my own space, the rhythms of the surats leaping off the page. I finished my section and was about to turn to the next when Taslima held my hand back. "Wait. I'm not done yet."

"Where are you?" She pointed to the third line up from the middle. "I'll read it." I breezed through the rest of her half. We were done in no time.

I stared at my mother to get her attention. Finally, she felt me and glanced up.

"Done," I mouthed.

She tilted her head, her way of giving permission, then kept reading. Taslima's mother noticed, looked at Taslima, and gave her permission too. We got up slowly, not knowing exactly what to do with the new longer leash.

As soon as we stepped into the hallway, Taslima tugged her dupatta off. "Man, I depend on you reading my part."

Her dark, curly hair erupted in perfect round black curls. Instead of letting it be curly, her mother usually made her comb it out until it became frizzy. Then she made Taslima put teyl on it to calm it down. We both hated the funky, greasy mustard smell of the teyl and how it made us look so oily, it was embarrassing.

Taslima laughed, catching me staring. "My mother was too rushed to make me comb it out. She asked me if I'd gotten a perm. As if she would ever let me! Then she asked if I was putting Vaseline in my hair!"

"What does that even mean?"

We both started laughing.

"I have no idea. She thinks I'm trying to make my hair like this."

Taslima always joked about it, but I knew, like me, she got frustrated by her mother's constant criticism.

We walked through the dark hallway to the kitchen. My mouth started watering as soon as we entered. The counters had been scrubbed down for the Vaz. They were filled with the aunties' best dishes: aluminum pans and platters full of tandoori chicken, aloo keema, unda kofta, chana chaat, and fruit chaat. All the dishes were covered with foil, but the delicious smells still came through. I was starving, but I knew we had to wait until the Quran was finished to eat.

Bahar and Aliza, Taslima's older sister, were making chawal. They were only a few years older than us, but so different. While me and my friends still tumbled around like wild weeds, getting lost in abandoned parking lots, they were the older girls who stayed in the kitchen making chawal, since chawal was most delicious when made right before eating.

Bahar was at the stove, frying onions. She was only eighteen, but she was already engaged to a man from Pakistan. She could talk of nothing else. "He has three Mercedes and ten servants and five bedrooms in his house. He saw my picture and he picked me from all of the girls he wanted to marry." Bahar still had a Pakistani-British accent, which made all of this sound extra snotty.

Aliza looked bored. She was more into books than marriage. She sat at the kitchen table, lazily swishing water in a bowl of soaking rice. Her legs were crossed, and she was kicking her top leg up and down, wiggling a shoe on and off. I wondered how she'd gotten away with keeping her shoes on. But Aliza was like that. She only followed some of the rules.

She got up with the bowl and poured the water into the sink, cupping her hands so the rice didn't fall out. She turned on the faucet and gave the rice one last rinse, then brought a glass of water for Bahar to pour on the frying onions. This was the step in making chawal that always scared me.

Bahar put the water in and the hot oil burst into angry droplets. She laughed when she saw me jump. Aliza lowered the flame, put the rice in, and put the lid on.

They still had barely acknowledged us.

"Are you going to live there?" I blurted out.

Bahar turned to look at me. Her eyes glittered and her teeth sharpened like fangs. She started laughing. "Live there? Stupid! Live there? So stupid!"

My skin felt hot, as if I'd been slapped.

Bahar was not a princess. She was a witch.

Aliza didn't laugh, but she didn't defend me either. She rolled her eyes, sat down at the table, and stretched her legs out.

Taslima stood up for me. "You two don't have to be so mean."

Aliza glanced at Taslima. "If you can't stand the heat, get out of the fire."

Taslima pulled me out of the kitchen. "Whatever. Let's go."

We walked back to the front of the house, toward the TV room. When we opened the door, smells of boy musk and dirty socks rushed into the hall. The brothers had commandeered the TV room before us. They were watching *Batman* and acting out scenes. They made the sounds of fists and punches, cymbals crashing against trumpets, vases being smashed.

"Close the door! Close the door!" they shouted.

There was nowhere else in the house to go. We had used up all the rooms. We stood by the front door, feet-deep in shoes.

Taslima looked down at the pile. "Let's go outside." When she saw my hesitation, she added, "We'll just sit on the front steps."

My stomach growled. "Okay." Anything to pass the time until lunch.

As soon as we stepped outside, the heat hit us. Steam came off the street in waves. A slight breeze shook the leaves of the one tree on the block. The paint on the cement steps was peeling in gray layers, flaking in some places, gone and missing whole in others. If I looked long enough, I could see patterns of animal shadows.

"Look, there's a dragon." I pointed to a blotch that seriously looked like a dragon.

Taslima squinted at the spot. "I swear, Razia, I don't know what you see. Are you sure you're not losing your mind?" It was mean, but the way she said it made me laugh.

I looked back at the dragon. It had transformed into a snail. Then it became a barking dog and a little mouse. I decided not to tell Taslima. Instead, I looked up and down the street.

Two-family houses lined both sides, connected to each other like fifties relics and jumbles. Most of the houses, including Bahar's, had dirty aluminum siding, white gone off-white, gray gone sooty gray, or green gone dark and dusty.

There was very little going on.

"Stoooopid." Taslima imitated Bahar's way of saying it, and I laughed. "Stupid! That Bahar's the one who's stupid. I bet that guy doesn't even have all that stuff!"

"Really?" I hadn't thought of that. Pakistan was a distant fairy-tale land our parents had come from, a place where everything was supposed to be better, a place they said they would return with us to live. This last part made us very nervous.

Taslima didn't drop it. "God, that Bahar is such a snob. Don't you remember when she slapped me?"

I laughed. "Oh my God."

Taslima frowned. "I'm glad you think it's so funny."

"It's not funny." I laughed even more. I couldn't help it. It was just so crazy.

"I don't even know why she slapped me."

"Because you asked if her bracelets were real gold."

We both started laughing at how snotty and ridiculous Bahar was.

A mother and four little children walked by. They were all roly-poly, holding balloons and birthday banners on their way to a birthday picnic. Our eyes followed them up the hill that went to Taslima's house and past that to Flushing Meadows.

Taslima got a look in her eye. "Let's go to my house."

It was one thing to sit outside at Bahar's, but leaving in the middle of a Vaz to go all the way to Taslima's house? That would get us into trouble. I stalled. "Why can't we just stay here?"

Taslima didn't care for my hesitation. She said the magic words. "We could drive the Car."

The Car was Shafiq Uncle's broken-down gray four-door. Taslima's family had a yard big enough, and her father was generous enough, to let uncles leave their broken cars there when they didn't have the money to fix them.

The car doors were unlocked, so we could make-believe drive whenever we wanted. Taslima and I spent whole days pretending to journey all over the country, passing red mountains and green fields, playing pretend radio and singing down long stretches of make-believe highway.

I sucked breath between my teeth, then looked back inside.

"Come on," she insisted. "We'll get back before the dua. They won't even notice. Didn't you see how many saparahs were left to read?"

Her house was only two blocks away and there could easily be another half hour until our mothers and aunties were done reading Quran.

Taslima stood up and brushed off the back of her kameez. "Don't worry. We'll make it back in time."

"Okay," I finally said, and stepped off the cement stairs and brushed off my clothes too. We headed uphill.

On the first corner, there was a bodega with a string of light bulbs like theater lights. I wished we could stop to get something to eat. A bag of chips, even a Tootsie Roll or Mary Jane to stick to my stomach, but there wasn't enough time. We crossed the street and kept going.

Taslima wouldn't let it go. "I can't believe she called you stupid. She's the one who's stupid."

I finally responded. "She's the one who's stupid for marrying someone from Pakistan. I'd never marry someone from there."

Taslima laughed. But we both knew we didn't have a choice. We'd have to marry someone from Pakistan, someone our parents picked. But we pretended we were freer than that.

"Who are you going to marry," she teased, "George Michael?"

I fake-sighed. "Oh, George Michael. I'd just look at him all the time."

"Yeah. I don't think he's going to want to carelessly whisper into your ear."

"Ha. Ha. That's not even funny."

"I still don't know what you see in him. He wears so much makeup."

"That's Boy George. Not George Michael. And I like how Boy George looks in makeup. What about your Ralph Macchio? He's not all that."

Taslima made a face. She hated anyone saying anything about her Karate Kid. "All I know is—" She threw her arms up in the air and channeled Whitney Houston, "*I want to dance with somebody.*"

I laughed and joined her, "*I want to feel the heat with somebody!*"

Together we kept singing: "*Yeah, I want to dance with somebody. With somebody who loves me!*"

We were out of breath by the time we got to her corner. I saw our shadows on the sidewalk, dark under the bright sun, our shadow torsos overlapping, our shadow fingers holding hands. I was about to say something when I heard a growl.

I turned to see two stray dogs behind us, their fur long and mangy, their teeth yellow, their gums red and swollen. They snarled and moved closer.

All the hair on my arms stood up. Sweat broke and froze on my skin. A third dog joined them. The three growled, an even lower growl.

I became light-headed. The world had just shifted gears.

"Is Benji with them?" I whispered. I don't know why I thought Benji would convince the others to have mercy on us.

Taslima didn't answer. She was afraid to look. There was something in their eyes we didn't want to see. She whispered, "These dogs have been coming around the house all week. Just walk slow."

We walked slow, slow, slow, as they snarled low and followed.

Taslima's house was just half a block down. Maybe we would make it. But then with some secret signal, the dogs started moving faster. They knew where Taslima lived.

Taslima's eyes had become dark pits. I couldn't hold it in anymore. "Run!" I screamed.

We both broke into runs. We had fear on our side and youth. Our breath came fast. Our jellies hit the pavement. We flew.

I could feel and see nothing, only the pain in my chest. Taslima was right behind me.

There was a short chain-link fence around her house, a door with a curved handle. We slammed into the door, but the handle was stuck. Taslima pushed my hands away. She pulled at the handle with all her strength and opened the gate.

We ran!

In our hurry, we didn't lock it. The dogs only hesitated for a second, then rushed after us.

"The garage!" Taslima screamed.

There was a broken-down garage at the end of her driveway. It had once been gray-blue, but the paint had faded and peeled off like tree bark. We ran toward the cracked wood of its accordion doors. One of the doors had been left open and there was just enough room for us to get through. We threw our bodies against the door and pulled and pushed with all our might until it closed.

The dogs surrounded the garage. We could see them through the small broken panes of glass.

Ruff! Ruff! Ruff!

Their madness was electric. I was afraid they'd jump at the doors, like wild dogs in movies, but they stood a few feet away, barking, barking, driven mad by our presence. Taslima and I shrank back into the garage, hiding behind all the broken bikes and appliances. Each bark felt like a punch. I covered my ears and cringed. The dogs were making me feel crazy. Their barking was breaking into my skin.

"This was a stupid idea!" I snapped.

I'd never yelled at Taslima before. She began to cry and I felt wretched, the pit in my stomach a hollow hole someone had shot out.

It was forever before the dogs stopped barking. They settled down in front of the garage, waiting for us. I got up and looked out the window. More dogs had come. There was a black Labrador, a German shepherd, and mixes of all kinds of strays, each different from the other, but all large and terrifying. They were sitting in a semicircle like a pack of wolves. It had gotten hotter, and their tongues were hanging out of their mouths.

A half hour had definitely passed. Our mothers were going to find out any second we were gone. I looked over at Taslima. She wasn't crying anymore, but her eyes were red and her nose was still running. She wiped it with her dupatta.

I looked away. "I'm sorry. It's just when my mother . . ." I trailed off.

Taslima was quiet. She knew what would happen when my mother found out. She'd seen her in one of her moods, chasing me around the house with a slipper. When my mother got like that, Taslima's presence didn't stop her.

She sniffed, then said, "Maybe she'll be worried."

"Maybe," I said. I didn't deserve Taslima's kindness.

She let out a little whine. "I really have to go to the bathroom."

As soon as she said it, I realized I had to as well. Keeping it in became immediate torture. Minutes passed but they felt like hours. Just when I thought I couldn't hold it anymore, we heard: "Hutt! Benji! Hutt! Hutt!"

I looked out the garage window. It was Bahar's mother. Right behind her was Taslima's mother and then mine. They were holding pans and metal spoons, banging on them, unafraid, screaming at the pack of dogs. "Chalo niklo! Go on! Get out of here!"

The dogs whined and ran away. Through the broken glass of the window, I could see our mothers walk toward us. My fear grew. Taslima's mother opened the garage door. Taslima and I stood in front of them, hungry, about to pee on ourselves. I choked back tears and looked at my mother. Her eyes were red and beneath them was a cold, hot fierceness that would always protect me, a fear from which I would never be able to hide.

BOOK THREE

Fall 1987–Summer 1988

CLOCK RADIO

On Saturday mornings, I went to Taslima's house as early as possible so I could catch Casey Kasem's *American Top 40*. We were like junkies at the racetrack. If our songs were called, we felt we were winning. When our songs fell behind, we were personally insulted.

Taslima got away with listening to music in a way I never could. She had a mother who wasn't as religious, a door she could lock, and a clock radio. Well, it was Aliza's clock radio. Their father had given it to Aliza so she could get to school in Flushing on time, not realizing that now Aliza, and by extension me and Taslima, could listen to music as much as we wanted with just the press of a button and the turn of a dial. We listened every second we got, the volume turned down low.

I loved that clock radio. The time was told in neon red digits. There were smooth buttons all along its light purple surface. "Not light purple," Taslima always insisted, making fun of the way Aliza said it, "*lavender.*"

One Saturday, we were propped up on Taslima's pillows, our heads close to the clock radio. Our talking was interrupted by the prerecorded chorus: "Casey's Coast to Coast . . ." and then the distinct rasp of his voice: "Hello again and welcome to *American Top Forty*. My name's Casey Kasem and we're counting down the *Billboard* top hits. These are the records you're buying and record stations are playing all across America as rated by *Billboard* magazine."

I turned to Taslima. "Isn't it a catch-22? The radio plays the songs people buy and people buy the songs the radio plays."

"God. Ever since you read *Catch-22*, you think everything's a catch-22. I'm going to tell Aliza to stop lending you her books."

The chorus sang, "*American Top Forty*," and Casey Kasem continued, "Now what you've been waiting for. This week's number one song in the land." We sat up, excited. "'I Think We're Alone Now.' From the album *Tiffany*, that's the girl herself. Sixteen-year-old Tiffany with 'I Think We're Alone Now.'"

Taslima and I jumped out of bed.

For weeks we'd been doing endless renditions in front of the mirror. Even though we made fun of the way Tiffany danced, it ended up becoming the way we danced, putting our hands through our hair, winking, and doing a weird herky-jerky wave with our chests. We strained our voices trying to hit Tiffany's high notes: "*I think we're alone now . . . Doesn't seem to be anyone around . . .*"

There was a banging on the door. It was Aliza. "Taslima! What are you doing in there? It sounds like an earthquake. And you're not alone. We can all hear you!"

We turned off the radio but couldn't stop laughing.

Aliza banged again. "I told you a million times not to play with my radio. I mean clock! Ammi!"

We heard her run downstairs, but we knew Aliza wouldn't really tell because then the radio would be taken away and Aliza wouldn't be able to listen to music either.

We lay down on the bed, out of breath, not opening the door, in case Aliza was waiting outside to pounce.

After a few minutes there was another knock.

"My God, what does a girl have to do around here to have some peace and quiet?" Taslima whispered in an exaggerated voice, like Blair from *The Facts of Life*. I broke into more laughter.

The knock came again, gentle this time. "Taslima?"

"Abu?"

We sat up and she quickly turned off the radio and opened the door. Instead of coming inside, Taslima's father stood outside and peered in. He was different from the other fathers. He read Urdu poetry, kept a vegetable garden, and cooked the most delicious biryani. For the last few years he'd been sick with an illness no one understood. His work clothes hung on his skeletal frame.

"Razia!" He acted like he hadn't seen me in forever, when the truth was I spent more time at Taslima's house than I spent at mine.

"Asalaamu alaikum, Uncle."

"Wa alaikum asalaam." He smiled at me, then turned to Taslima. "Beta, what are you doing?"

Taslima looked at the clock radio guiltily. "Nothing, Abu." She tried to change the subject. "Are you going to work?"

"Oh yes, work, work, work." He sighed and came into the bedroom. "Did I ever tell you about my first job when I came to America?" Uncle took any excuse to sit down and tell a story. He sat now on the edge of the bed. Taslima and I moved over. "You know those places that make food very quickly?"

"You mean fast food, Abu?"

His eyes lit up. "Yes!"

"You worked at McDonald's?" I was amazed.

He shook his head. "No. The one with the girl with the red hair."

"Wendy's?"

"That's the one. It was my first day, so the manager gave me an easy job. He said, 'You! Wash the dishes.' So I gathered all the dishes"—he imitated carrying a large stack of plates—"and put them in the sink. Then *boom*!" Uncle blew his hands up in the air. "The sink exploded!"

"What? Why?" Taslima and I burst out.

"I thought it was a sink, but it was really a deep fryer. You know, where they make the French fries?"

"Yes, Abu, I know! But how did you not know?"

"You know American sinks are full of dirty water with dishes soaking in them. I thought it was water, not oil." He shook his head. "The manager was so angry. They had to close down the kitchen and throw out the oil. Very dirty oil. They used it for months. The manager said to me, 'You're fired!' But I didn't speak English well then. I didn't know what 'fired' meant. I thought he was saying I started a fire, so I nodded yes."

Taslima and I were both trying not to crack up.

"Well, after that day, the manager was going on vacation. I just kept coming every day. After two weeks, the manager returned. I still didn't know I had no job. I just knew this was the man who was angry at me. So when I saw him, I hid under a table. The manager saw me and said, 'You! What are you doing here? I fired you weeks ago!'"

We couldn't hold it in any longer. Taslima and I burst into laughter, imagining her father getting caught hiding under a table. Taslima's father smiled. It was always this way with our fathers. They made stories of cruelty seem so funny.

The digits of the clock radio caught his attention. "Okay, Beta. It's time for me to go."

He patted his thighs a few times, as if he was revving himself up, then lifted himself slowly. He smiled, looked at the clock radio, and said to Taslima right before walking out the door, "You're never alone, Beta. You'll always have me."

He was so thin, walking away from us, the shadow of the young man inside him tugging at his sleeves.

LAST CHRISTMAS

It was the day before Christmas, and there was a sleepy happiness in the streets. Snow was gently falling. I loved Corona like this, the snow making everything look clean. The garbage cans were frosted like vanilla cupcakes. The streetlamps were decorated with wreaths mysterious elves had put up at night, green grass necklaces swinging "Season's Greetings" from lamppost to lamppost.

Of course, we didn't celebrate Christmas, but we still had the time off, and in that way, it felt luxurious, with days and days of no school. I was especially excited because I was sleeping over at Taslima's house for Christmas Eve.

Taslima's mother had made a joke of it, laughing with my mother over the phone. "Why shouldn't we celebrate Christmas-Shristmas? Let Razia stay." My mother had agreed. The Christmas spirit was hitting everyone.

It was a cold walk over. Salwar kameez was not winter wear, even with sweaters, coats, and long johns. I rubbed my arms, then put my hands in the pockets of my thin coat and walked faster. I tried singing to warm myself: "*Last Christmas I gave you my heart . . . but the very next day you gave it away . . .*"

It was more than the words that warmed me. George Michael opened up a window in my soul. When I thought of him, my whole body felt like a meadow of light, a poppy seed, an electric tornado ripping through a field of dandelions. Aliza and Taslima made fun of me endlessly about my crush.

I walked up the driveway. Covered with snow, their old garage looked like a gingerbread house, its broken windows like open eyes. "Merry Christmas," I said to the garage.

The side door to Taslima's house was always open, no matter how much everyone warned them to keep it locked. Up a few more stairs was the doorway to the kitchen where Taslima's mother was busy at the stove. The delicious smell of her cooking melted away the cold that had gone deep into my bones.

"Asalaamu alaikum," I said, always a little shy around Taslima's mother.

"Wa alaikum asalaam." She gave me a wry smile. "Merry Christmas."

The kitchen led to what they called the family room, or the TV room. There, Aliza was folding clothes and watching *Miracle on 34th Street*, a black-and-white movie about a Macy's Santa who said he was the real Santa. A little girl was looking at Santa out of the corners of her eyes, wondering if she should listen to him or to her mother, who was pleading with him: "Could you please tell her there really is no such thing as Santa Claus?"

"But there is," Santa insisted.

The TV mother's white skin looked gray in the black-and-white of the old-timey film. Her face was pinched. "You misunderstand me. I want you to tell her the truth."

"But I am telling the truth. I am Santa."

Aliza stopped midfold and looked at me. "Taslima's upstairs. And in case you're wondering, there is no Santa."

I knocked on Taslima's bedroom door, saying, "Knock, knock."

Taslima whispered through the door, "What's the password?"

"The password is 'Password.'"

She opened the door so quickly, I fell in.

"Merry Christmas!"

"Merry Christmas!"

We hugged, faking a festive feeling that became real.

I caught a glimpse of myself behind Taslima in the mirror on top of her dresser. The cold outside had made my cheeks rosy, my face almost pretty. Every Pakistani home I knew had a dresser like this, with a mirror surrounded by combs, clips, nail polish, dark lipstick, and a small jar of Vaseline, all arranged neatly on a hand-embroidered cloth with roses blooming in red thread.

Taslima was trying to put her hair up in a banana clip. Her curly hair was thick and the banana clip kept being overpowered and popping open. Taslima threw it down on the dresser in annoyance.

"Ugh. I hate my hair."

I never knew what to say to Taslima when she said she hated anything about herself. She was so much prettier than me. She turned heads wherever she went.

Finally I said, "Come on. Are you kidding? Don't you remember when we went to Bahar's Valima and all her boy cousins were staring at you? All the aunties started hitting you up with marriage proposals."

"Well, Razia, that *hardly* means anything, those idiot boys wouldn't know beauty . . ." She dropped her fake snobby accent. "I just want to get my hair layered."

I was shocked. "You can't do that."

"Why not?"

"Hello? We can't get haircuts."

"Who says?"

I paused. No one ever *said*. It was just known. It was in the air we breathed. We weren't allowed to cut our hair, no questions. We had two braids now and when we got older, we'd have one long braid like our mothers. We were Pakistani and that was the way it was.

Taslima didn't pursue it. She started braiding her hair.

I turned on the clock radio, high enough so we could hear it in the room, but low enough so no one could hear it from the other side of the door.

The DJ filled our silence. "It looks like we're going to have a White Christmas, folks, the snow is falling, your friends are calling, 'Yoo-hoo!'" He slipped into a recording of the carol, "*Come on it's lovely weather for a sleigh ride together with you . . .*" He spoke over the music, "Hope you're with someone you love this Christmas . . . but for those lovelorns who aren't, this one's for you . . . He's been slamming us this year with hit after hit, from his number one album *Faith*, but here's an old favorite from the Wham! years . . ."

"*Last Christmas, I gave you my heart . . . but the very next day, you gave it away . . .*"

Violins raced like agitated birds, beating their wings, and I sighed. "Why would anyone give away George Michael's heart?"

Taslima stopped midbraid. "Um, hello? Me. I don't need his heart."

"You wouldn't turn down his heart!"

Before she could respond, there was a frustrated turn of the doorknob and then a banging. "Taslima! How many times have I told you? This is my room too. Don't lock the door!"

I jumped to open it. Aliza stormed in and went right to the mirror. Taslima moved out of the way fast. Aliza was as beautiful as Taslima, but she looked at herself and frowned. She noticed the song and teased me. "Oh, it's your boyfriend." She straightened out her bangs. "How can you love him when you don't even know him?"

I smiled at her reflection. "Our love is impossible to explain."

She burst into laughter, then stopped suddenly and said, "Okay. Enough fun." This made me laugh even harder. She looked at Taslima. "Ammi wants you to put down the dastarkhan."

We didn't have to be told twice. It was time to eat and we were hungry. Taslima tied up the end of her braid, and we both ran downstairs.

We placed the dastarkhan on the floor and brought out plates and cups and water, then the dishes Aunty had filled up to the top with aloo salan, gobi, chicken, rice, and roti. A Christmas feast!

"Food, food!" Taslima's brothers ran into the room.

Atif, Taslima's older brother, turned the TV back on. *Miracle on 34th Street* was still playing. Instead of sucking up everyone's energy, their TV was like a fireplace where everyone gathered around talking. At this point, Santa was being evaluated and the psychologist was getting angry because Santa was showing concern for the psychologist's agitated behavior. There was a running commentary from the family. "Of course he's not a real Santa. You're not a real doctor either!"

Right then Aliza walked down the stairs like a queen, and Aunty came in, carrying the last roti. "Turn it off."

We turned the TV off, but it was still with us, because Taslima's family liked making fun of the way families on TV talked. If anyone needed something like yogurt, they'd say in an exaggeratedly proper voice, "Could you *please* pass the yogurt?"

Then we'd all laugh as the yogurt was passed the wrong way around the circle, each person saying, "Could you *please* pass the yogurt?"

This banter occupied much of our eating time.

Taslima's mother smiled at first but when she had finally had enough, she said, "Stop! Just eat!"

It was quiet for a few seconds, then out of nowhere, Suheil, Taslima's youngest brother, said, "I wonder if Santa's going to come this year."

No one said anything, so I finally told him, "Santa doesn't come to Muslims' houses." I was trying to prepare him for a life of disappointment during Christmas.

"Yes, he does! I saw him! I saw him last year!"

Taslima whispered in my ear, "Our neighbor came dressed as Santa."

I was amazed. Taslima's neighbor was one of the old Italians. Maybe not all of them hated us.

"Is he going to come again this year?" Even if he didn't have anything for me, I was excited at the idea of seeing a Santa deliver presents.

"No. He's not going to come this year," Aliza said, glaring at Taslima.

Everyone became quiet.

I looked around. "What happened?"

"He died," Aliza said flatly.

"Santa died?" I didn't mean to laugh, but a snort escaped from my nose.

Suheil looked horrified.

"Aliza," their mother said sharply, "make a tray of fruit for the neighbor and take it over to her."

"Now?"

"Yes, now."

Aliza took one last bite and then got up. "No one better touch my food."

When we'd all had seconds, thirds, and fourths until we were stuffed, it was time to clean up. Taslima's mother went to lie down and I helped Taslima gather all the dishes and bring them to the kitchen. The boys kept watching TV.

In our families, the boys never had to do any housework, just like the boys in Pakistan. Meanwhile the girls were expected to do everything: the dishes, sweeping, laundry, vacuuming on top of our homework. I didn't have brothers, so it wasn't as obvious in my home, but it definitely was in Taslima's.

Aliza had fought the battle many times but had been outnumbered by the boys, who didn't want to do anything, and by their mother, who insisted Aliza needed to learn how to do housework for when she got married. Aliza had just groaned.

When Taslima tried to bring up the housework issue when it had started to fall more on her, the boys had laughed and Aliza had just said, "Good luck."

I didn't mind doing dishes when I did them with Taslima. She soaped and I rinsed. But I still knew the whole system was unfair. "When I have my own family, I'm going to make my husband and sons wash dishes too."

She laughed. "You're going to make George Michael wash dishes? That reminds me . . . we got a present for you."

I got flustered. "Wait, we're doing Christmas presents? I don't have anything."

Taslima wiped her soapy hands on her kameez. "Don't worry about it. It was Aliza's idea." She looked excited. "I'll go get it!"

"Shouldn't we wait for Aliza?"

"She said we didn't have to. I'll be right back."

"I hope this isn't a trick to get out of doing dishes."

She smiled and ran up the stairs without answering. I scrubbed the burnt crust from the cauliflower pan and wondered what the present could be.

Taslima came back down with a small package, not much bigger than my hand. When she put it in my palm, the weight was just right. My heart started beating fast. I hoped, hoped, hoped it was what I imagined.

"Oh my God. Oh my God." I ripped it open and gazed down at George Michael's beautiful face on the cassette cover, his stubble black against his golden skin. He was gripping the collar of his leather jacket, pulling it over himself as if he didn't really want to bare himself to the world. I pulled out the booklet. The lyrics for every song were laid out like tiny little poems.

Aliza walked in through the side door just then. She looked pale and exhausted from her visit with Santa's widow.

We'd brought her plate to the kitchen table. She sat down and started eating as if she had been starved for months. She said between mouthfuls, "I see you gave her the gift."

"Thank you," I said, but the words could not capture what was in my heart.

Aliza stuffed her mouth with another bite. "Don't worry. It's more of a present for us."

"What do you mean?"

"Now you won't be coming here all the time pretending you want to hang out with Taslima but really wanting to listen for George Michael on my clock radio."

"Hey! That's not true. I like hanging out with Taslima."

Aliza smiled. "Razia, did you know there is no definition for the word 'gullible' in the dictionary?"

Her teasing didn't dash my joy. I knew it meant she loved me.

"Can we play it now?"

"That's the catch. You can never listen to it."

"I knew there had to be a catch."

"You two go upstairs," Aliza said. "I'll finish the dishes."

"Wow. You really got hit by the Christmas spirit," Taslima said.

"Whatever, I just don't feel like listening to George Michael right now. Go and get it out of your system."

Taslima and I ran upstairs, past the boys who had changed the channel and were watching wrestling. We made faces at them, but they didn't notice.

We went to her parents' room and got the family tape recorder. Every Pakistani family had one of these, flat with a handle like a purse, with eight colored buttons. It was essential to have these because most families in Pakistan still didn't have phones.

Every month, our parents filled cassettes with their voices: asking after everyone's health, giving news of their lives. They made us kids say salaam so our families could hear our voices, the grandchildren, nieces, and nephews they'd barely met. Then my parents would fill the rest of the cassette with instructions on which gift and which packet of money went to which relative. They mailed these or sent them with anyone who was traveling over.

For our families in Pakistan, our parents were the real Santa Claus.

I put the cassette in and hit Play. Church music erupted into the room. Organs straining against pipes. I couldn't believe it. I was getting to hear the full opening. Usually, the DJs talked over it. For them, the church music was too slow, but I knew what George Michael was saying. The church would always be with him, no matter what he sang.

There was a burst of guitar and then George Michael's gorgeous voice. I could feel through his gritted teeth, the frog caught in his throat, that he was experiencing what I was experiencing: desire.

We spent the rest of the night listening to the album and dancing. I never danced at home. It was only with Taslima that I felt I could move my body without judgment. She watched herself in the mirror and never looked at me. I closed my eyes and felt George Michael's voice move through my body, an electric charge, freeing me here and there and there.

Whenever I thought of him, I felt heavy, wet, damp, like a sponge soaking in rose water. I wished I could touch the stubble on his face, feel his arms around me. I wanted him to press his body against mine, to feel his warmth. I was transported into a fantasy. In it, George Michael and I were trapped in a cave. I don't know how we'd gotten there. An avalanche of snow had blocked the entrance. The stubble on his face tickled my soft skin. His lips were warm. Of course he'd have to be stuck in a cave with me to pay me any attention.

Taslima and I lost track of time. No one came to bother us, another Christmas miracle.

It was late, past midnight, when Aliza came back to the room. "I'm going to sleep. I've run out of Christmas spirit."

We were tired ourselves, with the sweet exhaustion that came from dancing. Taslima and I brushed our teeth while Aliza pushed the two twin beds together to make one full-size bed that the three of us could sleep on sideways. Aliza turned the lights off and the three of us got into bed.

"Aliza," I said, "do you think I'll ever marry a man like George Michael?"

Aliza whispered back in a voice that meant *I'm sleepy, stop talking*, "A man with a beard? I don't think you have a choice."

I smiled and snuggled in.

Outside, the snow was falling against the panes of glass. I drifted off, feeling the warmth of Aliza's and Taslima's bodies next to mine. Under the covers, a winter fire bloomed in my heart.

GARDEN OF ROCKET SHIPS

While everyone else had Christmas and Easter, we had Eid, and we treated it with all the glory of the other holidays rolled into one. The laws of gravity were suspended, and the work, work, work that kept our parents in a perpetual grinding of the soul was forgotten. Our parents came alive, remembering they were Pakistanis who loved nothing more than spending time with family and friends.

Early in the morning, while the world still smelled of dew and fresh bread, the streets of Corona filled with Pakistanis. Everyone stepped out in their shiniest best. All the men and young boys strutted in new kurtas. All the women and girls sashayed in gold, silver, and aqua, shades of mermaids and peacocks. We shed our ill-fitting school clothes, our out-of-date salwar kameez, and were transformed from the poor of fairy tales into royalty.

Even more Pakistanis had moved to Corona. I barely recognized anyone. My father knew everyone, though, saying "Salaam" a million times before we got to the park. Everyone came to the Gosht Dukan.

We headed together to Flushing Meadows, where my father and the uncles had arranged for us to read Eid namaaz in front of the Queens Museum of Art. As we entered the park, we passed the Hall of Science, with its rippling walls like waves and its garden of rocket ships. The rockets displayed there had been created to explore the wilderness of the universe but had somehow ended up parked for eternity in Queens. Their pointy tips, like silver pencils, scratched the sky.

Past the rocket ships was the Unisphere, an enormous sculpture of the earth. It rose to meet us, the silver metal of its globe shining. In the grass between the Unisphere and the Queens Museum, prayer sheets spread like moss.

Taslima, Aliza, Bahar, even Saima and Shahnaaz were in a circle. My stomach lurched. My throat became tight. Somehow I'd managed to avoid Saima and Shahnaaz since the last time I'd gone to Saima's house.

But feuds were forgotten on Eid, and when everyone hugged, saying "Eid Mubarak," Saima reached for me. I lingered in the hug, a familiar comfort coursing through me. When she pulled away, I hid my feelings by hugging everyone else, even Shahnaaz, who was as hard and thin as a street sign.

I stepped back, a little bit unsure of what to say with Saima there. Bahar and Shahnaaz were admiring each other's clothes and mehndi. The night before, we'd all decorated our palms with paisleys and patterns.

"You two know each other?" I asked, confused by their intimacy.

"Yeah," Shahnaaz said in a snobby voice. "Our families are from the same village in Pakistan."

"How come you never come to the Vazes, then?" I said in my own rude voice.

Shahnaaz laughed. "Oh, I'm going to come to the next one. My family was busy because we bought another gas station. It's in Long Island." She said "Long Island" as if it was some kind of fancy place. It was the land where the Italians had moved after we'd come to Queens.

I kicked myself. Now she was going to be at the Vazes.

Annoyed she wasn't getting attention, Bahar turned to me. "Your clothes are so pretty!"

I looked from her clothes to mine. Mine were nice, sky blue with patterns of silver sequins, but they were nothing compared to Bahar's. Her fancy emerald garara was blinding in its bling. She was pregnant but was still wearing her wedding finest, just let out. By the way she said "ahem," and jingled her gold bracelets, I realized she wanted a compliment back.

"Yours are beautiful too," I mumbled.

Aliza and Taslima started laughing at my insincerity.

Shahnaaz grabbed my hand. "Let me see if I can guess who you like."

I pulled my hand away. "What?"

"You're supposed to hide the initials of the boy you like in your mehndi." She looked at me pointedly. "Or the girl."

Bahar and Aliza laughed as if she'd said the funniest thing. Saima looked away but Taslima stared at her rudeness. Unlike me, she hadn't grown up with Shahnaaz and didn't understand why I'd let her walk all over me.

"Does it say 'Julio'?" Saima asked.

Saima remembered my crush on Julio, and it shook me. "No, he left. He moved back to the Dominican Republic."

"Oh, you really liked him." She sounded sad, and my whole body filled with longing. For her or for Julio, I couldn't tell. It was all mixed up inside.

Shahnaaz didn't like that Saima and I were talking again. "So who is it?" she asked.

Taslima turned to her. "Can you find a *G* and *M*?"

I could see Shahnaaz running the names of the boys we knew through her mind.

"It's George Michael, of course," I said, and everyone, even Shahnaaz, laughed.

The PA system screeched and we heard Hafiz Saab's call: "Allahu Akbar. Allaaaaaaahu Akbar," and then his commands: "Straighten! Straighten the lines!"

There was a sudden rush to find places to pray.

The Eid prayer was optional for women and I hoped Saima would stay with Taslima and me, even if it meant Shahnaaz did too, but when I turned around, everyone but Taslima had disappeared. She didn't seem to mind them being gone. She pulled me toward the Unisphere and its empty fountain.

For as long as I could remember, the Unisphere fountain bed had never held water. Instead, the park had painted the floor marine blue, to make up for the lack. We didn't know any better, so we preferred it. For us, it was a free roller-skating rink, the perimeter a walking path. Taslima and I stepped up onto the edge and began walking around the sphere, swinging our arms.

In the distance, there was a pavilion with two long columns, round disks at the top. They looked like brontosauruses lifting their long necks and blinking their eyes. When we'd been children, Saima and I had run from the pavilion with the towering heads as if we were running for our lives, screaming, "Dinosaurs!"

The fountain and all the mysterious structures were from the World's Fair. Ms. Cooperman had attempted a lesson on it once. It seemed the World's Fair was a time when the country was imagining its future, back when the future still seemed exciting and glossy, like a stainless steel science fiction movie.

She'd been trying to build our Queens pride, but she didn't realize we preferred to imagine the relics as a mystery. When we'd shown no interest in learning, she'd looked at us with confusion. "Didn't you ever wonder why those rocket ships and sculptures are there? Where they're from?"

"Aren't they from outer space?" someone had called out, and we'd all laughed, though it wasn't so different from what we thought.

Ms. Cooperman had given up on the lesson and we'd never learned much beyond the theme of the World's Fair that year: "Peace Through Understanding."

Taslima was chatting about something, but I couldn't get Saima out of my mind. I turned to Taslima. "Let's go there," I said, pointing to the dinosaurs.

Taslima smiled, always up for an adventure.

As we got closer, the stench of decay became stronger. We stood at the entrance of the pavilion. Sharp wires slashed the air, radiating out of the center circle like a spiderweb. Shattered glass and reddish-brown tiles lay on the ground, weeds cracking through them.

"What is this place?" Taslima whispered.

Before I could answer, glass crunched nearby and we jumped. This was what our mothers had warned us about, wandering away and falling into the hands of dangerous strangers.

Before I could hyperventilate, Aliza emerged from behind a column. She'd ditched namaaz and followed us.

"What are you doing here?" Taslima asked.

"I could ask you the same," Aliza answered. "Don't they teach you anything in school?" She must have overheard us. She knelt to the ground. "This is a map of New York." She reached down and picked up a broken piece of tile with half the name of a town written on it:——ntauk. "Actually, they didn't teach me either. You can't wait for anyone to teach you. Otherwise you'll learn all the wrong things."

"Our teacher did try," I said, defending Ms. Cooperman. "It's from the World's Fair, the year of 'Peace Through Understanding.'"

Aliza gave me the same incredulous look Ms. Cooperman had, but her eyes were tinged with barely hidden rage. "Peace through understanding? Pakistanis weren't even allowed in the country in 1964. Don't you think it's weird that there were no Pakistanis before us in Corona? That we're the first?"

"I don't know," I said, with the same sheepishness I'd felt in class.

Taslima waved her hand in Aliza's face. "Hello? It's Eid! We took off from school. We don't have to learn anything today."

Aliza laughed and let it go.

We spent the next part of the hour roaming among the decaying map, reading the broken names of New York. When we touched the map, chunks of tile fell off, and the wind blew dust all around.

In this broken map of New York, Queens was small, Corona invisible. I sighed. "I wonder if I'll ever get to see any place but Corona."

"I'm not going to be trapped here," Aliza said. "I'm leaving."

"You're getting married?"

She looked at me as if I'd been totally brainwashed. "If you think I'm going to marry one of those Pakistani guys who can't even pick up his own dish and put it in the sink, you're crazy. I'm applying to college. Far away."

I was amazed by Aliza's courage, but I also knew it would be easier for her and Taslima. Their mother had gone away to college herself in Pakistan.

Aliza pointed at a spot on the map. "This is where I want to go. Stony Brook." She paused. "Or this is where it would be if the tiles weren't all broken."

On the map, the distance from Queens was nothing, not even a footstep, but I knew Aliza would never come back. I knew I should want Aliza to be free, but I wanted her close too. If she left, it would all begin to unravel. There was nothing new about this. Our parents had left their homes and the thread had unraveled, then been woven again with us. This was how it always was, an unraveling and a raveling of the earth, the ground we stood on. Nothing was sacred, everything was sacred, everything changed, everything stayed the same.

The wind blew the last words of the Eid prayer toward us. "Assalamu alaikum warahmatullaah. Assalamu alaikum warahmatullaah." Namaaz was over.

We looked at one another and, without words, began to run back to where our parents were praying out in the open, under the sky, among the rocket ships and planets that had once spoken of the future's promise. Our slippery silver shoes miraculously kept us from flying off the ground.

THE PLEASURE OF FLAMES

Our mothers had been so busy, they'd let the Vazes fall to the wayside. Then they seemed to realize, all at the same time, that us younger girls were becoming women. We'd gotten as tall as them, which was not hard because they were mostly less than five feet. One after another, we'd sprouted hairs over our lips. The blood had come, and our mothers had given us insanely large boxes of maxi pads to take care of it. We needed spiritual guidance and fast.

The Vazes were still at Bahar's house, even though it was no longer Bahar's. She and her husband were living in New Jersey, with, from what I heard, a new baby boy who cried constantly.

On the day of the Vaz, I had my period, which meant I couldn't read Quran. I was surprised when Taslima also said she had hers. Aliza had stayed home with the same excuse. The odds that we were all bleeding seemed questionable, but our mothers left us alone.

We must have touched some soft spot in them, some lost tenderness. Maybe they weren't ready to force us into being women. Maybe they were trying to protect the girls inside them, the ones who'd gotten married so young. Or maybe they were just happy to see each other and wanted to have adult conversations without us being around. Either way, they didn't question.

When Shahnaaz and her mother showed up, though, it caused a stir. It was their first time at a Vaz. I wished I hadn't mentioned it on Eid. While the mothers caught up, Shahnaaz, who also said she had her period, kicked the brothers out of the TV room and took it over for us girls. The brothers didn't seem to mind. They went out to play baseball in the empty schoolyard next door.

"Look at this!" Shahnaaz pulled the doily off of Bahar's mother's new VCR. None of us would have dared. "She got it as a gift from Bahar's husband."

I wondered how many hours Bahar's mother spent with it, trying to fill the empty space left by Bahar. Shahnaaz turned on the TV and pressed Play. Music erupted into the room.

"Turn it down!" Taslima and I whisper-screamed.

Shahnaaz laughed but lowered the volume.

It was an Indian movie I recognized, *Silsila*, a scandalous one starring Amitabh Bachchan and Rekha, about an affair between a married man and an unmarried woman. The craziest part was Amitabh and Rekha were really having an affair and Amitabh's real-life wife, Jaya, was playing his movie wife. The sparks, the jealousy, the anger weren't pretend at all.

Shahnaaz forwarded the video until she found the part she was looking for, the scene where Amitabh and Rekha first meet at a wedding party. Rekha looked gorgeous. Her hair was in one long braid down her back like our mothers', but she was doing what our mothers never did, dancing, spinning in the center of the room, impressing everyone, especially Amitabh, who started praising her in song: "*Pehli-pehli baar dekha aisa jalwa! . . . Ho aisa jalwa! Ye ladaki hai ya shola!*"

She was a firecracker, a burning ember setting him ablaze. Amitabh pretended to pull her toward him with an imaginary rope and she let him. When she came close to him and spun, her braid flew in the air and snaked around his neck.

Shahnaaz jumped up and started imitating both Amitabh and Rekha. Shahnaaz could really dance. She knew all the moves and moved with a passion that took us by surprise. Taslima and I laughed and clapped, forgetting our mothers were next door.

When the song ended, Shahnaaz's forehead was shiny with sweat. She was breathing heavily, but she stopped the video and pressed rewind. Amitabh and Rekha unwound themselves from each other's bodies. Rekha's braid unroped itself from around his neck. They moved farther and farther away. At the right moment, Shahnaaz stopped the tape to start the dance again.

She pulled Taslima up. "Now it's your turn!"

I thought Taslima would protest. No one in her family even watched Indian movies, but she didn't hesitate.

"You know this dance?" I asked, but she didn't answer. She'd seen the video once and it was enough for her to memorize the sequence.

This time, Shahnaaz acted like she was Amitabh and Taslima became Rekha. Shahnaaz looked at Taslima intensely and pulled her close while I stood to the side like Amitabh's jealous wife, my mouth in a straight, grim line. Why was she asking Taslima to dance and not me?

Suddenly there was a banging on the door. "Darwaza kholo!" Shahnaaz stopped midmotion, and Taslima ran to the other side of the room, her face flushed.

Bahar's mother yelled through the wood. "What are you doing in here?"

Shahnaaz quickly turned off the TV, but the VCR was still running when the door opened. I noticed Bahar's mother kept her keys in a bunch tied to the end of her sari and tucked in at her waist, just like the grandmothers from Indian movies.

She stepped into the room and looked at the doily on the floor, then walked slowly over to the VCR. We held our breath. She turned on the TV and music burst into the open. Amitabh and Rekha were still dancing. She looked at all of us and then started laughing. "Arey!"

Shahnaaz's mother appeared in the doorway. Now it was Bahar's mother who quickly turned the TV off. She smiled, looking guilty.

"What's this she-devil doing now?" Shahnaaz's mother looked at Shahnaaz, but there was no real anger in her voice.

"Is it time to eat?" Taslima asked.

Bahar's mother smiled. "Dua first, then khana."

They herded us out of the room. We followed, feeling lucky we hadn't gotten into more trouble.

Bahar's mother stuck her head out the front door to call the boys in for the final prayer. "Larkey! Ajao! Dua ka time heyn!"

I looked out from behind her, through the metal-and-glass door, remembering when the stray dogs had chased us. They'd disappeared from the streets. The dogcatchers had come for them. I imagined the kind of dogcatchers from *Tom and Jerry* cartoons, crawling through the streets with giant butterfly nets. Somehow the fantasy ended there. Our stray dogs would have ripped those butterfly nets to shreds.

The boys were taking their time. Bahar's mother bellowed, "Arey!

Jaltee!" When they finally appeared, there were dirty streaks of sweat running down their faces. Down the hall, Shahnaaz and Taslima had gone ahead of me. I saw Shahnaaz put her arm around Taslima's shoulder. Jealousy filled my throat with bile. I couldn't believe Shahnaaz was trying to steal another friend.

When everyone, including the boys, were all seated, my mother began leading the final group prayer. When she did dua, she always adlibbed a short sermon beforehand. Today was no different.

She began, "When we die, we'll come to a place with a long line, a line into infinity, a checkout like Key Food. If you think the lines there are long, this one will be much longer!" The aunties laughed. They knew this was not in the Quran, but they loved the pictures my mother created in their minds. "You'll have to put the items of your heart in front of the register. Allah will ask, 'How did you spend your time? Helping others? In charity?'" She paused and looked at us girls pointedly, but with a slight smile. "'Or in dancing and singing?'"

I looked at Bahar's mother. She looked down, guilty.

My mother continued. "But if you read namaaz, if you read dua, if you meet others and come together in prayer . . . then you can go on the express line!" The aunties burst into laughter. "You will have so few sins and so many good deeds, you won't have to wait at all. You can just rush ahead of everyone into Heaven. Now for the dua. Let's pray."

We cupped our hands, while my mother recited surats from the Quran. I imagined putting my sins on the conveyor belt in front of the cashier for the Day of Judgment. I saw miniature versions of me, Shahnaaz, and Taslima enjoying *Silsila*, me clapping, Shahnaaz and Taslima dancing. I saw the cashier press a button and felt panic as we began to roll into Hell.

My mother quickly glanced at me. How did she always know when I wasn't paying attention?

She closed the dua by thanking Allah for all our blessings and asking for protection. She prayed for all the families in Palestine being brutally forced out of their homes. She asked Allah to help us all become better Muslims. I raised my voice and joined hers. "Alhamdu lillahi rabbil alamin . . ." The prayers kept me close to her, a thin thread, a kite string keeping me from losing her, from losing everyone I loved completely.

MARIANNA'S BEAUTY SALON

Every time Taslima and I walked by Marianna's Beauty Salon, we looked inside. Always there was a group of Dominican women, their hair the dirty blonde of lions' manes, frozen as if the wind had left it that way, held in place with industrial-strength hairspray. Their skin was brown from summers of going to DR, quick dashes of blush across their cheeks like hot-pink scars. The windows were foggy from all the steam inside, from hair being blow-dried and washed.

"Look," Taslima said. We looked through the smoky windows. "She's not afraid to be sexy."

She was pointing at the woman I had named Marianna in my head. She was old, but from the way she was dressed, I could see she was not ashamed to show her body. She was proud. As we stood there, she spun around, pulled a black comb out of a jar of sticky blue liquid, and, in a quick motion, flicked her wrist so the drops fell off. She did this like it was a dance, and I thought yes, she was not afraid.

Taslima reached for the door handle. I pulled her arm back.

"What are you doing?"

Taslima had been saying for weeks that she was going to get a haircut before we started high school.

"You said you'd come with me."

"I didn't know you were serious."

"Well, if you won't come, I'll just invite Shahnaaz."

"Shahnaaz! You have her phone number?"

"Yeah, she gave it to me at Bahar's."

With an exasperated sigh, I pushed open the door.

From behind me, Taslima laughed. "I'm just kidding. I wasn't going to call her."

But we were already inside. It was like stepping into another world, a forest of sounds, women laughing like birds in trees, the smell of hair spray thick and overpowering. All the Dominican ladies stopped what they were doing and stared at us. I saw us in the mirrors and my face grew hot. We were two skinny Pakistani girls, long, dark braids down our backs, breasts barely hidden underneath our baggy kameez.

The woman I thought was Marianna stepped forward. Her eyes were heavily made up, and her full legs were wrapped in spandex, lace on the bottom at her ankles. Taslima was looking at her in awe. She wanted those spandex.

Marianna smiled and opened her arms out to us. There was lipstick on her teeth, but it didn't take away from her splendor. "Sit down, sit down." She brushed the hair off a turquoise barbershop chair and motioned for us to sit.

The ladies started talking to one another again, only glancing at us here or there, out of the corners of their eyes. There was hair everywhere, cut-up hair all over the floor, cut-up hair on the chairs. There was an armory of Aqua Net hair spray on shelves that looked like they'd been hastily built.

Taslima sat down and I stood beside her. I couldn't believe we were *inside* Marianna's Beauty Salon. Taslima adjusted herself in the chair, nervously moving around.

I looked at her face in the mirror. She was becoming more and more beautiful every day. Her skin was smooth, her cheekbones sharp like a model's. Meanwhile, my hair frizzed out along the edges and my front teeth seemed as if they were living in the wrong mouth.

Marianna was giving an older woman highlights, tying shiny aluminum foil around her hair, then painting it with a brush. The woman was speaking fast in Spanish and Marianna was sucking her teeth and nodding. Then the woman said something that made Marianna burst out into laughter. She laughed so loud the other women all turned. Marianna repeated the joke, and they all started cracking up. A woman, her hair in curlers under a blow-drying machine, added something to the conversation. They all burst into a fresh round of laughter.

Marianna looked over at us and smiled. "One minute, baby!"

"They're all busy, we can still get out of here."

Taslima shook her head. "No."

She fumbled with her braids, undoing them. I thought of my mother, Taslima's mother, and all our mothers. Sometimes they'd be so busy, they wouldn't even comb their hair for days, and when they did, they simply opened their braids, pulled a comb through, and then braided their hair back up again. It was not like this with women all around, laughing.

When Taslima finished unbraiding her hair, it hung down thick and curly.

Marianna finally came over. "Look at this hair," she shouted to the other hairdressers. She held up a handful of Taslima's thick hair. We were the only ones in the salon with long, black hair. Everyone else's was short, tinted brown and red, curled, straightened, cut to pieces. They looked at us with approving smiles.

Marianna touched Taslima's hair. "I used to have hair like you, baby. Beautiful." We stared. It was hard to believe her hair had ever followed the rules of gravity.

I wanted to open my hair and have them say it was beautiful too.

As if she knew what I was thinking, one of the other hairdressers came over. "Girl. You're mine! I want some virgin hair too." Up close, I could see a bout of chicken pox had ravaged her face. Her makeup was shellacked on, the foundation filling up the crevices.

I backed away, grabbing hold of my braids.

Marianna said, "Leave her alone," then put an apron around Taslima. "Baby, you sure you want to cut this?"

Taslima flicked her hair. "Yes, I want to get it layered. Like Blair from *The Facts of Life*."

"Who?"

Taslima looked around the room. There was a poster of a Dominican Farrah Fawcett on the wall. "Like her," she said.

Marianna smiled. "You got it."

I stood next to Taslima and watched Marianna comb her hair gently, starting from the bottom and working her way up. When she started cutting, chunks of hair fell to the floor. Taslima was looking at herself in the mirror as if she was seeing some lost familiar, as if she was pushing herself down the birth canal and letting Marianna hold up the mirror.

I felt the heaviness of my own hair as I saw Taslima transform into a stranger, her face no longer a child's.

"Beautiful!" Marianna said as she brushed away the snips of hair from Taslima's shoulders. She turned to me. "Okay, baby, you want to go next?"

"I . . . um . . ." I had the strongest desire to become beautiful like Taslima.

A sudden recklessness took control of me. "Yes," burst out of my mouth.

Taslima gasped, but Marianna smiled. I sat down and she put the heavy cloth around me.

Just then, the woman whose hair was being straightened started screaming, "Me quema!"

Marianna hurried over. She turned to the hairdresser who'd wanted my hair before. "Julia, you do this one."

Julia walked over and immediately my fears were unleashed.

I stood up as if to run, but she said, "Sit down."

I sat down, not knowing how to say I'd changed my mind.

Taslima stood next to me. "It'll be great!" She tried to muster bravery for both of us.

Julia put the plastic apron around me and started cutting. She cut my hair as if she was chopping away at overgrowth, hacking her way through a forest.

I closed my eyes and felt a lightness I'd never experienced before. It made me dizzy. The ropes of hair tying me down loosened. I imagined my layered hair floating in the breeze. Maybe Julia was a secret genius.

When I opened my eyes, I saw Taslima's face in the mirror first, looking horrified. Then I saw myself. My hair stuck up straight in patches, like a baby bird's. I felt queasy.

Julia saw our faces. She puckered her lips. "That's okay, honey. It's not a thing a little hair spray can't fix."

She pulled a neon-blue can of Aqua Net from the shelf. Without even telling me to close my eyes, she began spraying at my hair the way I'd seen my mother spray at roaches. My eyes shut tight but the smell invaded my nostrils.

"Sorry, baby. It burns a little bit."

She went to get a broom to sweep up the hair that had fallen. As soon as she left, I felt hot tears slipping down my face, picking up small threads of clipped hair on their way down. I pulled my arm out from underneath the plastic sheet and started wiping them away.

"It doesn't look so bad," Taslima said. But she couldn't hide what I could see. She switched tactics. "It'll grow back. I mean, doesn't your hair grow like a gorilla's?" I knew she was trying to make a joke, but I felt numb. "Your mother won't even notice if you put your dupatta on."

My mother! What would she say? Maybe I could hide out in Marianna's Beauty Salon until my hair grew back. I imagined Marianna finding me cowering behind a chair as they swept up the hair at night.

"Do you want me to come to your house with you?" Taslima asked. Volunteering to come home with me was real courage.

"No." She didn't need to see my mother screaming at me.

Taslima handled the money, paying Marianna for both of us. It was only two dollars a haircut, but it was still a lot. I knew it was Taslima's way of saying sorry for getting me into this mess.

When I got home, my mother was making roti in the kitchen. She turned in slow motion and stared at me as if a stranger had walked through the door. I braced myself, but my mother just stared. She didn't raise her hand to slap me. She didn't take her slipper and throw it at me.

Instead she said slowly, so each word could be stamped on me: "You look ridiculous. Like a crazy person. A crazy person is someone who thinks they're something they're not." She flipped the roti on the tava and pressed down on it with a cloth.

THE AUNTY

A few days later, I woke up to find an aunty had come to visit. There was no announcement or discussion, just an aunty at the dining table, a cup of chai at her lips. I stumbled to the kitchen, rubbing my eyes. The air felt slightly slick, greasy warm with the smell of frying Crisco. There was a dream troubling me. I'd been trying to get somewhere. It was a familiar place, but I was lost in a gray, cloudy darkness.

I was so disoriented, I thought the Aunty was my mother, even though I rarely saw my mother sitting in the morning. When she turned, I jumped. It was the Aunty. Her glasses were thick, her wrinkly skin the color of chai. Her lips were pursed, the lines around them pinched, like an orange.

I don't know how long I stood staring before my mother came into the dining room with a plate of parathas and elbowed me in the back. "Say salaam."

"Asalaamu alaikum."

The Aunty looked at me like she smelled something unpleasant in the room. She glanced at my head. Each butchered layer of hair was held down by a line of barrettes. Pointy wisps poked out all over like a crown of thorns.

Nothing went by my mother. "Where's your dupatta? Go get it!"

I was annoyed but happy to leave. Maybe try to go back to sleep.

I heard the Aunty behind me: "She doesn't wake up for Fajr?"

My mother's voice was startled. "Yes . . . she does . . . usually."

My mother was lying. For years she'd tried to wake me up, nudging me in a coaxing voice that drove me insane. Finally she'd decided I was in charge of my own soul. At my age she'd already been married off. I read Fajr when I woke up and never missed my other namaazes, so we'd found a kind of peace. With one question, the Aunty was about to ruin the balance we'd come to.

My mother noticed me standing in the doorway.

"I'm going, I'm going," I said before she could say anything else.

On my way to the bathroom, I passed the living room and saw two tan-colored Samsonite suitcases side by side. They stood, mean and foul-smelling, like oxen in a stall. Their weight settled on my chest. Maybe the Aunty was just visiting for the weekend. Sometimes random people stayed with us, stopping in Queens before flying to Pakistan.

When I opened the bathroom door, I was shocked. The sink and floor were splashed over with water. The Aunty! She hadn't used the sponge my mother left on the edge of the sink. Ever since my father had gotten a new sink, my mother was extra careful to make all of us wipe up after ourselves.

I used the sponge now, trying not to get grossed out while I squished the runoff water from the Aunty's body down the drain. I couldn't believe I'd just woken up like this was any old Saturday.

When I was done reading my late Fajr, I cupped my hands for dua and let loose. "Allah . . . now what? Who is this lady and is she as much trouble as she looks? Sorry, sorry. I know that's rude. But I thought I was going to hang with Taslima today. This aunty better not get in the way!"

Taslima and I had been planning a hang for the last few weeks. It was becoming a careful balancing act for me to get permission to spend time with Taslima. Ever since Marianna's Beauty Salon, there had been tension. My mother still loved Taslima's mother, but she was becoming suspicious of Taslima's influence on me.

I cursed the strategy Taslima and I had chosen for the weekend: the Surprise Ask. The Surprise Ask meant we waited until the morning of to ask if I could visit. This was usually the best tactic because it wasn't until the last minute that my mother realized it was easier to have me out of the way.

Of course, the danger of the Surprise Ask was that anything could come up last minute. Intense irritation filled my body. There was no way my mother was going to say yes with the Aunty visiting.

There was a phone in the kitchen and another in my parents'

bedroom. I picked up the one in the bedroom and dialed Taslima's number. My mother usually eavesdropped on my conversations, so I always had to listen with one ear cocked for the click, which meant the other line had been picked up.

Taslima answered on the second ring. I burst out, "Aunty. Staying. Can't come over!"

"What? What are you talking about?"

I slowed down. "An aunty just came last night."

"Ooooh. Did you get presents?"

I thought of the Aunty and her pursed lips, the two tan suitcases in the living room. They were definitely not full of presents. She didn't seem like a present-giving aunty.

My mother picked up the other line just at that moment. "Razia! Why are you on the phone? Did you read Fajr?"

"Yes, I was just . . . talking to Taslima."

"Can you give the phone to your mother?" My mother acted as if she'd been the one calling and Taslima had answered.

Taslima went to get her mother. I tried to linger on the phone and do a reverse eavesdrop. I knew my mother would tell Taslima's mother everything. I could find out who this aunty was and how long she was staying.

But my mother said, "Razia, get off the phone," and I had to hang up.

My stomach grumbled, but I didn't feel like going into the kitchen with the Aunty there.

Safia woke up and started crying.

I went into the bedroom to get her, and as soon as she saw me, she started to jump up and down. I hid out with Safia and did a show with her toys. Whenever I played with Safia, I could forget everything bothering me. We were both giggling uncontrollably by the time my mother came into the bedroom.

My mother smiled, seeing us playing. "We're going to go to Alexander's to get Aunty some socks and things. Do you want to come?"

Socks and things? Did that mean the Aunty wasn't on her way to Pakistan? Or maybe she wanted to bring socks and things to people there? My mind spun with questions. How long was this aunty staying?

Then I saw my opportunity. I left Safia with the toys and followed my mother back to her bedroom. "Ammi, can I go to Taslima's?"

She paused for only a second. "Go ahead."

I couldn't believe it. The Surprise Ask had worked.

The only way out of the house was through the dining room and kitchen and I'd have to pass the Aunty again. I put my dupatta on tight and steeled myself, but the Aunty had retreated to the living room. She was rifling through the suitcases as if she was an animal eating the carcass of a beast. I ran to the kitchen, where there were still a few parathas left on a plate. I wrapped one up in a napkin and ran out the door.

It was early in the day but it was already getting hot. Aliza and Taslima were sitting in their backyard, drinking iced tea. Aliza was putting on bright cherry-red nail polish. She always did her nails outside because there wasn't enough ventilation in their bedroom.

"Hey!" Taslima called out. "Want some iced tea?"

"Of course!" I loved the way Taslima made iced tea. She always used double the amount of powder, then put in lots of ice. Tangy at first, the taste mellowed out and became less sweet as the ice melted.

Taslima had already brought out a glass for me.

"How'd you know I was coming?" I was disappointed. I'd wanted to surprise them.

She laughed as she poured the tea. "Who do you think is driving your mom and your new aunty to Alexander's? My mother's the one who said you should come."

Alexander's was far and Taslima's mother was the only aunty who knew how to drive. No wonder my mother hadn't hesitated at my Surprise Ask. The mothers were always a step ahead of us.

Taslima handed me my glass. "So who's this aunty?"

I was just waiting to vent. "I don't even know where she came from, but from the first second, she was asking my mother why I wasn't reading Fajr, why I wasn't wearing my dupatta."

"Why aren't you?" Taslima said in a serious voice. I gave her a look and she started laughing.

Aliza held up the bottle of nail polish. "Want some?"

"No, I have to read namaaz. Plus who knows what this aunty will say if she sees me wearing nail polish?"

Taslima laughed. She finished her iced tea and poured herself another glass. "If she's so horrible, maybe you can go through her suitcase and find something incriminating."

I rolled my eyes. "Incriminating? What, like she's a spy or something? There's probably just aunty underwear and Suave shampoo."

Aliza blew on her nails. "Well, my mother's going to invite your favorite aunty over for a dawaat."

"Really?"

Aliza always got this kind of news first. But it wasn't surprising. Having dawaats was what our mothers did when someone came to visit.

I took another sip of my iced tea. "Well, then you'll see. She's not a normal aunty. I can already tell. But maybe—" I thought. "Maybe she's one of those aunties who fakes a nice personality around other people." I sighed. "Why does she have to stay with us?"

Taslima shook her head. All our houses were rotating hotels of relatives and pseudo-relatives. "Everyone in Pakistan thinks we live in mansions."

I looked around the yard. The latest in a series of broken cars was resting on two cinder blocks. Caterpillar weeds and overgrown grass filled every inch. The fence was leaning over as if ready to collapse.

Aliza finished her last nail and blew on her fingers. "Razia. I think you don't have enough drama in your life, so you're making more drama. You have to take one for the village. This aunty is your father's cousin's wife. She was living in Texas with her husband until"—she looked at me pointedly—"he had a heart attack and died." Taslima gasped and I felt sufficiently ashamed. "Now she's trying to figure out if she can move back to Pakistan to live with her sister or stay here."

I suddenly remembered a phone call my father had gotten a few weeks ago. How he'd left the room right after. "You knew this the whole time and you didn't tell me? You didn't even stop me from complaining?"

"I thought you needed to vent."

"Agh!" I fell back in my chair. "I guess I should be nice to her. But I really hope she's not planning on moving in with us forever."

"It's not her fault," Aliza said with the new tone she'd been using since getting into college. "Cultures that tie women's worth to their husbands and children also make it impossible for women to have their own money. Like all of us, the Aunty's trapped in the patriarchy. She wants to go back to Pakistan to live with her sister, but her brother-in-law is the one who has the final word. Without a husband and children, the Aunty is at their mercy. Her only power is her controlling behavior over the rest of us girls."

Taslima and I stared at Aliza.

"Haven't you ever heard of patriarchy?" she asked.

We shook our heads.

"Feminism?"

We continued to look blank and Aliza started laughing at us. Soon we were all laughing. I felt light. At the very least, a dawaat at their house meant one less awkward meal with the Aunty. In Aliza's family, there were so many people, I could get lost.

Back home, the Aunty was slowly taking over. Now when I got up in the morning, it would be the Aunty at the stove, alongside my mother. She'd be there making paratha or kneading dough. I began to wonder if it was part of the Aunty's master plan to make herself indispensable so she could move in. If it was my fault the Aunty had come, my own stubbornness, my own laziness when it came to housework. Was she my punishment?

Finally, the day of the dawaat came. My mother let me go ahead so I could help Taslima's mother set up. Her mother had already made chicken biryani, unda kofta, chicken salan, and even gulab jamun for dessert. All of her best dishes. Taslima's mother lowered the flame under the chawal, right as the back doorbell rang.

"They're here!" Atif shouted.

"Then open the door!" Taslima yelled back.

Taslima's mother and brothers were watching the baseball game in the family room. Taslima's mother was a huge Mets fan, but now she pretended she didn't care about the game. "Atif, go do your homework."

When she said "Atif" she meant both Atif and Suheil, but not Taslima. The boys cleared out and Taslima's mother opened the door.

My mother, the Aunty, and Safia stepped into the kitchen. Taslima's mother picked up Safia and hugged her close. She had a soft spot for Safia. There were salaams all around and then everyone went to sit in the family room. I tried to hide, but the Aunty's eyes found me and narrowed.

I looked over at Taslima, for her to see I wasn't imagining this, but Taslima was busy getting out the drinks tray. She put three glasses on the tray and filled them with ice and Coke. She brought the tray out to the family room. I followed her.

My mother took a glass and granted Taslima a smile. Maybe she was beginning to forgive her for the haircut.

"Diet?" the Aunty asked. I was surprised because she'd never asked for diet anything at our house.

"Uh, no," Taslima said.

Taslima's mother said quickly, "Go see if we have a can of Diet Coke in the pantry."

I whispered to Taslima as we went back into the kitchen, "It begins."

Taslima laughed, but she had no idea how bad the Aunty could get. We returned to the living room with the Diet Coke. We were about to go upstairs but our mothers stopped us. "Sit down," they said, and we sat down awkwardly in the corner, across from them.

Aliza came down the stairs. She'd taken a shower and had a towel draped over her shoulders. Her wet hair was hanging loose. She was stunning, a mix between Cleopatra and a wildflower.

"Asalaamu alaikum," she said to the Aunty and my mother.

My mother gave her a genuine smile. She thought of Aliza as a good role model and proper daughter, even though Aliza was really the one who put all the radical ideas into my head.

I expected the Aunty to say something to Aliza about her uncovered hair, but she simply stared at Aliza, taken by her beauty.

"Looks like your aunty likes Aliza," Taslima whispered.

"Just wait," I whispered back. "You'll see."

Aliza had only come down to say salaam. She went back upstairs to finish getting dressed. Taslima's mother was being very circumspect and gentle. It was obvious she already knew what she needed to know about the Aunty's situation.

At first she said, "You must come and visit. Razia can bring you."

My mouth dropped open in horror. I'd been planning on using Taslima's home as my escape.

Instead of accepting the invitation, the Aunty asked, "Your older daughter, is she engaged?"

Taslima's mother smiled. "Oh, she's not engaged yet. She's going to start college in the fall."

The Aunty frowned. "College? Before she's engaged?"

Taslima's mother laughed. "Our family doesn't follow the old customs here."

The Aunty sniffed, then said in a slightly nasal voice, "I would think it's more important to follow the old customs here." She took a long, drawn-out sip of her Diet Coke.

She looked at Taslima's mother with the disapproving look that had become too much a part of my life. My mother shifted in her seat. The Aunty caught herself and transformed her face into what she thought was sweet. "My sister's son is an engineer at the University of Management and Technology in Lahore. If you'd like I can make an introduction."

Taslima looked at me, horrified. I made my I-told-you-so face, then whispered, "Hey, she can be your aunty too!"

Taslima's mother laughed nervously. "I don't think—"

My mother finally spoke. "Aliza is a good girl. There's nothing to worry about with her going to college."

Taslima's mother looked at my mother in gratitude, then said, "Let's eat." She looked at us, remembering we were there. "Taslima, bring out the dastarkhan."

We were hungry and did as she said, spreading the dastarkhan on the floor, bringing out the water, plates, and glasses, then each dish one by one. The boys came running down the stairs, hungry. Aliza followed, walking in slowly, her hair freshly braided, looking pretty. She would be a catch for the Aunty's nephew.

It was a long lunch, made longer by the awkward pauses the Aunty's questions brought on: if the boys were studying Quran to become Hafizes (they weren't), if Taslima was learning how to cook (she wasn't), or if Aliza was studying to be a doctor (maybe, maybe not).

There were no silly jokes, no asking to "please pass the yogurt." Even my mother and Taslima's mother seemed awkward with each other. Taslima and I looked at the Aunty out of the corners of our eyes. She was the fear we'd been trained for, the one our mothers warned us we'd become if we didn't listen to them: a widow, a childless woman.

But I knew the flaw in their thinking. The Aunty *had* listened. She *had* gotten married. She *had* tried to have children. That was why she was so bitter. She'd still ended up alone.

As if reading my mind, the Aunty sighed. "You're blessed to have your children," she said to Taslima's mother.

I gave Taslima a let's-get-out-of-here-fast look. I knew where this was going. We began to pick up dishes and head to the kitchen. The boys had already hightailed it out of there, supposedly to do homework but really to play Atari. They'd left their plates on the floor, expecting us to pick them up.

The Aunty continued in a sad voice. "I regret I never had a Quran khani for my husband. I was so overwhelmed when he died. So alone. I never did a Khatum, where we lived for so lo—" Her voice broke and she began to cry.

I looked over at my mother. I knew what the Aunty was hinting at. She wanted my mother to host a Quran khani. I could see a million thoughts pass across my mother's face: the cost, the cleaning, the destruction of the bathroom sink, but if my mother refused to host a Quran khani it would appear unreligious. The Aunty was saying it in front of Taslima's mother to put pressure on my mother. However, the Aunty had neglected one thing: Taslima's mother was not judgmental of my mother.

The silence stretched out until my mother said, "Yes, that's a good idea. We haven't had a gathering in so long. We barely see each other, much less gather to read Quran. We've lost so much of our free time. Perhaps we've truly become American."

My mother was making a joke and Taslima's mother laughed, but the Aunty frowned. "Muslims must make time to see each other and read Quran."

The smile disappeared from my mother's face.

Taslima's mother added quickly, "It's a good idea. We can do a one-dish."

My mother looked at her gratefully, and I felt thankful my mother had a real friend.

After chai, it was time to go. There was no long lingering at the kitchen door, the way there usually was, the adults saying endless goodbyes. Taslima's mother said to the Aunty, "If you'd like to visit, come anytime," but her voice didn't have the kind of enthusiasm it had the first time she'd put out the invitation.

The Aunty just nodded. Saying a quick "Khuda hafiz," she walked out, expecting us to follow.

"Ammi, can I stay and help clean?"

My mother saw the piles of dishes covering the counters and filling the sink.

Taslima's mother looked at me with pity and said, "Yes, let her stay."

My mother nodded, then took Safia by the hand and rushed to catch up with the Aunty.

As soon as they left, Taslima's mother turned the TV back on to catch the last few innings. Baseball games were endless, so the game was still on.

We started picking up dishes and bringing them to the kitchen.

Aliza scraped food off a plate into the garbage. "What's up the butt of your aunty?"

"Oh my God," I said. "You can't say things like that about aunties."

"Really? I just did." She threw the plate into the sink. "But we're going to have to figure out how we're going to save you."

Aliza was right. I needed all kinds of saving.

When I got home, the Aunty was with my mother in the kitchen, chopping onions. Even if we'd just eaten a large lunch, dinner had to be started and ready by the time my father got home.

The Aunty was still talking about her nephew. "He's such a good boy, but he's having trouble because he's looking for a religious girl."

My mother was rinsing out pieces of chicken in the sink. "Well, that shouldn't be a problem."

"He's looking for a religious girl *here*."

Oh, so he wanted a green card too.

"Don't worry. All the girls here are mazbhii." My mother rinsed out a chicken neck. "The only thing is they are less mature. They don't know the things we did, how to talk to people. They're not ready to be wives."

"As if we were ready," the Aunty said with a smirk. From the way she said it, I knew she was referring to sex. Awkward.

I shifted in my discomfort. They noticed me lingering in the doorway. My mother looked embarrassed, but the Aunty eyed me up and down.

"Asalaamu alaikum," I said, walking out of the room as fast as I could. "I have to read Asr."

I kicked myself. I hoped I hadn't put the idea in the Aunty's head that I was the kind of girl she was looking for. Was I a religious girl? I still read all my namaazes, even if Fajr was always late. I still read Quran even though it was mostly on the weekends.

But I knew "religious girl" was code for something that had nothing to do with Allah. It had to do with how a girl did whatever her husband and the community said, how a girl wouldn't question the way things were set up.

I knew the Aunty's nephew was like the young uncles from my childhood. For them, us first-gen Pakistani girls were a forest of green cards. We were groomed like Christmas trees, thinking we were in the beautiful woods, thinking we were growing, but we were just being readied to be cut down. They were coming for us.

THE KHATUM

All week my mother was on the phone, calling all the aunties to invite them and figure out who was bringing what dish, so everyone didn't show up with chana chaat. We went into a frenzy of cleaning, and I got sucked up into it. My mother mopped the floors; I swept the stairs. My mother dusted the shelves; I vacuumed the rooms. My mother cleaned all the windows and mirrors and told me to change all the bedsheets and pillowcases, even though no one would be using the beds.

The Aunty just watched us, saying her back hurt. It didn't hurt enough, though, for her to follow me around, her eagle eyes noticing every speck of dust and dirt I missed.

The morning of the Khatum, our house was set up like a showroom, clean and pristine, the carpets vacuumed and the floors gleaming. Although it was a one-dish, my mother and the Aunty had made fruit chaat, chicken, kebabs, and of course later there would be chawal. Although the time that was given was eleven, no one arrived until noon, and when they did, they all arrived at once.

Taibah Aunty was the first. She came in carrying two trays of home-made samosas. As soon as she got near me, I got a whiff of rose oil. I cringed, remembering the day we'd gone to the Exorcist. Taibah Aunty smiled knowingly and walked off to the living room to greet the Aunty.

Bahar's family was next. Bahar's mother was at the head of the crowd, weighed down with a tray full of food. She looked happier than I'd seen her in a long time. I immediately saw why. Bahar was behind her, carrying her baby boy in her arms like a prince. He was round and adorable with thick surma around his eyes. He was wearing a perfectly ironed white salwar kameez, while Bahar was wearing a heavily embroidered pink suit and had braided flowers into her hair. Leave it to Bahar to get herself and her baby super dressed up for a Khatum.

I was surprised to see Shahnaaz at the end of the family caravan, pushing the baby's stroller, which contained a large diaper bag. She looked like a miniature Bahar, the same haughty look on her face, wearing clothes too fancy for just a stroll in Corona.

There was a flurry of hugs and salaams as everyone entered the house. I followed them to the living room, holding Safia. She put her head on my shoulder and sucked her thumb. So often, just holding Safia made me feel calm.

As soon as my mother and Taibah Aunty saw Bahar's son, they went insane with joy. He was passed from aunty to aunty. He kept a bored look on his face, as if he was used to this kind of attention.

Bahar's mother, Bahar, and even Shahnaaz looked on and beamed. "Say salaam, Mittoo," Bahar said in the voice people used with babies.

When she handed him to the Aunty, she held him awkwardly. She tried to smile, but her face twisted into a grimace. She didn't really know how to be with children. She passed him to my mother, who held him and cuddled him.

Safia squirmed in my arms, wanting to go to my mother, so I put her down. She ran over and clung to my mother's side. She tugged at my mother's salwar, but my mother didn't look down. I was about to go to her when the doorbell rang.

"Get the door," my mother said to me, finally picking Safia up and putting her on her other hip.

I ran down the stairs, hoping it was Taslima. For me, even a Quran khani was not a party until she was around. When I opened the door, I was surprised to see Hafiz Saab's wife. I'd only met her once a few months ago when she'd first arrived in the States. Everyone had been shocked by how strikingly beautiful and young she was. Especially compared to Hafiz Saab, who seemed so old and run-down.

Before I could get over my surprise, I saw who was behind her and froze. Saima. She was no longer the young girl of our childhood. She looked like her mother, with the same round moon face, but more beautiful, like the paintings of Mughal princesses I'd seen in the library.

I'd heard Saima had found religion, but I hadn't believed the rumors because she'd never been even a little religious before. I'd been the religious one. But it seemed the rumors were true. She was wearing a scarf instead of a dupatta.

"It's me!" she said, making fun of the look on my face.

"Razia," Hafiz Saab's wife said, taking my hand. "I've heard so much about you." I wondered what she'd heard. "Saima says you read Quran so beautifully."

Saima smiled. "I also heard you got into Stuyvesant! Congratulations."

"Thank you," I said, becoming embarrassed. I'd gotten into the top specialized high school in New York City. My parents hadn't wanted me to go, but the aunties and uncles had encouraged them to let me. There was a myth that if you went to Stuyvesant, scholarships to college would just be given to you. Every door would open.

Everyone thought the smartest kids went to Stuyvesant, everyone except Taslima. She hadn't even applied. "Why would I go so far away to a harder school with more homework?" she'd said, tapping her forehead. "Use your brain."

"Where are you going?" I asked Saima, hoping she'd say Stuyvesant too.

She saw my hope but shook her head. "I didn't get in. I'm going to John Bowne."

I felt uncomfortable, the way I had ever since I'd found out everyone I knew hadn't gotten in.

"It's okay. I didn't really want to go all the way into the city. But congratulations! I always knew you were the smartest."

I realized Saima was the first person to sincerely congratulate me. I felt a deep, piercing pain as the time capsule of our friendship, the one I'd kept locked away, punctured.

"Where's your mother? I'd like to say salaam," Hafiz Saab's wife's voice broke through.

Before I had a chance to answer, my mother came into the kitchen and exclaimed over both Hafiz Saab's wife and Saima. After a moment of hesitation that maybe only I noticed, she gave Saima an extra-long hug. I'm sure she was relieved her mother hadn't come.

We all went to join the group, and I was surprised when Shahnaaz and Saima said formal, distant hellos to each other. Was it because Saima had become religious? Shahnaaz would have run from any religious lectures, the way she used to with my mother.

The bell rang again. I ran downstairs, welcoming an escape from the feelings that were overwhelming me.

Taslima's family had finally arrived. Aliza was carrying a large aluminum-foil tray filled with tandoori chicken. It smelled so good, my stomach gave a twang. Taslima hugged me while her mother smiled and nodded, giving me the kind of smirk that always made me crack up. I was so relieved they were here.

Now the guests were complete. I closed the front door and followed Taslima's family upstairs. My mother and Taslima's mother hugged as if they hadn't seen each other in years. The house was suddenly crowded, more full of life than it had been in a long time. My mother was happy to be connecting with everyone again. She'd seen her friends so much less since the Aunty had arrived. Maybe it wasn't such a bad thing to have a Quran khani.

For a while everyone mingled. Taslima's mother joined the circle of aunties cooing over Mittoo while Aliza and Bahar caught up on the sofa. I had a feeling that when we weren't around, Aliza enjoyed talking to Bahar. Shahnaaz and Taslima had their heads bent together. I would have been jealous, but now all I could think about was talking to Saima.

I went to look for her and saw the Aunty had cornered Saima and Hafiz Saab's wife. I went and stood next to them. Saima was quietly listening while Hafiz Saab's wife consoled the Aunty.

I whispered to Saima, "I'm so glad you came."

She smiled, but before she could say anything, we were interrupted by Taibah Aunty, who said in a loud voice: "Arey, Quran khani hai. Milna shilna choro!"

The aunties laughed. It was time to read Quran.

Taibah Aunty helped my mother put down a clean sheet and all the aunties came down off the sofas. The sheet was one of my favorites, with yellow roses on a blue border. Everyone began to take saparahs and sit in the circle.

Hafiz Saab's wife and Saima sat in a corner together. Before I could, the Aunty sat down next to Saima, and Taibah Aunty sat down next to Hafiz Saab's wife. Luckily, Taslima had saved me a seat next to her, expecting we'd split reading a saparah.

I looked at my mother. "Ammi, can I—"

My mother looked at the Aunty, then cut me off. "No. You and Taslima are getting too old to share saparahs." The Aunty!

Then, I don't know if she did it on purpose or by accident, but my mother handed me the twenty-third saparah, the one with Surat Yaseen. My bitterness disappeared. I loved reading Surat Yaseen. I went deep as I read and began to feel calm and quiet.

My mother had placed table fans throughout the room. They whirred back and forth, circulating the perfumes of the aunties: rose oil, jasmine, Charlie. The sounds of the outside dimmed. I stopped being annoyed about the Aunty and anxious to talk to Saima. For the next half hour, I became lost in reading Quran.

When I finished, I noticed the aunties were starting to get fidgety. They stretched their legs, cleared their throats, and fixed their dupattas. Saima and Hafiz Saab's wife were the only ones who stayed focused in their bubbles of light. Their headscarves were pinned, while our dupattas were draped loosely around our heads. We had to fix them continuously.

I looked over the room. Taslima was mouthing the words as she read and Aliza was staring out the window. Shahnaaz was bent over her saparah. She was still on the first page. I wasn't sure she could even read Quran. She caught me staring and I quickly looked away.

My mother saw I was done with my first saparah. "Razia, go to the kitchen and get the chawal started."

"Chawal started?" I got scared. My mother had never given me such a big cooking task. What was she thinking?

The Aunty laughed. "She doesn't know anything about making chawal."

The other aunties all chuckled. I filled up with anger, but I couldn't show it.

"Just wash the chawal," my mother said, "and someone will come help you."

Taslima looked up hopefully, but her mother said, "Finish your saparah first and then you can help."

Hafiz Saab's wife said politely, "I'm done. I can help."

"No," my mother insisted. "You're our special guest."

The Aunty scowled. She probably wanted to be the only special guest.

I went to the kitchen, grumbling to myself, wishing my mother and the Aunty hadn't embarrassed me like that. I did know how to wash rice. That's all my mother had to say. Wash the rice, not make chawal!

I prayed the Aunty would go back to Pakistan to live with her sister. Maybe there was extra magic at a Quran khani and my prayer would come true.

I measured the rice into the bowl and began to think about Saima. How had she gotten so close to Hafiz Saab's wife? Who was Hafiz Saab's wife anyway? Why had she married an old man like Hafiz Saab? Had she had a choice?

My thoughts were interrupted by a noise behind me. "Can I warm up this formula?" It was Bahar, carrying Mittoo on her hip and a bottle in her hand.

"Okay. The pots are there." I gestured and almost dropped the rice.

Bahar laughed at my nearly disastrous mistake. "Can you do it for me? I have Mittoo." She motioned to him, as if trying to explain something to someone who was too slow to get it.

I wanted to say, "Um, I'm washing chawal," and motion to the bowl as if *she* was too slow to get it, but I couldn't talk to Bahar that way.

For one thing, she would probably slap me.

I washed my hands and warmed up a pot of water and put the bottle in it. Finally, after what felt like forever, with Bahar watching my every move, she said, "That's enough." I handed her the bottle. She squeezed formula on her wrist to test the temperature. Satisfied, she put the bottle in Mittoo's mouth. He drank it hungrily.

Instead of leaving, Bahar sat down on the chair the Aunty had brought to the kitchen to rest her aching back, while my mother did most of the cooking. Suddenly, Mittoo started crying. He wouldn't take the bottle. Anger and annoyance flashed across Bahar's face. "Ugh." She shoved him into my arms. "Take him to my mother."

He whimpered, tears clinging to his eyelashes. "Sorry she has to be your mother," I whispered to him as we left the room.

When I brought Mittoo to Bahar's mother, she glowed. At least he had this love. Then again, being a boy, he'd have more love from the world than any of us. Now fully distracted, the aunties all offered to take him, but Bahar's mother held him close.

I was about to head back to the kitchen when my mother said, "Aliza, can you help Razia? I'll finish your saparah."

"Okay, Aunty," Aliza said, getting up, looking relieved.

Taslima frowned, annoyed she had to keep reading. I looked at her apologetically, but I was glad it was Aliza. She knew how to make cha-wal and she could also distract Bahar.

When we got back to the kitchen, Bahar had made herself even more comfortable, putting her feet up on a large tin of ghee my mother kept near the stove.

"Done reading Quran?" Aliza asked her.

"For today."

Aliza laughed. She lifted the lid off the pot. It turned out my mother had already cut the onions and put them in. She hadn't said that to me either.

Aliza put the oil in expertly. She leaned against the counter and began to peek under the different tinfoils. "Oh! Samosas!"

"Bring me one," Bahar said. "I'm hungry."

Aliza must have been hungry too because she took a samosa for Bahar and one for herself.

She offered one to me but I said no.

Bahar and Aliza were in their own category of behavior. They had aunty-privileges without the aunty-restraint. If my mother walked in and saw me eating before everyone, she'd lose it.

Soon, the onions were jumping around in the oil, dancing. Aliza mixed them with ease.

Bahar got a wicked look on her face. "So I hear you're going *away* for college?" She had an accusatory note in her question. In our community, we were expected to go to college, but we had to live at home. Wanting to go away to college was practically an admission of guilt that we were going to be going wild, partying, and forgetting about Islam.

Aliza's tone was neutral, guarded. "Yes, I am."

I knew Aliza wanted to go away to college, to experience all the things we were denied. But I didn't want her to tell Bahar that. It was dangerous to share information with someone who loved to gossip like Bahar. I started to send Aliza psychic messages: *Don't say anything. Don't say anything.*

I didn't have to worry. Aliza knew Bahar.

"What's wrong with going to schools here?" Bahar asked. "You could have gone to LaGuardia." Bahar had gotten into LaGuardia but decided to put it off until after she got married, and then she'd had Mittoo and here we were. Bahar got a mischievous look on her face. "Do you think you'll meet anyone there?"

Aliza didn't answer right away. "No boyfriends, if that's what you mean. I'll be studying."

"Just studying?" Bahar arched her perfectly threaded eyebrows.

Then Bahar did something I'd never seen her do. She went after Aliza. "What do you think you're going to do with all this studying? When you get married it doesn't help you change a diaper."

Aliza looked at her coolly. "Maybe I won't be changing diapers."

Bahar gasped. "Do you want to end up like her?"

We all knew immediately who she meant by "her."

"I think," Aliza said, "there are other options."

Bahar got up and filled a glass of water, then poured it over the frying onions. Even though I'd gotten less scared over the years, I still jumped at the explosion.

Bahar smirked at my sensitivity. Then she abruptly changed the subject. "Do you think Hafiz Saab's wife is as perfect as she seems? Girls in Pakistan are more clever than girls here, you know. They have more freedom than we do."

Aliza smiled. "You would know."

"Why do you think she married Hafiz Saab?" I asked. "He's twice her age! And he doesn't even make any money."

"He's not just any Hafiz Saab," Aliza said. "He's a Hafiz Saab who lives in America."

Before she could say more, Shahnaaz came in. She didn't even acknowledge me or Aliza. She turned to Bahar. "Mittoo needs his diaper changed."

"Can you change it? I'm soooo tired." Bahar was being dramatic, but Shahnaaz fell for it.

I was amazed. What kind of power did Bahar have over Shahnaaz?

Bahar smiled. "She's always over at our house now, so I let her take care of him."

Aliza gave Bahar a pointed look. "Do *you* even know how to change a diaper?"

Bahar shrugged.

Taslima came in next, sweating. "Oh my God, I thought I'd never finish that saparah. Your mother finally felt bad for me and took over. Are you sure all the saparahs are the same length?"

We all laughed at how bad Taslima was at reading Quran.

Aliza's chawal timing was perfect. As soon as she lowered the fire, we heard the call from the living room.

"Dua time, girls," Taibah Aunty yelled out.

When we walked into the living room, my mother and Taibah Aunty were going back and forth.

"Would you like to lead the dua?" my mother asked Taibah Aunty.

"No, you should," Taibah Aunty replied.

The Aunty cleared her throat. "May I?"

Everyone turned to look at her.

My mother flushed. "Yes, of course, I'm sorry, I didn't realize you wanted . . ." She flailed.

The Aunty gave her a flat smile. "It's okay. I understand." What exactly she understood, I didn't know.

We all put our hands together for the dua, but the Aunty began to talk instead. Slowly and awkwardly, we all put our hands down. Immediately the Aunty's sermon was different. Our mothers usually started with surats from the Quran, then prayers for guidance, protection, and care. But the Aunty spoke in a voice that was loud and harsh. At first it sounded like one of her many complaints.

"The other day as I was walking to Key Food, I saw a young girl. She was surrounded by a group of boys. Four boys and one girl. She was wearing shorts so short, you could almost see her *thing*."

The Aunty said "thing" with such revulsion, as if she wasn't carrying her own around. She'd been living in Texas this whole time. Hadn't she seen people in short shorts?

"In Islam we teach that women are jewels. We are precious and strong. We're so precious, we must be hidden from the world, as jewels are hidden first in the earth and then in safes. When we flaunt our bodies, we become less precious. We shame ourselves and our families."

The Aunty's logic didn't work for me. What about men and their responsibility to not stare at women? No one ever enforced that rule. Was I the only who thought it was unfair? I looked around to see that all the aunties, even Saima and Hafiz Saab's wife, were nodding in agreement. None of the other girls seemed to be paying attention. Is that how they handled it, by zoning out?

Shahnaaz was staring off into space. Taslima was playing with her dupatta. Aliza was looking at her nails. Bahar was cuddling Mittoo. For a second, when she thought no one was watching, a look of deep love transformed her face. Perhaps she was a good mother after all.

The Aunty was only beginning. "And then these children, they turned to me and started calling me a Hindu!"

My stomach dropped. It was deeply shameful for an aunty to be bullied by kids on the street. My allegiance to them swerved like a car trying to avoid hitting a tree.

"I said to them, 'I'm Muslim, not Hindu!' Can you imagine, calling me a Hindu?"

My allegiance flipped again, like a car out of control. It was so hypocritical to be hateful if the Aunty didn't want to be harassed herself.

The Aunty took a dramatic pause while everyone but me shook their heads in sympathy.

"There is no mercy for those who harass Muslims. There will be a special place in Hell for them. They will burn alongside the ones who mocked Muhammad (Peace Be Upon Him) and tortured his followers. Those who have been burning all this long time."

There was an uncomfortable shifting. The Aunty's sermon was definitely more fire and brimstone than anything we were used to.

She noticed the discomfort and tried to rein it in. "We are Muslim. We live among kafirs, but we are Muslims."

Calling our neighbors kafirs led to more uncomfortable shifting.

In Corona, our parents had neighborly relationships with, well, our neighbors. We shared our food, our sidewalks, our streets. Yes, the old Italians had hated us, but they had left.

Sensing she was losing her audience, the Aunty shifted tactics. "Allah didn't bless me with children." She shook her head back and forth. "And that is for my own sins . . ."

Or maybe Allah just has a soft spot for children, I thought.

"But now I feel it was a blessing to not have daughters in this country. There are so many dangers for them." The Aunty's voice broke. "Oh, Allah, where have you brought us? I buried my husband in this country. No one, no one, no one from his own family could come . . . When our parents passed, when our brothers and sisters passed . . . we mourned them alone so far from home . . ." She broke into tears.

Suddenly all the aunties were wiping their eyes. This had never happened before. I'd never seen a Quran khani turn into a crying fest. The Aunty!

After the dua, Saima and Hafiz Saab's wife got up decisively. I thought they were going to offer to help set up the food, but instead Hafiz Saab's wife turned to my mother and said, "I'm sorry. We have to go."

My mother was surprised. We all were. "Where are you going? We were just going to eat."

Hafiz Saab's wife turned toward Saima, who was looking down at her feet. They had planned it this way.

"We can't stay to eat," Hafiz Saab's wife said.

"How can you not stay?" the aunties protested.

Then it dawned on us all at once. The feud was still on. An exception had been made to read Quran for an uncle's memorial. But that was it. No socializing. No friendship. I wondered if Hafiz Saab's wife had brokered this deal. Bahar was right. Young women from Pakistan were much smarter than us, more able to navigate the ways of the world, or at least the ways of Pakistani people.

You could see the aunties' minds were swirling with gossip. Out of kindness to my mother, though, they held their tongues.

My mother was the first to recover. "Take food! Take food! Razia, make some plates."

Hafiz Saab's wife protested but my mother insisted until she accepted. I tried to catch Saima's eye, but she wouldn't look at me.

As if breaking a spell, there was sudden motion and a few people jumped up to help, but my mother said, "No, Razia can do it."

As I began to leave the room, Saima whispered to me, "I'm sorry. I wish I could stay."

Somehow, it was not until then that I realized Saima and I would never be friends again. Her loss, the one I'd never allowed myself to believe, began to bleed. My throat closed and before anyone could see me crying, I rushed into the kitchen. I filled Styrofoam plates with chawal, samosas, and kebabs. The plates overflowed. I stuffed my tears away inside them, under the tinfoil.

By the time Saima and Hafiz Saab's wife came into the kitchen, with everyone following them to say goodbye, my face was already stone. I gave Saima two plastic bags bursting with food. She hesitated, wanting to say something, but there were too many people around. Hafiz Saab's wife gently pulled her away.

After the dua, there was a strange feeling among the aunties. Usually they were cheerful when it was time to eat. Now they seemed uneasy. It wasn't just the sudden departure of Hafiz Saab's wife and Saima. It was a feeling in the air. The mothers were looking at us daughters. Would we soon be wearing shorts so short they reached all the way up to our *things*? Would we be hanging out with boys, four boys to a girl? It was as if a storm was coming and they'd just caught a whiff of it in the wind. The only one who seemed unworried was Bahar's mother, who'd already locked Bahar down.

I overheard Taslima's mother say to Aliza, "When you go to college, you need to still read namaaz."

"Ammi," Aliza said, "I barely read namaaz at home."

Normally Taslima's mother would have laughed at Aliza's sassiness but now she just frowned. "It's not funny."

As soon as her mother walked away, Aliza looked at me and said, "We have to figure out how to get rid of this aunty."

Soon, the kitchen was a frenzy of activity as all the girls came in to pull off foil from the trays; set up the cups, plates, and forks; place the chawal in a dish; and warm up the samosas and rotis in the oven. We'd been doing it for so many years, it was a choreographed dance. In no time, the table was set with a feast.

The aunties got their food first and we stepped to the side and let them fill their plates, piling them high with chicken, rice, and salan. There was so much deliciousness! The more people took, the more it grew. It was Barkat. The law of sharing.

The aunties took their food and went to the living room and the girls crowded around the small dining room table. Taslima had saved me the seat next to her. I wondered what Bahar would do, if she'd go with the aunties or sit with us. For now, she was standing at the front of the food line talking to the Aunty. As we watched, she decisively walked over to the dining table where we were sitting.

Aliza sat at the head of the table. Bahar usually took that seat, but Aliza acted innocent. "Sorry, we didn't think you were coming." She motioned for Bahar to take the seat to her right.

"I'm not an aunty yet," Bahar said with a huff, but she sat down.

Shahnaaz slipped into the seat next to Bahar, who immediately asked, "Is Mittoo okay?"

"Yes, your mother's feeding him," Shahnaaz said. I wondered what secret was between them to make Shahnaaz act so different.

Bahar looked through the doorway. I followed her gaze to see Mittoo squirming as Bahar's mother brought a bottle to his mouth.

We dug into our food, starving. "You seemed to be best friends with the new aunty," Aliza said to Bahar in between bites.

Bahar leaned in toward all of us. She stage-whispered, "Do you know what the Aunty asked me? She asked if Saima was engaged! She's trying to find someone for her nephew. When I told her Saima was Pathan, she asked me if there were *other* girls in the community who weren't at the Quran khani."

"Oh, dis!" Taslima said. "To Pathans and us!"

I felt a surge of intense protectiveness. How dare the Aunty think she could move in on Saima?

"Is her nephew cute?" Shahnaaz asked.

I smiled, somehow relieved Shahnaaz was being herself again.

"You don't have to worry about him being cute," Bahar said meaningfully, but before I could find out more, Bahar's mother yelled from the living room.

"Bahar! Mittoo threw up!"

I could see through the door that it wasn't just a little baby throw-up. It was a whole bottle of formula.

"Ai! Shahnaaz, come with me." Shahnaaz listened. She got up with Bahar and went to Mittoo.

As soon as they left the table, I let it all out. "I can't believe this aunty! She planned the whole Quran khani like some kind of game show to find a bride for her nephew."

"You're mad?" Aliza said. "I thought I was the top choice."

Taslima frowned. "How come no one ever asks about me?"

"Oh my God. Why do either of you want to marry this guy?"

"I don't want to," Taslima said, pushing around her rice. "But it would be nice to be asked."

Aliza frowned. "My mother showed me a picture of him the other day."

Taslima almost spat up some of her food, laughing. She'd clearly seen the picture.

"What did he look like?"

Always proper, Aliza finished chewing before answering. "You know how Pakistani people never smile for cameras?"

"Yeah," I said. "It always makes them look so serious."

"Well, he looks like the Aunty, but with a mustache."

I laughed. "Do you have the picture on you?" I was becoming more and more curious about this nephew.

"You think I carry it around? Are you crazy? My mother wanted me to talk to him on the phone. She acted like it was just a conversation, but you know these guys. You have one conversation with them and they think you're engaged."

I shook my head. "It's so weird to be told your whole life you can never talk to boys and then suddenly be forced to."

"I'll tell you one thing," Aliza said. "No matter what, you always have to have your own money. As soon as I get to college, I'm getting a job. That's the only way to avoid this whole mess."

After chai, one by one, everyone left. Taibah Aunty rushed off to do a million things, as was her way. Mittoo was crying and Bahar's mother said they needed to get him home.

"Shahnaaz," Bahar said, "come with me!" Shahnaaz followed under Bahar's spell.

Taslima and I hugged, promising to see each other soon. The house felt emptier than ever.

Cleanup was my job, but my mother still came in to instruct me. The Aunty shadowed us. My anger came back tenfold when I saw the Aunty. She didn't really care about honoring her husband. She'd just been screening prospective brides to get herself a ticket back to Pakistan.

That very night the phone rang. It rang urgently and it rang late. I'd just fallen asleep and I woke suddenly to find Safia curled up next to me. She had crawled into my bed. She did that when she was having bad dreams. She was having them more with the Aunty around.

I heard my mother answer the phone in a muffled voice. My father was still at work.

In a second, my mother sounded wide awake. She began to talk loudly, and I knew it was a call from Pakistan. Whoever it was hadn't bothered to figure out the time zones. Immediately, I knew it was a call from the Aunty's sister.

I got up, pretending I needed to go to the bathroom. My mother saw me as I walked past her room.

"Go see if Aunty is awake."

Before I could answer, there was a sound in the hallway. The Aunty walked toward us looking disheveled. Her kameez was wrinkled and strands of hair slipped out from underneath her dupatta.

"Your sister's on the phone," my mother said, as if it was normal for the Aunty to receive a call in the middle of the night, as if this was not the call we'd all been waiting for.

For the first time, I saw a look on the Aunty's face I'd never seen before. Fear. It blended back into her features, but in that split second, I saw fear was the foundation of her entire face.

The Aunty turned and walked to the kitchen to pick up the other line. I knew my mother was sitting up awake, listening through the thin walls like me. We could hear the Aunty clearly.

There were salaams and asking after health and greetings. Then the Aunty said something and my ears perked up. I wondered if I'd heard her correctly.

"Yes, yes, there are a number of girls here. It won't be a problem."

Who was she talking about?

"It's late here . . . No, no. You didn't wake anyone." There was a round of goodbyes as long as the greetings and then the Aunty hung up.

It was quiet for a moment.

Then I heard loud sobbing. My mother got out of bed. I followed quietly behind her and stood hidden in the doorway. The Aunty had pulled the long phone cord out of the kitchen and was sitting at the dining table, just like the first time I'd seen her. She'd taken her glasses off and was wiping her eyes.

When she saw my mother, an animal cry came through her. She began to cry. "I'm going home," she said. "I'm going home."

BOOK FOUR

Fall 1988–Spring 1989

GOODWILL

Fall was humidity slaking off, flaking; hot, wet air becoming a ghost of itself. Suddenly the ground was covered with acorns and squirrels scurrying past, carrying them in their mouths. The sun clocked out earlier and earlier each evening. As soon as night hit, it bolted, not wanting to be caught dead in these parts. The last of the cicadas' song was a surprise. "They're still here," I said to myself, to the air, to no one in particular.

Taslima and I had the pull of new schools, new lives. Taslima was going to Flushing and I was going to Stuyvesant. Going to separate schools wasn't new for us. Our zone schools had always been different. But this was on another level. Flushing was going deeper into Queens-style preppy, into old Italian and Jewish territory. Stuyvesant wasn't even in Queens. It was in the East Village, where punks walked around like zebras in the wild, lingering on every street corner, their pierced faces and rainbow mohawks disturbing the air.

On St. Marks Place, desi uncles lined the sidewalks, selling stall after stall of scarves, leather pants, sunglasses, and fake silver necklaces with crosses and pentacles. The very first week, I bought myself a green crystal sphere clutched in a hawk's claw. I wore it constantly, much to my mother's horror.

Even though Stuyvesant and Flushing were as different as could be, Taslima and I both realized the first week that we needed better clothes and fast. For years, we'd complained about the clothes our parents bought us: baggy shirts and ill-fitting pants from Alexander's. In Corona, most kids had worn the same. Now we were up against a whole new kind of classmate whose parents took them to Macy's or the Gap. These kids had money.

It was a miracle when we discovered Goodwill on Junction Boulevard. Goodwill was a gold mine. It was filled with woolen sweaters with the prettiest buttons, velvet blazers, and dusty rainbows of vintage dresses.

As amazing as it was, our shopping at Goodwill had to be a secret. I had to employ all my skills to avoid getting caught. If my mother knew I was buying clothes from a thrift store, she'd be furious. Buying used clothes was not something Pakistani people did. It was considered dirty. We never saw any fellow Pakistanis there, but Taslima and I didn't care. More clothes for us.

Finally we were wearing the kind of clothes we wanted to wear. Not salwar kameez that made us targets. Not clothes from Alexander's that looked like they were rejects from the factory, never quite fitting, with strange pinchings at the shoulders and neck, the sweaters always riding up.

Thanks to Goodwill, we were making a style of our own. My favorites were the rows and rows of funereal black dresses that made me look like a ghost nymph of myself. Taslima's style was more eclectic. She could find anything and, with her mother's sewing machine, transform it into a unique outfit.

We went almost every Wednesday, leaving school as soon as our last class ended and meeting at Junction Boulevard. Our mothers thought we were doing extracurriculars and didn't say anything. Extracurriculars were good for getting scholarships after all.

I was running late and rushed into Goodwill. America, an old Dominican man, was at the front counter, tagging clothes, looking depressed. America never said anything to us. Like everyone else, he had thought Taslima and I were Dominican. He'd tried to speak to us in Spanish and when we'd said "No habla español" in terrible accents, he'd realized we were Pakistani. He'd stopped speaking to us in Spanish, which meant he'd stopped speaking to us.

The store was empty of customers, except for Taslima in a far corner. She already had clothes draped over her arm.

I walked toward her and mock-gasped. "Sweaters! No! I don't want winter to come!"

She shook her head. "Whether or not you want, it's coming." She glanced at the long black dress I was wearing. "Why are you always wearing black? Who are these new friends of yours at Snoyvesant, vampires?"

Taslima had come up with the nickname Snoyvesant after I told her how many snotty kids there were. The school was full of upper-class kids whose parents were trying to skimp on a few years of private school tuition and overachieving immigrant kids like me who, Taslima said, began to act snotty after they'd gotten in.

I wasn't hanging out with vampires, I was barely hanging out with anyone, but the Goth fashion of the East Village was rubbing off on me like charcoal.

"You sound like my mother. Except instead of 'vampires'"—I deepened my voice—"she says 'Shaitan.'"

Taslima laughed. "Your mother always brings in the devil."

We began to make our way through the store, *click click click*ing through the racks. Something caught my eye, a black velvet T-shirt with silver-white sequins forming the face of a furry cat, whiskers, and fur. I held it up as a joke. "Oooohh. This would be perfect for you!"

Taslima opened her eyes wide. "No! It would look amaaazing on you!" She scanned the rack across from me and picked up what looked like a prom-slash-bridesmaid dress. It was aquamarine, like the waves from under the sea. "You'd look great in this!"

"Oh no! You should take it. I insist."

Taslima's eyes narrowed. "Hmmm. I could just *alter* . . . it." With her fingers, Taslima made two quick strokes. What I saw in the air did look fashionable.

We kept moving through the racks.

"What about this?"

Click. Click. Click.

"What about this?"

The sound of our hangers rang through the silence. Maybe it was the darkness. Maybe it was because for the first time we were in a place where we felt rich. Our giggles threw dust in the air.

Then a quiet came upon us, as sudden as a door opening. Through the racks, I could feel the clothes calling me. At Goodwill, each piece had a vibe, a personality, even if the garment had been, I hoped, washed before being donated. It wasn't like shopping at regular stores where all the clothes looked and smelled the same, cheap cloth and plastic. Goodwill was filled with clothes people had loved enough to pass down.

When we came to the blazers, Taslima walked ahead, but I stayed. I loved blazers, how they covered up my Betty Boop boobs. My sweaters and shirts clung to me, making me feel exposed. But blazers made me feel strong. I had a special collection I kept hidden in the back of my bedroom closet.

I let my fingers drift over the rack until I felt the pull of a blazer. I touched its soft velvet sleeve. It was olive green, a warm color between moss and a deep darkness falling in a forest. I slipped it on. It fit, snug around the waist.

Taslima reappeared, buried in clothes. She peeked at me from behind her pile.

"Go ahead, make fun of green velvet," I said, but she was already walking to the Mirror.

The Mirror lived in the far back of the store, surrounded by bags, cardboard boxes, and suitcases filled with hand-me-downs. It was dirty and smudged but was the ultimate judge, the game show host, the guillotine. Whole piles of clothes were made or unmade, orphans rejected or chosen, in front of the Mirror.

I could have sworn it came from a fun house, the way it made my body look different on different days. Everything looked good on the racks or even carried in my arms, but after visiting the Mirror, I could end up empty-handed at the end of an hour.

Although I wasn't done, I followed Taslima. I wanted to see if the blazer would withstand the Mirror's scrutiny.

Taslima pulled out a red corduroy miniskirt from the heart of her pile. She began to shimmy it up her legs. Her jeans were tight, and the skirt went right up. She turned around slowly, looking at herself. "What do you think?"

It looked amazing, so I didn't say the obvious, that we weren't allowed to wear miniskirts. Instead, I looked past Taslima and gazed at myself. I was thrilled. The blazer made me look smart, like a college girl from the fifties. It felt like a good-luck day at Goodwill.

"I'm going to keep looking."

Taslima didn't hear me. She was engrossed in her own pile of finds.

I walked over to the dresses. A light green one caught my eye. Someone had hung it at the front of the rack. The fabric was a pattern of ivy and flowers, the material translucent. There was a silk slip underneath, sewn to the top layer. I held it against my body. The dress went below my knees all the way to my ankles, so my mother couldn't say anything about the length.

I walked back to the Mirror. Taslima was busy buttoning up a shirt. I pulled my blazer off and slipped on the dress. It hourglassed at the waist and rippled from the bottom half, pulling the attention down and away from my breasts. It surrounded the shapes of my body and made them flow in a smooth motion down to my feet.

Taslima reached out and touched the hem. The bottom opened like wings. As she let it go, the fabric poured like water. "Not bad."

I smiled and straightened my spine. My hair had grown out a bit and it was beginning to look like the style I'd originally envisioned, with long, black layers like Jaclyn Smith from *Charlie's Angels*. "What are you getting?" I asked.

She held up the red miniskirt.

"Are you really going to buy that? It's cute, but—"

"But what?" Taslima acted oblivious. Before I could answer, she laughed. "I know. I know. I'll just wear it in my room." She looked away from me and glanced at her watch. "Oh my God! It's almost five o'clock!"

"What?" We were expected home by five. I thought of leaving the blazer and dress behind and rushing home, but there was a no-hold policy, and I was afraid someone would buy them before I came back. I couldn't bear to lose them.

"Here, let's pay together to save time." Taslima grabbed the clothes and we ran to the front.

America's movements felt even slower than usual. He must have been particularly depressed. I shifted from foot to foot, hoping my anguish would inspire him to hurry up. Finally he said, "Eleven."

We had our money ready. We threw the bills on the table and grabbed our clothes. "No bag!" we both said, stuffing the clothes into our book bags and running out the door.

Our eyes had adjusted to the dimness of Goodwill, and the suddenness of the bright light dazed us. We smelled slightly of must. Taslima pulled out a yellow Jean Naté spray bottle. She spritzed herself, then held it out to me. I shook my head. If I came home smelling like perfume, it would be more obvious than smelling musty.

I buried the clothes at the bottom of my book bag. We ran up the subway stairs, flashed our train passes, and ran to the platform. The 7 train came right away and I sighed with relief. A few minutes later, we were saying goodbye.

"See you this weekend," we said at the same time, then laughed. In front of our mothers, we'd act like we hadn't seen each other during the week.

I speed-walked home, calculating when I would have a chance to secretly wash and dry the blazer and dress so I could wear them to school.

In our front yard, there was a cloud of crayon red. The cherry tree was turning color. A wind blew and the leaves rained down on me. I felt a sudden sadness. It had been so long since I'd sat in the cherry tree's branches. I spent so much time on the trains, going back and forth to school, and then there was so much homework. I sighed and said, "One day soon, I promise, Cherry Tree."

I rang the bell and Safia opened the door. She hugged my legs and smiled. I carried her up the stairs, even though she was getting big.

My mother was in the kitchen. I could tell immediately she was upset. The kitchen felt hot and stuffy. There were two pots on the stove. The pressure cooker's top spun, emitting the sound of an old-fashioned train.

There was an edge to her voice. "Why are you so late?"

I looked at the clock above her head. A way to not look in her eyes. It was well past five.

"I was at a club."

"What club?"

She'd never asked before. I blanked for a second, then recovered. "Yearbook."

I was a terrible liar. I could barely meet her eyes. Ever since I'd started going to the city, I'd begun to change, and my mother was suspicious of any change.

Her voice was tense, tired. "Go read namaaz."

I went to do wuzu and hid the blazer and the dress at the bottom of the hamper, underneath a week's worth of dirty laundry. My salwar kameez was hanging on a hook. I changed and got ready to read the namaazes I'd missed in school.

My mother was standing outside the bathroom door, waiting for me. "Where did you go after school?"

I was caught off guard. Before I could answer, there was a crash from the kitchen. We both ran at the same time, to make sure Safia hadn't spilled boiling salan all over herself. Thankfully, she had just pulled open a kitchen drawer too far and it had fallen. She sat in a circle of spoons and knives.

I fled to my parents' room and began reading Zohar, then Asr. I felt my mother come and stand in the doorway. But she couldn't say anything. Not even my mother could interrupt namaaz. Finally, she left.

When it was time for dua, I cupped my hands and confessed. "Allah, I'm finally wearing school clothes I like. Is that so bad? I hate having to lie, but there's no other way I can make them happy and still live my life. If there is, please show me." I ended my dua as I always did. "Allah, please protect my mother, father, and Safia." I blew two breaths, one to either shoulder, so the angels could bring my prayers up to Allah.

I folded up the janamaaz, took a deep breath, then slowly walked to the dining room, where I knew my mother would be setting out food. She didn't say anything about the club again. She was too tired. She put roti and salan in front of me. I was starving and grateful. I felt such a pinching, thorny love for my mother. I wished I could hug her. But that would have been impossible. We never showed love in that way.

Before I could do anything, she said, "Can you watch Safia? I need to go to Key Food."

"Okay," I said, my mouth full of roti. It was perfect timing for me to rescue my new clothes.

By the time my mother returned, I was doing my homework in the living room, Safia was on the couch next to me watching *My Little Pony*, and my newly washed olive-green blazer and dress were hanging in the back of the closet with the rest of my collection from Goodwill.

The next day I rushed home to appease my mother and my guilty conscience. She was in the kitchen hunched over the sink, cutting onions. Safia was sitting on the counter, swinging her legs, flipping through a picture book. The onion fumes made my eyes smart.

My mother was so busy cooking I knew I had time to model my clothes, now that they were all clean and washed. I rushed to my bedroom and opened the closet door, but I could look and look. There was nothing but emptiness. All my clothes were gone.

I dug under the winter blankets my mother kept in a box in the closet. I don't know why I thought they would have ended up there, but I kept looking, my insides starting to bleed. Maybe my mother had put them in the laundry. Believing this was the only way I could keep calm.

I tried to breathe. "It's going to be okay. It's going to be okay. Maybe they're still somewhere in the house."

Slowly, I walked back to the kitchen. "Ammi."

Safia looked between us with fearful eyes. I knew then my clothes were gone.

Without turning around, my mother asked, "What is it?"

We both knew what it was.

I tried to make my voice normal, to not let her know she'd gotten to me. "Do you know what happened to the clothes in my closet?" As if they might have walked off by themselves.

She turned. There was a dark look on her face. "I threw them in the garbage."

The garbage? The horror of it moved through my body.

"How could you do that? You can't throw away my clothes!" I had never raised my voice to her. Terror filled my body, but I stood my ground.

Her voice was louder than mine. "Those dirty things are not clothes. They're garbage. And why are you lying to me about where you are going? This is what the Aunty said! Raising girls here is impossible!

Enough of this school! You're going to be going to the regular high school like everyone else."

Rage surged through me. I hated that she was listening to the Aunty. She'd left, but her fumes lingered. "You can't make me leave Stuyvesant. Just because you never went to school—"

I'd gone too far. My mother's face grew hard. She said slowly, "I am your mother and you will respect me."

I don't know what demon took over my mouth. "Respect has to be earned."

She slapped me so hard, I fell back. Safia tried to put her body between us, but my mother pushed her away. Safia stood to the side, silently crying, the tears flowing down to her chin.

Before my mother could slap me again, I ran to my bedroom and slammed the door behind me. I knew she wouldn't follow me. I threw myself on the bed and cried until I felt a million years old.

I only realized I'd fallen asleep when I was woken by my father's voice. "Razia?" It had gotten dark. I sat up, still, tense. He was still wearing his work clothes. There were dark bags under his eyes.

"Asalaamu alaikum," I mumbled.

"Wa alaikum asalaam." He sat down next to me on the bed. "Are you okay?" I stayed silent. After a moment, he sighed. "Ammi is feeling really bad for what she did." I turned my face into a mask so he couldn't read my thoughts. "She didn't mean to hurt you. Your Ammi, she's upset. She's just very worried about you. She loves you."

My mother? Love me? I burst into tears, surprising even myself. My cries shook through my whole body and left my father speechless. He awkwardly patted my head.

"Your Ammi just wants you to listen. You can't lie to us about where you're going. Who you're with. It's not safe here. Your Ammi, she didn't want you to go to a school so far away but I told her we should let you. Now you're starting to lie to us, cut your hair, wear these strange clothes. Behave different. We don't know the meaning."

"It's just clothes," I managed to say.

He sighed. "It's not just clothes. No matter what you do, if you try to be American, they will never accept you. They'll turn against you in the end."

How could I explain that I wasn't trying to be American, I already was?

When I didn't say anything, he continued. "I know you're a good girl."

"But I . . . I'm not good." A fresh wave of tears choked my voice. I kept trying to stop them, but each time I thought it was over, there would be a new wave.

My father let me cry. Finally, he got up to leave and as I watched him walk out the door, I caught a movement out of the corner of my eye. It was my reflection in the mirror. My face was ravaged, my eyes red. My father was wrong. It was too late. I'd already begun to change.

I looked into my eyes. "I'm going to get out of here one day."

As soon as I said the words, I felt a lightening, as if my head was lifting off, everything inside me falling away. In the mirror, the green crystal swung like a pendulum, dangled from my neck, like the promise of another world.

BETHESDA FOUNTAIN

"I have something to show you." Taslima locked her bedroom door behind me, then reached under the bed and pulled out a thin brown bag. "Asmi Khala brought it for Atif, but he didn't want it." Asmi Khala was Taslima's youngest aunt, who'd just come from Karachi with a suitcase full of gifts.

I turned the package over in my hands. The smell of Pakistan came from it. Inside, there was a black velvet vest with gold piping making patterns of swirls and flowers. In the center of each flower was a tiny round mirror. I'd seen these vests before. On Eid, the younger boys wore them, looking handsome and serious, like tiny Mughal princes.

"Let me guess. You made up an 'Outfit.'"

"But of course . . ." Taslima said in her fake British accent. "Now turn around and I'll show you."

Ever since "The Incident," as Taslima and I had begun to call the Goodwill debacle, I'd been depressed, but Taslima had worked to keep us "fashionative." She created outfits for us from whatever was at hand.

She found inspiration in the *New York Times Magazine* I brought over on the weekend. My father had been sent a "free" subscription, but when he'd been too busy to call and cancel, the bills and the Sunday edition had kept coming.

Taslima couldn't get enough of the fashion, of the models draped all over New York City in clothes that fit them like gloves. Wearing black, they floated in boats in Central Park. Wearing blue, they looked startled near the Hudson.

I wasn't as into fashion as Taslima, but her outfits did cheer me up. While she changed, I looked through Aliza's bookcase. She'd filled it with books she'd stolen from school or bought from secondhand book-stores. I picked up *The Catcher in the Rye* and started reading. I'd read it so many times I could open to any page and jump into the story. Holden had just woken up with his favorite teacher stroking his hair.

Taslima turned. "Okay, I'm ready!"

I pulled myself out of Holden's world. Taslima was wearing tight blue jeans and a white V-neck T-shirt with the black velvet vest on top. The velvet brought out the black of her eyes and the gold highlighted her black curls.

"Wow! You look like a model."

She smiled at herself in the mirror. "I want to go to Central Park and wear this." She said it to her reflection and me, daring both of us to defy her.

"Outside?" We couldn't go outside dressed like this. Ever since "The Incident," I'd been afraid of stepping out of line. I didn't want my parents to pull me out of Stuyvesant.

She rolled her eyes where I could see in the mirror. "Yes. Central Park is outside."

Central Park was where our favorite fashion shoots were. There the models pressed themselves against the granite arches of fountains and acted like they were in Europe. We pretended with them and felt an American stirring, a child's longing for its parents. We were all part of the bastard culture of England. Us Pakistanis, doubly so.

I looked at the vest, touched its beautiful black velvet. "Would I wear the same thing?"

Taslima stared at me, as if I was brainless. "No. You're going to wear what Asmi Khala brought *me*."

She reached under the bed again and pulled out a folded chador. It was covered with a pattern of white flowers against a blood- and rust-colored background. The flowers were the part of the cloth that had not been dyed. They popped like they'd been carved out of clay.

"It's batik." She opened up the chador and the pattern of flowers exponentially increased. We were supposed to wear it like a dupatta, but she doubled it and wrapped it around her waist. "Look, it's a mini-skirt!"

"How are we going to leave the house dressed like this?" I touched my cheek, remembering my mother's slap.

Taslima continued looking at herself in the mirror but raised her eyebrows pointedly.

"We're not going to. We're going to change *after*."

"But how are we even going to go to the city on a weekend?"

"My mother and Asmi Khala are visiting Aliza this weekend. I'll ask my mother if you can come over to keep me company."

"Why wouldn't you just come over to my house?"

Taslima sighed. "You know your mother doesn't trust me." I couldn't deny it. "Even more, she loves having you out of the house."

It was true. Ever since "The Incident" my mother and I were avoiding each other. I slunk around hiding from her. When she'd see me, she'd get flustered and make an excuse to leave the room. The whole thing made me so sad.

I took a breath. "Okay. Show me what you got."

Taslima was thrilled. She loved having a model for her outfits. I stood still while she wrapped the skirt tight around my hips, then pinned it with a safety pin.

She pulled out one of her father's white undershirts. It was new, blindingly white. "You'll wear this on top."

Taslima turned while I put on the shirt. The combination of the undershirt and chador was brilliant. The undershirt brought out my eyebrows and dark eyes. They shone against the white. Through the thin material, I could feel my breasts like headlights. I crossed my arms over them.

"Can I wear a dupatta?"

"Of course not!" But then seeing how exposed I was, Taslima said, "Hold on." She pulled something out from her dupatta drawer. It was thin and black with round, flat sequins around the edge. "You can wear this like a scarf."

I was just about to say "Otay butay buffet," our secret way of saying yes, when there was a knock on the door.

"Who is it?" Taslima said quick.

"Taslima! Open the door!" Aliza knocked harder.

We started to change as fast as we could. I pulled off the chador skirt while she struggled to get out of her tight jeans. I could see the door push in when Aliza leaned against it. "What are you doing in there? It's time to eat. Ammi wants you to put down the dastarkhan."

Taslima shoved the vest into the dupatta drawer and I slid open the lock.

"Hi, Aliza!" I said.

The tension dropped immediately when she saw I was there. She came into the room, looked in the mirror, and pulled at her bangs. "What are you reading?"

"*Catcher in the Rye.*"

She frowned at herself in the mirror. Then picked up tweezers and plucked a stray hair between her eyebrows. "You can borrow it."

"Really?"

Taslima sighed. "Great, now she's going to be reading for the rest of the day."

I got up, happily holding the book to my chest.

Taslima rolled her eyes. "Okay, if this nerd love fest is over, can we go?"

Aliza took my spot on the bed, choosing a novel for herself. She stretched her legs out on the bed and disappeared into her book before we'd even left the room.

The next morning, I woke up nervous. I was afraid my mother would know what Taslima and I were up to. I didn't want her to catch me lying again. How could she not? My mother knew everything.

She was in the kitchen, a cloud of smoke above her head. She'd been up before me, making breakfast for my father, and had stayed up to make breakfast for me.

"Nashta?"

I sat down at the table. Safia sat across from me, smiling. Even though she should have begun to speak, she never said a word, as if she had absorbed the silence of the house. My parents took her to doctor after doctor, and after examining her, they all said there was nothing wrong with her vocal cords. She would speak when she had something to say.

My mother put the paratha down in front of me. "You're going to Taslima's?" my mother said, exhaustion in her voice.

"Yes," I said, not meeting her eyes.

"Behave yourself there."

"I"—the paratha lodged in my throat from the lie—"will."

When I got up to go, my mother followed me into the hall and watched as I buckled my sandals. I squirmed under her gaze and left as quick as I could.

Taslima had it all planned. Instead of going to her house, we'd meet on the 7 train. My stop was 103 Street–Corona Plaza and Taslima lived one stop away on 111th. The plan was for her to get into the first door of the first car of the 7 train. Then when she pulled into my station, she'd put her head out. If we saw each other, I'd jump in. If we didn't, she'd step off.

I had to show my train pass before going in, but the station lady in the booth was busy with a long line. There was a young woman, fixing her makeup with a small compact. A few older men were behind her, the sort who looked drunk early in the morning. I held up my train pass, but the station agent didn't look at me. He had no way of knowing if I was doing anything school-related or not, but he was going to give me a hard time.

I heard the train in the distance and frantically waved my train pass at him. The attendant finally glanced up. He sighed and pressed the button to open the side door. I got ready to run up the stairs, but there was a mother with two little kids, one in each hand, a boy and a girl. She was pulling them up the dirty stairs.

I felt the rumble of the train. "Hurry, hurry," I whispered.

The mother scolded the kids to move to the side. The little girl did, and I sprinted up to the top of the stairs, just as the brick red and purple of the 7 came down the tracks.

I was far from the meeting point. I braced myself and ran alongside the train. When the first car passed, I saw a flash of Taslima's face. I ran faster. The train stopped, the doors opened, and Taslima put her head out and yelled, "Come on!"

I got energy from my secret reserves and ran. I jumped in right when the doors were closing and got my back leg caught in the door. Taslima tried to pull me in. The doors opened, and I fell on top of Taslima.

We both started giggling. The rest of the subway car gave us an annoyed look, one that was not so different from the look our mothers often gave us. Our mothers had started calling us Khee-Khees, for the sounds we made when we were together, always laughing for what seemed like no reason.

"Did you bring the clothes?" I asked, out of breath.

Taslima held up a large plastic Busy Bee bag. "No, I brought my teddy bear."

We khee-kheed about one thing or another all the way to Queensboro Plaza, where we switched to the N heading to Central Park.

When we got off at 59th Street, we were hit with the smell of horse dung. There were carriage horses and caricaturists drawing people with enlarged heads. There were watercolorists and old men selling photographs of John Lennon with the word "Imagine." I knew who he was because Taslima sang "Imagine" all the time in a passionate and overly dramatic voice.

We walked down the stairs into the park and I saw the lake. My heart raced. "Hey, look, it's the lake from *Catcher in the Rye*, the one with the ducks."

Taslima shook her head. "Sometimes I don't know if you come to my house to visit me or Aliza's books."

"Aliza's books, of course."

The lake lay poised with stone skyscrapers and a dramatic backdrop. The water was a deep, dark green with little islands of floating moss. Sure enough, there were ducks.

"You know, I never understood the ending of *Catcher in the Rye*. They never answered the main question. Where the ducks went."

"Why do you care so much about what a whiny, rich white guy thinks?" Taslima saw my surprise. "What? I read books too, you know. It's not just you and Aliza."

I laughed. She was right. Holden was spoiled and annoying, but I still read the book every year like clockwork.

She pulled at my arm and we kept strolling, copying what other people did.

"When are we going to change?" I asked.

"Patience, patience."

We walked up a hill, past an old building called the Dairy and then through a cathedral of trees. The light in Central Park drenched the trees golden yellow and orange. There were couples and families from all over the world. We stopped to look at street art, watch a magician, then a juggler. There was music everywhere. We were in the world of the Sunday magazines.

Past the cathedral of trees, we saw men and women dressed in rainbow colors roller-skate-dancing to Michael Jackson. They were spinning, moonwalking on skates, whirling in circles. I was filled with a strange sense of excitement, one I hadn't felt since I was a kid. Maybe I never had to go to school again. We could just come here every day.

"Come on," Taslima said, pulling me forward. "We still have to change."

We came to a stone terrace. There was a dark gray angel in front of us, her wings spread out, her feet soft from not touching the earth. I jumped back, imagining she'd been sent to capture us and bring us home.

Taslima brought me back to reality. "It's a fountain!"

Now I saw it. Water fell from the angel's feet. There were pigeons on her wings. "I feel like I'm in Venice."

"You don't know what that feels like," Taslima said.

Laughing, we walked down the terrace stairs to the fountain. The stench of urine from the tunnel rose to greet us, but we held our breath and descended.

There was a woman singing in the tunnel. Her voice echoed as she sang, "*I see my light come shining . . . From the west down to the east . . . Any day now, any day now, I shall be released . . .*" I was filled with a strange sensation, as if I was being lifted into the air.

The water came down the fountain like rain. We walked around clockwise, so we could see the angel from every angle. My shoulder blades started to itch and ache. From one angle she had her wings up, waiting. From another she was straining forward, running away from us, wings lifted. From another she was leaping on top of us.

Only the angel's face didn't change. With solemn eyes and mouth, she moved through the air with purpose. Taslima had a similar look on her face. She scanned the surroundings and pointed to a boathouse near the mossy green lake. "Maybe there's a bathroom in there."

Sure enough, there was a public restroom tucked in the side of the boathouse. It was a bit dark, but it would serve as a place for us to transform.

"Good luck," I joked to Taslima as we walked in. She handed me my clothes.

In the stall I took off my pants, trying not to let them touch the floor or toilet. I wrapped the chador carefully around my waist and pinned it like Taslima had shown me, then pulled off my shirt and put on the undershirt. I put the dupatta around my neck like a scarf and stuffed the other clothes in my bag.

When I stepped out of the stall, I felt naked. I considered running back in and changing, but I didn't want to disappoint Taslima. She was waiting for me outside, looking sophisticated, standing next to the boathouse gate. She had added a black derby hat to the outfit. It looked amazing. She turned to me. "We can rent boats here."

"Let's do it!" It seemed to be the thing to do with our new outfits.

She looked closely at the sign. "It's twenty dollars!"

"Let's not do it!" I said with equal excitement.

We laughed and walked toward the fountain instead. I could feel the sun on my legs, my arms. I looked around slowly, then realized no one was ogling me. I felt a lightness in my chest, rising up to the sky.

No one in the park seemed to notice what an epic and surreal event this was. How I wished this could be my life. This freedom to move in the world without anyone bothering me.

I looked at Taslima. She was walking proud, turning heads. Her light grew. The looks we were both getting from people were so different from the ones in Corona. Instead of feeling naked and soiled, I felt lifted up.

"I forgot to tell you," Taslima said. "I have a surprise." She opened her bag and pulled out a little yellow-and-black disposable camera. "We can do our own photo shoot!

"Come on," she said, seeing the look on my face. "Everyone's taking photos. No one's even going to notice." She put the camera in my hand and sat down on the edge of the fountain, tilting her head back, a rapt look on her face. Her eyes shone. She looked beautiful, her cheekbones as sculpted as the angel's.

She managed to stay still the entire time I was trying to figure out the camera. I took a few pictures of one pose. She sat up, put her hand under her chin, and looked off in the distance. I got into it, snapping and directing her on how to move.

"Now look at me! Now look at the water! Blow the angel a kiss!"

We were having a blast.

"Wait!" Taslima said, seeing how fast I was snapping pictures. "Don't use up all the film. We have to take some of you too."

"No way. I don't want evidence of this."

"Come on. I did it."

I gave in. "Okay. But not here." I brought her to the bottom of the terrace stairs. There were carvings in the stone, gray granite baby birds crying out from their mother's nest. I stood next to them. "Here."

She took the camera and I put my hand on my hip. It looked so awkward, we both started laughing. Sexy was not my thing. I crossed my arms in front of my chest and Taslima said, "That's good! Look angry." Once I realized I could be a sullen model, I got really into it. I scowled an ugly scowl. I let go of my body, threw my head back, and laughed.

"Just perfect," Taslima said, snapping away.

We felt it, before we heard or saw. There was a shift in the air, a slight turn of heads, like a herd of antelope sensing a leopard. We turned. There was a man dressed extra heavy for the heat, in a blue polyester suit, maroon shirt, church hat, and tie.

He was coming down the terrace steps, carrying a sign painted crudely with red paint. It said JESUS!!! We'd seen plenty of crazy men in Corona, but this man had a different energy. I couldn't look away.

He looked up at the angel and proclaimed, "For an angel went down at a certain season into the pool, and troubled the water, the healing water of the fountain of Bethesda." His was a voice that could command a church room, a voice that had gotten lost in the wilderness of New York City. "And when Jesus saw the crippled man, and knew he had been waiting a long, long time, he said unto him, 'Are you willing to be whole? Will you be whole?'"

"It looks like he's gotten his geography mixed up," a woman said to a man passing by us. The woman was divinely dressed for the middle of the day. She was wearing an ethereal shirt, high heels, and a perfectly tailored skirt. The man was just as well groomed, smoking a thin cigarette. They might as well have been under parasols.

"The woman who designed that fountain was a lesbian," he stage-whispered to his friend as they breezed by.

The word "lesbian" floated toward us, disturbing the air. I felt a stirring in the pit of my stomach. The religious man started moving toward the fountain, closer to us. He moved unnaturally quick for a man so old. "It was here, at the fountain of Bethesda, house of mercy, where Jesus was labeled a sinner, where the tides turned against Him for curing a lame man on the Sabbath, a day of rest. He was cursed for telling the lame man to rise, but He said, 'My father and I work all the time . . .'"

I looked over at Taslima. She was mesmerized.

"My father works all the time too," I said, close to her ear, trying to break the spell with a joke.

Taslima laughed. The old man must have heard our khee-khee sounds. He suddenly locked eyes on us.

He started to walk toward Taslima and me, pointing his finger, as if he was pushing telephone buttons in the air. The tiny mirrors in Taslima's vest flashed in his eyes. The mirrors were getting the maddening going in his brain. "If you believe in Jesus, if you want to be saved, come heal yourself at the fountain of Bethesda!" He glanced at my chest, then my legs. I felt he knew everything about my sins. As if my mother had sent him.

The people who had been lounging near the fountain turned to look at us. Even the well-dressed woman and man stopped and stared.

I pulled at Taslima. "Let's go."

But the man followed us. "If you believe in Jesus, if you want to be saved, come heal yourself at the fountain of Bethesda! Where the harlot will be saved as well as the lamb!"

We started walking faster, then broke into a run, passing the well-dressed man and woman again. They stared at us and I overheard the well-dressed woman saying, "The Bible's not my cup of tea, but that doesn't sound quite right."

We ran back the way we had come, past the rainbow roller-skate dancers and the Dairy. By the time we got to the lake, we were out of breath. We looked at each other and collapsed into laughter. We hadn't run like that in years.

We spent the rest of the afternoon by the lake. We treated ourselves to warm pretzels covered with salt and fed bits of the soft white insides to the ducks.

"You know," Taslima said, "I don't think the ducks go anywhere, not when they have people feeding them all the time."

I realized we were all like the ducks. We would do anything, even go against our natural instincts, so we could be taken care of.

A few weekends later, I was back at Taslima's. Her bedroom door was, surprisingly, open. She was lying on the bed doing her math homework.

I handed her the latest Sunday magazine. "I haven't even looked at it yet."

She sat up, excited, and flipped through the pages to the fashion section by finger memory, knowing how many pages to turn.

I saw her face erupt. "Oh my God! Oh my God! Oh my God!"

"What is it?" I leaned over her shoulder to see.

Taslima pointed. There she was, a woman with straight blonde hair hanging in bright kitchen curtains around her face, her eyes as green as mossy water. She was wearing a batik chador that looked like *our* chador wrapped around her waist and the black velvet Eid vest. The vest and the chador clashed. Taslima would never have put them together, but the model dared us to defy her.

I saw the angel fountain, the granite baby birds, the terrace stairs. They'd even taken our place for the photo shoot and struck Taslima's and my poses.

"I can't believe it! They totally copied us." I felt robbed, cheated.

But Taslima looked smug. "See, I told you it was good fashion."

STUYVESANT

At Stuyvesant, most of the students were extremely competitive. There were some with money, connections, and ambition. They'd be going to their parents' fancy alma maters without worrying about having to get scholarships. But the rest of us, the majority, were children of not-so-rich immigrants. We were the dreams, the ones expected to take our paper airplanes and turn them into rocket ships rising into higher orbits. We had to get money for college. The heat was on. The pressure was intense.

I was a rocket ship, but for me things were slightly different. My parents cared about school but at the end of the day they didn't believe in the importance of this world other than as a spiritual test. The ultimate test whose grades mattered more than anything else.

It was hard for me to make friends those first few weeks of school, but I noticed Angela on the first day. We were in the same homeroom and both of us were the only ones who laughed out loud when our home-room teacher told us he was really a famous novelist in France. Then, during sixth period, I discovered we were in the same English class and the only ones who seemed excited about the books.

It was hard not to notice Angela. Her hair was dark brown and curly, electric, as if she'd stuck her finger in a socket and had her hair blown out into a wild tree. She wore blackberry lipstick and thick black eyeliner over her lids. The way she drew the line, it curled up a little bit, as if she had been heading toward a spiral and then just stopped short.

I was drawn to her, the way a spaceship might get pulled into a black hole, then into another dimension of space.

But it wasn't until weeks later, when I saw her on the platform at Grand Central, that underground humid pit of Hell, also sweating and waiting for the 7 train, that I took a chance, found the courage to approach her and say hello.

"Don't you go to Stuyvesant?" I asked, an obvious opening.

She turned to me, then glanced at the platform. "Yeah. Are you also taking this slow-ass Seven train?"

"I am."

"Great. I'll have some company besides the perverts."

I smiled. "Oh my God. It's not even funny how many there were on the train this morning. It's on the pedophile schedule to get up early to molest girls on their way to school."

Angela burst into laughter, and I felt an unexpected thrill.

She shrugged her book bag up higher on her shoulder. "So what do you think of Stuyvesant so far?"

I sighed. "It's far."

"I'm glad you didn't say it was amazing or a lifelong dream. I would've had to stop talking to you immediately."

There was a shrill sound in the distance, a harsh screech of brakes echoing through the tunnel. With a rush, the 7 train pulled into the station. Angela and I pushed in. The train was crowded but we found a spot near the end of the car by the window. Soon, we were hurtling through a tunnel toward Queens. I grabbed onto a pole and braced myself. The train took a bend and we were thrown to the left. We held on tighter.

"What's your stop?" Angela asked.

"103rd Street–Corona."

"Corona. Like Rosie, Queen of Corona?" She sang a song I hadn't heard before. When I looked at her, confused, she said, "Paul Simon? You don't know Paul Simon? Simon and Garfunkel?"

The wonder in her tone made me feel the kind of musical awkwardness I'd been experiencing ever since starting Stuyvesant, where I'd learned quickly that "George Michael" was not an acceptable answer to the question "What kind of music do you listen to?" No one had ever asked me my whole life in Corona what kind of music I listened to.

"I'll play it for you sometime," Angela said with a smile, and the awkwardness between us disappeared. "I'm going to my father's in Astoria for the weekend. He just moved back in with my grandmother last year." She looked out the train window, even though we were in a tunnel and there was nothing but blackness moving quick.

I tried to act as if having divorced parents was no big deal. "I've never been to Astoria."

Without missing a beat, she said, "I've never been to Corona."

We laughed. Queens was like that. You basically didn't cross neighborhood lines.

"I used to go to Astoria to see my grandmother on holidays, but going there for the weekend every weekend . . . it sucks."

We were quiet for a second, holding on for dear life as the train took another rough turn before pulling suddenly aboveground. We traveled over a track yard. It was a wasteland, except for the silk water of the Citibank building. It was all tall blue glass, a lonely skyscraper hanging out on the fringe, exiled from the tribe, acting like it was okay to be all alone.

"Do you ever feel sorry for the Citibank building?" I asked.

She pushed a tangle of dark hair back. Silver hoops shone from her ears. "No, why?"

"I don't know. It's just like this awkward tall kid in the classroom, standing in the corner away from all the other skyscrapers. It can see them across the river but it can't join them to play."

"You have a funny way of seeing the world." But she said it as if I was interesting, and I felt my face getting warm.

The 7 began to make a wide circular turn. We were tilting so much, I could see the last car. If the train was a snake, it would be eating its own tail.

Reading my mind, Angela began to sing, "If the train falls off the track . . ."

I answered, "Do you want your money back?"

We both started laughing. All the exhausted riders stared at us, but a little girl in braids, sitting next to her mother, smiled.

Before I knew it, we were at Queensboro Plaza.

"I've got to switch here," she said. "But if you see me in the park, come hang out."

A strange longing came over me. I didn't want her to leave. "Sure. I will."

The train built up speed as it left the station. When we passed Angela, she turned, waved, and made a silly face. I waved back, smiling, until everything began to blur.

I knew which park she meant, Stuy Park. Stuyvesant didn't have a courtyard, so we claimed the nearest city park as our own. It was where everyone hung out when they should or shouldn't be in school. Stuy Park was filled with benches arranged in concentric circles. There was a broken fountain in the center, with a thick cast-iron fence enclosing it.

Our park was one of a pair. There was an eastern twin and a western twin cut through by Second Avenue. Maybe that's why the public was willing to let one get overrun by teenagers: there was a spare. Outside of homeroom, attendance wasn't taken. The teachers thought we were so nerdy we'd just go to class on our own. Clearly, they were mistaken.

In Corona, I'd always felt loved by my teachers, but at Stuyvesant, the teachers couldn't care less. My presence in class was slightly necessary at best. I could pass by just handing in the homework. No teacher even knew me by name. I was getting the kind of grades I'd have been horrified by before, but I didn't care about getting As anymore. The effort suddenly felt meaningless. Instead, I spent all my time at Stuy Park, reading novels, writing in my diary, sometimes falling asleep on a bench.

The morning after I met Angela, though, I was excited for school. I wore one of my father's gray suit jackets, a plain white T-shirt, and my favorite jeans. Taslima had advised me on the outfit and I knew my mother wouldn't throw away anything belonging to my father. She didn't say anything about my clothes, even though I could see she was upset by my outfit.

The 7 train was slow and sluggish, the 4 crowded with sleepy workers, and the L had broken down, so by the time I got to Stuyvesant, I'd already missed homeroom. Angela was probably long gone. Bummed out, I went to the deli to get a cup of coffee. With the first sip, some spilled on my father's jacket, and I cursed my life.

I walked to Stuy Park, sadness jostling my brain, but every dark feeling fell away when I saw Angela. She was drinking a peach-vanilla Mistic, *The Village Voice* open in her lap. She was reading my favorite column, Real Astrology by Rob Brezsny. A circle of Flushing Goth girls surrounded her like beautiful butterflies, wearing thick-heeled Doc Martens, dark lace dresses, torn black tights, and fishnets like tattered wings. Their heads were shaved and their hair dyed in all kinds of combinations. Silver earrings and crosses climbed up the arches of their ears, safety pins snaked up their tight black pants.

Angela was wearing a Skinny Puppy T-shirt and black jeans that were ripped at the knees. She wasn't fully Goth, but it didn't matter. Angela's magnetism worked on everyone.

She looked up at my arrival. "You made it!" She turned to her audience. "Everyone, this is Razia." Before I could get their names, Ed, a senior I recognized from the halls, a floater between circles, graced us with his presence.

Like everyone, I kind of liked Ed. He was a Korean Sylvester Stallone. He thought he was the coolest and smartest, but at Stuyvesant, most of the kids thought they were too, or at least used to, before they got to Stuyvesant.

"Ed," Angela said in a mock flirtatious tone. "What's your sign?"

Ed flipped his dark hair with a toss of his head. "Whoa, man, I'm not telling you my sign. How do I know you're not the Zodiac Killer?"

"What?" Angela started laughing.

The Zodiac Killer was a copycat serial killer who was on a spree in New York City. He'd ask people what sign they were and if they were the sign he was hunting, he'd kill them. He'd already killed four people.

Ed held up the *Daily News*. "Look!" The front page was a grainy black-and-white photo of the night sky with astrological constellations. There were red ink splashes, meant to be blood, on the signs that had already been hit. Ed looked at it a little more closely. "Oh wait. Boom. Virgo's done. I'm safe. Read my horoscope."

Angela laughed. "I don't need to read it. I already know it says: 'Your pompous head will explode like a hot-air balloon over Sweden.'" Her entourage of Goth butterflies laughed, enjoying the show.

Ed flushed. "I don't need this abuse. I'm leaving."

Almost on cue, there was a movement. Third period had ended, and fourth was about to begin. There was a subtle, then more obvious wave of kids heading out of the park, toward school. The rest of us, those skipping class, settled deeper in, taking the benches left behind.

The Goth girls dispersed but Angela continued flipping through the *Voice*. I stayed, feeling like I'd take a chance on hanging out.

When it was just us, she asked, "Did you just get to school? I didn't see you in homeroom."

I nodded. "It was a hellish commute."

She took another sip of her Mistic. "Do you want to skip the rest of the day and come over? I live around the corner."

"I thought—"

But before I could say anything tactless, she interrupted, "With my mom."

"Oh yeah," I said, recovering. Then it hit me. "You live in the East Village?"

"It's not that great. Wait till you see our place."

I tried to act cool. "I'm already marked absent, so it makes no difference to me."

"Great." Angela capped her Mistic, stood up, and brushed off her jeans.

We gathered up our belongings and walked out of the park.

I realized too late that we should have taken a different route. We were passing right by the main entrance, the final threshold where kids either got sucked into school or pulled out by their friends. The side-walk was narrow and there were kids swarming around, perched like crows on parked cars.

One of the crows jumped up and headed toward us. It was Ed again. He'd decided not to go to class after all.

"Where you heading? Pizza?"

He was addressing Angela and ignoring me. I hoped she wouldn't invite him.

"Sorry, Ed." Angela drew close to me. "We're having girl time."

"Oh no. Do you have your periods? Are you going to shop for tampons? I can help. I'm good with that kind of stuff. I have three sisters."

Angela started laughing and even I smiled, imagining Ed in the maxi pad aisle with his three sisters, who in my imagination all seemed like slightly larger, feminine versions of Ed.

"We just don't want you around, Ed," she said.

He put his hand up. "Okay, okay, I'm going to Calc anyway. Peace."

I was thrilled to have Angela to myself.

She really did live around the corner from school, in a skinny building that looked like a normal-size building had been shrunk and turned gray. She unlocked the three locks on the downstairs door with a snap of her wrists, as if she'd been doing this since she was a kid. I was impressed. I was the opposite of a latchkey kid. My mother was always home. The few times I had to unlock our door, I had struggled and freaked out when the key got stuck.

The building was cramped. We walked up dank, tight stairs. There were all kinds of smells in the hallway. I felt a chill, a ghost memory of tenement living, of families living close and hungry and cold. Sometimes these memories came into my head and I didn't know where they came from.

"Do you know all the people in these apartments?"

"You mean my neighbors? Sure. I grew up here." She pointed to closed door after closed door. "My neighbor there is from Russia. He has a little dog he treats like his child. And in that apartment, there's a Republican vet who loves all things pink. And in that one is a widow who's been wearing black for as long as I can remember. No one ever moves out of the building. Unless of course they have to," she added bitterly.

When we reached the top floor, Angela unlocked one last door and we stepped in. It was a box of light, spider plants spilling over shelves. Books were piled onto every surface of every table and chair. Books inched their way over the floor, books and books and books reached to the highest walls, their spines soft with wear. I thought of Aliza's tiny bookshelf, of the few books we all shared.

"Wow," I said, walking around, immediately feeling comfortable in the mess of it all. "Does every door in this building open onto a magical world?"

She laughed. "My mother and I like reading."

The front room was one large room. The only thing that separated the kitchen from the living room was a sofa, and the only thing that separated the living room from the dining room was a stack of books.

Angela was already walking ahead of me down a short hallway. "My bedroom's in the back."

My heart started beating fast. My palms became sweaty. I didn't understand what was happening to my body.

Angela's bedroom was tiny, like a closet. In Queens it would have been a closet. There was just enough room for a dresser and a twin bed. A teddy bear was propped on top of her pillow.

She picked him up, held him to her chest and then out to me. "Here, meet Huggy Bear. I've had him since I was little."

I stood awkwardly in the doorway. Huggy Bear's fur was matted. His eyes were scratched away by dust, making them look alive. He stared at me, and I felt an old fear my mother had instilled washing over me.

"I don't know if I want to meet Huggy Bear."

She laughed. "Why not?"

"My mother never allowed me to have dolls or stuffed animals. She said they came alive at night."

If I'd said this to Taslima, she would have just nodded and said, "Of course," but Angela started laughing. "What?"

"You don't know. One time my friend Saima made a doll out of paper and cut her out, just so we could have some dolls to play with at my house. I woke up in the middle of the night and the doll was standing over me, clapping her hands. I'll never forget how crazy-looking her smile was."

Angela laughed even harder.

"I'm glad you're amused by my pain!" But I loved hearing her laugh, so I kept going. "Saima had made her with one of those blue Bic pens. She wasn't a very good artist, so it was a terrifying drawing. I mean, we were children. Who can draw a non-freaky human then?"

Still laughing, she said, "I'll put Huggy Bear in a box when you come over."

"You would put your beloved bear in a box for me? I'm touched."

Catching my mocking tone, she threw Huggy Bear at me. I jumped out of the way with a real fear. The bear missed me and fell to the floor.

I reached down to pick him up. I looked into his eyes and a strange feeling swept over me. I realized what it was. He looked just like the bear that used to molest Saima's Barbies. It made sense. Huggy Bear was as old as that bear would have been.

In a flash, it all came back to me. The spider dreams. The way Saima and I would wash our faces again and again with cold water so we wouldn't fall asleep. It could've happened once. It could've happened all the time. I didn't know.

"Razia, hey! What's the matter?" Angela snapped her fingers in my face. I must have gotten frozen like a statue. "Earth to Razia." She laughed, not knowing what I was thinking. "Did a stuffed bear come alive at night too?"

"Something like that," I said, my voice sticking in my throat. It was time to change the subject. "Hey, can you play me that song?"

She looked puzzled. "Which one?"

"The one about Corona."

She smiled. "Oh, right. I only have it on vinyl."

I had no idea what she meant but I went with it.

"My father left his records. He said he was going to come back for them, but he never did." She pulled a milk crate out from under her bed. "I have to hide them in here because my mother doesn't want to see anything of his."

I unstuck myself from the doorway and came to sit on her bed. She lifted the milk crate, placing it in the middle of the bedspread. I sat down on the other side of the crate and watched her flip through the records. We didn't have albums at my house, only cassettes filled with naats and Indian movie songs, so I was amazed at how large the records were.

"I like listening to his records. It's as if he's here. But I can only do it when my mother's not around. She hates hearing his music."

"Do you miss him a lot?" I kicked myself. What a ridiculous question.

Luckily Angela didn't notice. "I do, but I don't miss all the fighting. God, they used to fight so much."

We were quiet for a second. Huggy Bear continued to stare at me.

She hadn't put him away. I gave him the kind of glare I gave pervert men on the streets.

"Here it is!" She held up the album. There was a white man on the cover. He could've been Greek, Italian, Jewish. His eyes were dark and his eyebrows thick. He was wearing an army coat, the kind I'd once seen in Goodwill, green turning to silver-gray with a big fur mane. He was looking to his left, away from the camera, as if he was already figuring out how to get out of there.

"Let's see. Here it is! 'Me and Julio Down by the Schoolyard.'"

I sat up. "Did you just say 'Julio'?"

"Yeah, that's the name of the song. 'Me and Julio Down by the Schoolyard.'"

"Wow, maybe he does know Corona. Julio would be the first person I'd sing about."

Angela laughed. "Who was Julio? Your boyfriend?"

"No . . . he was a boy I knew a long time ago." I hadn't thought of him in so long. Julio with his hair in his eyes, his arms full of roses, his laughter when his friends had yelled "Pajama People!"

Why was I having so many memories at Angela's?

She smiled, oblivious to the crashing waves of feeling that were coming over me. "I used to have a crush on a boy named Joseph when I was in elementary school." She stood up, holding the album. "Come on. The record player's in the living room."

Tucked away among all the books, there was a small rectangular box with a clear plastic top and black wood bottom. I watched as Angela opened the lid and then pulled the record out of its sleeve. Sleek, black, and fragile, it looked like a postmodern plate, easily broken.

"My dad would go crazy whenever I got any fingerprints on these. I still can't believe he just left them behind. Especially this one. He loved Paul Simon." She smiled. "You know, the Queens connection. Let's see if I can find where the song begins."

I went to sit on the velvety green sofa. It was like soft sand. I sank in, then struggled to sit up. "How do you know where the song begins?"

"It's easy. If it's not the first song, you look for the deeper grooves, count to the number of the song, then put the needle on it. It's the first song on the B side, so this'll be easy."

She handed me the album, and I looked at the pictures inside. There was Paul Simon standing in front of one of those tan brick homes. He really was from Queens.

As soon as Angela put the needle down, music burst into the room. There was a fast rhythm and, underneath it, I could almost hear the sounds of a schoolyard. The song was about two kids, Julio and the storyteller. Something terrible was happening to these kids. They were getting into trouble, being threatened with the house of detention, but the music was filled with happiness.

Angela smiled, seeing how I was getting into it. She walked toward the kitchen. "Would you like some popcorn?"

I stirred. "Do you need help?"

"No, keep listening. Wait till I tell my father you love this song. He's going to be thrilled."

She sounded happy and all of a sudden, I couldn't sit still. The music was getting into my body and making me want to jump around. But I felt shy to dance in front of Angela. I walked over to the window. Down below, the cars looked like tiny boxes. I imagined I was standing at the window of my own apartment in the middle of the city, an apartment filled with books and music.

I felt a quivering sense come over me. The noises of 14th Street became quiet and dim. It all began to disappear, what my parents wanted from me, who they wanted me to be, the future they had so carefully planned.

THE MET

Brown leaves swirled in mini-tornadoes along the sidewalk, hiding under the benches like crinkly dust bunnies. The sun was shining, a late autumn gold. I knew everyone would be in Stuy Park, huddled in their coats, joking and laughing around the broken water fountain. Sure enough, as soon as I passed through the wrought iron gates, I saw Angela surrounded by the Goth butterflies and Ed, dressed like a Benetton model.

From far off, I could see he was telling a story, throwing back a slash of emo hair that kept falling in his eyes. The sun cut through the gaps between buildings and reflected off the car windows, blinding.

Everyone else nodded in my direction, but Ed continued narrating his story about a pool hall fight where Bronx Science and Stuy kids had gotten into a brawl over a table. Sticks had been broken over heads and legs. I rolled my eyes. It couldn't have gotten that rough. I mean, it was just kids from Bronx Science and Stuyvesant.

"And I was like *bam*! Take that. And that. They ran like pussies . . ."

"You mean they were running like cats?" I asked.

Ed stopped and looked at me, as if just now registering my presence. "Ha! That's a good one, Razia, running like cats." With his finger, he pulled the neck of his collar back and we saw three inches of a red gash, a Frankenstein curve of a smile. "Look at this!"

Everyone oohed and aahed, everyone but me.

"Ugh," one of the Goth girls said, looking at her watch. "I've got to get to Chemistry." She rustled her wings and together the Goth girls all flew off.

Ed stayed. He spoke just to Angela as if I wasn't there. "You going to class?"

"No, I'm hanging out with Razia." She moved closer to me, and I felt an electric jolt.

"Can I come along?"

I hated him with a sudden passion.

"Nope!" She grabbed me by the hand and pulled me away. I felt electricity move through me. All the hidden molecules in my skin burst to the surface.

Ed shrugged, then slunk away with his gash and his bravado. Angela seemed oblivious to his crush.

She squeezed my arm. "Thank God they're all gone."

My head spun. It hadn't seemed like she wanted them gone. She looked like she was enjoying herself. I was the one who'd felt like gum on the bottom of her shoe.

"So . . ." I said, suddenly blundering.

Before I could say more, she asked, "Want to go to the Met?"

The Met! I'd dreamed of going to the Met ever since I'd read a book about these children who ran away and lived there. I couldn't remember the title, but I'd loved the book. I smiled a gigantic smile. "Of course!"

The whole train ride over, I felt like we were in our own world of laughter. Everyone stared at us, as if trying to understand the mystery of our happiness.

We got off at 86th and Lexington and zigzagged our way down the street, going south then west, west then south. All of the Upper East Side was filled with majestic stone apartment buildings and people who looked like they'd just stepped out of magazines to walk their fluffy poodles and let them pee on every inch of sidewalk.

As soon as we turned onto Fifth Avenue, the air became festive. There was no mistaking the Met. It spanned blocks. As we walked toward the entrance, I felt chills. My eyes traveled up to the sculptures. There were floating heads of Athena, perched high above in concrete headdresses, lining every inch of the roof.

At the foot of the museum, we stood and stared at the rows and rows of stairs, the majestic columns like the entrance of a grand temple. Instinctively, Angela and I moved closer together. I could feel my whole body melt like butter in a dish.

Angela laughed. "You are so into this."

I smiled. "I am. Did you ever read this book about these runaway kids who live in the Met?"

Angela scrunched up her eyebrows. "Was there something about a fountain?"

"Yes! They took money out of the wishing fountain at night to pay for food. That's what I would totally do if I ran away from home."

Angela began walking up the stairs. "Would you ever run away from home?"

I stumbled, then righted myself and laughed. "I don't know. I mean, maybe if my parents tried to get me married off to some guy in Pakistan."

Angela's eyes got wide. "They wouldn't really do that, would they?"

"No," I said, "of course not." But I was lying. They would, but why tell her? I knew she'd judge my family without understanding.

The security guards at the entrance of the Met were half-asleep. They nodded to us and didn't seem to think anything of the fact that we weren't in school.

I saw why as soon as we stepped inside. We entered a grand hall with domed skylights filling the space with a murky light. All around us there were people from every country, maybe planet. The halls were filled with a blend of languages, as if everyone in the Tower of Babel had been reunited. We could have been teenagers from anywhere in the world.

As we tried to pass through an archway, which opened onto a grand staircase, a security guard stopped us. He was jumpy, much younger than the guards out front. He gave us a harsh look. I went on guard myself.

"Your button?" He pointed to his collar, where there was an aluminum tin of a button choking him, a round robin's-egg blue, with the letter *M* in fancy curlicues.

"Button?" I asked innocently.

"Yes, you have to purchase one." He pointed to the ticket counters tucked into each side of the hall. There were long lines on both ends.

"How much is it?"

He smiled and I could see his teeth were crooked like mine. "Whatever you wish to pay."

Angela jumped in. "Really? What if we want to pay nothing? Can we come in now?"

She was half joking, half serious, but his smile faded, quick.

"You still need a button," he said in a cold voice.

I could feel Angela tightening up. "Even if we want to pay zero?"

I pulled her away. "Angela, we've got to be classy. We can't just walk into a fancy place like this and act like we have no money."

"But we don't have any money."

"This is true."

We both started giggling. People were beginning to stare at us. We were blocking the flow up the grand staircase. We slipped away from the crowd and hid behind a pillar. We rummaged through our bags and counted our coins. I had a dollar and fifteen cents and she had three dollars and thirty cents. We decided to save four dollars for lunch and pay forty-five cents for the both of us.

I pointed to the line to our left. "That lion seems shorter."

She started laughing. "Did you just say that lion seems shorter?"

I smiled at the slip of my tongue.

Stuck on the crowded line, we moved closer together. I breathed in her scent of citrus and patchouli.

When it was our turn, we stepped up to the woman at the ticket counter. She was fancy-looking, with gray hair and fake-diamond-studded cat glasses.

I smiled my most winning smile and pushed our coins across the counter. "We'll pay forty-five cents for both of us."

She looked from Angela to me to the barely existent space between us and gave a smile with a secret message in it. It was like she was Marie Curie, and we were giving off signals, like radiation coming off a rock.

"Enjoy the museum, girls," the woman said. She passed us two buttons that were like the guard's, robin's-egg blue, round, metallic, with a small bendable handle to attach to our collars.

I handed one to Angela and she surprised me by leaning in and pinning her button on my collar. Her arm brushed against my chest and I shivered. She smiled. "Let's go this way." She pointed to a different entrance, away from the guard at the grand staircase. This new guard looked barely out of high school. He gave us a quick nod and we were in.

"Have you noticed the guards keep getting younger and younger?" I asked.

"Maybe the next one will be a baby."

We entered the Greek and Roman wing, laughing.

The entire space was filled with lifelike sculptures of young men, galleries branching out in rooms filled with objects and antiquities. Angela spun around. "That's what I'm talking about, my people!"

"Your people are very white."

"It's marble!" she said, hitting me on the arm.

"And very naked," I added, covering my eyes when I came to an immaculately carved, anatomically correct statue of a young, buff man.

Angela looked even closer. "Oh my God. His balls are just hanging out. No penis. I guess over time it must've fallen off."

We fell over each other laughing.

A young couple, so exquisitely dressed they were clearly from another country, looked at us and smiled beautiful smiles. Our joy was infectious.

As we passed from room to room, I gravitated toward the one spot of color in the whole space not dominated by shades of white and gray marble. It was an enormous black urn so huge I could have crawled into it and hid.

The entire surface was a detailed line drawing of a family scene. As I got closer, I realized the vase was painted black and the orange lines of the drawing were unpainted clay. What was not drawn came forward.

I read the museum note. The urn was from 465–460 BC. The scene was of a mother hanging laundry and the father, the god Dionysus, sitting with a baby in his lap, although the baby looked more like a tiny man than a baby. The Greeks had clearly improved some of their artistic skills over the centuries. But in other ways, how little things had changed. The mother looked tired, while the father was sitting, bonding with the baby.

I read what the urn was for and started laughing. "Oh my God! Angela, come here."

Angela was staring at one of the particularly muscular men, but she came over and read the sign out loud. "'Four sixty-five BC.' Damn, that's old! 'Terra-cotta bell-krater, bowl for mixing wine and water' . . . So?"

"How much wine do your people drink?"

"It's not that much wine. They watered it down. See!" She pointed at the note.

I shook my head. "I wouldn't know. My people only water down milk."

"Between this and the Carlo Rossi side of my mother's family, I better be careful I don't turn into an alcoholic."

"I wonder if your ancestors ever imagined the Greek empire would be over and gone, broken up into pieces and kept in a museum for their descendants to find."

"I don't think so." She said it so seriously, we both started cracking up. "I wonder if that will ever happen to New York? Then the City would just become a mellow old island and we can drink wine. Mixed with water, of course. Isn't that better than ruling the world?"

"You would think people would know that," I said, "but they never do."

We wandered through the rest of the wing, past sculpture after sculpture of beautifully carved bodybuilders. "Does this really remind you of your people?"

"No, no one in my family is this fit after those gallons of wine."

I smiled, but as we kept moving through the galleries, one thing was true: it was Angela's face looking out at me from every sculpture and painting of a woman. They all had large eyes, strong noses, and curly black hair always drawn to look like waves: waves cascading down their shoulders, waves captured in buns.

Angela touched her hair. "Maybe that's what I should do. Put my hair in a bun."

"Don't," I said, "I like it open." Then I blushed, feeling as if I'd said too much.

We came to an enclosed courtyard filled with enormous sculptures. There was a brick wall along one end and, along the other, a wall of windows.

Angela and I were both immediately drawn to a statue of a woman. She was epic in her stature, in her intention and tension. Surrounded by nakedness, she stood out with her clothes on. Her head was tilted while her right hand clenched her chest. Her left hand clutched a small harp. She was slumped in her chair. Her toes curled up out of her sandals.

"That's exactly how you sit when you're studying," I said.

Angela's posture annoyed our English teacher, but I knew it was her way of concentrating, as if she had to let the rest of her body go limp to focus all her energy into her mind.

Unlike the other sculptures, which had long notes explaining the background story or myth, this note simply said: "Sappho."

Angela came up behind me. "Sappho . . . isn't she . . ."

We knew the story of Sappho, like everyone else. It was a rumor surviving centuries.

"A lesbian," I said, finishing her thought.

The word hung over us, and a charge flowed through the air.

"She's beautiful. Like you," Angela said quietly.

No one had ever told me I was beautiful before. I leaned into Angela, and she leaned into me. We became two wood nymphs intertwined at Sappho's feet, freezing into place like marble figurines.

CHRISTMAS SPIRITS

On the first day back from Christmas vacation, there was a happy bustling in the air. The auditorium balcony was crowded, filled with sounds of laughter, hugs, and "Happy New Year's." Everyone had come back to school refreshed, having enjoyed parts of life we were normally encouraged to forget, spending time with family, eating lots and well, becoming full and round. Most everyone came back with rosier cheeks, wearing new gloves, hats, sweaters, and coats.

I felt a twinge of jealousy. When I was younger, I'd learned to never care about Christmas presents, but now I thought how nice it would be to be showered with gifts once a year. Especially new clothes.

The only thing that kept me cheerful was knowing I was going to see Angela. I'd missed her so much during the winter break. We'd talked on the phone only once, and it had been awkward. She'd immediately started talking about cutting and going over to her house. I'd quickly made an excuse to get off the phone. My mother had a knack for picking up the other line at the exact time when someone was saying something they shouldn't. Taslima and I had learned to talk in code, but Angela had no idea how.

I spotted her sitting by the balcony edge. We ran to each other and hugged, saying "Happy New Year's!" at the same time.

She looked so pretty, her curly hair bursting out of the sides of a new winter hat, so white it shone. She was wearing a dark brown parka and black-and-gold-striped leg warmers. She saw me admiring them. "My dad got them for me." Then her eyes lit up. "Oh my God, you won't believe what else he got me. My mother's so furious. She told me to throw it away, but I've been keeping it hidden in the back of my closet so I could show it to you."

"What? A puppy?"

She started laughing. "How can I keep a puppy in my closet? You really don't understand about pets, do you?"

I smiled. Angela liked to poke at the strange places my mind went, but I knew it was out of love.

She gave me a mischievous look. "I know we just got back, but want to come over and see what it is?"

Of course I wanted to, but I still asked, "You can't just tell me?"

"No, you have to experience it."

I held out my elbow. "Twist my arm."

We pushed our way out of the auditorium doors through the warm throngs of kids hugging and having their own reunions. In the main hallway, in the curve at the bottom of the hall staircase, there was a portrait of Peter Stuyvesant. It was a large painting of his full figure, wooden leg and all. He had a long, hooked nose, balding head, and watery, beady eyes. He was . . . ugly.

Not just outside but in. He had hated people of all religions except his own, Dutch Reformed, and was best known for stealing land and starting battles. Our history teacher hadn't taught us any of this. I knew it from reading between the lines of the *Encyclopaedia Britannica*.

In the hallway there were a few white faces, but mostly, like me, it was immigrant kids. There was probably not a Dutch Reformed in the house. It gave me pleasure to think of Stuyvesant's failure.

"Happy New Year's, you old perv!" I said to him.

I'd told Angela all about Stuyvesant and now she never lost an opportunity to give him the finger. She had to be careful that the security guards didn't see her and think she was giving it to them.

We ran down the soft, worn marble stairs, spilling out onto the front sidewalk. It felt wonderful to be out of the confines of school and on the wintry streets.

The sun was shining but the air was frigid. It had snowed and frozen, snowed and frozen all during the break. The sidewalk was just a thin cut between two miniglaciers of gray and yellow snow. We walked against the wind, slip-sliding all the way to her apartment.

As soon as we got to her place, Angela shouted, "I'll get the present," and disappeared down the hallway to her bedroom.

By the time I'd taken off my coat and boots, she was so deep in her closet, the top of her body was buried. I could only see her gold-striped leg warmers and socks. She was throwing clothes out behind her so fast, the floor was soon covered.

I plopped down on her bed. She'd left her father's record crate on it, and I began to flip through, recognizing some of the albums now. I had to admit, I really liked her dad's hippie music. I'd learned about Janis Joplin, Jimi Hendrix, the Velvet Underground, and the Grateful Dead, and Angela had learned not to say things like, "How did you not know John Lennon was one of the Beatles?"

"Hey!" A flung shirt hit me in the face, and Angela emerged with a board game in her hands.

"What would make your mom so furious about a board game?"

"It's not just a game."

She brought it to the bed. Instead of the cartoonish characters that were usually on the covers of board games, there was a faded brown sepia photograph of two disembodied hands touching each other's fingers.

I edged away. "It looks creepy."

She laughed. "That's what my mother said. She said it was just one more of my father's stupid toys she didn't want in the house. Sometimes I wonder how they ever got together in the first place. Oh yeah, the sixties."

I'd learned enough about the counterculture to get the joke.

Angela sat down across from me and looked at the box longingly. "My mother won't play it with me. I really want to show you how it works. It's the craziest thing I've ever experienced. You can talk to spirits."

I got nervous. "No way. I do not mess with spirits."

She tried to mask her disappointment, but not so well that I couldn't see it. "Can I just show it to you?" She looked with pleading eyes, and I found myself melting. Could there be any harm in just looking at it?

"Okay," I finally said.

Her face brightened. She opened the box and pulled out a simple wooden board, laying it out between us. The alphabet was printed out in two rows. A third row contained numbers. On the top right, there was a thick crescent moon with a star in front of it.

"It's like the Pakistani flag," I joked. But when I looked closer, I saw the moon's face was perplexed, reacting to a big NO in its face. In the left corner, smug and round, there was a sun, with the word YES printed in its face.

"I don't get it," I said. "How do you talk to spirits with this?"

Angela pulled out a peg with a circle of plastic glass cut in the center. "You ask a question and it spells out the answer."

I was amazed. "The spirits just spell it out? What if we get possessed?"

"Don't you think it would be in the news if people were getting possessed by Ouija board spirits?"

I didn't think that logic held with the news cycle. I thought about the Jinn that used to haunt me and shake the bed. Then again, how amazing would it be to have a direct conversation with a spirit, to be able to ask the questions that were starting to freak me out? Like how I was ever going to get out of marrying someone my parents picked?

The years of high school were speeding by fast, and my parents were not going to let me go to college without at least an engagement. No other girl in the community had except for Aliza, and the rumors had already started about her. People said she was on drugs, having sex. That she was ruined.

Although my mother didn't participate in the rumors, she wasn't interested in anyone saying those things about me. The rumors, not the truth, were enough to destroy a girl's reputation.

A wild feeling seized me, of desperation and fear. I took a deep breath. "Just let me know. How do you stop the sprits from talking once you start?"

Angela was fiddling with the peg. She realized I was being swayed. "It's easy. You just say goodbye."

"That seems so simple." I didn't think spirits were that simple. No matter what Angela said, I was going to read special duas and tasbihs. Maybe even read Quran, which I'd sadly stopped doing because my homework had just been piling on like crazy.

I said the Ayatul Kursi under my breath, then said, "Let's do it."

She smiled and the room went brilliant. "Really? You'll play with me? I don't want to make you do something you don't want to do."

I looked her in the eyes as if to prove it to myself. "I want to."

"Okay. Put your fingers on the edge." She put the pointer in the center of the board. "Don't remove your fingers until the spirit says goodbye."

I was about to ask what would happen if we did remove our fingers, but then I thought better of it. We both put our fingers on the pointer. When they touched, they made a spark.

She began to talk as if she was a professional clairvoyant, with a seriousness appropriate to the situation. "Spirits, are you here?"

The peg started to move toward the sun's face, to the YES.

I pulled my hand off as if I'd been bit. "Are you moving it?"

She shook her head. "I'm not."

"How is it moving if you're not moving it?"

"This is why I wanted to show it to you. Should we continue?"

I hesitated but now my question was burning a hole in my tongue. I felt a thrill of excitement and chills at the same time. The portal had been opened. Why not take a tiny step in? I nodded and we both put our fingers back on the peg.

"Okay," Angela said in a whisper, "ask your question."

"Spirits, will I get to marry who I want to marry?"

A sudden wind rattled the windows. Angela and I flinched but kept our fingers touching on the pointer. Nothing happened for a moment. Then the pointer started moving. It scraped against the board, like chalk on a chalkboard, putting my nerves on edge. It moved to the center of the board, all the way across to the *R*, then to the *A*. What were they spelling? The peg rushed across to the next letter, *Z*, and the hairs went up on my arm.

"Is this normal?" I whispered, as if the Ouija couldn't hear.

Angela looked unsure and scared. "I don't know . . . I've only played it once with my dad and they didn't spell out anyone's name."

"At least they spelled it right," I said, but my joke was feeble.

The spirits weren't done. They began to spell more and more quickly. Our whole bodies were pulled by the force and speed of the peg. R-A-Z-I-A-Y-O-U-M-U-S-T-P-R-A-Y R-A-Z-I-A-Y-O-U-M-U-S-T-P-R-A-Y.

Even though it was cold in Angela's apartment, I began sweating. I couldn't believe it. I got it from my mother. I got it from all the aunties. Now I was getting it from a Ouija board.

"Say goodbye! Say goodbye!"

Coming out of her own fright, Angela said, "Goodbye. Goodbye."

The board went quiet. I pulled my hands off the peg. We were both shaken.

"I didn't know it was going to do that. It didn't act this crazy when my dad and I asked questions. It just said yes or no."

"Oh my God!" I shook my head. "They sell this in a store? In the toy section?" I lay back on the bed but then sprang up again, afraid the bed was beginning to shake.

Angela scrambled to put the game back. She buried it deep in her closet and then came and sat at the edge of the bed. "I'm sorry, I didn't realize it would go berserk like that!"

I was quiet, feeling strange, dark shadows creep over me.

Angela looked over at me, worried. "Do you want some hot chocolate? My mom got me this special Godiva cocoa for Christmas. She even got whipped cream and marshmallows."

I finally smiled. "I like the way your mom thinks about presents a lot better."

She laughed. "I think it's as much for my mother as it is for me."

"I'll take whipped cream but no marshmallows."

I'd already be reading a million nafls. I didn't need to be eating any haram marshmallows to get me into deeper trouble.

The sky had gotten dark. It looked like it was about to snow again. There was a blanket of dark clouds over everything. I sank into the sofa and closed my eyes. I could hear her, warming up milk on the stove. The board had not really answered my question. Was I going to have to marry someone my parents picked?

"Why are you sitting in the dark?" Angela came into the room and began to turn on all the reading lamps. Her mother collected lamps from thrift shops like she collected books. With each click, the room began to glow with spheres of light.

We both heard sizzling. "The milk!" Angela ran back to the kitchen. After a second I heard, "Saved it!"

I knew that feeling all too well from making chai.

I noticed a movement out of the corner of my eye. I quickly turned, thinking it was a Jinn, but it was only the first snowflakes of the evening. The city fell quiet, the way even the city falls quiet with snow.

I prayed, "Allah, please protect me from evil spirits." After a pause I added, "And please protect me from marrying someone I don't want to marry."

I was praying just like the Ouija board had told me to do. Angela came in with two steaming mugs of hot chocolate, one with marshmallows and one without. She held out a cup of hot chocolate and smiled. All my fears dissolved, like snowflakes hitting the ground.

RAMZAAN

Aliza, Taslima, and I were like wet noodles laid out on the bed, so hungry we could barely move our limbs. I was so thirsty I was trying to drink my own spit. It was late afternoon, only the first week of Ramzaan, and the clarity hadn't set in. Unlike our parents, who went about the day doing everything they needed to do with cheerfulness, we were not yet buffered from hunger and thirst by the joys of Ramzaan.

We were woken up at dawn, as if part of some secret society. Like ghosts haunting the kitchen, our mothers would already be up making parathas, smoke hanging over their heads in question-mark clouds, the sound of the stove fan disturbing the stillness of the predawn hours. We'd come down groggy and our mothers would say, "Hurry, hurry, eat. Sehri's almost over." With bleary eyes we'd look out the windows but it would still be dark, with no hint of light creeping over the horizon.

I was at Taslima's because we were going to be having an Iftari party. My mother had sent me over to help prepare. But their kitchen was small and four people were too many. Taslima's mother shooed us out, sending us upstairs to study.

I had a giant book of integrated algebra in front of me, but my brain just wouldn't work. The numbers danced in front of me. My head hurt when I thought of all the work I had to do. I wasn't doing well at Stuyvesant. It was a secret I'd been keeping to myself.

I just wanted to sleep, to close my eyes. I wouldn't mind fasting if all I had to do was rest and read namaaz and Quran. Maybe if we were back in Pakistan it would be like this, but the pace of the city and the heartlessness of my teachers at Stuyvesant didn't let up.

They didn't care if it was Ramzaan. I still had to do homework and take tests and quizzes and be present and awake in class. I'd learned early getting sympathy was impossible. It was generally thought by our teachers that being Muslim was our fault and our odd, tortuous traditions were not their problem.

Taslima's voice came to me from far away. "What if I brush my teeth and I swallow a little bit of water? Would that break my Roza?" No one answered, but she continued. "What if I'm showering and I lean my head back and I accidentally swallow a bit of water? Would that break my Roza?"

Aliza's head was under a pillow. She wasn't happy her spring break coincided with Ramzaan. She'd been looking forward to some home cooking. She had tried to read but then decided her head was more comfortable under a pillow. "How many hours until Roza ends?"

I looked over at the silent clock radio. During Ramzaan, we didn't listen to music or watch TV. Without those worldly distractions, we were stripped down to our essence. That was the point of Ramzaan.

"Two hours," I replied, and Aliza groaned.

"You know what I really miss?" Taslima continued as if Aliza hadn't said a word. "The way when water comes out of the tap, it fizzes. Then you wait for the clouds to pass . . . and then you drink it."

No one said anything for a while.

"How long now until Roza ends?" Aliza asked.

"One hour and fifty-seven minutes."

She pulled the pillow off her head and looked out the window, glaring at the sun, trying to make it move faster. "How can you even study?"

"I have to. I can't keep up at Stuyvesant."

Taslima tried to assure me. "It's hard to focus on anything when you have Roza." When we'd first come upstairs, Taslima had tried to type a paper, but after typing "t-h-e," she'd said, "My fingers are tired," and flopped back on the bed.

"It's not Roza. I'm just not smart anymore."

They both stared at me.

"What are you talking about?" I could sense the annoyance in Aliza's voice. I should've known better than to irritate her so close to Iftari time, but I couldn't help myself.

"The teachers just make me feel so stupid. They're not like the teachers in Corona. They're not nice."

"I don't know what nice teachers you got in Corona but proceed."

"Like in math, anytime I get anything wrong, the teacher screams at me, 'How did you get into Stuyvesant?'" I flushed, remembering how embarrassing it had been. He always seemed to pick on me, the only Muslim in the class.

"Razia, I'm just gonna say this once . . . I cannot believe I'm even going to waste these calories on you, but you're either smart or you're not. If you passed the test to get in, that means you belong in Stuyvesant. Plus you wouldn't last a day in John Bowne. You'd get eaten alive."

Aliza was right. In John Bowne, grades didn't matter as much as survival. Boys came on strong, girls fought with fists and nails, and exasperated teachers were as likely to throw a punch as the students.

"You're right, Aliza, you're right." I tried to sit up, but as soon as I moved, my bra strap cut into my skin, tightening around my shoulders. I pulled at it to try to stretch it out.

"What are you doing now?" Aliza snapped. "You're making me crazy."

"Sorry. My bra . . ."

"You've got to stop buying those cheap Junction Boulevard bras."

How did she know? My mother, angry at my jiggling around the house, had taken me to Junction Boulevard. My body was an embarrassment to her and myself. Just when I thought my breasts were done growing, they'd grow even more.

There weren't any fitting rooms in the stores. The management thought we were all thieves. So there in the stacks of cheap clothing, my mother made me strap bras over my kameez while a group of little girls stared at me, giggling.

"If you want to buy a real bra, get one from here." Aliza reached into her desk drawer. "Oh, a Hershey kiss!" She pulled off the silver wrapper and popped it into her mouth.

"Aliza! You just broke your Roza," I said, horrified.

"It's okay, nobody knows."

"Um. Allah knows."

Aliza rolled her eyes. "Oh my God, Razia. Please. Your mother's not watching. You don't have to act that way."

I wasn't acting, though.

Aliza tossed the catalog and it hit me in the face. That was Aliza, one moment she'd be telling me to be strong and believe in myself and then the next she'd be throwing an underwear catalog in my face.

I opened it, and my breath stopped. The pages were filled with beautiful women. They were in nothing but bras and skimpy panties. They held their bodies like Amazons, stretched out between tall grasses and jungle foliage. They stood under waterfalls but were not drenched. In empty rooms of elegant apartments, they posed under chandeliers and were not embarrassed. Instead of stooping and hiding their breasts the way I did, they pushed out their chests and stretched their arms over their heads. They looked straight out of the pages, daring us to say, "Hey, you're just wearing underwear."

I felt a warm electricity start in my stomach and move through my body. The image of Angela floated into my mind. I'd never seen her in anything except concert T-shirts and ripped jeans, but I saw her now, with her thick eyeliner and wild hair, wearing black angel wings, in nothing but her underwear.

"Stop drooling. What's wrong with you?"

I became defensive. "You're the one who gave it to me."

"Yeah, but I meant to look at the underwear, not at the women. What are you, a lesbian?"

The word hung in the air between us like a neon sign.

"Aliza! Taslima!" their mother called from downstairs.

"Speak of the devil," I said, but my joke fell flat as we hadn't been speaking about their mother at all. Still, I thanked their mother for saving me from Aliza's and Taslima's questioning eyes.

As we came downstairs, we could hear Aunty in the kitchen. I wondered how she cooked such delicious food without getting tempted. Even when she couldn't taste the salt, she would still get it perfect.

She had three different pots going on the stove. She turned off the flames and said, "Okay, I'm done in here. You three make the samosas."

Samosas! We all got excited. Samosas, flaky and crispy on the outside and filled with delicious keema on the inside. I could almost taste them in my mouth.

With memories from Ramzaans past, we formed ourselves into an assembly line. Aliza rolled out the dough and cut it into squares. Taslima placed each square on the samosa maker. I scooped out spoons of meat filling and put them in the center of each samosa, then Taslima put on another layer of dough and we took turns with the rolling pin. The pin pressed the dough and filling down through the samosa maker. Then, we picked each samosa up and pressed our fingers around the edges to close them.

Each step was agony with my bra. Every time I pulled at it to loosen it, I thought of the women in the catalog. I was grateful no one was bringing it up. I didn't know if it was because they were being kind or because they just didn't care about anything but eating.

Afraid Aliza would restart the conversation, I began to talk about anything. "Your mother seems so happy."

Taslima closed up a samosa. "She's happy because the mice have all disappeared."

I laughed. "Does she think they're keeping Roza?"

Aliza shook her head. "No, she thinks it's a Ramzaan miracle, but I think it's because there isn't food out everywhere."

I imagined the mice looking up at the moon with our fathers on the rooftops, hiding near our fathers' feet. When the announcement was made that Ramzaan would start, I imagined the father mouse saying to his family, "Pack up your bags, we're going to the Catholic family next door. We need to eat."

"Hey, Razia, keep it moving!" Taslima had already put down the bottom layer of dough and Aliza was holding the top layer ready.

"Oh, sorry," I said, scooping in the filling.

The last hour before sunset was a blur of frying and preparation. Aliza deep-fried the samosas. They sizzled and popped in the pan. I stood awkwardly in the corner.

"Razia, make yourself useful. Help Taslima make fruit chaat."

Aliza was giving me the easiest job, but I still had questions. "Where—"

"Everything's in the fridge."

Taslima brought out fruit in different stages of decomposition.

Green apples and yellow pears with bruises all over them, reddish-purple grapes, clementines and bananas that had seen better days. That was what fruit chaat was for: to save dying fruit and bring our bodies a meager amount of vitamin income. Together, Taslima and I cut the fruit, our hands becoming slick from the juice.

Aliza came over to check up on us. "This isn't fruit chaat. It's fruit salad. It becomes fruit chaat when you add the chaat masala." She opened up a cupboard over the kitchen sink. It was filled with jars of spices. She rummaged through to find the jar Aunty had labeled "chaat masala" with ink and masking tape. Aliza heaped a spoonful and sprinkled it over the chaat. "Now it's fruit chaat."

The salty earth tang of the chaat masala mixed in with the sweetness of the fruit. The scent drifted up and combined with the cloud of smoke from the samosas, filling the small kitchen. My mouth watered for all the things I was hungry for, all the things I could never have.

STATEN ISLAND FERRY

There was the smell of wet dog in the air, from the old seats, stage curtains, and everyone's slightly damp Benetton sweaters. Angela and I were sitting in the auditorium balcony. We started every morning off with coffee and a Hershey bar each from the corner deli. I had my feet up on the railing alongside Angela's.

We'd become closer and closer, electrons circling each other, until the whole rest of the world, including the Goth butterflies, had fallen away. We didn't care. We liked being together without anyone else around.

On the balcony, we always hung out in the seats closest to the railing so we could watch the S.I.N.G. kids rehearse. Instead of regular theater, we had S.I.N.G., where students wrote and produced whole musicals from scratch. They didn't just put on endless renditions of *Bye Bye Birdie* and *Our Town*. I'm not saying the shows were better, but they were definitely original.

Angela liked to make fun of the S.I.N.G. kids, how seriously they took themselves. Taking sips of her coffee, she began her morning observations on the production. "Like we need another musical written about a physics test."

I leaned over the edge to get a better look at the stage manager as he walked briskly across the stage. He had long brown hair that was always bushy and disheveled.

Angela smiled at me. "Why don't you just ask him out?"

"Who?" I innocently took a sip of my coffee.

"That S.I.N.G. boy you're always staring at."

"Ha!" I said. "Unless he has opera binoculars, there's no way he even knows I exist. Plus, my family would never let me go out with him."

"They won't let you go out with anyone!"

Angela knew about my family's ban on dating, but it didn't mean she understood it.

"Why are your parents so against intermingling?"

"You make it sound like we're talking about dating between alien species."

"What about me? My parents are from two different countries. And," she emphasized, "I'm just fine."

Angela seemed pretty happy with herself that morning. She stretched out her legs. She was wearing her favorite sparkly black-and-gold-striped leg warmers over jeans so ripped I could see her knees.

"But they're not really different. They're both, you know, white."

"Oh my God, Razia! I can't believe you just said that. I'm Greek and Italian! Don't you remember when Ms. McManus gave us a whole random feminist mythology lesson in English? My people have been warring for *centuries*. Helen of Troy, ever heard of her?" She drained her coffee and I noticed the blue paper cup had fake Greek letters and the Acropolis on it. No, it wasn't the same.

"That's why my middle name is Helen. My parents thought it would be a good joke. Something for me to think about later in life." She shuddered. "Helen? Gross!" Angela pulled her legs down, so our feet were no longer touching. "It *was* a big deal. My father was Greek Orthodox and my mother was Catholic, and both their families disowned them. My grandparents didn't even come to see me, their adorable grand-daughter, for the first year. It makes me so angry! Families who don't accept who their kids want to marry!"

Just as suddenly, she deflated and sank down into her seat. "Sometimes I wonder if my parents would have had such a hard time if their families had just accepted them."

I understood then why she was so upset. I thought of my own family. What would they do to me if they found out I was dating someone, especially someone not Pakistani? They'd probably do worse than not speak to me. They'd ship me to Pakistan to get married.

The S.I.N.G. boy gestured to a group of stagehands and they began dismantling a living room and turning it into a forest.

Angela sat up so suddenly she almost knocked me over. "Let's get to more serious matters. What do you want to do for your birthday?"

I smiled. Angela and I had planned to cut school and have an adventure. It had been up to me to decide where we would go.

In English, we'd been swooning over Walt Whitman and reading "Crossing Brooklyn Ferry."

"Let's take a ferry ride."

"Yes!" She threw her arms around me. I'd given an answer she liked.

On the early-morning trip to Staten Island, the boat was empty. Well, almost empty. There was a young mother with sad eyes and a sleeping baby at her feet, a middle-aged woman looking dazed, her blonde hair defying gravity, her black purse the size of a child. A few benches away a homeless man was fast asleep.

Angela and I seemed to be the only ones awake. She walked toward the back of the boat and I followed. "It's the best view back here. No one's out here this early."

"How do you know so much about the ferry?" I whispered, not wanting to wake anyone.

"Remember that cousin I told you about who had to go to rehab?"

"Oh, right." I had hung on to every word of that story. I couldn't imagine anyone in my family ever going to rehab.

"I used to visit him in Staten Island where he was locked up."

We pushed open the white metal doors at the back of the ferry, and I caught my breath.

There was nothing but an accordion fence between Angela and me and the churning water. The ferry cut through the water, and a gust of wind whipped at my face. Angela was right. No one was out there. It would be too hard to fall asleep.

We walked to the railing and hung over its edge. I felt the rush of waves passing beneath us, the skimming of the boat, a calming buzz at my feet, a quick and gentle vibration.

As we moved away from the city, the skyscrapers collapsed into miniatures. I gazed at the Twin Towers. They were surreal, the way they stood against the sky.

There were binocular machines on the deck, the kind that looked like silver alien lollipops with robot eyes shooting out of their faces. Angela started to swing around and around them. "Want to look in the slot? I might have a quarter. It'll be your birthday present!"

Angela had been saying this all day about everything, whether it was my breakfast Hershey bar, coffee, or subway ride, which was a joke because we both got in for free with our subway pass.

But I didn't want to look too close. Somewhere behind those miniature buildings was Queens, and in Queens, Corona. It all felt so small and far away, and I wanted to keep it that way, if just for a moment.

The ferry moved farther and farther. One of the Towers hid behind the other like a shy twin. At that moment I had a flash of a photo. It was a Polaroid of Saima's father on the ferry, eating an ice cream cone. Vanilla ice cream was dripping over his chin and shirt. He was laughing. Saima's mother and my mother were sitting on benches, smiling, with us in their laps. The Twin Towers were behind us, like two ancient pillars to Heaven.

It had been one of our rare family excursions to the city. My father must have taken the photo. I felt suddenly so deeply sad at how many years had passed since our families had hung out. I remembered how happy my father had been whenever he was with Saima's father.

I took a deep breath, squinting my eyes against the light. I would never have imagined doing something like this when Saima and I were girls: cutting school, having adventures in the city. It seemed like another lifetime ago, when Corona had been my whole world and there had been nothing outside of the neighborhood.

"What are you thinking?" Angela had learned to ask this question whenever I seemed to drift away.

"I used to have this friend, Saima—"

"The one who made the scary-looking dolls?"

I smiled. "Good memory."

I'd never told her the story of our families' break, of how I'd lost Saima. I still didn't. "We used to play this game whenever our families drove into the city. Saima and I would pretend we owned one of the skyscrapers—the Empire State Building, the Chrysler. I always picked the Twin Towers because I could get two buildings for the price of one. And, of course, because I'm a Gemini." Being a Gemini, someone with two selves, made more sense to me than any other identity.

"I knew a girl who thought she was a Scorpio and then found out she was adopted and really a Virgo. But she'd been acting like a Scorpio her whole life."

"Not her whole life. I mean she probably wasn't even reading the horoscopes until she was like eleven."

Angela suddenly jumped up. "Oh my God! Look!" She pointed behind my head.

I turned. It was the Statue of Liberty. She was green and stunning, so close, she felt miraculous. We ran to the railing on the other side and stared. Old-fashioned sailboats crossed in front of her. I felt transported hundreds of years, as if I was someone coming to this land for the first time.

We stared in quiet until Angela started giggling.

"What is it?"

"We're so close we can see her armpit hair!"

I burst into laughter, and a gale of wind blew the white doors open. Just at that moment, an old lady with a blue-frosted helmet of hair, who'd been dozing inside by the door, woke up and glared at us. We kept giggling as the door fell closed again.

When we arrived in Staten Island, the ferry ground to a slow halt, bumping up and down as we pulled in. Trees and plants were growing out of the docks. The wood felt ancient.

"Want to see Staten Island?" I asked.

"Not really," she answered.

Outside of the sleeping man on the bench, it was all women, young and old, shuffling off. Angela and I stepped away from the doors and windows, pressed ourselves against the wall of the outer deck. Unless someone came onto the deck, they wouldn't see that we had stayed back.

We peeked through the window to see the boat fill with the next load to Manhattan. There were crowds of Staten Islanders heading to work in the city. Their costumes were almost identical. Young women with platinum-blonde hair, flesh-colored pantyhose, and white sneakers heading to the city with their high-heeled shoes peeking out from their faux leather purses. I never understood why anyone wore heels. If you couldn't walk in your shoes, what was the point?

When the ferry began to move, we came forward. We were braver and leaned harder on the railing, watching the city grow as we got closer and closer. The wind picked up, and Angela started yelling into it:

> *"Flow on, river! flow with the flood-tide, and ebb with the ebb-tide!"*

I joined her, our voices echoing the river's sound:

> *"On the ferry-boats the hundreds and hundreds that*
> *cross, returning home, are more curious to me than*
> *you suppose,*
> *And you that shall cross from shore to shore years*
> *hence are more to me, and more in my meditations,*
> *than you might suppose . . .*
> *Just as you feel when you look on the river and sky,*
> *so I felt,*
> *Just as any of you is one of a living crowd, I was one of*
> *a crowd,*
> *Just as you are refresh'd by the gladness of the river and*
> *the bright flow, I was refresh'd,*
> *Just as you stand and lean on the rail, yet hurry with*
> *the swift current, I stood yet was hurried . . ."*

Angela stared at me. "Whoa. Do you have the whole poem memorized? Can you show me your trick?"

"Sure." I smiled. I didn't tell her she'd have to spend years with my mother, reading Sabak and memorizing the Quran.

When we got back to Manhattan, there was a garbled announcement. The ferry slowly pulled into the dock, bumping up and down like crazy.

After a few moments, the sleeping man shook himself awake. We figured if he was getting off, we should too. Exiting the ferry, we blended in with the crowds of people hurrying to work.

I looked at Angela. "Want to go again?"

"Razia, that's why I love you."

I blushed.

The next ferry was leaving soon but from a different gate. We pulled out of the wave of bodies and ran through the terminal, ducking and darting between clumps of passengers. Giggling and out of breath, we made it just in time.

The ferry was even more empty on the way back to Staten Island. For a second I thought we were the only ones on the boat. We took off with a jerky start and almost fell on top of each other. We started laughing and walking through the cabin, swinging our bodies back and forth through the center aisles, bouncing when we hit waves and bouncing on our own some more.

Angela started singing, "*Yo, ho, ho and a bottle of rum!*"

The words were easy to pick up, and I sang along.

We were laughing so hard, I walked right into someone without realizing he was there. He was a young man, and for a second it didn't hit me that he was wearing gold wings on his white shirt.

He stared at us. "Shouldn't you girls be in school?"

"Um, what?" Angela and I exchanged guilty looks.

Our hesitation gave us away. It was over. My parents were going to find out I'd been cutting school. My mother was definitely going to take me out of Stuyvesant.

I heard Angela through my cloud of panic. "Captain! Oh hi, Captain." She pointed at me, as if there was anyone else on the boat. "It's my friend's birthday, and since there isn't any school today—it's Staff Day—and she loves ferries, I thought I'd bring her for her birthday."

My temperature was flashing hot from adrenaline. I looked at Angela open-mouthed. There was enough truth to make her story float.

His eyes focused on me. "You're interested in ferries?"

He was kind of cute, like a young George Michael. "Yes. Yes, I am."

He grinned. The skin around his eyes crinkled. "Would you like a tour of the captain's cabin?"

Angela and I looked at each other. "Sure!"

We followed him up the flights of stairs, smiling and nudging each other at my birthday luck.

His cabin was at the top of the boat. The young captain unlocked the door with a big key. Inside, there were valves with clockfaces, a steering wheel that looked like the steering wheel of a car, and hand brakes that looked like brakes on a spaceship. There was a phone that looked like a pay phone, with a curved black handle, a thick mouth and earpiece.

Angela was already at the monitors. "What does this do?"

The captain spun around. "Don't touch that!" Then he softened his voice. "Why don't you girls just sit down?" He pointed to two swivel chairs.

I did, but Angela kept hovering over the panels, like a child trying to control herself. I leaned into the center window. The view was amazing. The ferry seemed to be moving even faster from up high. The captain came and stood by me, and I became flustered. Why wasn't he standing next to Angela? She was usually the one who got attention wherever we went.

Nervous, I started asking questions. "What's the craziest thing you've ever seen out here in the water?"

He smiled. "Dolphins. Whales."

"Wow . . ." I whispered. How I wished I could see dolphins and whales, any ocean creature. I wasn't even allowed to go to Coney Island because there were too many naked people there.

He seemed to enjoy my impressed look and kept going. "Once three dolphins just swam alongside my boat."

"No way!" Angela put her hands on her hips and stood up straight.

She was still at the monitors. He seemed annoyed but then acted as if he didn't care.

He leaned in closer. "I know there's no such thing as Staff Day. But is it really your birthday?"

I swallowed. "That part is true. It's my birthday."

"How old are you?"

"I'm fifteen."

He smiled. "Fifteen. Since it's your birthday, we'll let it pass." He reached into a bag that was hanging from the chair I was sitting in and held out a silver can. "Do you want a beer?"

"What?" I was startled. "Are you allowed to drink at work?"

He winked. "Just one a day. One won't hurt anyone but me."

I hesitated but then thought: What the heck? It's my birthday. I wanted to do something I'd never done before. I took a small sip. My face tightened. It was disgusting. I remembered how much Saima and I had hated the smell of beer. What would she think of me actually drinking it? I handed him back the can as fast as I could.

He started laughing. "Haven't you ever had beer before?"

I swallowed, trying to get the taste out of my mouth. "No, I've never had alcohol."

He looked surprised but then said, "It's an acquired taste. Here, have another sip."

Angela, who'd been secretly touching some of the controls, noticed what was going on and came over. She took the can and drank the whole thing like it was Coke.

I was shocked. So was the captain. I wondered where she had learned to drink like that. There was so much about Angela I didn't know.

The captain's eyes opened wide. Before he could say anything, the phone rang. I was amazed again at how the phone looked just like a regular pay phone.

"Uh-huh, uh-huh. Uh-huh, uh-huh." He hung up and looked at us. "Sorry, girls, you have to leave. Time to dock. My co-captain is heading back. But you can stay on the boat. Just wait out in the back. No one will check."

We didn't tell him we already knew that.

I got up so fast, I half fell off the chair. I had only had a sip of the beer but I felt drunk. Angela, who had begun to look glazed, straight-ened up. We stumbled out of the cabin. I heard him call out behind us, "Happy birthday!"

We ran down the steps, the white metal clanging underneath our feet. The sun glinted over the vanishing skyscrapers. There was noth-ing blocking the light. It was all light, reflecting off the buildings and water.

"Do you want to go again?" Angela asked.

"Can you imagine if I said let's move to Staten Island and we never went back?"

She laughed and her laughter filled my being. We went back to our spot by the accordion fence. I leaned over the railing and took a deep breath of air. I could hear the water whispering, "What if? What if? What if?"

Seagulls flew alongside the ship, dipping and swaying, their wings large enough to break the city down. They were floating on air, invisi-ble wind. They didn't even have to flap their wings. They wheeled over our heads, their undersides catching the sunlight, dipping down and near us.

In the distance, I saw rain clouds inching their way toward us on the horizon. The wind picked up. The water became choppy, push-ing up against the boat. The waves elongated their fingers, reaching into the air. The water was alive, each wave pushing up, churning the earth.

The sun was still out. In the water, there was the reflection of the sky and halos of light around our heads. I felt eyes on me but when I turned around, there was no one. I was about to tell Angela the ghost of Whitman was visiting us, but when I turned back around she was smiling wide, holding a packet of Ring Dings in her outstretched hands. "Happy birthday!"

"Oh my God. When did you get these?"

"At the deli when you weren't looking."

She put the Ring Dings in my hand and leaned toward me. I thought she was going to give me a birthday hug, but instead she kissed me on the lips. Her mouth, her lips were soft. Her kiss was like warm bread, salt, hunger. Everything around me buzzed.

There was a sound behind us and we jumped apart. A young man and woman had come out onto the deck. I touched my fingers to my lips. The man had a black mustache. The woman had long black braids. She was pushing an umbrella stroller with a sleeping baby.

The man looked right at me. "Will you take our photo?" he asked.

I hesitated, but then hurried over and took the camera. My hands shook only a little bit as I took the picture.

SURPRISE

As soon as I got home, I called Taslima. She answered the phone singing, "*Happy birthday to you. Happy birthday to you . . .*"

"Taslima—" I tried to interrupt her, but she was in full-on birthday-singing mode. "Taslima, stop. I have to tell you something."

"What?"

I fell silent. I couldn't say it. "No, forget it."

"Oooooh, did that S.I.N.G. boy ask you out?"

It was so far from what I wanted to tell her, I lost my words even more.

"No . . . I'm . . . I'm afraid to tell you . . ." And I did feel afraid. I remembered the way Aliza had made fun of me for looking at the women in the catalog. Would Taslima do the same?

Taslima sighed, annoyed that I'd interrupted her singing for no reason. "Did you kill someone?"

"What? No!"

"Well, then it can't be that bad!"

Her crazy logic snapped me out of my paralysis, and I blurted out, "Angela and I kissed."

"Angela?" She seemed confused for a second. "Your friend?"

"Yes."

There was silence. Finally she said, "What are you going to tell George Michael?"

We both burst into laughter and, just like that, the turmoil I was carrying became calm.

"Does this mean you're a lesbian now?"

"I don't know. Does it?"

"I don't know. Does it?"

We both started giggling. This back-and-forth could go on forever.

"I didn't know there could be Pakistani lesbians," Taslima said.

"I didn't know it was possible either." My mind was in a whirl.

Taslima had a million questions. "Is she your girlfriend now?"

"I don't think so."

"Did you talk about it?"

"No."

"You didn't talk about it? Why?!"

"Well, someone wanted us to take their picture."

"What?"

"We were on the ferry."

"You went on the ferry without me?" I could hear the hurt in her voice. I'd forgotten we'd been planning on taking the ferry to see the Statue of Liberty on our next cut day.

"I'm sorry, I forgot we were going to go."

"Hmm. You forgot?" She was quiet. But then her curiosity won over her annoyance. "Well, why didn't you talk after you took the picture?"

"I don't know. We just stayed out on the deck with the family."

She gave an exasperated sigh. "Oh, Razia . . ."

"Well, I mean there was a really nice view. You could see the Twin Towers and the Statue of Liberty."

"Oh my God." Taslima started laughing. "Razia, you're the worst lesbian ever."

"Well . . ." I said, feeling like I *was* the worst lesbian ever. "Angela was feeling a little nauseous."

Taslima started cracking up. "You must be a terrible kisser!"

I began to feel even worse but I defended myself. "She was feeling sick because she drank a whole can of beer the captain gave us."

"Whoa whoa whoa. Back up. What captain? The captain of the ferry? What the heck happened today?" Taslima took a deep breath. "Razia, just because you turned fifteen doesn't mean you have to squeeze every haram thing into one day! What are you going to do for the rest of the year?"

Something inside me pinched. Did she think kissing a girl was haram? Like drinking?

"Ask your mother if you can come over." Taslima's tone was suddenly much too casual.

"Taslima. I know you and Aliza are going to throw me a surprise party."

She let out a breath, the secret off her chest. My kiss with Angela had distracted her long enough. "How did you know?"

"Because Aliza only said to me a million times that I shouldn't make plans for after school on my birthday."

Even if Angela had wanted to hang out, I wouldn't have been able to miss Aliza's surprise party. I'd offered to go home with Angela but she'd said she wanted to go home and sleep, then hugged me and kissed me on the cheek.

Taslima interrupted my thoughts. "Well, hurry up because Aliza just finished frosting the cake and she's going to be mad if her masterpiece sits out too long."

Just then my mother came into the room. "What are you two Khee-Khees laughing about?"

"Ammi, can I go to Taslima's?" I knew she'd say yes. Birthdays and *Days of Our Lives* were two traditions my mother wholeheartedly embraced.

"Yes, but read Asr first and come home before Maghrib." She smiled and said, "Happy birthday," then bent over to pick up some clothes I'd left on the floor.

I had a sudden irrational desire to hug her, but there was so much distance between us. My birth had been only the beginning of our separation, the first time I was cut loose. From that moment until now, I'd just been going farther and farther away, my body a lifeboat pushing into the ocean.

I read namaaz quickly, and during dua, I said nothing to Allah about the kiss, although I imagined Allah already knew. I figured we would talk about it later, when I wasn't in such a hurry to avoid Aliza's real-life wrath.

As I passed Linden Park, the scent of the flowers on the trees over-whelmed me. They were in full bloom, with a perfume like honey, like the smell of baking sugar bread floating over Corona in the early morning. It was dawning on me, what my feelings for Angela had always been. I knew I should be afraid, but instead I felt elated. Is this why I'd always felt different? Was this why I'd always felt repulsed by the idea of weddings, of being a wife? Things it seemed no one else had a problem with. Things people even seemed excited about. Had my mother always known? Is that why she'd always kept a close watch over me? Had tried so hard to control me?

I wondered: Is this how a lesbian walks?

I was so lost in my thoughts, I was at Taslima's house before I knew it. I opened the gate and walked down the driveway. The garage was there at the end, looking older and more sunken than ever. Its blue paint had almost all peeled off.

I walked through the back door into the kitchen but there was no one there. I continued through the family room and there was no one there either. If I hadn't known they were throwing me a surprise party, I would have thought Taslima's family had been abducted by aliens.

"Hello?" I yelled up the stairs, adding a little pretend fear to my voice for their benefit, as if I was in a horror movie.

I walked into the formal living room, which was separated from the family room by a curtain. Taslima's mother was sitting there in the dark like Norman Bates in *Psycho*. Aliza, Taslima, Atif, and Suheil jumped out from behind the sofa, yelling, "Surprise!"

I screamed for real.

The lights turned on and everyone started laughing, gathering around me, feeling the postsurprise thrill.

"Were you surprised?" Suheil asked.

"Yeah, she was," Atif said. "She jumped. She was really scared."

"Happy birthday!" Taslima said, hugging me.

"Ahem!" Aliza said. She gestured with her eyes toward herself and then to the table.

Aliza thought of herself as a Pakistani Betty Crocker, but even she had outdone herself with a three-layer yellow cake, each layer covered in chocolate frosting, and a rose from the garden on top. The cake said "Happy Birthday Razia" in hot-pink icing with Aliza's distinctly beautiful handwriting.

Aliza had always aspired to a kind of elegance, like a character in a Jane Austen novel. She'd practiced calligraphy as if she really had attended a British finishing school. She felt it was her curse and her cross to bear that she'd been born in Corona, into a Pakistani family. I felt there was some truth to what she was saying. It had been some kind of mistake, her being born among us.

I smiled. "Thank you so much for the cake, Aliza! I love the rose touch."

"It's classy," she said, "and don't forget it. The rest of this stuff is their fault." I took in the whole spread. There were neon-orange cheese puffs, potato chips, chocolate chip cookies, and even gifts wrapped up in old Christmas wrapping paper that must've been bought on sale.

While everyone began to devour the snacks, Aliza put the candles in the cake. They were thin, pastel pink and sky blue. She fit the candles in between the swirls of the letters of my name and in the spaces between the "Happy" and the "Birthday."

"You're so old you're ruining my design," Aliza said, trying to squeeze in one extra candle for good luck.

She pulled out an oven lighter. The fire illuminated her face as she lit a candle for every year I'd been alive.

Everyone, even Taslima's mother, sang: "*Happy birthday to you . . . Happy birthday to you.*"

Atif and Suheil added, "*You look like a monkey and you act like one too.*"

"Make a wish!" Taslima yelled.

"Hurry, you're ruining the cake!" Aliza snapped. Indeed, the wax was melting all over her masterpiece.

All that came into my mind was Angela. I wished for Angela.

I couldn't believe there were presents as well. I unwrapped the small one first. Aliza had gotten me my own copy of *The Catcher in the Rye*.

"So you'll get your grubby hands off mine. Now that I think about it, you should get the worn copy and I should get the new one."

I couldn't believe I had my own copy. Leave it to Aliza to get me the perfect gift. As if she had taken a class in Victorian Gifting. "Either way, Aliza. Thank you."

Taslima's present was in a Christmas-paper-wrapped Alexander's clothing box.

"You got me something from Alexander's?"

She rolled her eyes. "Look inside."

The box was filled with gray-blue tissue paper. Inside, something shone, reflecting the light.

I pulled out Taslima's black-and-gold vest, the vest Asmi Khala had brought from Pakistan, the vest she'd worn the first time we'd gone to Central Park.

I got choked up. "Oh, man. Thanks."

Taslima leaned in close to my ear so her mother couldn't hear. "And your mom won't throw it away because it's Pakistani!"

"Hey! Didn't Asmi Khala give that to me?" Atif asked.

Their mother, who hadn't really been paying attention to us, looked over. Taslima shushed him and he didn't push it. He was too happy eating all the cheese puffs.

When the party was over, everyone settled in for TV. *Quantum Leap* was on. I was about to sit down but Taslima dragged me upstairs. As soon as we got to her room, she locked the little sliding lock on the door and sat down on the bed.

"So. What did it feel like?"

"What?"

"Ah . . ." Taslima rolled her eyes up to the ceiling. "What? The kiss, of course!"

"Oh my God, Taslima! You keep asking me that. But how can I describe a kiss?"

The truth was that in that moment there had been a sweet giddiness, nothing but me and Angela in the world. Somehow, I knew I couldn't tell Taslima this.

She prodded me. "Come on. It's the first time one of us has kissed someone. I thought it was going to be a boy first, but of course you can never do things normal."

There it was. A little seed of judgment. Taslima always made fun of me for being strange, but this was different. She was acting like she was okay but then there was that part of her that wasn't.

"Oh, man," she said. "Are you gonna tell Aliza?"

"I don't think so."

"Yeah, don't," Taslima said. There it was again. Disapproval. Pinpricks of shame started coming over me, little drops of sweat.

I wanted Taslima to understand, to convince me to tell Aliza. Wasn't Aliza the one who said it wasn't crazy to want to live my own life? I sighed, realizing I couldn't tell Taslima everything.

"Thank you for the vest," I said instead.

"You are most welcome. Oh my God! That reminds me. I have a new outfit I want to show you. You know I wouldn't give away one of my favorites without coming up with a backup. But you have to go outside."

"Why do I have to go outside?"

"You know . . . because." She pointed to her lips.

It was so rude even I had to laugh.

"Taslima! I'm not into you like that! Just because I kissed a girl doesn't mean I'm going to kiss every girl in front of me now."

"I know, I know." She waved her hand dismissively.

But I continued, feeling hot. My emotions were spiking up and down. "When you kiss one boy, it doesn't mean you will kiss—"

"Okay, okay. I get it. But you still have to turn around."

"I always do," I huffed.

"Shoo! You never had good taste in crushes anyways."

I couldn't help but laugh. I shook my head and opened *The Catcher in the Rye*.

Since it was my own book, I felt superstitious that it had to be read from the beginning.

If you really want to hear about it, the first thing you'll probably want to know is where I was born, and what my lousy childhood was like . . .

But I couldn't focus. I pretended to read, but my mind was whirling between Angela's kiss and Taslima's comments. I knew I shouldn't be so mad at Taslima. For all of our breaking of the rules, for all of our schemes and desires for adventure, this was unprecedented. We'd been so vigilant with the boys, we'd forgotten about the girls. Wouldn't I have been surprised if she'd come to me with the same news?

Maybe, maybe in the future one of us would have gotten a boyfriend. I'd always imagined it would be Taslima first. That was it. Taslima was jealous because I'd kissed someone before her. She'd become so good at being sneaky she could've pulled it off. I'd probably have gotten caught with a boyfriend. But with a girl, I realized, I could always say she was my friend.

"Are you going to ask her to be your girlfriend?" Taslima asked, interrupting my thoughts.

I pretended to take a moment to stop reading. "I don't know . . ." It was suddenly a blessing she couldn't see my face. "You already asked me that."

She sang, "*You're going to have a girlfriend. You're going to have a girlfriend.*"

"Shut up!" I said, getting flustered.

How did it even work? I'd never known anyone gay, on TV or in real life. I'd never seen girls holding hands or kissing. Even at Stuyvesant, where kids thought they were so cool, I'd never met anyone who was gay. Although, I had met . . . me.

I felt suddenly afraid. "Don't tell anyone."

"I won't. No one," Taslima said, but then added casually, "So I can't even tell Aliza?"

I couldn't believe it. She couldn't have it both ways, telling me I shouldn't tell Aliza and then wanting to tell her herself.

Before I could say anything, she said "Ta-da" and turned around. She held up her arms. "Look!"

Her outfit was amazing. She was wearing a Nehru jacket, dark blue jeans, and beautiful black boots.

"Wow. Where did you get that jacket?"

"It was my father's! He used to be stylish like that."

"Whose boots are those?"

"Aliza's."

"Is she going to let you wear them?"

"We'll see."

I knew that meant that Taslima was going to sneak them. Taslima was a moral person but she definitely felt that anything that stood between her and fashion was fair game to be torn down.

The phone began to ring but no one was picking it up because they were all watching *Quantum Leap*. I looked out the window. The sun was going down. With a jolt I realized it was my mother.

"Yikes, I have to get home. It's Maghrib time."

"Do you have time for me to change?"

"No, just stay and admire yourself. I'll see you next weekend."

Downstairs, Taslima's mother was laughing on the phone. It was definitely my mother. "Razia—"

"I know, Aunty, I'm going. Thank you for the party!"

She smiled, awkward, unable to take the compliment.

Everyone else's eyes were glued to the TV, but Aliza turned before I left. "Happy birthday," she said, giving me a rare and brilliant smile.

The front yard was covered with cherry blossoms. Cherry petals were raining down like snowflakes in late spring. I'd been walking by the tree for days, admiring it, saying hello, but never stopping to sit up in its branches.

But it was my birthday and Angela and I had kissed. I climbed up to my favorite perch. All the light in the world was changing color. The sky was becoming purple with gorgeous hot-pink clouds. I could see the place where the old Greek couple used to sit. A few months ago, they'd moved away to be closer to their grandchildren.

I thought of Angela and understood for the first time what that slant of light must have felt like for them. I started to feel like I was floating. A spring breeze whispered past and I watched the flower petals rise, catching the wind and floating up, defying gravity.

BOOK FIVE

Summer 1989

THE STRAND

The last few days of school passed in a blurred flurry. Roses, pink as cherry blossoms, waved to us from every corner. Angela wanted to pick them, but I said to let them live. New York City felt more beautiful than ever, the air heavy with the smell of honeysuckle.

We became even more inseparable, making every day a half day of school. We'd mix it up, attend different classes on different days, hang around the fading hieroglyphics of Cleopatra's Needle in Central Park, or go back to the Met, where we'd get in with a smile and a penny and spend the whole day at Sappho's feet.

But mostly we just hung out at Angela's because it was the only place we could be all over each other. I never knew touch could feel like this, like a steady stream of joy, just flowing through my body.

Angela didn't want to tell anyone at school and I agreed. Anyone who was even rumored to be gay was treated brutally. Plus, I was terrified of my family finding out. I never brought Angela to Corona. I wanted to, but I knew my mother would be able to see right through us.

The only place I could talk about Angela was with Allah and in my diary. After I'd read namaaz, I'd cup my hands for the dua and tell Allah everything I was feeling. "Allah, I just can't believe this is wrong. It's the other stuff that feels wrong. All the ways you've set it up with men and women. How can it be wrong when she's my best friend? But don't tell Taslima I said that!"

I was joking but also serious. Taslima and I hadn't been talking much since I'd told her about Angela, and I didn't need her getting more mad at me.

After doing dua, I always felt a deep calm. But by evening, my mind would be spinning, and I wouldn't be able to sleep until I wrote in my diary. My diary was just loose-leaf paper stapled together, but it had become my most precious possession. Sometimes I'd write about our adventures, reliving them in my head. Sometimes all I could write was "Angela and I kissed. Angela and I kissed. She tasted of salty chips."

One day, Angela said she wanted to take me somewhere special. We walked down Broadway to the Strand, where barricades of books lined the sidewalk. As soon as I walked in, I sneezed. There were piles and piles of books, about to topple over, and a buzz of quiet excitement, of discovery. Book clerks rushed about, some wearing glasses, some nose rings, many with brightly dyed hair, purple or green. I thought of Aliza's small bookshelf. Even the Corona library had less books than this.

Angela squeezed my hand. "I want to get this book for us, *Even Cowgirls Get the Blues*. It's about these two girls who fall in love. I read about it in *Seventeen*." She disappeared into the stacks on a treasure hunt, leaving me behind.

I tried to get the attention of the book clerks, but they all buzzed by, ignoring me.

"Don't mind them. They all think they're writing the next great American novel. They can't stoop to help anyone. Can I help you find something?"

One of the clerks was talking to me. I turned to see a handsome man with a gold earring in his left ear. Gray threaded through his full beard. He pulled down his reading glasses and looked me up and down, taking my measure. His name tag said "Ben, Ask Me."

So I asked. "My friend is looking for this book, *Even Cowgirls Get the Blues*."

A smile moved across his lips. "Your friend?"

I blushed.

He turned and started walking to the back of the store. "Well," he said, then, knowing I wasn't following him, commanded, "follow me."

He brought me to the fiction section and began to whisper to himself. "Yes, this and a little bit of this." He was barely looking at the shelves, just pulling books down.

He handed me a stack. "You don't have to buy them," he said, "but you should read them."

He had given me *Bastard Out of Carolina*, *Song of Solomon*, and even *Even Cowgirls Get the Blues*.

"And if you can handle it . . ." He placed one more book in my hands, *Close to the Knives*. "It's a memoir but it ended up in fiction. These clerks are charming but distracted." He gave a loving but frustrated look at one of the clerks walking by. "David Wojnarowicz. A gorgeous artist. He died too soon."

I looked at the cover, a black-and-white photograph of buffalo running off a cliff. "How did he die?"

"AIDS."

A chill went through me. I remembered the day Julio and I had seen Mr. Nichols crying, when Julio had crumpled in the hallway.

Ben leaned in and whispered, "Seventy-five percent of the staff here died." He tilted his head to a tall, thin man in the art section. He looked up at us and smiled. "Only Robert and I survived. Robert used to say, 'Ben, everyone's going to think we were boring.'"

He laughed and I couldn't help but smile.

He looked at me closely. "Where did you come from? You're like a bear cub lost in the wilderness."

"Queens."

"That makes sense."

"How did you . . ." I didn't know how to finish the sentence.

"Live? I just never got sick." With a wave of his hand, he walked away to help someone else. "Let me know what you think of the books."

Angela found me, standing in place, looking through the books. "I found *Even Cowgirls*," I said to her. "I mean, someone helped me." I looked around but Ben had disappeared into the piles of books.

Angela insisted on buying everything. "My dad doubled my allowance. This parents-competing-for-my-love thing is really working out. Now, let's go to the Waverly and get some hot chocolate. We just have to head to the Village."

"Aren't we in the Village?"

My unfamiliarity with city geography made Angela laugh. "This is the East Village. I'm taking you to the West Village."

We walked crosstown through cobblestone streets. After the black and gray of the East Village, I had to blink my eyes with wonder. I felt as if I was Dorothy, entering the Land of Oz. There were rainbows everywhere, gay couples holding hands in the open. Angela's hand was trembling as she reached for mine. I pulled her toward me, feeling as if I'd become divine.

TAIBAH AUNTY

Angela and I learned to rest our heads on each other's shoulders on her Friday train rides to Queens. We acted as if we were two friends tired from a grueling day at school, two girls who looked like they could be sisters, but who lived by listening to the steady thump thump of each other's blood.

We held hands under our sweaters or book bags, not caring if they got sweaty. Sometimes people raised their eyebrows at us. Then we shifted away, pretended we were just friends. We'd been hearing about attacks on the train and went more and more to the West Village to escape.

One afternoon, I was resting my head on Angela's shoulder. All around, the sounds of the train, the bing-bong of the subway doors chiming, were bringing me to the edge of sleep. I thought of Adam and Eve. Eve had been created from Adam's rib. It's what my mother had taught me. Didn't it make sense then for two ribs to come together, like ribs really did?

I saw Angela and me, with bleeding hearts in between our rib bones, the kind of hearts I used to see on the loteria playing cards they sold in the bodega. When the bloody hearts started beating, I realized I was dreaming.

I woke with a start. We were at Queensboro Plaza.

Angela smiled. "I was just going to wake you up. I'm getting off."

I didn't want her to go. "I'll wait with you." Sometimes I waited at

Queensboro Plaza where the N and 7 trains met on the platform. I'd stay until the N arrived, then take the 7 home.

We got off, letting the long, roaring worm of the 7 flash away with one last blast of heat. It was muggy on the platform, sweltering. After the frigidness of the subway, the heat was an insult. My face became sticky with sweat. I fanned my T-shirt while my jeans stuck uncomfortably to my thighs.

All the beautiful people of Queens were wilting on the platform. An older lady with blue hair and a cart of groceries pushed past us. A subway worker was emptying the garbage in slow motion, releasing the smell of rot in the air. There was a group of boys with book bags strapped to their backs or hanging from their fingers. They'd normally be shouting and hollering, but even they were subdued.

"Come on." I pulled Angela behind a dark green rusty pillar, plastered with subway advisories spelling out the delays for the rest of the week.

"It's so hot," she said, but she didn't pull away.

Ever since we'd started spending time in the West Village, we'd become bold. We kissed and the silver glint of the buildings shone on us with mirror heat. Our atoms collided into each other. I felt Angela's heart beating against my chest. She tasted of peach vanilla iced tea and mint. A cicada, perched somewhere close on a tree overhanging the plaza, sang as if this was its one night of glory at an open mic in the East Village.

Out of nowhere, I smelled baby powder and rose oil. Then I heard a gasp. Matter realigned itself, and I turned in slow motion.

It was Taibah Aunty. Her face was wooden, her mouth a grim line.

Angela and I instinctively jumped away from each other. Angela dropped my hand, but the stickiness from where our fingers had intertwined clung to my skin.

Had she seen us? Had she seen us? The question hammered through my head. Every sense in my being sharpened.

"Asalaamu alaikum, Aunty," I said in my calmest voice possible. I let my reputation stand behind me. All the years of being the perfect Muslim daughter, reading all my namaazes and Quran, the only one from the neighborhood who'd gotten into Stuyvesant. I pulled my disguise over me like an invisible shield.

"Wa alaikum asalaam," she said to me while staring at Angela. She took in Angela's Nine Inch Nails T-shirt, her dark raspberry lipstick, the ring in her nose, the black eyeliner that turned up in a swirl at the end.

Taibah Aunty sniffed, and in that sniff was everything.

"Hello," Angela said, never one to be ignored.

In the distance we heard the rumble of a train. The track curved far in the distance, and for a moment we wouldn't know if it was the 7 or the N. A rat darted across the tracks. I smelled the sour smell of garbage festering in the heat. I smelled Taibah Aunty's sweat underneath the rose oil and baby powder. I began to gasp for breath.

The 7 roared into the station, and Taibah Aunty moved quickly. Drama or no drama, she was going to get a seat. When I didn't move, she looked back at me. She was already at the front of the crowd by the doors. "Aren't you going home?" It wasn't a question.

Angela and I exchanged a look. We both knew I needed to go.

"Bye, Razia," she said, trying to sound casual.

When I still didn't move, Taibah Aunty said, "Come with me!"

Of course, I had the ability to turn the other way, to resist, to do anything but follow her, but when Taibah Aunty spoke, I was lifted with such force off my feet, I floated to her side. There was a thin leash from her worn-out hands to mine, a leash made from centuries of tradition.

The moves I made in the next few moments would decide everything. I needed to convince Taibah Aunty she hadn't seen what she'd seen. I needed to make sure I got to my mother first.

I didn't turn back to look at Angela as we pushed onto the train. Because of the split second I'd wasted, Aunty hadn't gotten a seat. I joined her in the corner and held on to a pole. It took all my energy to keep standing.

Taibah Aunty could reach the strap hanging from the ceiling, but she dared not put her arm up over her head. It was too revealing. She ceremoniously pulled a handkerchief out of her purse and placed it around the same pole.

As soon as the train doors closed behind us, she scanned the train car. Seeing there were no desis, no one who would understand us, she asked, "Who was that girl?"

My knees buckled, but I answered. "She's my friend. From school." As if that last part was not obvious.

Her questions came rapid-fire. "Why were you waiting there? I thought your school was in the city?"

"Because the Seven was going to go express." It was a plausible excuse. The 7 often went express for random reasons. Then I'd have to wait at Queensboro for the local.

She kept her gaze steady on me, as if trying to push through my brain with her X-ray vision. She peered and probed, with the expertise of a neurosurgeon.

Every time the train stopped, as the 7 did almost every minute, I took the opportunity to break her gaze and look around, as if trying to find her a seat. Although she was older than most of the other passengers, no one offered her one.

The air became impossible to breathe. The bodies in the subway, the motion of the train, the smells unnerved me. Fears of what would happen next closed in.

Shame began to creep in and break through, like tentacles of a jellyfish pulling into my stomach, my heart, my nether regions, my lungs, my shoulders, my armpits. Shame was there, waiting for me with its beach blanket, wearing sunglasses and drinking iced tea from a container of powdered Lipton.

Finally, we reached Corona Plaza.

"I'll walk you home," Taibah Aunty said. My stomach fell into a crater.

Taibah Aunty walked briskly, and I tried to keep up with her. The streets of Corona were packed with kids coming home from school. Yet to me everything felt removed, moving in slow motion.

When there were no people near us, Taibah Aunty slowed down and looked at me again. "Razia, when I was young, in school, we all had friends like this, close friends." She paused. "Some girls would even write each other letters in blood." My mouth dropped open and I closed it quickly. "These were things we did before marriage. It can't be taken further than school, not for us. You know that, don't you?"

I couldn't believe what Taibah Aunty was saying. Had she had a girlfriend in school in Pakistan?

"It's very important that you're going to that special school. I won't tell your mother, but you have to promise me you'll stop being friends with that girl."

The words rushed up my throat so fast they got clogged like long hair and soap in the drain. I began to improvise wildly. "Aunty. I don't know what you're talking about. She's just a friend. Her parents are going through a divorce and she was feeling upset about it. I was just giving her a hug." It was what I'd watch Angela do: lie, but thread in parts of the truth, letting it guide her eyes and mouth. "I don't know what you think you saw. It's not—it's not like we write each other letters in blood."

"That's not what I meant," Aunty snapped.

We walked the next few blocks in silence. She didn't respond to my made-up story at all. I didn't know what my next move was. Except to survive.

When we arrived at my front door, Taibah Aunty looked at me expectantly. "You don't have a key?"

I shook my head. I was fifteen and I still didn't have a key to my own home. My parents didn't see the need as my mother was always there. Not having a key meant I couldn't get in by myself, but it also meant I couldn't leave, as leaving the door unlocked wasn't safe in Corona.

She reached over me and pressed the doorbell. It buzzed like an angry wasp. I knew we'd have to wait. My mother was always busy. If she was washing dishes, she'd have to wipe the soft bubbles from her hands. If she was cooking, she'd have to mix the salan once more before turning the fire down, in case the conversation at the door went long. If she was vacuuming, she might not even hear the bell at first. Whatever she was doing, she'd wrap her dupatta around her head if it had fallen low and come downstairs at her own pace.

I peeked at Taibah Aunty through the corner of my eye. She stood tall and straight, willing my mother to open the door.

Was it only for me that Taibah Aunty was choosing not to tell? Taibah Aunty, like most of the aunties, was a little frightened of my mother. Maybe she was recalling neighborhood legend, the fight with Saima's family. After my mother had cut off ties with Saima's mother, all the other aunties had stopped hanging out with her as well. Saima's mother had only spoken Pashto and had never been friendly to begin with, so it hadn't been too hard for them to exclude her.

Taibah Aunty didn't want my mother to hate her. Even if—especially if—Taibah Aunty was right, and she was, my mother would avoid her for the rest of her life. I understood, then, her love for my mother.

She turned to me. "I won't tell your mother, but you have to stop being friends with that girl." She was no longer asking for a promise. I noted the distinction.

When my mother came downstairs, her face was shining with sweat. It was a hot day and she'd probably spent hours in the kitchen. Her face showed surprise at seeing Taibah Aunty and then even more surprise at seeing me behind her.

"Asalaamu alaikum," Taibah Aunty said, taking control of the situation. "Razia and I were on the same train and I thought I'd walk her home."

My mother's suspicion warmed into a smile. "Wa alaikum asalaam. How amazing. What a big city and the two of you see each other. Come up for chai."

Taibah Aunty hesitated, as was polite, but of course she was going to drink chai. She stepped inside, and I followed her and my mother up the stairs. My mother had carried me up those stairs as a child. She'd taught me how to walk on them when I'd been a child. I'd swept those stairs as soon as I could hold a broom. Now I climbed them feeling as if my life was ending.

In the living room, Safia was watching cartoons and rocking back and forth on the sofa with her thumb in her mouth. Safia still hadn't spoken a word. For this, my mother saw her as a dream. She showered affection on Safia in a way she'd never done with me. My mother told me I'd been difficult. I'd cried and cried as a baby and never been happy. I'd never been her favorite, even when it was just me.

As soon as she saw me in the doorway to the living room, my mother said, "Razia, what are you doing? Go make some chai. And change your clothes!"

I didn't want to leave them for even a moment. I hurried to the bathroom and changed from my school clothes into salwar kameez, tossing everything to the bottom of the hamper. I rushed to the kitchen to get the chai going. In my haste, I pulled a tea pan from the shelf too fast and all the pans fell hurtling to the ground with a clatter. I heard my mother's and Taibah Aunty's laughter and could imagine the conversation my clumsiness had unleashed.

Sure enough, as soon as I got the pot filled with water and crept back to eavesdrop from behind the curtain between the dining room and living room, my mother was saying, "You know girls these days. Even making a cup of chai is beyond them."

I crept back to the kitchen, not wanting to hear more, hoping the water was boiling and I could put in the tea bags and get the whole thing over with, but there was nothing in the tea bag jar. I rummaged through the kitchen closet and found a box of White Rose. My mother liked Lipton but she got White Rose whenever it was on sale. It tasted stale but it was cheap and came with little animal figurines.

We already had a seal, an owl, and a fox. My mother lined the kitchen window with them. The figurines gave me something to look at all the hours and hours I spent washing dishes. It was better than staring at the brick wall of the building next door.

My fingers trembled as I tried to pull off the tightly wrapped plastic. Taibah Aunty had said she wouldn't say anything if I promised, but I had not promised.

I dug through the tea bags until my hand touched something hard and smooth. It was a miniature lion, the color of chai, his face somber.

The lion watched as the water began to boil and I put the tea bags in. I wanted to go back to eavesdropping, but I needed to give the tea a few moments to steep. I found a box of tea biscuits to give along with the chai.

When the tea had steeped enough, I poured the milk in. It swirled into a tornado of white, blending into caramel and then brown. The aunties all liked their tea milky, so I poured in a little more for good measure. Maybe if I made a superior cup of tea, it would win Taibah Aunty's loyalty and prove I was worth saving.

I tiptoed back and hid behind the curtain. The conversation of how us girls knew nothing practical had flowed into a discussion of school.

"I never made Razia work in the kitchen," my mother said. "I always said, you do the schoolwork. You do well in school. And she has, now she's going to one of the best schools."

I'd never heard my mother boasting about me this way. I felt ashamed for lying to her about how I was doing in school. I'd been hiding all my report cards and my parents never asked to see them. They'd trusted me.

"It's a very good school," Taibah Aunty agreed. "She's a smart girl, but she must be careful. The city is so far away. The kind of friends she meets . . . could be different."

Taibah Aunty couldn't help herself. She couldn't keep her promise. She had to plant a seed of doubt in my mother's mind.

"Razia doesn't have friends from this school. She always comes home right after."

"Yes, but—"

My mother interrupted her. "I'm sure I have nothing to worry about, Taibah." The mothers usually never said one another's names. My mother calling Taibah Aunty by her first name was a warning and Taibah Aunty changed the topic.

"Did you hear about Amir?"

My mother sighed. "It's horrible."

I became alert. Amir? Shahnaaz's older brother?

"Did the police find the men who did it?"

"Of course not. They won't even try."

"Is the family still in Pakistan?"

"Yes, all of them. They wanted to bury him there."

I had been so wrapped up in Angela, I hadn't heard anything of this story. Amir had died? Amir who used to say he'd beat us up if we said Shahnaaz wasn't beautiful? Amir who'd ridden his bike into the fence, making the hole so we could see the sunflowers in the Old Italian's yard?

I leaned in to hear more and the floor creaked.

They fell silent, realizing I was listening. Then we all heard it at the same time, the sound of chai boiling over, the sizzle of milk burning on the stove.

"Razia!" my mother screamed. I ran back, trying to save as much of the chai as I could.

A volcano of brown milky foam was spilling over the edge. I turned off the fire and raised the pot up to bring the volcano down.

There was just enough chai left for Taibah Aunty and my mother. The extra cup I'd put for myself was gone.

I couldn't believe the news about Amir. I hadn't seen Shahnaaz since the Khatum we'd done for the Aunty's husband. I couldn't even cry, I was so stunned. The lion figurine watched me from the side of the stove.

When I brought the tea tray to the living room, the conversation had shifted. Taibah Aunty was talking about her nephews and how well they were doing in their schools in Pakistan.

I put the tray down, and my mother began to pour the chai. I offered Taibah Aunty a tea biscuit. "Thank you," she said. She looked at me as if to say *Remember what I said.*

I excused myself and went to the kitchen, where I paced back and forth in the small space. What had happened to Amir? Was Taibah Aunty going to keep my secret? I picked up the lion figurine and kept pacing. Holding it in my hands calmed me down a bit.

There was a sound behind me. It was Safia. She didn't seem surprised to see me pacing around the kitchen.

"What are they talking about now, Safia?"

Safia didn't answer. She looked at the figurine.

"Oh, this? It's a lion."

She took her thumb out of her mouth. "Lion."

"Oh my God! Safia! You said 'lion'!"

I hugged her close, realizing for the first time that I'd lose Safia if my parents found out about Angela. I'd lose everything if I got caught.

PROM

The collective horror over what had happened to Amir hung over the community, fueling a new fear. A group of Italian boys had beaten Amir up at the family's gas station on Long Island. They'd thrown a book of matches into a pool of gas, setting off an explosion, destroying the station, burning Amir alive. Every time I thought of it, I couldn't speak. I worried all the time with choking breath. I worried about our fathers and brothers getting killed. Of Taibah Aunty breaking her promise and telling my mother about Angela. Of failing out of Stuyvesant.

It was finals, and the reality of what I'd done by missing so much school was hitting me. I was hopelessly lost in all my classes. I had to ace all my finals to get at least "Satisfactory"s on my report card. It was impossible.

It had been raining for days, so we couldn't even go to Stuy Park to study. I felt stir-crazy in her apartment, which now seemed dark, cramped, and filled with dusty books. I still hadn't told Angela about Amir, even though I thought of the explosion at the gas station all the time. It lay inside me, a dark pit of fear, a stone. I kept imagining it in my mind, but I couldn't find the words to speak of it.

"Ugh." Angela sighed. She was struggling with her own pile of makeup assignments. "Do you want some popcorn?"

"Yes, please." I closed my textbook, then my eyes. "Chemistry is giving me a headache."

Angela put a bag of popcorn in the microwave. Quiet at first, the kernels began to pop.

Angela's voice floated in from the kitchen. "Ed asked me to the prom."

"That Ed. He never gives up."

There was nothing then but the sound of exploding kernels. I lay on the sofa, listening to the steady pop, pop, pop.

Her voice came to me from a faraway tunnel. "I said yes."

For a second I didn't know what she was talking about. "Wait, you said yes? Are you joking?"

She came back into the room. "We're just going as friends."

"Does *he* know you're just going as friends?" My voice was more accusatory than I wanted it to be. My heart was racing. The popcorn was popping faster and faster, rushing to a crescendo.

"Of course he does. I told him. Just friends. Come on. I knew you were going to get the wrong idea . . ."

I'd always known there was something between her and Ed. Even if she never admitted it, she liked his attention. It wouldn't be just-as-friends. But all that came from the tumult of my thoughts was: "Why didn't you ask me first?"

"You don't trust me?"

"I don't trust him!"

Her eyes flashed. "Well, it's not like you and I could go together. You're so worried about your family all the time."

My breath caught. My mind went: *What?*

"You were the one who said we shouldn't tell anyone at school. Now I know why!"

The air between us was bitter and heavy. The popcorn had gone silent and there was a smell of burning kernels. Without a word, Angela got up and walked to the kitchen.

I went to the window, trying to calm my breathing down. Drops of rain streaked across the glass. The rain poured down and drenched the earth and, where there wasn't earth, cement. Broken umbrellas sprang from cracks in the sidewalk. The streets filled up. Cars drove through the puddles, splashing passersby.

She came back with burnt popcorn and fresh ammunition. "It's not like you ever let me come to your house!"

I turned around, ready to fight. "Why are you changing the subject? This is about *you* going to the prom with Ed."

But she kept going. "I'm always asking you to sleep over and you never do!"

"I already told you. I can't sleep over at people's houses."

She slammed the popcorn down on the table. "Then why am I always hearing about your sleepover adventures with Taslima?"

Oh my God. Was she jealous of Taslima?

"Angela. It's how—"

"I know," she said, "it's just how your family is." The bitter way she said it made me realize I said the phrase a lot. "I know how *insular* your family is."

I bristled. "What do you mean by that?"

"You know, insular." She said it as if I didn't know what the word meant.

My anger shot up. I thought of the Italian boys who'd burned down the gas station. Who'd thought nothing of killing Amir. "Well, maybe we have to be insular to protect ourselves from people like you! Your people aren't just insular. They kill anyone that's not like them."

"What are you talking about?"

"I'm talking about history! I'm talking about all the hate that comes from white people! I can't believe I ever trusted you!" I was shouting at her in a way I'd never shouted at anyone. It was as if the gas station was exploding in my body. My fury kept building. "And it's not like you're telling your family."

"Even if I did, my family wouldn't chop my head off."

I went cold. The atoms of my hot fury flipped and went below freezing. I needed to get out of there before I started really showing my Corona side and cursing her out. But when I tried to get up, I sank into the sofa like it was quicksand.

I pulled with all my energy to get unstuck. I was so angry and the only thing I knew I could take away from her was me.

I slammed the door behind me.

She didn't follow.

I began to cry as soon as I stepped out the door. On the train ride I kept crying. People noticed and looked away, saying nothing.

At home, my mother was in the kitchen making roti. Safia was eating cookies on the counter. When I saw them, I burst into tears and ran, slamming the bedroom door closed. Still crying, I phoned Taslima. As soon as she answered, I let out all the loud sobs I'd been keeping in the whole train ride home.

My mother began to yell through the door. "Razia, what happened?"

When I didn't answer, she started banging on the door. "Open the door!" There was a terror in her voice I'd never heard before.

Taslima was scared too. "Razia, what's going on?"

I blurted out before my mother could think to go back to the kitchen and pick up the other line, "Angela's going to the prom with Ed."

Taslima was quiet. For weeks, I'd been so consumed with Angela, I'd barely talked to Taslima. Now that I thought about it, Taslima hadn't been reaching out to me either. Even when she'd called to talk about Amir, it had been a short call. We hadn't even talked about ourselves.

Finally she said, "Well, at least you don't have to be a lesbian anymore."

I went silent, disbelieving.

My mother started to bang harder on the door. "Razia! Open this door right now!"

"I gotta go." I hung up the phone. I'd never felt so alone in my life.

I wiped away my tears and opened the door. My mother's face was a mask of fear. "What is it? What happened?"

I looked down. "Nothing. I just had a problem with a friend."

She became angry. "You're crying about a problem with a friend!" She went back to the kitchen, muttering to herself over how soft American children were.

I stayed in the bathroom and cried while vines of shame circled my ankles, covered my legs, and choked my heart. I broke down between the mirrors, my pain blossoming like a rose unfurling.

WILD ROSES

The wild roses had been silently biding their time. Now they erupted over fences, walls, and NO PARKING signs. In the courtyard of Bahar's house they grew thick, their hot-pink heads bent close together. Their petals unfurled, bright and billowing like the saris Bahar's mother always wore. She was the only Pakistani aunty I knew who wore saris.

Bahar's mother tended to the wild roses like the stray dogs she'd adopted long ago. Like the stray dogs, the roses were always on the verge of going feral. She'd say, "When I feel sad, the roses begin to die, so I always smile when I'm around them. The thing is, the roses still know what I'm feeling."

The summer the ants attacked the wild roses was the summer of Amir's funeral. Everyone was surprised when Shahnaaz's parents decided to stay behind in Pakistan and send Shahnaaz back home, a month later, married to one of Bahar's cousins. They moved into Bahar's basement, and he began to manage the family's remaining gas stations. The aunties all criticized Shahnaaz's parents until they were reminded that most of them had been married at fifteen and were just fine.

But when Shahnaaz dropped out of high school, my mother was furious. For days she muttered to herself, "They should have let her finish. What's the use of coming here if they do the same things they did back home?" Then she'd look directly at me. "When you get engaged, we'll tell the family they have to let you go to college."

Before, I would have said, "Ammi, I don't want to get married," but I barely said anything anymore.

I was broken. Angela and I had avoided each other all through finals and prom. Each remaining day of school had been torture, and as soon as school ended, I never left the house. All I did was lie on the couch.

My mother didn't know what was wrong with me, but she did know she'd had enough of me watching cartoons all day with Safia. She came into the living room and stood in front of the TV. The ponies from *My Little Pony* jumped around behind her on the screen. Safia looked over at me, her thumb still in her mouth.

"Did you and Taslima have a fight?" My mother's eyes searched mine. I knew she wasn't necessarily wanting me and Taslima to hang out, but the mothers had been talking.

"No," I said, but I was still mad at Taslima, and my mother could tell.

"Well, if you don't want to see Taslima, go visit Shahnaaz. She's been alone ever since she came back."

"What about her husband?" The peevishness in my voice was too much. I'd never have spoken to her that way before, but the pain I felt toward Angela had become a festering wound. The bile spilled over.

My mother became angry. "You're going." Then, catching herself before she lost her temper, she said, "When I was a new bride it was so hard for me."

I couldn't stop myself. "But, Ammi, you moved to a whole new country. Shahnaaz is just back in Corona."

She gave me a look of disgust. Shahnaaz had lost her brother. She'd gotten married to a stranger and dropped out of school. What kind of heart did I have? One that wasn't functioning at all.

"Her parents aren't here," my mother finally said. "Your country is where your parents are."

I followed my mother to the bedroom. "I'm sorry, Ammi," I said. She was looking through the cabinet where she kept her most precious possessions: her jewelry, money, a bag of Hershey's Kisses.

"I'm sorry," I said again. "I'll go."

She sighed. "I don't know what's gotten into you lately."

All I could do was say sorry. I felt like the worst person in the world.

She found a book in her cabinet and held it out to me. "I want you to give this to Shahnaaz."

"Are you giving her a Quran?"

For a second I thought she was going to slap me. "You don't know the difference between the Quran and another book? It's the *Bahishti Zewar*." I now saw the cover had ornamental Urdu writing on it, flowers with the ink spilling out. "Your Maji gave it to me after I got married."

Feeling jealous my mother would give Shahnaaz something so precious, I said, "Does Shahnaaz even read Urdu?"

"I taught her to read Arbi, so she can figure out how to read Urdu."

I remembered all the times Shahnaaz had run off during Quran class. I wasn't sure she could read Arbi, but I didn't correct my mother.

"This is a book all women should read. It taught me everything. You would benefit from reading it too." She opened to a random page. "Mahr . . . This is what a boy's family must pay the girl's family before marrying her."

"So he buys her?"

"Oh my God, you misunderstand everything! The money goes to the girl's family and then they give it to her so she can have her own money if anything happens. You don't understand this, but Islam is good to women."

My mother gave me another withering look. Maybe it would be good to get out of the house and visit Shahnaaz.

When I got to Bahar's, her mother was in the courtyard, fussing over the wild roses.

"They're dying," she said. And indeed they were brown and shriveling. She had a bottle of neem oil in her hand and, being careful of the thorns, she was oiling each stem, as if it was a strand of thick hair.

Our mothers couldn't help but put teyl on everything.

"Come in. Do you want some chai?"

I was being offered chai? Shahnaaz becoming a married woman had suddenly made me an aunty too.

With one last look at the roses, she ushered me inside.

"The stove downstairs isn't working. You can have chai upstairs."

"No, that's okay, Aunty." I knew chai meant a long visit and I was already feeling like I should be in and out fast.

"I think Shahnaaz is in the kitchen making dinner."

Shahnaaz cooking? I tried to hide the stunned expression on my face.

Sure enough, she was in the kitchen over two pots, stirring. Shahnaaz used to be like all of us, wearing worn-out salwar kameez, with dirt on her face and cheeks. Now she looked like a miniature aunty. She was wearing thick makeup, like a dangerous circus bear wearing lipstick. It made me wonder who all the aunties had been before.

When she saw me, she acted like she didn't know me. As if we had no history. Not knowing what else to do, I handed her the *Bahishti Zewar*. "Congratulations."

As soon as she opened her mouth, though, she was still the same old Shahnaaz. "What's this? A book?" She took it from me like it was a dirty sock.

"It's a book every married woman should have," I quoted my mother.

But instead of laughing, Shahnaaz frowned. "Yeah, you know, I don't really like books."

Even when we'd been young, Shahnaaz had fled from the Quran, from schoolwork, from any printed word.

Bahar's mother laughed nervously. She'd been standing behind us, watching to see how Shahnaaz would act. Why was everyone being so weird? Marriage made people weird.

"I'll finish making dinner," Bahar's mother said. "Why don't you go downstairs and see how Shahnaaz has fixed the apartment up?"

The door down to the basement was right next to the kitchen. Each step we descended, the smell of mold and the sickening smell of air freshener, canned roses, grew stronger. There was a sitting room at the bottom of the basement stairs. The ceiling was low, the room dark. There was too much furniture: one armchair, two mismatched chairs, a lamp that had no shade, just a light bulb floating in space.

There were suitcases piled in the corner. All our homes had these suitcases out in the open, as if we were ready to escape at any time. I noticed Shahnaaz's book bag cowering in the corner like a mouse.

I recognized the television and VCR as the ones that used to be in Bahar's TV room. There was no doily on it to keep it safe from dust. Was it only last summer that Taslima and Shahnaaz had danced while watching *Silsila*? It all felt so long ago.

On the wall there was a framed photo of Shahnaaz and her husband. It was the first time I was seeing him. He stood a head taller than her. He had a mustache, a scared look on his face, as if he was being hunted. Shahnaaz was wearing a hot-pink garara and was heavy with gold jewelry. Unlike Bahar, who had worn her bridal clothes majestically, Shahnaaz looked like she was wearing a costume. It was clear they'd been asked to stand together. Their bodies angled in different ways with inches between them.

I don't know why I'd thought Shahnaaz would be hosting me. She plopped down on the sofa and turned on the television. She flipped through the channels. *Days of Our Lives* was just coming on and she stopped.

I knew better than to interrupt. "What do you do all day?" I asked when a commercial came on.

"What do you mean what do I do? My husband, he goes to the gas station. I talk to my parents on the phone. I watch TV. It's easy."

"So you're not going back to school?"

"What do I need school for? I'm set. My husband gets me whatever I want."

I remembered how her father used to buy her things, like the golden locket she'd shown off.

"Do you ever see Saima?" I tried to sound casual, even though saying her name still brought up a deep ache.

"Nah. She spends all her time with Hafiz Saab's wife." She had a name but we still called her Hafiz Saab's wife. "Now that I have my husband, I don't need anyone else."

Tears filled my eyes and I turned away so Shahnaaz couldn't see. I had felt that way with Angela. We hadn't needed anyone else.

Shahnaaz made it clear that she didn't want to talk. We sat in our thoughts, watching TV, like two girls on opposite sides of the fence, so close together but in two different worlds. For the rest of the hour we sat in silence, watching the characters on *Days* struggle to live and still love each other.

The next weekend, Bahar's mother hosted a tea for my mother and Taslima's mother. When we walked in, Taslima was sitting in a circle of chairs around the tea table with her mother, Bahar's mother, and Bahar, who'd come to help her mother host. Shahnaaz was still in the basement getting ready.

Taslima got up to say hello but I gave her the cold shoulder and instead brought Safia to the bedroom where Bahar's son was watching cartoons, his eyes glazing over. I was relieved Taslima didn't follow me. I wanted to tell her how angry I was, I wanted to tell her how much I was hurting, but I knew she'd just make a comment that would make it worse.

I stayed with Mittoo and Safia, watching cartoons until my mother called me to come back out. She didn't say anything about me being rude. She probably didn't want to draw attention to my odd behavior.

Bahar poured chai for everyone, then put the teapot down. "So who's next to get married?"

Taslima almost spat out her chai. I couldn't help but laugh.

"It should be Aliza," Bahar continued, "but she's not here. Are there any plans for her, Aunty?" Bahar was asking casually but there was barbed wire in her comment, broken glass on top of a wall. Everyone in the neighborhood still gossiped about Aliza going to college without an engagement.

Taslima's mother smiled. "I didn't get married until after I finished college."

There was an awkward silence. None of the other aunties had gone to college. Some, like my mother, hadn't gone to school at all. In defending Aliza, Taslima's mother had accidentally taken on airs.

Taslima and I looked from one to another. Taslima took a cookie to break the tension. Her teeth made a loud noise, cracking it open. Her mother shot her a dark look.

Bahar, though, couldn't be deterred. "But, Aunty, Aliza has to get married!"

I don't know what came over me, but I blurted out, "But why, why do we all have to get married?"

I'd taken it too far. The mothers yelled in unison, "You have to get married!"

Mittoo, scared by all the raised voices, came running for Bahar. She picked him up and cuddled him. "Don't you want to have children?"

I did want to have children. I just didn't want to get married.

"Why can't we just get jobs and have babies?" Taslima asked. She looked over at me and I could tell she was trying to be friends again.

Bahar's mother threw her hands up in the air. "Oh my God, these American girls are crazy. You can't get a baby from a job."

"But you can have children without getting married," I said.

They looked at me, shocked. "Who told you that?"

My mother glared at me to stop talking.

I tried to backtrack. "I mean adopt them."

It was at times like this that I missed Aliza terribly. She would know what to say to make the aunties laugh and change the subject.

Bahar's mother took a sip from her chai. "One day you're going to be old. Then who will take care of you?"

"But won't our husbands be old too?" Taslima asked. "Maybe even older?"

"Not your husband! Your children will take care of you." Bahar's mother shook her head. It was like they were talking to the stupidest people.

"You won't always be young and beautiful," Bahar added. "You have to get married while you still are."

I'd never imagined myself as young and beautiful to begin with.

My mother pointed to Bahar's mother. "She was beautiful before, now look at her."

"And what's wrong with me now?" Bahar's mother responded. They all started laughing. Even Bahar's mother.

"But what if I want to travel?" Taslima was not realizing she was up against experts in circular logic.

"You can travel *after* you get married," my mother said, "with your husband."

Then Taslima asked the real question. "But what about love?"

All the aunties began to laugh. It was as if Taslima had said the funniest thing in the world.

"Love?" Bahar's mother tried to stop laughing. "You mean what Americans call love? That's lust! When the attraction goes, they move on to the next thing."

I felt a stabbing feeling in my body. Had Angela moved on to the next thing? Was she already with Ed?

"Look at these Americans!" Bahar said. "They marry for love and then the next thing you know they're getting divorces. The women are the ones who are left behind to take care of the children."

There was a perverse logic to everything they said. Most of the kids I knew from school, their fathers were out of the picture. Even Angela was still upset because of her parents' divorce. Is that why she couldn't love me?

"Americans don't understand the first thing about love," Taslima's mother added. "If they understood love, would they do all the terrible things they do in the world, bringing war everywhere?"

The aunties nodded. They were all news junkies. They didn't just watch the nightly news. They listened to BBC, watched CNN. They knew more about what was happening in the world than I did.

My mother shook her head. "If they understood love, they wouldn't do such things, killing so many innocent people for money and power."

Safia came into the room, needing to go to the bathroom. My mother got up to take her.

"Where's Shahnaaz and her husband?" Taslima's mother asked, looking to move on. When she said "husband," the aunties giggled in an awkward way that made me nervous.

Bahar's mother turned to me. "Razia, can you go get her?"

I got up with relief. Taslima looked at me, as if I was going to ask her to come, but I walked away. I felt like a buried land mine, upset at everyone.

At the basement door I heard voices. At first I couldn't tell if Shahnaaz and her husband were being really loud or if the sound just traveled up the basement stairs. Then it was unmistakable. Shahnaaz was saying something to her husband, impatience in her voice. She began to scream at him. He screamed back. Then there was a thud. The screaming stopped abruptly.

I ran back to the living room. My mother still wasn't there. Everyone was sitting frozen. The teacups shivered and trembled in their hands as a steady thud thud thud began to come from downstairs.

Taslima and her mother stood up, confused. Just then my mother returned with Safia. "What's going on down there?"

"Ammi, you have to come!" I grabbed her kameez and pulled her to the basement door. Hearing the blows intensify, she almost ripped off the handle. Minutes later she was upstairs with Shahnaaz. Her hair was messed up. Her lip were smashed. One of her eyes was swollen and starting to shut.

We heard a car door slam. He'd gone out through the back door and run off.

Shahnaaz locked herself in the bathroom and my mother came back to the living room. She glared at Bahar and her mother. "What kind of Muslims are you?"

They looked down into their tea cups, ashamed.

Shahnaaz came to live with us. She took over my bedroom and slept morning till night, or at least pretended to. I waited for my mother to say something, but she didn't.

In Shahnaaz's heartbroken body, I saw my inert shadow body. Shahnaaz could grieve like this out in the open, while I had to carry my pain over Angela hidden, under folds and folds of blankets. Then again, everyone looked at Shahnaaz and felt pity. Everyone knew her business. I didn't know which was worse.

On the third day, my mother woke Shahnaaz up and said, "I need your help."

Shahnaaz's hair was wild and uncombed. Her breath stank from far off. My mother took on the voice she'd used when we were children and she was teaching Sabak. "Take a shower. I've put some of Razia's clothes on the bed. You can change into them." Before I could say anything, my mother shot me a look. I realized we'd left the house without any of Shahnaaz's belongings.

My mother put a sheet down in the living room in the sun. In the center she put an empty bowl. Then she brought out a bag of garlic and three peeling knives.

Shahnaaz came out of the shower. She was much thinner than me and floated in my salwar kameez. The sun streamed in through the windows. She peeled in silence, until my mother began to tell a story:

"There was a girl in our village. She was my best friend. We were such foolish girls. We didn't know anything. We used to be like you two and Saima, always getting into trouble, always running around, tearing and dirtying our clothes. Our mothers called us junglees."

With a jarring feeling I realized my mother had always known what we'd been up to as children. I'd always thought we were invisible from her eyes.

"She was the first to get married. Back then, we all got married as soon as we got our 'you know.'" If Taslima had been there, she would have teased my mother: "Our what?" But we didn't interrupt.

"All the brothers in that family beat and terrorized their wives. Everyone told her family not to marry into that family." My mother sighed. "But what choice did they have? This man had fields to work in. Most in the village were hungry."

I thought that Shahnaaz would get angry at my mother for bringing up a story like this, but she was riveted. "What happened to her?"

"He killed her."

"Oh!" Shahnaaz was not as used to my mother's stories as I was. Even I stopped, knife in midair, until my mother said, "Keep peeling!"

It was as if my mother knew Shahnaaz needed a horror larger than the one she was going through to bring her back to her senses.

"In the days after she was killed, the villagers kept saying they saw her. One saw her wandering near the graveyard, another on the side of the road. Then the younger brother said she was lingering near the bathroom. Back then the toilets used to be outside. Her hair was wild and uncombed but otherwise she looked the same. When he looked down, though, he saw her feet had been twisted backward. She'd become a Chureyl."

"A Chureyl?"

"Yes, they're demon women who hunt the men who've killed them."

I imagined Shahnaaz as a Chureyl, wandering the streets of Corona. "Would a Chureyl ever hunt a woman?" I asked.

"Why would they?" My mother was annoyed by my question.

Shahnaaz looked at me and I saw something cross her face.

My mother continued. "The youngest brother disappeared one night when he was coming back from his work in the fields. Then the second son disappeared and finally her husband, the eldest, the one who'd killed her. All their bodies were found mangled on the side of the road. Their clothes had been torn off.

"My friend, she didn't have choices the way you do." For a moment my mother was silent, peeling garlic. "It's a terrible thing to become a demon forever."

After that, Shahnaaz began to follow my mother around. I'd walk in on them, their heads bent together, reading the *Bahishti Zewar*. They'd watch *Days of Our Lives*, gossiping about the characters as if they were people we knew from Corona. My mother began to teach her how to cook. She'd never even let me into the kitchen. She always said my schoolwork was too important.

My mother said, "Do you see how Shahnaaz has gotten so good? She was such a wild thing before." Then, seeing the look on my face and re-alizing what she was saying, she said, gruff, "Not all husbands do that."

"Then why do we allow it?"

"Didn't I go and get her?" With all the patience she had with Shahnaaz, she had none left for me.

I secretly began to wish Shahnaaz would go back to her husband. Then I'd feel guilty and pray to Allah to open my heart.

One afternoon, it was just Shahnaaz and me. It had only been a week, but it felt like years. My mother had gone with Safia to Key Food. Tak-ing advantage of my mother not being home, Shahnaaz was lying down in my former bedroom and I was in the living room. I still had the stacks of books from the Strand, untouched. I picked up the book on top, *Song of Solomon*, and began to read, hoping to disappear from my own life.

When I came to the story of Milkman's lonely sisters: *His sister made roses in the afternoon. Bright, lifeless roses that lay in peck baskets for months* . . . my heart ached so much, I had to stop reading. As soon as I did, I got lost in the memory of going to the Strand with Angela.

The phone rang, but I didn't want to get up. We didn't have an answering machine, and the phone kept ringing. Still, I was surprised when Shahnaaz picked it up. She was really making herself at home.

"Razia!" Shahnaaz yelled out. "It's some girl named Angela."

The world blurred. I lost my place.

Shahnaaz came into the room and eyed me. It was odd for anyone outside of our community to call me at home. I went into the bedroom and picked up the phone receiver, afraid to hear her voice. Afraid what it would do to me.

"Razia?" I remembered all the times she'd whispered my name. "I just wanted to see how you were?" I was silent. "Razia, I miss you."

"How was prom?" My words were a knife.

"It was terrible."

Was that why she was calling me? For comfort?

"I have to go." Without waiting for a response, I hung up. Shahnaaz came into the room. I realized I hadn't heard the click of Shahnaaz putting the other line down. She'd heard everything.

"Who's that?"

"Someone."

I saw the old Shahnaaz in the way she studied me, mocking. I became wary.

"She's your girlfriend, isn't she?" She sat down across from me. "In Pakistan all the girls have girlfriends before they get married."

What was this about Pakistan and everyone having girlfriends?

But Angela hadn't just been someone I was going to be with until I got married. Then it hit me. Maybe that was what I'd been for her.

Shahnaaz didn't say anything at first. She stared at me until I had to look away. I wasn't in the mood for a staring contest. I got up to leave the room. When I was almost out the door, she said, "I used to hide the places he hit me with makeup."

I stopped, my back still to her. "But didn't Bahar's family know?"

"If they did, they didn't say anything."

I turned. The child Shahnaaz began to grow in my eyes until she fully emerged.

"What? Why are you staring at me?"

"You look like you did when we were kids."

"When we were kids," she snorted, "that was terrible."

"What do you mean? We were always playing."

"You and Saima always left me out of everything."

"Left you out?" And then I saw her at the fence, her hands grabbing at it, trying to get our attention. For the first time, I saw the lonely look on her face.

"My husband is the only person who cared for me." She said "husband" like it was a broken vase she still loved. "We were so much happier in Pakistan. Every evening, we'd go out for ice cream. In Pakistan, people know how to live. It's not like here with work, work, work all the time. For our honeymoon, he took me to the mountains in Swat. Pakistan is so beautiful, like the scenes in all those Indian movies. It's nothing like this." She waved her arm at Corona. It shriveled under her gaze.

"Here there's so much responsibility on him. He has to manage all the gas stations. And the people who come through. You don't know how these people can be. How they treat him." As she spoke I saw it, the sudden gripping of her chair. "Terrible. They're murderers." Her voice broke. "Every night I'm afraid he won't come home."

She had not mentioned Amir at all to me or anyone. The ghost of Amir grew and grew until it filled the room. Neither of us breathed. Shahnaaz was like me, we'd never allow ourselves to cry in front of anyone.

"So she was your girlfriend?"

"I don't think she would have called it that," I finally admitted.

Shahnaaz began to spend all morning in the bathroom. I would be dying to go, my legs twisted together like pretzels, begging her to hurry up. One morning I heard her throwing up. I went and told my mother. She looked alarmed.

My mother leaned into the door. "Shahnaaz? Are you feeling okay?" My mother never showed me so much care when I threw up. She usually just seemed annoyed because it was more work for her.

When Shahnaaz opened the door, though, she looked terrible. Her face was bloated. Her hair stuck up everywhere. My mother and her looked at each other and something boundless passed between them.

Shahnaaz began to talk to her husband on the phone when my mother went out. When I caught her, she looked guilty. "You keep my secret and I'll keep yours."

"What secret? I don't have a secret." But I was a terrible liar.

I was so lonely I thought I was going to die. Finally, I called Taslima. She seemed surprised but didn't say anything. She just let me vent about Shahnaaz.

"She has a stomach virus, so what? My mother babies her so much."

"Don't you know anything, Razia? When a married woman throws up, it's different."

"How?"

Exasperated with how little I knew, she said, "She's pregnant, Razia!"

"What?!"

"Razia!" my mother said sharply. "Get off the phone. I need to make a call."

There was a collective forgetting among the aunties.

"The child needs a father."

"How will she work and take care of the child?"

"She'll be in trouble. How long can she stay with others?"

"She didn't even finish high school."

But whose fault was that?

My mother began to send me to Key Food to get fruit for Shahnaaz. One afternoon, I came home and Saima and Hafiz Saab's wife were sitting at the dining table with Shahnaaz and my mother. There was a bowl of wild roses on the table. Cut at odd angles, their hot-pink heads floated in the air above the bowl.

"These are from him," Shahnaaz said to me, as if I was the only one who didn't know.

I stared at them. Their leaves were as sharp as teeth, asking for blood.

Hafiz Saab's wife and Saima had brought Shahnaaz's book bag to pack up anything she needed. I watched Shahnaaz pack one of my favorite salwar kameez but I said nothing. My mother was helpless to stop her. She wasn't Shahnaaz's real mother.

Saima and Hafiz Saab's wife led Shahnaaz out, the way brides were led out on wedding days. They left the wild roses behind.

As soon as they left, my mother picked up the whole bowl, roses and all, and threw it in the garbage.

I became afraid. "Ammi," I said, "what if Shahnaaz turns into a Chureyl?"

My mother became angry at me, as if I was being naive, childish. "There are no Chureyls in Corona. Here there are no forests, and the bathrooms are inside. Here there's no place to hide."

GRAND CENTRAL

The next morning, the air was different. Safia was gone. It wasn't just that she wasn't in our bedroom. I couldn't hear a sound of her anywhere else in the house. I got up to look but stopped short when I passed my parents' room.

My father was sitting on the bed. I'd never seen him home during the day. Then I saw the pile: my diary, photos, notes from Angela. Everything I'd kept hidden. He held up my diary. "Razia. What is this?" His hands shook. I thought of everything I'd written about Angela and felt my insides shriveling. He flipped through the pages and stopped at one. His face turned red. "What you write about this girl. In Pakistan, they'd kill you. For this you'll burn in Hell."

I was used to my mother saying I'd burn in Hell, but coming from my father, the words shook me.

My father closed his eyes in real pain, as if he could already see me burning. "Do you know Allah will make us watch you be tortured for allowing you to do this? Do you think we could bear that?"

I'd heard this teaching before, but now for the first time, I felt enraged. Even when it was me burning in Hell, it still somehow became about them and how it would make them suffer. They never saw how selfish they were. I mean, I was the one burning. They just had to watch.

But there was no way I could argue with them and what they believed. I knew this. So I did all I could in the situation. I lied. "Just because I wrote it doesn't mean it's true. I was just writing."

My mother stepped into the room. She'd been listening from the other side of the door. "If it's not true, then why did you write it?"

"I just wrote it. I had to."

"Just wrote it!" My mother's voice rose. "Just wrote it!"

"Had to?" my father asked. "Who made you do this? Who made you write this?" There was relief in his voice. Perhaps it was someone else's fault.

"Taslima?" my mother asked. "That friend Angela?"

"No, not Taslima," I managed to say. I didn't need her to get into trouble.

I didn't deny Angela. I was afraid to say her name, afraid of my body trembling like grass. I clasped my hands to stop them from shaking.

"You can stop lying," my mother said. "I got a call from Hafiz Saab's wife this morning. Saima told her."

"Saima? I never even talk to Saima!"

"She heard from Shahnaaz."

I felt the ground give way underneath me. Shahnaaz! I remembered the phone call, and then with a sickening feeling all the times I'd felt my diary had been moved, when I'd felt the touch of another hand on it. Shahnaaz had been reading my diary. Fear surged through my body. Why hadn't I hidden my diary somewhere else? What had I been thinking?

I knew Shahnaaz would do something like this, but Saima? Had she thought she was trying to save my soul? She didn't know. She didn't know anything about me or my soul.

"I was crazy enough to defend you," my mother continued. "I said it was a lie, but now your father has read it in your own words . . . He talked to Uncle Fadi in the embassy. He can get us a rush visa. We're going to Pakistan."

Everything was happening in fast motion. I knew what all this was code for. They thought they were tricking me. But I knew what happened to girls when they went to Pakistan on rush visas.

A strange sense of unreality kicked in. I became oddly calm. I breathed in and out. And then I saw the strangest thing. A mouse just sitting there watching us. When I blinked it was gone.

I took a breath and began. "But—"

"No 'but'!" My mother's voice rose. "We've trusted you and spoiled you for too long."

I looked at my father. I could tell he was trying to keep his voice calm. "You made a mistake. But we can fix this."

I couldn't believe what I was hearing. I'd always thought my father understood me, but if he did, how could he ever think of marrying me off to someone I didn't know? I knew he thought this was the way it was done. But for me? For me?

I loved my father. I wanted to be the daughter he wanted me to be, but I couldn't, couldn't, couldn't get married to a stranger from Pakistan. This was not how my life was supposed to be. There was something else there, right behind the curtain. I didn't know what it was, but if I could just put my hand through, I could almost touch it.

I couldn't keep it in anymore. I started talking like I was outside on the street. "Are you kidding me? Are you kidding me!" Then it came to me in my fiery rage. The light. I raised my voice louder. "No! I can't! I won't do it! I won't!"

My father's face turned to a mask of ash. I'd become a stranger to him. He'd become a stranger to me.

My mother got up suddenly from the bed. Terrified she was going to hit me, I jumped up and, without thinking, ran out of the room. I grabbed my book bag, slipped on my shoes, and ran down the stairs and out the front door.

I ran past the bodega, past the masjid, past Linden Park. My breath came out ragged, my chest burned. I didn't stop until I got to the 103rd Street train station.

There was a pay phone at the bottom of the staircase. I looked in my book bag and found a quarter in the front pocket. I dropped it into the slot and dialed Taslima. It didn't matter if I was angry at her, or if she didn't support me and Angela. She'd know what to do.

The line was busy. I tried again. I listened to the steady *toon, toon, toon* of the busy signal, until it started to bore holes in my head.

I heard the train from above and ran up the subway stairs. There were people exiting through the emergency gate and I pushed past them, not waiting to get the station person's attention. I barely caught the train heading to the city.

With no real memories of how I got there, I ended up at Grand

Central station. I was so used to getting out and switching to the 4 that I just stepped out of the train without thinking. The platform was crowded. I couldn't breathe. I needed to get aboveground.

I took escalator after escalator. Instead of ending up on the street, I found myself in an enormous cavern, all marble and light, like a cathedral. The air was hushed. In the center there was a clock with a gorgeous globe of a head, gold plated with four round faces turned in each direction. All the movement circled around the clock. There were men in suits, moving fast, a blur of families, flashing camera bulbs, and a kind of quiet that was odd considering how many people there were. The noise rose and disappeared.

I looked up to see stars. Almost a century of ash and soot had floated its way to the ceiling and gotten caught in the night sky, hiding the constellations, but I could still see little points of light shining through the dark layer of dust.

I slid to the floor in a corner, under a bank of pay phones. The metal railings I'd been using to keep my body from crumpling collapsed. I had no one to call. I didn't have Aliza's number. Taslima wasn't answering. For a second the longing to hear Angela's voice was so strong, I felt faint.

I picked up the phone handle and put it back down a dozen times, my fear and desire dissolving my anger. I knew I shouldn't forgive her, but I needed help. I took a breath, fished the quarter out of my pocket, and put it back in, holding the receiver to my ear, cradling it near my cheek.

Angela answered after a few rings. "Razia?" She sounded nervous. "Razia, I'm so sorry. I should never have said yes to Ed. I shouldn't have gone to the prom with him."

"Angela, I can't even think about that right now. It doesn't matter anymore." I knew I was being harsh, but I was hardening myself, putting parts of myself into storage, conserving my energy. Nothing mattered other than escaping, other than getting away as fast and far as possible.

"Angela, my parents. They're sending me to Pakistan to get married."

"What? What are you talking about?"

"They're getting me a visa to go there right away."

"They can't do that. It's against the law!"

Angela would never understand. It didn't matter if it was against the law. My parents would get me to do it. I could only hold out for so long if they put the pressure on me.

"But why are they doing this all of a sudden?"

"They found out about us."

"Oh my God."

"I guess you were right about them. It's not chopping my head off but—"

"I'm so stupid. I should never have said anything like that. Can you come here, please?"

"No, I have to get out of here." As soon as I said it, I knew it was true. I sank back down to the floor, still holding the phone cord. It uncoiled like one of Angela's curls in my fingers.

She was silent for a moment before she said, "I have a cousin, Rebecca. She's living in this town. It's next door to Salem. What's it called?" I could hear her click her teeth on the other end.

"Angela!" I snapped. "Why are you telling me this story?"

"Oh yeah, Beverly. She kicked her boyfriend out and now she needs a roommate. It's easy to get there. Well, almost easy . . ." She trailed off. "Where are you?"

"Grand Central."

"That's good. The bus to Boston is close, in Times Square."

"Times Square? I can't go to Times Square! Hustlers will smell the runaway on me!" My life was starting to spiral into a terrible after-school miniseries.

"I'll come meet you."

"You will?" My head cleared a bit. "Wait, Beverly. Isn't—"

"Yes! That's what made me think of my cousin!"

We both said it at the same time: "*The Crucible!*"

The Crucible was the last book we'd read in English.

"Oh man. I didn't bring anything to read." It was so random and ridiculous that we both started laughing. My laughter felt hysterical, my throat raw, but it felt good.

"Where are you in Grand Central?"

"By the phones."

"Well, duh. You're *on* the phone!"

I looked around. "I'm next to a water fountain that looks like a lion."

"What?"

A gush of people rushed by. They were coming from a doorway cut into the marble wall. I looked at the numbers carved above the entrance. "I'm next to Track Twenty-Nine."

The recording of the operator cut in. "Please deposit twenty-five cen—"

"Save your quarter. I'll be there as soon as possible."

I sank back to my place on the floor and looked up at the stars on the ceiling. My life felt as unreal as those stars. It was as if my body was floating. I leaned my cheek against the marble, only to be hit with a shuddering cold, as if I really was in outer space.

A memory came back to me. When I was first learning how to answer the phone, it was always my father calling. I'd pick up the phone, say salaam, and ask, "Do you want to talk to Ammi?" My father would always answer, "No, I want to talk to you."

My heart clenched. How could I leave my father, who'd sacrificed his life working himself into the ground for us; my mother, who'd done nothing but take care of the family? How could I leave Safia behind? What would happen to her without my protection? What would they tell her about me?

I didn't know how long I stayed on the floor before I had the energy to get up and call Taslima again. This time she answered.

"Oh my God," I breathed. "I've been calling and calling."

"Your mother's been calling too!" She lowered her voice to a whisper. "Are you okay? Your mother came here in the morning and dropped off Safia. Now my mother keeps asking me where you are. What happened?"

"My parents found out about Angela."

Taslima gasped. "What? How?" This was the Code One emergency we'd been preparing for ever since we started rebelling.

"Shahnaaz."

"Shahnaaz! How dare she!"

"Well, she told Saima, and Saima told Hafiz Saab's wife. My parents said it wasn't true, but then my father read my diary."

"Oh my God! Razia! Why do you have to write about everything?"

"I don't know," I said. "I just have to." My voice broke and she realized she wasn't being helpful.

"I'm sorry. What—" She stopped midsentence. "Oh no, my mother's home. Where are you? I'll figure out how to get to you."

I didn't know if I should tell her. If I didn't, then they couldn't get the information out of her. But I really needed Taslima. The recording interrupted again: "Please deposit twenty-five cents."

"Grand Central!" I said quickly. "I'm in Grand Central. Track Twenty-Nine. Next to a water fountain that looks like a lion."

"Razia, you know there's no such thing as a water fountain that looks like a lion!"

The call cut off while we were still laughing.

Angela arrived first, carrying a half-stuffed duffel bag. She looked like a humpback whale or turtle. She dropped the bag and ran to me. We stood in front of each other, awkward. Then she hugged me. I leaned into her, but then pulled away, embarrassed by my need.

I touched the green army bag with the tip of my sneaker. "Where'd you get this?" Then, with an irrational hope, I asked, "Are you running away with me?"

"I can't. My parents would kill me . . ." She stopped, thinking she was offending me, then asked, "What's going to happen?"

I stared at the duffel bag, hiding my face. "I don't know."

She blinked away tears and looked down at the bag. "It's my dad's from when he almost went AWOL in Vietnam. But the war ended, and he didn't have to run away. See, you're helping this bag fulfill its purpose." She opened the top of the duffel bag like an army Santa Claus. "I brought you some stuff. There's some jeans in here, I figure we're almost the same size, and oh—this." She pulled out a forest-green sweater with tiny bottle-glass-green buttons. "It's a little colder up there, and I wasn't sure if you had a sweater."

Not only did I not have a sweater, it occurred to me that I didn't have underwear, socks, anything.

She saw the look on my face. "Don't worry. My cousin will help you go shopping."

"But—" I was about to say I didn't have any money when Angela reached into her book bag and pulled out an envelope.

"This is money I've been saving from Christmases and birthdays. I get double now with my parents being divorced. This is just half. It's still the same amount for me."

Inside, there was a small pamphlet of twenties. I couldn't believe I was holding so much money.

"It's for the bus ticket. Whatever's left is for food and sundries."

I smiled. "Sundries" was one of the words we'd started using after reading *The Crucible*.

"My cousin said you can stay the rest of the month for free at her place since she's not giving her boyfriend his rent or security back."

"Oh, man," I said. "I hope she changes the keys."

"She did! See? You two are totally going to get along." I couldn't help but smile. "My cousin said it's easy to get a job this time of year. Right before the summer rush. All the tourist places in Salem are looking for warm bodies. She's a server at the brewery and she makes good money there."

A bar?

Angela saw the look on my face and laughed. "Don't worry. You're too young to work at a brewery. But Rebecca said you're old enough for the witchy tourist jobs. She asked one of her coworkers who grew up in Salem." There were already so many people talking about me.

She rummaged more through the bag and pulled out a tissue-paper-wrapped bundle. She placed it in my arms. "I want you to have these too." I opened up the soft white paper. Her favorite black-and-gold-striped leg warmers were inside. "Now when you look down at your legs, you'll think of me."

"Of course I'm going to be thinking of you." All my feelings flooded through me. There was no space to even be mad at her.

She put her arms around me. The stone of ice inside me began to melt, and she was crying, and I was crying, holding her, not caring anymore what anyone thought.

When Taslima arrived, Angela and I were still wrapped around each other. Taslima stared at us but quickly recovered. I couldn't tell from her face what she was thinking.

I jumped up, a little flustered. "You got out!"

She looked back and forth between us, giving Angela her meanest glare. "Yeah. My mother was coming in the side door and I ran out the front door."

"Wow. I didn't even know the front door opened."

"It was jammed but I figured it out."

Angela stood up. "I can't believe I'm finally meeting you. You're famous in Razia's world."

Taslima gave her another look. Finally she just said, "But of course," in a fake British accent. She looked at the duffel bag. "What's that?"

"Angela brought it."

"I didn't have time to bring you anything."

"Are you kidding? I'm so glad you're here."

Realizing I needed time alone with Taslima, Angela said, "I'll get coffee. Three coffees?"

"Yes," Taslima said. She didn't drink coffee, but I knew she wanted Angela to leave. As soon as Angela walked away, she asked, "Are you back together now?" She sounded angry. "Do you trust her? Even after that thing she pulled with the prom?"

"She found me a place to stay at her cousin's near Boston."

"Boston! Are you kidding me? I don't trust her. How do you know you're not going to get sold into white slavery with this cousin?"

"Taslima! First of all, white slavery is when white people are sold into slavery. When it's called slavery, it's assumed white people are doing the enslaving."

"That's what I'm talking about! How can you trust her?"

"Come on, Taslima, you're sounding like my mother."

"Why don't you go to Aliza's dorm?"

"Because it'll be the first place they'll look."

I was amazed by my own survival skills. It was as if I always knew this day was going to come. Like there was another voice, an older voice, telling me what to do.

Taslima sighed. "Okay." She pulled a piece of paper out of her pocket. "Here's Aliza's number at her dorm. Call her and give her your new number. I'll get the number for the pay phone at my school so we can talk. You can call me from there."

"That's so smart."

"All the girls with secret boyfriends do it. If it's busy, just keep trying. I'll try to beat the girls off until I get to talk to you."

"Wow. Are you going to go to school every day?"

She laughed but then became serious. "Do you really have to leave?"

"Taslima, you know if I go home there's no way. They'll never let me out. I won't be able to . . . I won't be able to . . ."

I didn't have to explain why I couldn't. She understood.

"I can't be the person they want me to be. I can't get broken and I can't get religious and I can't be lucky and have your family. They'd never do this to you. I need to leave because of me. I don't know if I can totally trust Angela, but I can trust you."

"Okay," she said. "What do you need me to do?"

"Will you tell Safia I'm not an awful person? Will you watch out for her?" I couldn't continue.

She touched my arm. "I will. I'll watch out for her. I promise."

"Taslima, am I really doing the right thing?"

She looked into my eyes. She was more serious than she'd ever been. "Yes, you are."

Angela returned with a nest of coffees. She handed a cup to Taslima. She took a sip. "This is good. Thank you."

Angela smiled. "I always put a little extra sugar and milk in it."

She handed me my cup and sat down close to me. "I just called my mom. She told me there's a bus leaving at one thirty."

I looked at the golden clock. Its face was cut in half. One hand was pointing to twelve, the other to six. It was already twelve thirty.

"That's so soon!" Taslima said.

"If you catch this one, my cousin can pick you up in Boston and you won't have to figure out all the trains to get to Beverly. If you catch the one after, you'll arrive in the middle of the night and the trains won't even be running to Beverly."

Taslima looked at me and nodded.

I stood up. "Okay, that's it. Let's go."

Taslima and Angela stood up beside me. In a flash I had a vision, or was it a remembered dream? I was walking through a gate. The night sky was full of stars. I turned to see Taslima and Angela waving at me. I lifted my arm to say goodbye, then walked straight into the mouth of a lion.

ACKNOWLEDGMENTS

Thank you, Caroline Bleeke, your editorial brilliance and passionate care for this book was the greatest gift a writer could ever ask for. Thank you, Ayesha Pande, for your steady belief in my writing and fearless support of radical literature. Thank you, Susan Chang, for planting the seed and reading early drafts. Thank you, Bryan Borland and Seth Pennington, for believing in my writing and creating Sibling Rivalry, a fiercely beautiful resource for queer literature. Thank you, Sydney Jeon and the entire Flatiron Books team, for bringing *Roses* into the world.

Thank you, Kamilah Aisha Moon, Ben McFall, Anantha Sudhakar, Dr. Barbara McManus, Woodrow Bovell, John Savant, and Asif Bhai, for your light in this world and the hereafter.

Thank you, Rosina, for opening my heart wider than I ever thought possible.

Thank you, my family, for being my world. Thank you, Sa'dia Rehman, Ben Perowsky, Andrea Dobrich, Ambreen Khan-Landa, anastacia bolina, diedra barber, Rekha Malhotra, Saba Waheed, Sally Lee, Samantha Thornhill, Soniya Munshi, Tazeen Khan-Fitzgerald, Yvette Ho, Adele Swank, Adeeba Afshan Rana, Alykhan Boolani, Faria Chaudhry, Jesse Workman, Jonathan Ho, Jyothi Natarajan, Nadia Q. Ahmad, Nicole Counts, Nina Sharma, Rathini Kandavel, Tara Sarath, Vani Natarajan, Zainab Shah, Amna Akbar, Angie Cruz, Jess deCourcy Hinds, Chitra Ganesh, Daisy Hernández, Ishle Yi Park, Karen Russell, Dr. Ann Raia, Amy Hughey, Danny Blume, Frank Perowsky, Ginger Perowsky, Janet Savage-Blumenfeld, Kathy Warren, Karena Cronin, Robin Jones, Stas Gibbs, Blue Sky Bakery, and all the writers from Two Truths.

Thank you, Asian American Writers' Workshop, Barbara Deming Memorial Foundation, BIPOC Writing Party, Cave Canem, City Lore, Compound Cowork, Cullman Center for Teachers, Headlands Center for the Arts, Hedgebrook, Jerome Foundation, Kundiman, Main Street Coworking, Norcroft, Saltonstall, Soul Mountain Retreat, South Asian Lesbian and Gay Association, South Asian Women's Creative Collective, Women in Literature and Letters, and the Vermont Studio Center.

ABOUT THE AUTHOR

Bushra Rehman grew up in Corona, Queens. She is coeditor of *Colonize This! Young Women of Color on Today's Feminism* and author of the poetry collection *Marianna's Beauty Salon* and the dark comedy *Corona*, one of the New York Public Library's favorite books about NYC.

Recommend

Roses, in the Mouth of a Lion

for your next book club!

Reading Group Guide available at

flatironbooks.com/reading-group-guides